SIGIL

AL NICHOLSON

Copyright © 2024 Al Nicholson
All rights reserved.

Book layout by ebooklaunch.com

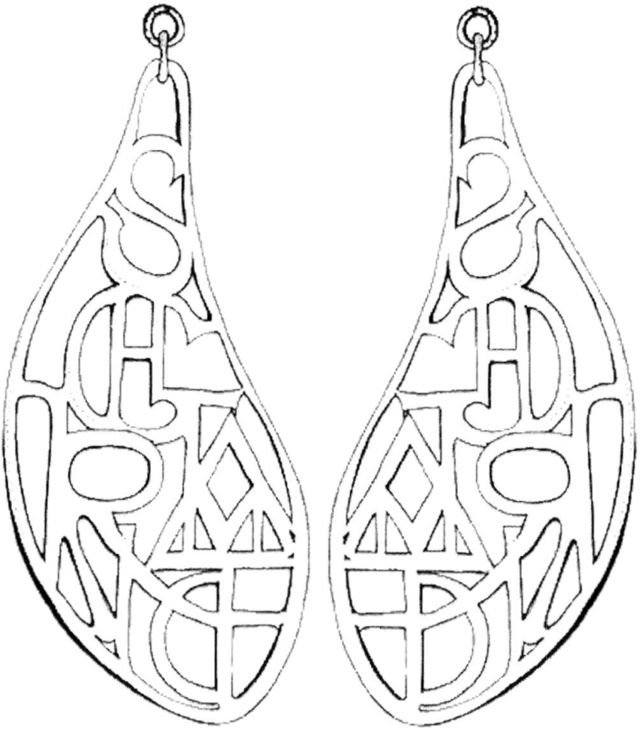

Preface

Many years ago, when our two children were very young, my wife and I took a vacation in the Dordogne region of France. The school holiday had just begun.

We drove to Newhaven in East Sussex and then took the four-hour ferry to Dieppe. We continued driving through the night, arriving at the charming town of Le Bugue in the early hours of the morning. It's about 600 miles from home.

A few days later we decided to visit Limeuil, a tiny village at the confluence of the Vézère and Dordogne rivers. It was a beautiful, balmy summer's evening and we chose to eat at a small, unassuming restaurant.

We were waiting in eager anticipation for the meals to arrive when my eldest daughter announced that the lady sitting by herself at the adjacent table was her teacher! Not expecting to recognise anybody – miles from home, in such an out-of-the-way place – we hadn't noticed.

What were the chances of such an occurrence? We had both chosen the same day and time to visit the village. We had both selected the same pizzeria and sat in the same area – even though there were many other spaces in which to sit.

My daughter's teacher had, no doubt, just completed an arduous summer term and was probably desperate for peace and solitude. So, we shared a few minutes discussing how improbable the situation was and then left her to enjoy her evening.

Coincidences do happen.

Chapter 1

They said it would be a challenge, and it certainly was. Fur Tor, the Queen of the Moor: one of the most remote and isolated places in South West England. Dartmoor's majestic peak, surrounded by very wet, inhospitable ground, would provide a difficult test for even the most experienced walker. And then there was the weather: unpredictable and, at times, extremely unruly. Sure, '...the whispers of the wind carried long-forgotten messages', but mist, hail, and snow blizzards often carried more prescient ones.

Unforgettable views of Hare Tor to the west – and, to the north, the heights of Yes Tor and the more immediate Little Kneeset – were obvious draws to the photographer. To the lover of the outdoors, it was the vast open landscape stretching out for miles with hardly a visible reminder of human existence. You could lose yourself out there and re-energise, though it made you feel very small and insignificant at the same time.

Jack was there because he'd planned to take several photographs to submit to a mind, body, and spirit website, as well as recounting his experiences in an associated blog. It was also, technically, one of a few days he'd put by to recharge his spent batteries and gather his thoughts. Two birds, one stone, as it were. The first day of February had not seemed the most ideal time to tackle such a venture, but – as luck would have it – the preceding icy cold month had set the ground hard. Consequently, the peat hags and the boggy ground of the South Tavy Head might be passed more easily. If your foot plunged into the moorland mire, it might only sink to boot level; in a wet March, it could mean finding yourself in it up to your waist.

Jack had approached the Tor from the southeast. The walk from Drift Lane over Broadun to the delightful waterfall at the East Dart River had been surprisingly easy; the ground was a little spongy in parts, but he had made good progress. The seemingly impenetrable marshy ground to the south of Cut Hill, however, was more problematic, and he was relieved to find the peat pass enigmatically named 'North West Passage'.

This Victorian 'thoroughfare' – a channelled stretch of firmer ground – had been created for huntsmen keen to pursue the wily fox into its unpredictable habitat. Wayfarers were grateful for half a mile of easier traverse and a chance to locate their exact position; the open moor had an uncanny way of making you lose all sense of direction. Identifiable features in this unforgiving, yet strangely alluring, desolation were extremely welcome.

The whites of his knuckles as he captured images with his camera, along with the grey, yellowish tinge in the sky, reminded him that he must press on to reach his goal. It was becoming colder, and the sky could darken in an instant. A six-hour excursion would just seem like a bit of a luxury if he came back with unusable material.

Dramatic and moody pictures needed the contrast of highlights. Muddy gloom just offered flatness.

A wave of excitement surprised him as he discovered the first evidence of the path that connected Cut Hill to the granite stacks of Fur Tor. The definition of the trackway was certainly rather odd; considering the lack of any recognisable path since the river, this was practically a highway.

Who or what has trodden this tough grass to a lower level than the surroundings? How many people even get to this spot in winter? Jack pondered.

Nonetheless, he buried his thoughts and felt himself almost rushing down the slope of the ridge. He could see the familiar shapes of the huge stone outcrop that gave each Dartmoor tor its own identity. A glance at the map and his watch reassured him that all was good, so Jack strode on purposefully, feeling just a little smug.

He had planned to eat a snack along the way, but his momentum had carried him on. It was only now, as he permitted himself to feel a little relieved, that he realised he was rather hungry. He was looking forward to finding a decent spot that was sheltered from the wind so he could eat something.

As he approached his destination, the granite rocks began to reveal themselves like great grey battleships, millions of years of weathering having produced these striking features. He then stood on a grassy platform, framed left and right by these monsters. Eerily, a sheep's skull had been placed on a ledge in full view – obviously someone's macabre way of reminding travellers that, out here, nature governs everything. To add to the almost gothic scene, a raven circled, landed on its nest, and peered menacingly in his direction.

The thrill of accomplishment and the panoramic view, easily as good as it had been billed, caused Jack to beam profusely. He turned to the left and gazed down at the Amicombe Brook below. He could have attempted the walk from that direction, but he'd decided against it. Turning to the right, he took in the impressive peaks of the northern moor. Vast swathes of golden brown grass tinged with russet lay before him. In the summer sunshine, shades of green would abound and granite tors would cast long shadows, offering sheep respite from the heat. Winter's last month would offer no such finery. At this moment it was bleak, but strangely addictive.

Fixated by the visual splendour, Jack momentarily forgot about his pressing need for refreshment. He raised his camera to his eye and scanned to the right. The main stack filled the frame.

At that moment he detected a movement behind the rocks, witnessed through odd gaps in the structure. Quickly, he panned left again to ascertain whether it was a trick of the light, or perhaps another raven. He noticed a quickening in his chest, perplexed as he was by a situation that eluded his understanding.

All became clear when a girl stepped out, into the clearing. She smiled and said warmly, "Hi, I saw you coming…" As he didn't immediately reply, she continued, "…from the crest over there." She pointed to where he'd come from.

"Yes, from Cut Hill, it's a great path down," he replied, as he lowered his camera and met her gaze. In truth, he was mildly put out that he wasn't going to have the experience all to himself. However, wanting to be sociable, he desperately tried not to show his true feelings.

"I'm Ruthven. I thought I was going to have this all to myself," she told him, as if mirroring his thoughts entirely, "and then you came along." She almost sang the second half of the statement so it wouldn't come across as unfriendly.

Jack had no notion of having been watched, albeit briefly, and he stupidly tried to recount whether he'd done anything embarrassing – like punching the sky in triumph or getting overexcited by the view. Perhaps it was because he'd just become aware that the girl before him was somehow captivating. She was also confident – the kind of confidence you gained through experience.

"Ruthven? I've never met a Ruthven. How are you spelling that? I'm Jack, by the way."

"Any way you like," she laughed. "It's been spelled every which way. You should see some of the birthday cards I got at school."

Jack smiled. "How long have you been here?" he asked. "I never expected to see anybody. I mean, maybe some wizened hill walker…"

"…But not a girl with make-up and coloured nails," she finished, guessing what he was thinking.

"No… I didn't mean…"

"Just a few minutes before you arrived at the ridge,' said Ruthven, quickly answering his original question.

They both let the response hang in the air, desperately trying to avoid saying something overly trivial or embarrassing.

"Well, you thought you'd have this *all* to yourself, but now you have *me*," she announced, playfully stressing the 'me'. Ruthven searched Jack's face for any telltale signs of disappointment.

"Be my guest," he laughed, happily passing the test he knew she had set. "You came from a different direction… I'm sure I would have seen you otherwise."

"Over Hare Tor from Lydford," she confirmed. "I crossed the brook and slogged it up from there. The last bit was effing awful."

He nodded, impressed that she'd taken on such a challenge by herself. He chuckled inwardly. He had always loved hearing cultured, intelligent women using bad language. "Listen, I was going to eat as I'm famished, but looking at that sky… I'd better crack on and take some photos." He pointed to the northeast.

She gazed in the direction he indicated and saw the darkening sky. "Business or pleasure?"

Her question was answered when he unpacked, from his backpack, a quality-looking camera with various lens attachments.

"It's what I do… I write blogs for various websites and publications. Can we eat after I'm done? Err… that is, assuming you haven't already eaten," he added, babbling nervously and hoping she wouldn't lose interest.

"Well…" she replied, stringing him along just a little, "I might share one of my homemade cookies with you… but your pictures do have to impress." With that, Ruthven turned and walked towards the main granite stack, pleased with her response.

Jack smiled, watching the way she walked. He couldn't quite fathom what was happening. They'd only just met moments ago – a chance meeting in a remote location, miles from anywhere – yet it felt like they were exchanging banter by the photocopier in an office. Jack wondered whether the oddness of the situation was the reason why both parties had committed. Maybe there was something elementally sociable about the human race; ignoring each other would have been an intolerable strain.

Jack could see that the clear skies wouldn't hold for long. Soon, the dark clouds that were forecast would bring hail or sleet. He would have to make the most, therefore, of this very fortunate situation. He had already researched the most popular viewpoints online, and these were now familiar to him as he scanned the ground. He figured that, even though two pictures were never the same, owing to the changing light, it would be advantageous to find some more unusual angles. Just one spectacular image could make all the difference between a successful article and an easily forgotten one.

Ruthven watched Jack with fascination as he worked across the tor, taking photographs from all angles. At times he would disappear from view for quite a while, hidden behind rocks or taking long shots from way off. On one occasion she began to wonder if he'd chosen to abscond altogether, leaving her behind as a worthless distraction. She was just debating whether or not she was surprised by her feelings about that possibility when Jack came back into view.

He beamed, obviously pleased with his results so far. "The light is fantastic!" he shouted, a little way off.

"Great, but I'm starving!" she yelled, her voice battered by the – now much stronger – wind.

He strode towards her. "Just a few more of this stack from here." He pointed in her direction and swept his arm to indicate the viewpoint. "Is there any chance you could move over there?"

"Well, really… I should be highly offended!"

"Why aren't you then?"

"Because…" she paused for effect, "landscape photographers don't usually like people in pictures – unless they help to scale the subject matter," she announced with a knowing grin.

"Very good. What camera have you got?" he asked, making an incorrect assumption.

"Only my phone, but you'd be surprised with what I know." She shifted her weight and began to move from her perch.

"Actually, I wouldn't," he said, revealing far too much about his interest in her.

"Now that you've got what you asked for, you'd better get an effing shift on because that light is going to change." She pointed to the darkened portion of the sky, where the yellowish tinge of grey was slowly turning to slate.

Jack worked for another ten minutes, taking pictures from all angles. It amused Ruthven to see his visible excitement and purposeful posturing. It was almost like a game hunter stalking his prey. One moment he would crouch low, the next he'd be lying flat on the tough moorland grass. At times he'd be searching for height and would scale the rocks to reach a good vantage point. With a 'selfie', all you had to do was hold the camera aloft and snap. This looked much too involved.

"All done," he finally announced as he placed the camera in his bag, "now you have my undivided attention. Lunch. I'm starving."

"Oh, I see… when *you're* ready. I might just have eaten mine. You were so preoccupied with your camera angles that you didn't notice."

"Yes, but you haven't… otherwise you would have tiny traces of cookie in the corner of your mouth, and you haven't." He gazed at her face searching for clues, enjoying the tit-for-tat conversation. Just then he noticed a tiny scar on her right cheekbone and felt himself become fascinated in its story.

"I fell on rocks like these when I was twelve or so," she said, "but I can't remember which tor. We used to holiday here every year. I love this place… but it can be scary."

Her almost telepathic response unnerved him. Was he so unsubtle? He thought it had gone unnoticed. It was, after all, just a fractional adjustment of the eyes to focus on a particular spot. He had never encountered someone who seemed to be so many steps ahead.

He was going to say that it looked like a beauty spot, but he managed to check himself. Instead, he chose to acknowledge his rather ungallant stare at her blemished skin before moving swiftly on. "I got stuck while climbing Combestone Tor, over near Venford Reservoir. I guess I was about eight or nine. A grazed knee and hurt pride are my only marks of honour," he replied, acknowledging his unfortunate mistake.

While Jack recounted his early years' experience, Ruthven rummaged in her surprisingly large bag and produced two large cookies. Then, sitting slightly uncomfortably on an uneven shelf of rock, sheltered from the now increasingly prominent wind by an overhanging ledge, the pair devoured the provisions they'd brought with them. A comfortable silence hung over proceedings; both stared out at the view towards the north, encapsulated by the changing light and how it played on the open moor.

Jack read the situation well. He refrained from attempting to fill the void with small talk, even though many minutes passed; somehow, they understood the need to be utterly consumed with their own thoughts. After all, neither had expected company or distraction, and they'd both battled the elements to be there. Almost as if by a prearranged signal, or a ceasefire, they had both withdrawn into their shells, huddled together yet separated by that tiny yet significant margin that delineated friends from lovers.

Jack scrunched his sandwich packet into a ball and placed it deep into his bag. He then stood up and lobbed an apple core into the distance, mindful to ensure it would be hidden from view. It was almost an announcement. A sort of 'what happens now?'

Ruthven continued to eat the last few pieces of cookie, noticing but ignoring his dramatic intervention. "Of course, we could have sex," she uttered almost casually, continuing to look outwards towards the horizon.

Jack reeled. This was the very last thing he'd expected to hear; he was completely floored and he found himself clawing for the correct response. What *was* the correct response? "I beg your pardon?" was all he could muster – the kind of reply that was useful when you were trying to buy time, yet it fooled no one.

"Sex, here… now… nobody about. We'll never see each other again; it will be just a moment in time. A memory." She looked up at him. Her calmness affirmed that she was actually serious. Then she almost giggled.

"You're crazy… you don't even know who I am…" As he trailed off he immediately realised that anonymity might be the catalyst for her rush of excitement.

"Let me see," she said, her eyes looking him up and down, seemingly scanning his imaginary barcodes,

"…happy childhood; roughly thirty; well-educated university type; not particularly money-driven; just finished a long-term relationship, or experiencing the dying embers of; a little sensitive and feels at a turning point in life. How's that for starters? Close enough?"

Astonished at her accuracy, Jack desperately tried to hide his feelings and not reveal that she had just uncovered many of his truths. He was also aware that her outrageous proposition required a very clever reply, but he simply didn't have one. So, using the mantra that attack was the best form of defence, he countered with his own observations.

"Okay then… also around thirty; sadness during your teenage years because of family issues; very intelligent, but didn't complete university for some reason; likewise, you too have just ended a relationship – in fact, you were engaged; you're confident and very astute… and you are also at some kind of turning point in life."

He wasn't even sure where the words had originated; they'd just tumbled out, like replies to word association when probed by a psychologist. Normally, Jack would be overly careful not to offend, but in an effort to be equally impressive, he had abandoned his reserve. It felt cathartic for some reason, as if he'd been harbouring these thoughts all along and wanted to confess them.

"Very good, or at least some of it. Of course, you were guessing wildly," she said.

"There's an indentation on your ring finger. That's quite recent, I'd say," he offered as proof of his conjecture.

"Proper little boy scout. Why engaged? Why not married?" she asked, unconsciously glancing down to her left hand.

"Maybe I thought that was too personal," he lied. What he really wanted to say was that she hadn't married because she obviously had issues concerning commitment.

"So, Jack escapes the fallout from his crumbling relationship and takes himself off to the one place he feels can energise him: Dartmoor. He chooses Fur Tor because it's a kind of rite of passage; it's all about the struggle." Ruthven zipped up her backpack, slung it over her shoulder, and stood up, facing him.

"Something like that," he confided, with a heaviness that revealed she'd touched upon a nerve. "Anyway, it's too cold. I'm beginning not to be able to feel my fingers, let alone anything else," he recovered, relying on well-worn banter.

"Just an idea," she said, affectionately resting her hand on his jacket, signalling that no damage had been done.

"And you? Is finding this spot some kind of bucket list endeavour? Most girls I know would choose backpacking in Thailand or paragliding in the Alps."

"Most girls? How dare you. I'm not 'most' girls," she gasped, feigning outrage. "What could be more exciting than wet boots, cold feet, tired limbs, hunger, and lack of alcohol?" She didn't wait for a reply, but struck a more solemn tone to her voice as she added, less stridently, "I suppose it was on a list of sorts…"

"And now you've ticked it off. Well done you!" Jack patted her shoulder in a similar gesture to the one she'd adopted moments ago. "What's next on the list?" he asked, expecting something unusual.

"You just turned it down…" she replied in a coquettish voice, waiting for the discomfort to show on Jack's face. "Not really!" she giggled, enjoying the moment.

He didn't know if she was being at all serious. He must have got quite lucky with her character assessment because he couldn't read her in any way. He was keen to joust with her and appear lively and interesting, but he always seemed to be the one to react.

"The bucket's going to remain empty for a while," she said, before walking away as if to take in the view for the last time.

The first icy flurries of sleet appeared like dissolving confetti; it was peculiar how it always seemed to feel wetter than rain. In an effort to preserve the shape of her hair, Ruthven unfurled her hood from her jacket and turned her back to the gathering wind.

Jack searched the sky and privately bemoaned his luck. He could easily have spent another hour with her. He hadn't felt this alive for ages. Common sense, however, dictated that it was time to leave; the sky offered no hope of respite as the last bastion of its brightness was consumed by a blanket of grey, menacing cloud. It would be difficult to walk in heavy sleet or hail, especially across a featureless landscape; darker skies made it difficult to judge distances and stinging hail made looking ahead torturous. His way back would be difficult enough.

Finding the path back to Cut Hill would enable him to locate the red and white poles demarcating the limits of the army firing range. If he followed the direction of these, it would bring him close enough to the East Dart River, and from there it would be relatively straightforward, as the ground was reasonably firm.

Jack was sure that Ruthven's way back would be more problematic; there were fewer actual paths and more areas of wet ground you could stray into. If they left now, he calculated that they probably had another two hours of usable light and a remaining hour of dusk. Not much margin for error, though.

"We ought to leave soon; the weather's closing in!" he shouted across to her.

She turned to face him.

"Where's your car again?" Jack spoke with authority.

"The other side of Hare Tor, over there." She pointed in the direction.

He wanted to ask her to join him walking back to his vehicle. He could then give her a lift to where she'd started… but what if she rebuked him? Clearly, she'd been perfectly capable of reaching this spot without any help. He didn't want to taint the occasion by becoming overbearing. He was confused.

"I'm parked back the other way," was all he said.

He knew that she knew this, but he felt he had to state the obvious. Social etiquette still held sway, even when miles from civilisation and standing next to a complete stranger. He walked over to her and stood closer than before.

"Yes, you said… I'll be fine, though," she answered, once again reading his thoughts perfectly.

"It was great fun meeting you. I'm sorry it was such a brief encounter… can't ignore that lot up there though." Jack pointed to the heavy, leaden skies. He tried to sound casual, but inside he was screaming. He was cursing his choice of words. When he needed it the most, his lexicon had deserted him.

"Me too. Sorry if I messed up your opportunity for peace and quiet. Oh, and I hope I didn't offend you…"

Stopping her from mentioning the unmentionable, Jack mumbled, "…Not at all… it's just that…" He trailed off. He was almost crushed by the fact that he should have acted differently.

"Life's too short, you know," Ruthven cut in abruptly, not trying to chastise him from turning down her offer, but attempting to justify her craziness.

Without saying anything, Jack plunged his hands into the bottom of his rucksack and located a small plastic box. Rather pleased with himself, he extended his hand towards Ruthven. "Here, you'll have more need of this than me. I'm not religious at all, but this silver St Christopher was given to me as a talisman for safe passage. A bit of a mixture of ideas, but you get the gist."

Ruthven's gloved hands received the gift, but she was unsure.

"Please," Jack begged, pushing his hand further forward.

She was finding it difficult to respond to such a random act of kindness, but she also knew that to refuse would greatly offend and make the parting even more awkward. "I'll be fine… but thank you," she said finally, taking the box and tucking it precariously into one of the netted side pockets of her backpack.

Jack wanted to tell her to bury it in the main body of her pack, otherwise it might fall out, but he worried about fussing her. Now was not the time for that. She had accepted his gift and, in any case, he knew the silver pendant wouldn't really aid her travel.

They looked at each other again, nervously, aware that the end of the fantasy was approaching.

Ruthven broke the momentary silence. "Sorry if I gatecrashed your private moments; you were here first." She shrugged. "It really is an amazing place."

They stood facing one another and smiled.

Jack rather awkwardly offered a handshake, figuring a hug would seem too intimate. In his world, such greetings and farewells were reserved for old friends and lovers. "Hope to find you again on some other distant tor," he said, realising he'd probably made the wrong choice.

Surprised that a handshake had been offered – it seemed far too formal – Ruthven accepted it more apprehensively than she'd intended. "Maybe I'll get locked up for terrorising strangers before then," she laughed. "You go. I need to stay here a moment longer."

She moved her left hand and clasped the handshake, sandwiching his hand between hers in a more touching embrace.

It was such a final, sincere gesture that any subsequent words would have broken the spell. To ask for a contact number or to arrange another meeting would be like walking out on an argument and then ringing the front door seconds later.

So, resigned to the situation, and not being able to think straight, Jack nodded and turned away.

Chapter 2

The girl lay motionless, face down in the icy cold water. Some of her tangled, mousy brown hair floated aimlessly to the side, while the remainder clung in a matted nest to her jacket and neck. Her left arm was outstretched, the other tucked underneath her body, still clutching the shoulder straps of her backpack. Her legs were twisted awkwardly, and her right boot appeared to be wedged between three or four large, water-worn rocks. Her lifeless, misshapen outline made her look incongruous with the natural beauty of the surroundings. It appeared as if she had been unceremoniously dumped there. However, her stone-coloured walking trousers, brown jacket, and faded black rucksack rendered her perfectly camouflaged. Consequently, she had gone totally unnoticed.

The Amicombe Brook – beneath Little Kneeset, and swollen by the January rains – was not a deep stretch of water by any means. However, its lack of flat, grassy banks and its boggy ground made it a respected obstacle.

Jim Bickle of the North Dartmoor Search and Rescue Team was pleased to see Detective Sergeant Sandra Baines and Detective Constable Mark Box; he had waited faithfully for two hours for their arrival. He was used to the inclement weather, and he loved the wild open country, but guarding such a tragic scene had affected him deeply. This poor girl looked around his daughter's age. Also, the abrasions to her face – which were just about detectable from a short distance – meant she could have been murdered. He was slightly apprehensive that he had, unwittingly, compromised a crime scene.

"And you do this sort of thing voluntarily?" DS Baines questioned as they shook hands. "I'm worn out. Why aren't there any decent paths around here?"

"Jim Bickle. Twenty years with the team," he announced proudly. "We're on call whenever we're needed. I've not touched a thing," he added.

Sandra immediately noticed his strong hands and weathered skin. He oozed practicality and dependability.

"Did you find her?" DC Box asked, also shaking hands with the ashen-faced volunteer.

"Yes, I did. I was just returning from sorting out a few lads who'd got into some difficulty about a mile north of here. I was following the brook back when I found her, and I called the police from here. That would have been about ten o'clock this morning," he answered, anticipating the next question.

"Yes, we have records of that call. Listen, Jim…" DS Baines softened her approach, as she could see that he'd performed an onerous task, "we'll just ask you a few questions and then you can be on your way."

"Yes, of course," he replied, quite glad to be nearing the end of his duty.

DC Box ushered Jim away from the immediate vicinity of the body and began the informal interview.

Meanwhile, DS Baines began making observations as she stepped nearer to the half-submerged body, ensuring not to contaminate any possible evidence.

This was certainly an odd one. The face of the deceased female was in the icy shallow water, yet Sandra could see that it had received a blow on the right-hand side. Her left hand was outstretched, unsurprisingly grazed from the impact of the fall. This would probably rule out death occurring elsewhere and the body being dumped. Still, she thought, that would be one for the Crime Scene Investigators who would shortly be arriving by helicopter thanks to the army, who occasionally helped the Devon Police gain access to remote spots on the moor. Anyway, where else could death have occurred?

She scanned the environment. The open wilderness offered no clues. There were no indications that the body had been dragged; there would have been evidence on the wet ground adjacent to the brook. Although half of the woman's jacket remained submerged in the water, the back of it was clean, suggesting it hadn't been hauled across a stretch of Dartmoor bog. The blow on the side of the face didn't look like it would have been fatal but, of course, there could be further – unseen – evidence of trauma. DS Baines wasn't about to destroy that by clumsily moving the body. The forensic investigators would be poring over the poor unfortunate girl in a matter of moments. All dignity would vanish with the flashlights of cameras, the bagging of personal items, the capture of DNA, and then the subsequent post-mortem.

How old did she look? Late twenties? Maybe even early thirties.

The detective stared into the middle distance, trying to envisage the woman's last movements. With such a bulky bag, she could have been camping out overnight. Why else would someone carry so much? Maybe there was an argument, a push, and she fell into the stream. Then, not expecting to be thrust into the fast-flowing brook, her left hand and the right side of her face took the brunt of the impact as she clung onto her backpack. It made a lot of sense, but it didn't explain the death.

What if her head had been held down under the water? That, thought Sandra, was a definite possibility, yet there wasn't any disturbance. The assailant would surely have stood astride the fallen victim and held her down while a struggle ensued. The boggy ground betrayed no slipping of boots, no crushed rushes or sedges, no flattened spearworts, sundews, pimpernels, or any other water-loving plants that her father had always been so fascinated by when walking out here with her when she was a child.

"Her boots..." Mark called out, striding towards the body.

"What about them?" Sandra asked. "Have you finished with the questioning?"

"Textbook Q and A. He's a bit shaken, poor chap. He might be great at rescuing the living, but nothing prepares you for this." He pointed to the lifeless form. "He's obviously not a suspect, and we know where to find him if we need him."

"Her boots?" Sandra prompted.

"Oh, yes," he said, continuing the thread, "do you see that her right boot is rather caught between these rocks? There are a couple of bigger rocks behind those that she could have stepped on... one more over here... and a possible flat rock that could have been a platform for a final leap to the other side. All a bit dicey, especially in icy conditions."

"But much better than wasting time trying to find a better crossing," DS Baines said, following the line of enquiry he'd offered.

"I reckon so."

"And are you implying that her right foot got caught?"

"It may have slipped off that stone there," he said, pointing to the offending smooth rock. "The girl may have been a bit tentative or nervous about her footing, especially with such a heavy backpack. Is that a tent she has in there?"

Mark stepped forward and examined the body more closely. "Her foot got wedged in between those two rocks there," he suggested, "and, with her foot trapped, she had nowhere to go but down. Presumably, the bulk of her backpack sent her crashing as her centre of gravity shifted violently."

DS Baines looked straight at her partner with a knowing smile. She was grateful for the theory and not a bit upset that she hadn't solved the conundrum all by herself. They made a good team.

"Left hand down to break the fall. The right hand clings onto the bag, unable to free itself in time–"

"And the right cheekbone and side of the head collide with these stones here, just under the surface of the water," Sandra cut in, agreeing with the possible sequence of events. "She must have turned her head, bracing herself for the fall."

They both nodded, happy with the conclusion, yet neither party was completely convinced. Lots of people lose their balance and fall, but only a tiny fraction will perish as a consequence. Something was missing.

DS Baines broke the momentary silence. "Are we saying that she was here by herself, and that she lost her footing trying to cross? If we are... how did she die?"

The attention of the two police detectives was diverted by the sound of the incoming helicopter that circled noisily above, searching for an ideal location to land. If DS Baines needed any more evidence to support her notion that everything was a supreme effort in this wild landscape, this was it. Owing to the wet ground that was ever present in this part of the moor, even the helicopter had to rest easy a good way off from their present position.

"I wonder if someone remembered to bring a flask of coffee!" DC Box shouted, trying to be heard above the din of the chopping rotor blades as the CSI team poured out of the open door of the helicopter.

"I wish! It's freezing cold when the wind whips up. I'm long overdue for a caffeine fix," the Detective Sergeant replied, aware that her energy levels were fading. It was going to be a long day.

Soon, the scene was dominated by busyness. In a carefully choreographed fashion, evidence was collected and processed by the team of forensic scientists, turning the lonely, inhospitable location into a hive of activity. DS Baines knew that initial observations would be available to the detectives within the hour, but more technical issues would have to wait until the next day and beyond. Lines of enquiry would have to be set in motion, and – even if this turned out not to be a murder investigation – there would still be much to do. She was hoping that identification of some sort would be forthcoming. Presumably, someone would notice that this poor girl was missing.

Sandra feared however that, in life, the girl had been a frequent visitor to this place. Some loved to camp in the most desolate spots, untroubled by the excesses of modernity. Out here, mobile phones, cash, and credit cards meant little to those seeking an alternative lifestyle. It was entirely possible, therefore, that she had ventured onto the moor without telling anyone.

The familiar face of Geoff Salter strode towards Sandra and Mark, bearing gifts; the welcome sight of white polystyrene cups produced an energetic reaction from the two detectives.

"Instant coffee in a plastic cup: normally an abomination, but right now… bloody marvellous!" Sandra beamed. "Thanks, Geoff. Tell me: as head of the unit, is this part of your job description?" She liked working alongside Geoff, and she loved teasing him whenever she could.

"Well," Geoff replied, "since you and I will be working together on this one, it's in my best interests to keep you calm. We all know what happens if you're without a coffee." He looked knowingly in Mark's direction.

"I'm saying nothing. She's a joy to work with at all times," replied Mark mechanically.

"Hmm… a conspiracy. I'd better try to keep you two apart." Sandra gratefully grasped the warm coffee with both hands, took a sip, and then got down to business. "What do you have for me, Geoff?"

"Early days, of course, but there are a few pointers. What don't you have?"

"Okay, so I know that you won't commit at this stage, but I could do with help in several key issues. Firstly – is this, in your view, a murder? Secondly – how and when did she die? And thirdly – have you found any identification?"

"I won't know, conclusively, if this girl was murdered until the autopsy… but you know that already, of course. Judging by the position of the body and the evidence of trauma that's visible, I'd say the girl lost her balance and fell. Whether or not she was pushed is debatable. At the moment, we haven't found any evidence to support that. We think she was alone." Geoff paused and waited for agreement before sharing his other initial thoughts.

"I think we're with you on all of that," Mark said, "in which case, could she really have drowned?"

"The crucial aspect here is the fact that the water is so cold," Geoff explained. "Water between ten and fifteen degrees produces cold shock. Water around five degrees is so painfully cold that it feels like it's burning your skin. At this temperature, your physiological stress greatly increases. Even the most hardened outdoor enthusiast would succumb; thinking is all but impossible in such circumstances. This girl slipped and fell. Unfortunately, the weight of her pack tipped her forward and she crashed. She was barely able to break her fall with her hand. Her face hit the icy water and the shock rendered her senseless. Hypothermia or a heart attack did the rest. Blood vessels constrict in response to a dramatic fall in temperature. Heart rate rapidly increases and so does blood pressure. It probably took less than a minute."

He paused for a moment to let his final statement sink in. "As to the *when*… early signs – and I must stress the word 'early' – indicate that death probably occurred yesterday afternoon. We can't be more precise than that, I'm afraid."

The three figures gazed at the Amicombe Brook winding its way towards Tavy Cleave, a few miles distant. It was difficult to believe that, in its present condition, it could take human life. The fast-flowing water clattered and burbled over the myriad stones and scree. Before, the brook had seemed to provide a mellifluous, almost chime-like backdrop to proceedings. Only now did it seem cacophonous and jarring, as if someone had turned up the volume.

"Do we have a name, or any clues to identification?" Sandra asked, keen to move the investigation on to its next phase.

"I'm sorry to disappoint you but, as yet, no phone or credit cards," Geoff revealed, aware that such news would be a blow. "Oh… also no rings, a bracelet, or a necklace. No visible tattoos either. Of course, any more intimate markings will be found in the post-mortem."

Sandra pondered the outcome. It was impossible to seal off the scene completely. In an area like this, it was difficult to police the movements of the general public and, although in February, visitor numbers were considerably lower, there were still walkers keen to access the more remote locations. If someone were to walk by, or see the obvious activity, one could be sure it would be on social media before the day had passed. That was a worry. It was always messy when families of the dead became aware of the tragedy via the internet. It was even worse when a local journalist knocked on the door. A name would have given them a chance, at least – a very small head start.

"Any car keys?" questioned DC Box, clutching at straws; he felt sure that if anybody had found them, they would have been offered up already.

"Afraid not," Geoff said, wishing he could have brought something more welcome than two cups of coffee.

"So, either she lived in one of the surrounding villages, or she intended to catch a bus. Perhaps she'd arranged to be picked up, but without a phone to confirm, it seems highly unlikely."

"Agreed," said Geoff.

"Where was she heading? Can we ascertain that, at least, from her decision to cross the brook at this point?" Sandra asked. Before the question could be answered, however, she cursed. "Damnation! I should have found that out from Jim, the search and rescue volunteer. Never mind. We'll give him a call."

"No need," cut in DC Box rather smugly, "that was one of the questions I asked him. Deadlake Foot was her most likely destination – in other words, the direction we need to take to get back to the car. There's that good path up and over Hare Tor. A bus stop on the A386 is only a mile or so away from that point, and Lydford is only half a mile from the main road. Another possibility was that she was crossing the brook and heading for Tavy Cleave. It's a very pretty walk, so I'm told. Maybe she lived in Horndon or Mary Tavy. However, if she tried to cross here at, say, two o'clock, she would have been cutting it fine to reach either of those destinations before it got dark. My money's on the way we came: from the direction of Lydford."

Geoff Salter left the two detectives. He knew that their investigation required momentum, and he and his team only had a few crucial hours left to gather data. Before he went, he wished them good fortune in their hunt for the deceased's name and informed them he'd be in touch, the following day, with any new developments.

Despite the poor signal, Detective Sergeant Baines managed to contact the police station at Plymouth; they would have to enable the procedure for identifying an unknown person. Sandra was going to be out of action for the next few hours, walking back, and couldn't afford to lose time.

"There's nothing more I can do here, Mark," she said. "I'm making a move. I need to be out of this wilderness to coordinate the operation." She sighed, shaking her head. "It'll be a late one tonight. I want you to stay here and hand over to a uniformed officer who will be here shortly – obviously, we need police presence until the CSIs have removed the body. You'll get a ride in the helicopter if you're lucky. Then one of the team will be able to give you a lift home. Oh, if you're really lucky, it'll be that new girl – that slim brunette, who I know happens to be single!"

"Very funny, boss," replied Mark, raising his eyebrows. He knew better than to say, 'Will you be okay walking across the moor by yourself?' so, instead, he adopted a sincere tone of voice and continued, "Remember, it's back the way we came. Use the compass on your phone and keep heading west from here. It's the best part of a mile to the Rattle Brook. Cross at the same place, and then it's easy to find the good path that leads up and over Hare Tor. If you recall, once over the other side, there's that good path all the way to the car." He looked at the sky. It was much better than the day before. "The weather looks clear; I think it will hold."

"I'll be fine. Let me know if the CSI team discovers anything of use. We need to get that girl identified."

With that, DS Baines turned to the west and began the march across the open moor. It hadn't gone unnoticed that the dead girl she'd just left behind had also been walking alone the day before. She had to admit that being alone in this vast empty space was certainly an uncomfortable feeling, yet it was also strangely liberating. It took a certain amount of courage to wander alone across difficult terrain with nothing but huge skies to accompany you. Was it managing to find the best path, or was it managing to deal with your own thoughts? Most people, she knew, would baulk at the thought of taking themselves off into the unknown with only a map to guide them.

When Sandra was a child, her father would bring her and her sister to these places and take photos of the prehistoric stones. He would show her gnarled and twisted oaks in ancient woodlands. They would climb tors and hop across huge flat stones in the clear, fast-flowing waters. She knew the land; she knew the dangers. She shared happy memories of those days, but she hadn't chosen to revisit them in adult life. As a result, Sandra hadn't walked across the moor in years. Once her father had passed away, the impetus had gone. Besides, if truth be known, she had always been a worrier.

What if we get lost? What if the mist descends and we walk in circles for hours? And, when she was really young, *What if the pixies get us?!* She chuckled to herself at that last thought.

Sandra continued to slog her way across the wet, uneven ground that occupied the space between the two brooks. After a while, she turned to look behind her, at where she'd just come from. It was always comforting to know that you'd covered ground. She looked ahead again but could ascertain no landmarks; there was still a way to go before Deadlake Foot and the crossing.

Her thoughts turned to the dead girl, and the type of person she might have been. Certainly, the woman had been confident enough to camp overnight by herself in February. That was quite remarkable. She was obviously resourceful and experienced; you could easily die of exposure if you didn't carry the right gear. Presumably, she had packed a high-quality sleeping bag and a state-of-the-art, lightweight tent. There would also have been a stove and high-energy food. She was certainly no shrinking violet to be able to carry all that weight. Sandra checked herself with the irony of the situation: the girl had been tough enough to survive the weather, but had perished crossing the water.

A simple slip of the foot; probably tiredness, she considered.

Sandra crossed the Rattle Brook at the same place as she had on the outward journey. Now, she prepared herself for the ascent of Hare Tor that loomed ahead. It wasn't a particularly difficult challenge if you were an ardent walker, but Sandra was currently feeling the effects of a carefree Christmas and the resulting January denial.

At 34, her life had been spiralling lately. Although she was in reasonably good physical shape, her mental state was rather fragile. Just how many failed relationships could one endure? It always seemed to place more pressure on the next one. She had never struggled to attract interest from male or female admirers, and this was half the issue;

she was probably too flattered to seek depth in the personality of potential partners. Consequently, she was often let down when a lover failed to match up to her initial, rather fleeting, assessment.

Sandra thought it strange that, in the workplace, she was a different animal. She had a 'nose' for good and poor practice, and she could anticipate and avert breakdowns in communication. More importantly, Sandra knew she possessed the common touch with members of the public. This was particularly handy when conducting interviews. She had gained quite a reputation for her technique – and for the positive outcomes that usually followed.

As she reached the summit, Sandra stopped to take in the glorious view. She had to admit to herself that the mantra, 'No pain, no gain', was certainly true of hill walking. Here, West Devon gave way to Cornwall in the distance. The iconic mound of Brentor and its 13th-century church – perched precariously on its peak – rose above the landscape like a surfaced leviathan.

She had missed this 'country' and, caught quite unawares, she suddenly felt crushed by the loss of her father. Her chest tightened, and she felt uncontrollably emotional. Missed opportunities to visit him, partners who disappointed, ridiculous arguments about nothing, moving out… it all flooded her conscience with a cascade of fleeting, guilt-ridden memories. It had happened a few times before, of course; the most insignificant visual cue could trigger an episode. To Sandra, it was profoundly shocking because it laid her bare. There was never any warning and certainly no answers either. It also hurt like hell – that deep kind of hurt that made you reel.

Recovering from the turmoil of the momentary attack of grief, Detective Sergeant Baines descended the slope and made her way to the path that led to where her car was parked. Her pensive mood lightened a little as she neared the end of her journey. She laughed to herself when, on an inspection of her phone app, she saw she had obliterated her 10,000-step target. She'd also had time to take stock of her meandering life. Outside of the work environment, it definitely lacked direction. Perhaps she needed to harness some of the pioneering spirit the unidentified girl had clearly had before her life had been cut so cruelly short.

The solo trek had undoubtedly invigorated her. If it had resulted in nothing else, it had allowed Sandra some valuable thinking time. Sure, she was dog-tired, but in her own, very small way, she had achieved something. Besides, she figured that, later on, a soak in a warm bath and a glass of red wine would go some way to cure her aching limbs.

When Sandra reached the car, she removed some of her heavy items. Her muddy boots were tossed into a box in the boot alongside her rucksack, and her walking jacket and inner fleece were laid on the back seat. She felt almost like a dancer in her flat shoes, owing to her newfound mobility.

Once in the driver's seat, she placed her mobile phone in its holder on the dashboard and turned on the satnav. She then glanced at the car key in her hand as if it were a weapon; it was almost as if starting the car was a metaphor for the next stage of her life.

She plunged the phallic object into its slot and smiled. Sometimes she amazed herself at how random her thoughts were.

Chapter 3

The blue-sky thinking of the previous afternoon had taken a hit. Cleaning a very muddy pair of boots had dampened her spirits. Coming home to an empty house and washing just about everything she was wearing had further darkened her mood. Then, to top it all off, a text – read over breakfast – had revealed that word was out: there had been a body discovered on the moor. Her worst fears had been realised. It seemed to Detective Sergeant Baines that even in the remotest corner of Britain, someone would always be watching. The irony was, in the busy streets of towns and cities, a person could walk around in a gorilla suit and nobody would notice.

However, although Sandra was rather miffed at this development, she wasn't at all surprised. The day before, anybody in the vicinity of the Amicombe Brook would have been drawn towards the spot by the sound of the incoming helicopter. Amateur photographers would have been drooling at the prospect of capturing shots of such a machine against the magnificent backdrop of the northern Dartmoor tors. Walkers conquering the challenge of Fur Tor, proudly casting their eyes over the valley below, would have been more than a little intrigued to witness the white-suited CSI team busying themselves – incongruously, like ants covered in ant powder – around something deposited in the water. They might as well have set up a grandstand and invited people to watch.

We're not going to get away with this one, she thought.

As she drove down the familiar streets of her neighbourhood, heading for the police station, Sandra considered her next steps. Presumably, newshounds from the local press had already picked up the story from social media. She would therefore have to brief her Senior Investigating Officer, Detective Inspector Beechcroft, on the current situation. He, in turn, would have to deliver the facts at a press conference. Low-key as it would be, that was the tricky part. Joe Public, losing his life in an accident on Dartmoor in the winter months, would – unfortunately – attract little interest; a lone, unidentified girl discovered face down in a brook would be a very different scenario. There would be salacious gossip aplenty. Speculation would run rife.

She was pushed! A killer is on the loose!

There was no doubt that the moor seemed to encourage exaggeration. A sheep killed in slightly unusual circumstances resulted in a hunt for a black panther. A stolen mobile phone left conspicuously in a car was part of an orchestrated campaign by a gang of car thieves. And then, of course, there were the pixies…

Trying desperately to shake off deeply emotional thoughts of her father inspired by the little folk, and then feeling extremely guilty for doing so, DS Baines parked the car in her usual place. It was about the only regular aspect of her life.

Two weeks ago she had finished with Sam, a lecturer at a local agricultural college. It had only lasted a month or so. The initial spark had been all but extinguished after only a few dates, but he was a sensitive soul; severing the fledgling relationship had seemed overly cruel. Then, a week ago, she had embarked on the polar opposite. Thinking about it as she gathered her coat and bag from the back seat, it must have been a reaction against being single again, but it still made her cringe.

Monica was, therefore, an even bigger mistake. After meeting in a bar and walking back to the car park late at night, things became difficult when her newfound friend discovered Sandra was interested in her on a different level. Sandra's lack of any experience in this particular area had made her misread the signs, and a very awkward moment ensued.

Time and time again she came back to the same conclusion: unlike most others, she didn't understand the binary choice. The trouble was… it was troubling. Far from closing your eyes and being perfectly happy with whatever chocolate was chosen from the box, you were often left in limbo land – especially in a place like Devon. People didn't understand; she didn't understand.

As she settled into her tiny office, she noticed DC Box walk past her doorway. "Mark!" she called out, hoping to attract his attention.

After a few seconds, the welcome sight of her trusted ally – and partner on this investigation – came back into view.

"Don't…" He purposefully paused with a rueful look on his face, pointing his finger in her direction.

"Don't what?" she asked, knowing that a game was being played.

"…mention the helicopter ride."

"Because…"

"Because… I felt like throwing up every time it changed direction."

"Not a good look in front of that new CSI recruit, eh?" she said, smiling whimsically and giving him a conspiratorial wink.

"Very amusing. How was your evening?"

"Very amusing," she conceded, quickly realising he'd immediately restored parity. Evens. She liked that; Sandra considered it the basis of a good friendship. "Hey, grab a coffee and let's get our heads together on the Dartmoor girl."

"Will do," Mark replied. "Oh, and we have a potential witness coming in at eleven…" He disappeared from the doorway then, leaving Sandra to ponder the development.

* * *

Jack was in turmoil. The spoon he'd been eating his breakfast with remained level with his chin. A teardrop of milk hung from the underside. It distended and finally plummeted towards his lap. Eyes fixed on the mini television screen and mouth wide open, he tried to make sense of what he was hearing. It was the last item of news:

"Tragedy on one of Dartmoor's rivers: a girl found dead near Fur Tor. We hope to have more details on that in our evening bulletin."

As soon as he heard the unemotional BBC voice, it was gone. No details. No pictures. His head was spinning as he finally managed to swallow his last mouthful.

He replayed his movements over the last few days, hoping to clear himself of any involvement. If the girl had been found yesterday, as was probable, she may have died the day before.

That's when I was there.

But surely the girl he'd met would have seen her? Jack bombarded his mind with questions, hoping to find convenient answers.

The stretch of water nearest the tor was the Amicombe Brook. You had to cross it if you approached from the west. The River Dart was to the east, about two miles distant. But Jack figured that the news presenter would have said, 'Tragedy on the River Dart' if that was the case... wouldn't she?

He'd just paused to make sure he was being logical when a cold realisation dawned on him. One that he must have subconsciously parked deep inside: the dead girl in the river could have been Ruthven.

Jack placed his hand on his forehead in dismay. Yes, there might be an alternative explanation, but what were the chances of that? After all, there hadn't been anyone else about on that part of the moor that day, not that he'd seen.

He immediately felt cold as he tried to make sense of it all. He'd only met Ruthven once, but he felt emotionally tied to her.

At once, Jack made his mind up to contact the police. Of course, he could pretend he'd never set foot on the moor, pack up the campervan, and return to Sutton in Surrey. There were no witnesses, and he doubted his image had been caught on CCTV. After all, the car park at the Postbridge Information Centre wasn't exactly Oxford Street in London. That way, he would save himself from becoming embroiled in the tragedy. He had planned to return home tomorrow, but now, in all probability, he would have to spend a couple more days down in Devon, explaining his movements and motives to the police. And then there was the press. Could he avoid speaking to local journalists?

It didn't take him long to decide that, if he did nothing about this, the situation would haunt him forever. He knew, therefore, that he couldn't simply ignore it. He owed it to her. He wouldn't abandon her now – even if her life had tragically expired.

So, with his head full of swirling thoughts, Jack packed away the breakfast things. He finished the last drop of lukewarm coffee and placed the mug in the washing-up bowl. That would all have to wait until later. Then he folded the table and slid it back into its travelling position, adjacent to the fridge. The roof was next. He started the engine and scrolled through the options on the electronic unit built cleverly into the ceiling of the van. One press of the button fired the motor into life and, after the warning signal, the roof slowly descended back into position.

Jack had never regretted buying 'Smudge', his three-year-old VW California campervan. These last few days had been another great adventure, and he was more than delighted with the results. Not only were the pictures he'd managed to take rather inspired, but he'd also managed to pen the accompanying blog with a good deal more panache than usual; Ruthven's ephemeral presence had definitely influenced him to write with more freedom.

Finally, with a very heavy heart, Jack slid the side door home, climbed into the driver's seat, and reached for his mobile phone.

* * *

Geoff Salter gathered the findings of the autopsy together. He would present these to the police later that morning but, for now, he would email the salient points to DS Baines.

Of course, he'd seen many dead bodies before. This unfortunate female was, essentially, not very notable. She was aged around thirty. She was of average height and weight and possessed few distinguishing features. She had a small tattoo – a symbol of some kind – underneath the bikini line on her left-hand side. He didn't really think it was significant, but he would obviously bring it to bear in discussion, seeing as though the identity of the girl had not, as yet, been established. She had sustained minor injuries to her face, hands, and knees in the fall. She was a non-smoker and had not had children.

Geoff reread the passage, always mindful of the mistakes predictive text could produce. 'Not very notable'. What the heck did that even mean? He always hated writing phrases like that. It confined this anonymous female to even further anonymity. He was under no illusion – he knew that 'really rather beautiful' was not at all scientific. They would think him unhinged if he had written 'her smile would have lit up any room'.

'Few distinguishing features' was also a travesty. Just sticking to the science enabled one to be objective and unemotional, but it had the effect of reducing the human body to meat. He shook his head. Perhaps he'd been doing this job for too long.

The circumstances behind her death had spurred Geoff Salter into updating his knowledge on cold water drowning, especially as the science on this subject was changing all the time. He knew there were many variables at play, and that it was difficult to be precise. Age, weight, the temperature of the water, the length of time spent in the water, injuries sustained, and rescue would all impinge on the end result. He was well aware that the colder the water, the better – if you were rescued in time, that is. The heartbeat slows. This stops the breathing and redistributes blood flow towards the heart, lungs, and brain. This phenomenon, he knew, was called 'the mammalian diving reflex'. The brain's need for oxygen wasn't so great when it was cold; therefore, it could survive for much longer without air. Studies of boating accidents had shown that, if unconscious, a body could stay afloat and be recoverable for up to an hour. However, Geoff knew of other studies that stressed reports of miracle cases, increasing false optimism.

He knew that, in this instance, the girl could have been saved; you didn't need a PhD to work out that if she'd been travelling with a companion, she would have been rescued. A friend's quick reaction, entering the icy brook and dragging her to the bank, would have saved the day. Maybe she would have needed resuscitation and medical help, but in all probability, she would have lived to tell the tale.

Basically, she fell so quickly that she couldn't use both hands to break her fall. She hit her head, and the shock of the cold water – coupled with her inability to move – killed her. She never regained consciousness.

The question remained: Could she have been pushed? Certainly, Geoff and his team had found no conclusive evidence of another party being present at the scene. There were no signs that the head had been held underwater. There were no injuries sustained suggesting that a scuffle or a fight had taken place. Her only injuries were those consistent with the fall.

However, it would only take a simple shove on the back and, with so many layers of clothing, this would be impossible to detect. The female was so laden; she would have been very unstable. Maybe the assailant, if there had been one, had intended to hold her head underwater. Then, maybe he or she had realised that this action wasn't required. Maybe… maybe…

Geoff didn't like maybes.

Above all, the fact that no identification had been found on her created an air of mystique that was becoming unavoidable.

* * *

Jack had offered information about the death over the phone, and he knew he was expected, but he still felt extremely apprehensive as he crossed the threshold and moved purposefully towards the front desk of the police station. A surprisingly cheerful police officer signed him in and told him to wait. She signalled to him where the coffee machine was but he declined and took a seat.

Jack tried to remember if he'd ever been inside a police station before. He certainly hadn't crossed the law enough to attend a trial in court. A speeding ticket and letting off a firework in the street when he was thirteen were all the misdemeanours he was prepared to own up to. Unless, he thought, you counted watching the late-night Channel Four television programme, 'Mile High', which was awfully cheesy. He smiled at his own nervous immaturity but was awoken by the presence of DC Box.

"Jack Reilly?"

"That's me," Jack replied, glad he didn't have to sit there a moment longer.

"If you come this way, DS Baines is waiting in her office."

He led Jack through a maze of corridors, flashing his electronic pass at various entry points. Eventually, they arrived at a very small room that could barely be described as an office.

DS Baines welcomed Jack and offered him a chair facing the two detectives. "Coffee?" Sandra asked, noticing he was without a drink.

"Er, yes, I will actually," Jack said, changing his mind owing to his now very dry mouth, "black, no sugar please."

Sandra looked at Mark and sheepishly grinned. He understood the non-verbal communication and left the room.

"So, Jack, you've come to give us some information about the death on Dartmoor. Is that correct?"

"Well… not directly, but I was up on the moor taking photographs of Fur Tor on Monday," he said, a little hesitantly.

"And what bearing do you think that has to our investigation?" Sandra asked.

At that moment, DC Box entered the room and placed three mugs of coffee on the table. He sat down next to the Detective Sergeant and produced a notebook and pencil.

Sandra smiled reassuringly at Jack and declared, "You're not under caution. This conversation is not being recorded. You're free to go whenever you like, but we'd like to make a few notes."

"I quite understand." He cleared his throat and took a sip of the hot coffee, wincing slightly at its bitterness. "I met this girl… on Fur Tor. We arrived at the same time but must have come from different directions. It was bloody unbelievable. I mean… it's in the middle of nowhere… and I didn't expect to meet someone like her."

The two detectives exchanged a knowing glance that was imperceptible to Jack. They were both aware that this was an important development.

"And how do you think this might be of interest to us?" DS Baines asked, knowing full well how it might be of interest.

"I heard about the death of a girl on the local news," Jack explained. "A brook near Fur Tor was mentioned. I was up on the Tor, and I met a girl there. I put two and two together…"

"Go on," Sandra encouraged.

Jack paused enough to mentally rehearse his lines before speaking out loud. "Maybe… the girl that I met at the tor was the girl who died in the river. I hope not… I mean…"

"Yes, I get what you mean, Jack. So what happened at the tor? Why does this girl mean anything to you? Not many people would have come forward."

Jack paused again, trying to think of the best way to explain a very crazy meeting with a girl who had affected him so much in such a short space of time. In truth, he couldn't stop thinking about her.

Sandra could see he was struggling to get started, so she decided to take him back to the beginning. They had plenty of time, and this was getting more interesting by the minute. "Why don't you start at the beginning?" she said gently. "How did you get to Fur Tor?"

"It's a tough one, that," Mark said, jollying the conversation to make Jack feel more at home, "I tried once with some friends, but we ran out of light."

Jack outlined the purpose of the visit, and described the southeasterly route from Postbridge to Fur Tor. He referenced the weather and the condition of the ground. He mentioned that he hadn't seen a single soul on his travels, apart from the girl at the tor.

Jack's explanation was very detailed and Sandra wasn't ruling out that he had, indeed, approached the tor using the route he described.

"When I reached the tor, I was elated. It was actually a good deal easier than I thought it would be. I guess I got lucky with the weather," Jack continued, gathering pace. "At that point, the light was amazing – all moody and dark to the distant hills and, in the foreground, shafts of brilliant, milky sunlight cascading over the rocks."

Realising that he was becoming too poetic, Jack brought his narrative back down to earth as he continued, "I started taking a few shots, but as I panned across one of the granite stacks, I noticed something moving behind. That's when I saw her."

Jack paused for a moment as a sudden flashback took hold of him.

"Describe her to us, Jack." Sandra spoke softly. She realised he'd reached a critical moment.

"My heart missed a beat, because I wasn't expecting any movement," he said slowly. "I thought it might have been cattle or sheep… perhaps a large bird. And then this exuberant bundle of fun appeared. She was not what I was expecting at all."

"How so?" DS Baines asked, allowing Jack to formulate an accurate response. DC Box unconsciously shuffled forward on his chair.

"It's February. It's a long hard slog to reach there. I thought it'd be some weather-worn character, and definitely not a lone woman. She was average height, slim, and athletic-looking. She had light brown hair of medium length."

"What was she wearing?" DC Box asked, pencil at the ready.

"Typical outdoor gear – you know, light browny-grey walking trousers, a darkish jacket, possibly black or brown. I can't remember... oh, and walking boots."

"Can you remember anything about her boots?" Sandra asked.

"Not really, no." He paused to think, and then said, "I wasn't looking at her boots."

"Good-looking, was she?" DC Box asked a little too eagerly.

"Well yes, but it wasn't that. She was like a whirlwind. She was witty, a bit flirty, and her face was *so* expressive. I've met a few people like that in my life, but I was... I have to say, immediately transfixed. I guess the situation was so odd... I mean, what are the chances of meeting someone there... at the same time?"

"Indeed," was Sandra's response. Then, concerned she might have betrayed her thoughts, she quickly fired off another question. "Did she have a backpack?"

"Yeah." He smiled. "She reckoned she couldn't be without her make-up..."

The rather odd reply made both detectives look at him inquisitively, as if more information should be forthcoming.

"That was a joke she made. She knew that, initially, I'd thought her a bit 'ditsy'. Not exactly the outdoor type – especially with her nails. She was enjoying making me squirm."

"Nails?" questioned Sandra, desperately trying to keep her voice as even as possible.

"Bright blue. They looked immaculate. Just a bit out of place, I guess."

Sandra was momentarily alarmed. Had she missed something? She didn't remember the dead female having brightly coloured nails. Surely she would have noticed? Geoff's notes hadn't said anything about nails either.

DS Baines composed herself before asking another question. "Do you remember if she had any other distinguishing features?"

Jack thought for a moment. "I noticed she had a small scar underneath her eye on her right cheekbone area. I was embarrassed about noticing, as she saw me glancing at it. She told me how she'd got it before I'd even asked. She seemed to have this ability to always be one step ahead."

DC Box hurriedly scribbled a few notes and looked up at DS Baines. They were both aware that the deceased had fallen and received an injury to the same area. Abrasions received during a fall would easily cover a small scar.

"So you have a photograph of her…?" Sandra posed, hoping beyond hope that he could confirm the identity of the girl.

"I wish I had, but I haven't," Jack replied, aware that an image of her would have helped. He cursed his own stupidity for not taking at least a selfie of the two of them.

"No photo for a photographer seems like a serious omission, Jack," Mark pointed out.

"I take pictures of landscapes, and I was working," he explained. "I knew I didn't have much time to complete my assignment. I actually asked her to move out of the way of a great shot. I can show you the series of pictures…"

"Some other time, Jack," Sandra replied, remembering the endless slide shows her father used to subject her to. "How about contact details? You said you were 'transfixed' by her. Did you manage to arrange to meet up again?"

Sandra looked squarely at Jack. She knew what the answer was going to be before he even spoke. He was reasonably tall, and rather striking without being boyishly good-looking. His thick, dark brown hair and olive, swarthy skin made him an ideal candidate for a knight in one of Burne-Jones's paintings. However, it was his vulnerability that made him attractive – but that was, she guessed, his own personal downfall. Women would fall for him, but he wouldn't even know it was happening.

"The weather began to turn and I knew we needed to get back. I… lost the moment," he admitted, in defeat. "I lost my nerve because it all seemed so unreal."

"So, no photo and no contact details. How about a name?" DS Baines asked, almost resigned to hearing the negative response.

"She said her name was Ruthven," Jack said, pleased to offer something tangible.

"Ruthven? That's unusual. I wouldn't know how to spell it," Sandra admitted.

"Me neither. But I searched for it on the internet and checked all social media. I came up with a big blank. I couldn't find her anywhere. It's all rather unusual."

"The whole story is unusual, Jack. You say you were there and, of course, you have the photos to prove it, but how do we know you didn't follow this girl off the tor?"

"She said she'd come from Lydford… over Hare Tor. My campervan was parked at Postbridge," he pleaded, trying to parry this unwelcome slight.

"…You ask to meet up, but she declines. You don't take no for an answer because you're smitten. You won't turn back. She tries to shake you off, but you won't listen…" Sandra became more and more intense as she spoke, trying to provoke a reaction.

"No."

"The weather is becoming worse and things get out of hand. You reach the brook below the tor, and she tries to cross quickly – too quickly."

"No, that didn't happen." Jack's heart was beating fast now, and he felt extremely anxious. He hadn't been expecting this sudden change of questioning. He felt like he was being pushed into a corner.

"You tried to stop her crossing the brook, but in doing so, you pushed her. She fell. She hit her head. She looked lifeless, like an unwanted ragdoll tossed into the water. You panicked. You ran." Sandra looked straight at Jack, her eyes boring into him, searching for answers.

"No, no, no." By now, Jack was getting a little angry about the injustice of it all. He also knew he had very little evidence to back up his version of events. He placed his head in his hands, desperately trying to think of something that would stop this unwanted barrage.

"Okay, you've got to help us, Jack," DC Box requested, adopting the 'good cop' role.

"Because one thing's for certain," Sandra added dramatically, taking out several photos from a folder, "this girl, here, died only a short distance from where you were, on the same afternoon."

She spread the images, one by one, across the table.

Jack stared at the photos of the lifeless form in the water. He picked up each one in turn, studying them carefully. Both detectives sat motionless, analysing Jack's reaction. The click of the dusty analogue clock hanging on the wall behind them punctuated the stillness.

Finally, Jack looked up at them and exclaimed, "It's not her – my God, it's not her!"

Chapter 4

The brightly-coloured nails had been a warning, but Detective Sergeant Baines hadn't really prepared herself for Jack's announcement. She'd anticipated a tearful collapse. Confronted with the evidence, staring starkly at him in the form of large colour photographs, she thought he'd buckle under the weight of guilt or shame. Instead, Jack had thrown the pebble into the pool, and the ripples were spreading in ever-increasing circles.

The ramifications hit home immediately, like a series of battering rams thudding against her castle wall. Another lone female on the moor – at the same time and in the same vicinity as the deceased – was a difficult thing to countenance.

What were the chances of that?

Jack's account, in all probability, was a fantasy, but it had appeared convincing. Nevertheless, Sandra had been a detective for many years, and in that time she had witnessed the most accomplished liars. Even so, she would need to consider the unlikely possibility that he was telling the truth.

As more ripples lapped the shore of her consciousness, she was suddenly hit by several 'what ifs'. Perhaps this

'Ruthven' knew the deceased, and they had argued and split up for some reason. What if Ruthven *murdered* the girl in the brook and, making her escape via the tor, met Jack? What if this girl knew nothing about the death and simply failed to see her on her way up to, and back from, the tor? Whichever way she considered the alternative series of events, it sounded more like a film script than an investigation into the tragic death of a young person. In all probability, the girl Jack had met *was* the girl who had lost her life.

"I don't know this person; I've never met her… it's not the same girl," Jack stated firmly, desperately trying to control his frustration.

"But what you're suggesting doesn't make sense. Are you sure you're not confused? It must be a shock," Sandra said, trying to keep the conversation as calm as possible.

She knew they had evidence of him being in the vicinity owing to the photos he'd taken, but other than that, it was all circumstantial. Up until the moment Jack had entered the police station, Sandra had concluded that the death must have been an accident. Somehow, this new development had cast doubt over that assessment.

"I can see I'm the only person around here who believes my story," Jack said, tossing a photo back on the table, "so are you going to charge me with anything, or am I free to go now? Because this has been a massive waste of time. I knew I should have just gone home."

He slouched back into the chair after taking a mouthful of coffee. It still tasted bitter – everything tasted bitter.

"Of course you're free to go," Sandra told him, "but we'd like a copy of all the photographs – pertinent to the day in question – that you have. We would also like your contact details and where you'll be staying here in Devon. We'll need a statement from you too. Oh, and we will be trying to find your 'Ruthven'. Her whereabouts are obviously vital to this investigation."

With that, Sandra gathered the photos of the woman together and tucked them back into the folder. She then signalled to DC Box that they needed to have a discussion.

Standing up, DS Baines opened the door of her tiny broom cupboard of an office and ushered Jack from his seat.

As he walked past her into the corridor, he spoke softly. "Rest assured, *I* will find her, even if you can't… or won't."

* * *

Ruthven had been waiting in the car – which she'd parked down the lane – for half an hour or so. Victoria's cottage was clearly visible and, from her vantage point, she was able to monitor any movements. She had to be certain that the house was empty.

Ruthven had chosen mid-morning because that's when people tended to be at their least observant. The initial early morning rush of activity gave way to the 'I need caffeine' slump. That was the theory, anyway. Hopefully, nobody would notice her slipping into the cottage.

There was a rear entrance, via a garden gate, that would allow her to enter unhindered. She also knew that there were spare keys for the doors. Even so, there remained two problems. First, she had to locate the spares, which were hidden in a magnetic box under Victoria's car, parked on the drive; second, she must get to them without being seen by a dog walker or, even worse, the police.

She knew that Victoria secreted a spare set of keys under her Mini because, several weeks ago, they'd had a discussion about losing important items. Her solution was typical of her analytical mind.

The arrival of the police was a very real danger, and if it happened, it would be catastrophic. After all, being found in the house would take some explaining. However, the rush of excitement – owing to the riskiness of the enterprise – was quite intoxicating. Her chest thumped palpably, every sense heightened in the moment. She certainly understood how some people got hooked on adrenaline-filled escapades.

Thanks to the television announcement, Ruthven knew that the police had no idea of Victoria's identity. She was also aware that it wouldn't take them long to discover it. She had to find what she was looking for soon, otherwise the chance would be lost.

She exited her car, careful not to lock it. Even though the chance was minimal, she didn't want the alarm to sound – her car tended to do odd things at times, and now was not the time for a comedy sketch. She walked casually over to the cottage, carrying a clipboard and handbag for cover. Dressed in a blouse, tight pencil skirt, and heels, she could easily pass as an estate agent.

She made for the nearside door of the parked Mini, figuring that the magnetic key holder would be located underneath. Miraculously, she was correct. She didn't fancy grovelling around beneath the vehicle, getting her hands dirty. She chuckled to herself mischievously. Being analytical was one thing, but in this life, you had to be savvy.

Now with the keys in hand, Ruthven made her way to the front door. Although emboldened by the ease of passage so far, she calculated that the side gate might be more problematic. There didn't seem to be any alarm, so she continued and turned the key in the lock. The front door opened with ease. Cautiously, she stepped inside.

Of course the cottage was silent; what had she been expecting? From past conversations, Ruthven knew Victoria had no pets. There was no scream of, 'What the hell do you think you're doing?' either.

The silly girl got herself killed.

Ruthven was sorry it had happened, but – at that precise moment – clearing up the awkward trail was the only thought she had.

She removed her heels and placed them in a plastic bag; if she had to move quickly, they would be a hindrance. The thrill she was experiencing was now reaching fever pitch, and it was difficult not to get carried away.

Ruthven took a moment to check herself. After all, she had a serious mission to accomplish. It was important to locate the books – and, of course, the earrings. She hadn't really got a clue about the reality of leaving evidence behind, but she was taking no chances.

So, Ruthven donned her slim white gloves and clothed her stockinged feet with disposable plastic elasticated covers. She then made for the living room, where she'd spied two large bookcases. Normally, she would have scanned the shelves with great interest, trying to glean what the choice of reading matter said about the character of the owner. In this case, the organisation of the books spoke volumes: it was like a library. There were no tatty covers, no books squeezed horizontally on top of others, no books out of place, and no books out of alphabetical order.

Her eyes took in the majesty, and then it became apparent: there was a void to the far right of the furthest bookcase. One book had created the only oblique line in the whole wall by leaning into the space. Ruthven's heart sank. She knew immediately what that meant.

She walked over and stood before the offending blemish. It was in the occult section. Her eyes flickered to the left as she read the authors: John Dee, Aleister Crowley, H.P. Lovecraft, Israel Regardie, space, Peregrin Wildoak. As her eyes locked on the gap, she knew that the two books she was looking for were missing.

It was a blow. So far, the crazy break-in had run like clockwork, but Ruthven had been lucky. Now was the time to think quickly. So, she moved rapidly towards the staircase and looked up. If anybody came now, she could still make her escape out the back door and hide in the garden. There were many trees and shrubs in the extensive grounds that led to the River Tavy at its far end. There might even be access to the riverbank and path. Once upstairs, though, her options would be very limited.

The expression 'in for a penny, in for a pound' came to her, and Ruthven realised she'd already crossed a big line by stepping over the threshold. So, she darted up the stairs and located the largest room.

It was easy to see that this was Victoria's bedroom. In keeping with the lounge and her library of books, everything was immaculately tidy and in its place. It was personalised with soft furnishings, photographs, and pictures. There was a dressing table and mirror, an old-fashioned wicker chair, and two very grand wardrobes. An old chest was positioned at the foot of the bed, and two bedside cabinets with Art Nouveau lamps framed the bedhead. It was like a scene from 1905.

Not being able to resist opening a few drawers, Ruthven wasn't at all surprised to see clothes skilfully and vertically stacked. In the left wardrobe, the shoes were beautifully paired and placed neatly on racks. The remaining shoes were stacked in their original boxes. For a moment, Ruthven wondered what an intruder would make of her own bedroom, shuddering at the thought. Then she snapped back to reality and focused on the job at hand.

"Where the effing hell are those books?" Ruthven muttered under her breath.

She scanned the room, but all the surfaces were devoid of reading matter. This meant that if they were anywhere at all, they would be in one of the bedside cabinets. She opted for the closest one. Her hunch was correct and there, neatly placed on the upper shelf, was one of the two books by Austin Osman Spare.

Picking it up, Ruthven rifled frantically through the pages in search of Victoria's notes and designs. She was desperately hoping for sheets of white paper to tumble out, but to no avail.

"OMG," she whispered in horror. "The silly cow only took them with her!"

It dawned on her that Victoria must have carried the missing book, hefty though it was, onto the moor. She must have made further notes and changes by torchlight as she camped. It was even likely that she'd performed some kind of ritual.

Her mind raced. The police would now have all the doodles, designs, and annotations, and the background reading to explain them. What incriminating evidence would be on them? Would they be able to decode the drawing to find what she was hoping to hide?

Once again, Ruthven snapped herself out of her reverie and became decisive. She closed the book and threw it, slightly angrily, into the plastic bag alongside her heels. She had made up her mind to spend a minute or two more trying to locate the earrings that she knew existed; Ruthven wanted to extract any further evidence of being a part of Victoria's life.

So, she looked around the room for an ideal location for a small box containing very intricate gold earrings. She discounted searching for a jewellery box because that's where Victoria would keep *her* things. These earrings were an undelivered gift from Victoria, who had started to become more and more overbearing. In fact, thought Ruthven, almost scarily suffocating. It was then that she hit upon the blindingly obvious: her underwear drawer.

It was the most private space in anyone's house. For a woman, if you dared enter without express permission, it represented a violation. Even though Ruthven knew Victoria was dead, she still baulked at clutching the two dropped bronze handles that would enable her to slide open Pandora's box. However, the thought of the potential treasure within egged her on. Realising that time was running short, and that staying for much longer would be pushing the boundaries of fortune, she slowly eased the drawer open…

At that moment, her worst fears were realised: a knock at the front door reverberated around the cottage like a hammer blow. Ruthven froze. Her instinct was to take in a short breath and hold it.

She waited.

Another knock, this time louder.

Strangely, Ruthven didn't move. Something inside her head kept her thinking logically. The second knock indicated that the person outside didn't have a key. Otherwise, they would have used it already.

A worried neighbour, a delivery, or a door-to-door salesperson?

She ran the possibilities through her mind and decided she could sweat this one out.

After what felt like an eternity, Ruthven heard footsteps crunching on the gravel driveway to the side of the cottage. Seconds later, the side gate to the garden rattled as the bolt was noisily slid back. The gate squealed as its weight moved against the dry, rusty hinges.

In order to discount the mystery person being a neighbour – who was about to gain entry via the back door – Ruthven crept, crouching low, over towards the bedroom window. She then raised her head like a U-boat periscope, slowly breaking water.

She squinted at the view outside. She could see the lane, but – more importantly – she could make out a white van with its side door open, revealing all manner of parcels.

Ruthven exhaled and composed herself. She judged that the package would be left by the back door and that an advisory note would shortly be posted through the letterbox. The van door would slide. The diesel engine would clatter…

The intrusion had certainly served as a wake-up call, and it had clearly rattled her. So, Ruthven quickly returned to the task at hand and unceremoniously yanked open the top drawer.

She was confronted with an immaculately displayed array of undergarments, grouped into colours. Even though she was expecting nothing less, Ruthven still opened her mouth in sheer wonder. Her own drawer was a tangled mass of knickers, bras, and tights that reminded her of Medusa's hair. This was a cathedral of lace.

Breaking the spell, and with her eyes almost closed, she dived into the intimate space. Both hands burrowed under like a pair of moles, disturbing the contents in a frantic search for a box of some kind. After her initial foray, Ruthven found nothing. Becoming more desperate, she began sifting through handfuls, as if she was making pastry. The delicate items were thrown upwards in the hope of flushing out the treasure.

Suddenly, a red box revealed itself. As she gathered it in her hands, her relief was considerable.

The sprung lid was quite stiff, and Ruthven felt rather ham-fisted as she attempted to open the container. Inside, the most beautiful, intricately designed pair of earrings lay on a bed of pearl satin.

With a smug grin, Ruthven snapped the box shut and swiftly placed it in her carrier bag.

Ruthven knew that her lack of time was becoming critical, but she had one last task to perform. She scanned the room for a framed photograph of the house owner but, unsurprisingly, she couldn't see any. In desperation, she opened her bag again and found the small box containing the St Christopher pendant Jack had given her. Taking it out, she placed it under the now tangled underwear before her.

"I wanted to place it next to your photo, Victoria, but here will have to do," she muttered under her breath. "I haven't a clue what happened out there, but you'll need this talisman much more than I do. Safe journey, my friend. Sorry if I let you down."

With that, Ruthven closed the drawer and escaped as fast as you could in a tight skirt.

* * *

The loud music pumping through the campervan was having little effect. Really, Jack should have selected something more soothing, but he just couldn't face it. He thumped the steering wheel with both hands, frustrated at the way the morning had so quickly and easily deteriorated.

With the best of intentions, he had tried to do the right thing. Only now, he realised what a precarious position he was in. If the police didn't believe that Ruthven existed, and thought it was just a cover story, they would conclude that he was more than likely responsible for the death. The aspect that was really gnawing away at him, however, was not being believed. It took him back to his school days. The worst thing that could happen to you was injustice. It affected your very being: your soul.

He took the main road out from Tavistock and headed up to Lydford and the pub car park where he was staying for a few nights. Many taverns were more than happy to have an arrangement with campervan owners, and the 'Lydford Castle' suited him perfectly. In exchange for 'free accommodation', Jack frequented the pub and bought meals there.

As Jack glanced through the driver's door window, he surveyed the rolling hills and tors stretching away to his right-hand side. A few days ago, he couldn't wait to get in amongst them. Now, they filled him with dread. They looked dark and foreboding –they certainly hid secrets. He thought it ironic that if, from where he was staying, he had taken the westerly route to Fur Tor, he could have walked back with Ruthven. That would have saved him the turmoil he knew he was about to experience. He ruminated how decisions, made by even the tiniest of margins, sometimes created chaos out of proportion to all else.

Are we always walking on such a tightrope? he pondered.

Jack turned off the main A386 at the Dartmoor Inn and then drove towards the pub in Lydford. Suddenly the music faded, and his in-car phone rang. It was his sister, Beth. He didn't want to worry her with his troubles, so he quickly composed himself.

"Hi sis… got nothing else to do so you fancied a chat?"

"Very funny. When I have a spare moment I'll be catching up with some sleep," his sister said, used to Jack's sense of humour.

"So, how is my little bundle-of-fun nephew?"

"Charlie's great, but he's exhausting, Jack. He's growing fast. You must come and see him soon." Beth let Jack ponder that for a moment and then announced,

"Remember, we need to clear out Mum's things from the house… it's been three months now…"

"Yes, of course, Beth… I… I don't know where the time has gone. Listen, I'm in the van. I'm just parking up. I'll call you back in a few moments… don't go away now."

He disconnected the call and reversed the campervan into the allocated space. He then switched off the motor and slumped in the seat. His thoughts ran straight to his mother and the car accident; it had been a great shock to Jack and his older sister. They had lost their father to a sudden heart attack a few years back, and now they both felt rudderless. He had obviously gone into denial; he'd been avoiding their old home ever since it happened. Just travelling down the familiar streets near to where his mother had lived was painful.

He picked up his mobile phone and called his sister back. She answered immediately.

"Jack… I thought perhaps you were going to sweep it under the carpet again. I'm glad you called back."

"You're right as always. We have to get this done… it's just that it's going to be awful."

Jack thought about the unenviable task of throwing out all their mum's clothes and possessions that had been so precious to her but that meant nothing to anybody else. It felt like a criminal act was going to be committed.

"Yes, I quite agree, but we'll need to get the house sold while it's in good working order. We don't want this dragging on past the summer. Can you make it this weekend? I'll meet you at the house. I'll get someone to look after Charlie."

Jack wondered if he'd be free of police interest by then. He was hopeful that it wouldn't take them long to establish he hadn't known the dead girl. Finding Ruthven was the issue; that might take a while.

"I'll see you there, Beth," Jack said, not being able to directly answer her question.

He just hoped he wasn't going to have to let her down.

* * *

Detective Sergeant Baines sat facing Geoff Salter. His office was grander than hers but a little less cosy. He had invited her over to discuss developments in the Dartmoor death case. He preferred the 'meeting of minds' to be face to face rather than via computer screens; he thought it a more human experience.

Sandra sipped her coffee and returned the cup to its rather fancy saucer. She reminded herself to replace her standard chipped mug and instant coffee granules. They had to go. Her mood was buoyant, but she'd come in need of support. Geoff could help her with that.

"So," she announced grandly, "we're pretty sure we have a name and address for the poor girl."

"Ah, at last. That must be a relief," Geoff replied, looking encouraged. "How did you find out?"

"Her work's risk assessment procedure kicked in. She didn't make contact that evening. They couldn't raise her, and she obviously didn't show up for work the next day. When they heard the news of a fatality near to where she was camping, they raised the alarm."

"Impressive."

"Victoria Kent is her name, and she lived in a small, out-of-the-way cottage near Mary Tavy. I think she must have been heading home via Tavy Cleave and the moor gate at Lanehead."

"A heck of a walk, that," Geoff said, raising his eyebrows in admiration.

"Well, that was the point. We think she was in training for some kind of expedition in Northern Canada; she was a research scientist working on the capacity to live in cold climates. She worked for a company called 'Enable', based in Plymouth. They provide advice and support to groups working in inhospitable environments."

"I guess that's why she was camping out, in February, in one of the most hostile places in the UK."

"Indeed," agreed Sandra.

"She was certainly carrying some hi-tech camping gear in her backpack: a super lightweight but weather-resistant tent, and a very high-quality sleeping bag, amongst other things."

"Anything of interest to the case?" Sandra asked, keen to gain information that would push the investigation forward.

"Well now, her choice of bedtime reading was a little unusual," he told her.

"How so?" Sandra asked, rather intrigued.

"Austin Osman Spare. Know anything about him?"

She'd been expecting racy literature, not an unfamiliar author. Her interest grew. "Should I?"

"Well, he was an artist of some renown," Geoff explained. "However, his paintings and drawings are… an acquired taste. They are not easily accessible – a lot of sexual imagery, monstrous figures, and so on. He also wrote books about the occult. To the layman he is unknown, but to people who have an interest in these things, he is very well regarded."

Sandra knew only too well that Geoff had something specific to discuss. She urged him on. "So our girl was conducting magic on the moor?" She raised her eyes and smiled, indicating that she didn't believe that for one minute.

"Well now, that's a moot point; however, she didn't carry the hardback book as extra weight to increase the challenge, that's for certain."

"Okay, now I'm interested, Geoff. I know you've found something."

Geoff nodded. "So, inside the book were pieces of paper with many pencil drawings of designs containing letters. There was also a separate scrap of paper with – what looks like – the end product: a sigil."

"A what? You've completely lost me, Geoff, but I'm sure you're about to help me out here?"

"Look, don't think that I'm the fountain of all knowledge on this. I've just been doing some reading on this myself." He drank some of his coffee, as if to compose himself, before he launched into his explanation.

"Spare was really interested in the power of the subconscious. He believed that through a state of meditation, or sexual ecstasy, a person could access the secret world of the supernatural. He thought that by condensing letters of the alphabet into a 'diagrammatic glyph of desire' – that means an artistic-looking symbol – you could use it to create energy. A sigil is like a seal."

"I'm just about with you… keep going."

"Wonderful," said Geoff, pleased that she was prepared to humour him a little longer. "Let's say you have something on your mind, and you want to make it happen. You are going to 'will' it to happen, but to help – according to Spare – you need to use a sigil. You write down a simple statement like, 'My will is to communicate more with others'. You cross out all letters that are repeated, and then, taking the others, turn them all into capitals. Next, you have to create a design from the letters that remain – and some letters, of course, could have duplicates. It doesn't have to be a work of art, but it does have to represent your best efforts. It could exist as a drawing, a seal, a piece of jewellery… and so on. This sigil helps you focus: it is the charged will of its creator. It is meant to bring your will a step closer to coming true."

Geoff finished his explanation and looked carefully at DS Baines for her reaction. "I know you're going to find that all rather weird, but more people are into these things than you think," he finished.

"Okay, I'm beginning to understand the thread of this," Sandra replied slowly. "By working in reverse from the diagram, it might be possible to understand what was on her mind just before she died… is that possible? Oh, and don't worry, Geoff, I don't think you've lost your marbles!" Sandra laughed, getting excited at the prospect of a promising lead.

"Two things," Geoff offered. "Firstly, that is possible, although very difficult, but it might turn out to be very mundane and have nothing to do with her demise…"

"And secondly?"

"Secondly, I think her tattoo, just above her pelvic area–"

"Is a sigil?" Sandra asked, in anticipation.

"Exactly," punctuated Geoff, pleased that DS Baines had followed his thinking.

There was a brief pause while both parties considered the ramifications.

Geoff broke the silence. "The thing is, Sandra, this may be nothing at all. This could just be an interest of hers. I mean, we're hardly talking about a secret code that could tell us the whereabouts of the Ark of the Covenant. Also, trying to find all of the capital letters that form the sigil, and work out the duplicate letters that got discarded, might be next to impossible."

Sandra thought for a moment. "I get that, Geoff, but it may be important. That was great work… a little off your patch, but it could be very useful. If you give me a copy of her tattoo and the sigil, I'll get Mark on it. He loves all this sort of stuff."

Geoff nodded. "Oh, and one other thing of interest…"

"Go on," said Sandra.

"We found a metal dish and a small box containing fragments of charred paper. The document was obviously burned on the dish."

Sandra took a moment to process this information. "The paper wasn't burnt to eradicate something – otherwise, she would have scattered the ash to the wind."

"Exactly."

"Therefore, the act of burning must have been important. This could have been some kind of ritual involving the sigil – that's why she kept the ashes."

"My thoughts entirely," Geoff agreed.

"Well, well, well…" Sandra said, finding herself using a phrase her father had often used, "that's a little unexpected." She shuffled in her seat, indicating that she had questions of her own. Alarmingly, she couldn't quite get the image of the tattoo – close to Victoria's pelvic region – out of her head, but she needed to move on. While she was with Geoff she wanted to see if he'd changed his mind about any aspects of the death. So, after a brief pause, she spoke again. "Are you still of the opinion that it was an accident?"

Geoff swung his chair from side to side, as people do when they're a little stressed, or indecisive. "I am, because nothing indicates otherwise…"

"But something's bothering you?" At this stage, she didn't want to inform Geoff about the interview with Jack, because it might have coloured his assessment. Even though Sandra considered him impeccably professional, she didn't want to muddy the waters in any way.

"I have to deal with the facts as we discover them," he replied. "There's nothing to suggest she was with anybody when she died. Obviously, it makes it hard when you know she was an experienced outward-bound type. Really, she was the last person you would have expected to fall into that brook."

"Unless she was pushed?"

"Those are your words, not mine," said Geoff, looking straight at her.

Chapter 5

Detective Sergeant Baines and Detective Constable Box stood in the hallway of the cottage belonging to Victoria Kent. It was immediately apparent that she'd been house-proud, as there were no signs of dust or clutter.

Sandra bent down to pick up a delivery note from the floor, noticing the date; someone had called earlier that day. A simple message – 'Round the back' – was scribbled in the space provided.

"It's either an ongoing arrangement or someone's just lobbed it over the gate. I've seen that before," Mark said, reading over her shoulder. "Shall I go and get it?"

"Good idea, but don't be long. I want to do this together. I don't want to miss anything."

While Mark was gone, Sandra made her way into the open-plan living room. At once she noted two tall bookcases facing each other with a large oak dining table in between. A cut-glass vase with fresh flowers was placed on a lace doily in the centre, but some of the flowers were beginning to wilt. This was no flat-packed, cut-price furniture, thought Sandra. Victoria either had a very well-paid job or an inheritance. The décor was very much in the style of the Arts and Crafts movement of the late 19th century. She nodded her head in approval.

DC Box returned from the garden with a medium-sized package. One of the corners was slightly crumpled, but the box hadn't been punctured.

"See what I mean?" Mark pointed out the damaged area – the result of the parcel being dropped. "Shall I open it?"

"I reckon we ought to, seeing as though she must have ordered it not long before she embarked on her trek. It might say something about her frame of mind at the time."

They grappled with the parcel tape and packaging like a couple receiving a shared present at Christmas. Gradually, the contents were revealed: a new pair of walking boots and gators. They looked at each other and raised their eyebrows; the irony of the situation had not gone unnoticed.

"Late delivery methinks," Mark said, softly.

"Indeed," Sandra agreed, pondering how the little things in life can often affect us disproportionately.

They moved into the living room and began looking at the bookcases. Victoria's interest in an author associated with the occult fascinated Sandra. She didn't have a great understanding of esoteric literature, but she had become curious about others' taste for knowledge that lay on the margins. If a person shared a passion for something quite niche or less mainstream, she thought they were more intriguing. Maybe it was because she, too, enjoyed the frisson of exploring life on the edge of 'respectability'.

They gazed at the library before them. It wasn't difficult to notice the missing books; the gap stood out like a sore thumb, the symmetrical splendour marred by the omission.

Sandra stepped forward and pointed towards the offending space. "Very interesting. We know she took one book with her... so where's the other? And why is it missing?"

"Maybe it's upstairs. Bedtime reading, perhaps?" Mark suggested.

"Could be. We'll check that out when we look in her bedroom," Sandra answered, not convinced by the obvious explanation. "There are quite a few books on the occult. I'd say she had more than a passing interest," she pointed out.

"I'd agree, but there's nothing else to suggest a passion for the supernatural." He scanned the room. "There are no ornaments save this pointed block of crystal here. No objects, art, or photographs... just books."

"What were you expecting? A pentagram on the carpet, a coffin for a coffee table? Some people like to keep things that are important to them close to their chest."

"Point taken," Mark replied, quite used to Sandra's facetious comments.

They continued the tour of the cottage by moving upstairs into Victoria's bedroom. The kitchen had yielded nothing of interest. They were rather hoping for scribbled notes on a reminders board, or correspondence containing bad news – something that might link her to Jack, or explain why someone wanted her dead. As Victoria had no identification on her when she died, they were expecting to discover her purse and phone. Common sense dictated they would be in the bedside unit she slept next to.

It was uncomfortably quiet as they searched the bedroom for anything of use; it always felt odd to be poking about in a private place. They knew, of course, that Victoria wasn't about to step through the door, but even so… it was as if the cottage had lost its soul. It was a feeling Sandra remembered well; visiting her old home after her father's death had been very painful.

"Well, that's odd," exclaimed Sandra, "no phone, purse, or book. I would have bet money on them being in one of the bedside cabinets."

"This is clearly her bedroom. I'll check the other rooms, but why would she leave them there?" Mark asked, already on the move.

"I'll check the drawers, they may be in there…" Sandra called out, after he'd left the room. She opened each drawer in turn, going from the bottom upwards. Sandra had never seen anything quite like it. Her own drawers were bursting through the hardboard bottom panel, she had so much in them. Here, all of the clothes were expertly folded and neatly arranged. T-shirts and tops were stored so tidily they looked brand new. She wondered how it was possible to live this way, and then she recollected how much time it took for her to find a precious item of clothing 'lost' in the jumble.

Mark re-entered the bedroom and shook his head. "Nothing at all. One very typical spare bedroom… the other, rather empty save for a couple of photographic screens, some lighting, a wardrobe, and a few props. Perhaps she was into photography. Any luck?"

By now, Sandra had worked her way to the top drawer. She slid it open. "My God, will you take a look at this!" she exclaimed.

Mark moved closer to the opened drawer and peered inside. He wasn't quite sure what to say, so he mumbled, "That's the lady's underwear, boss. I think this is your department."

"Yes, but what do you notice?"

"I'd rather not look…"

"It's in a tangled mess – don't you think that's rather odd?" she probed, hoping he'd fall into line.

"Everywhere else is amazingly – almost scarily – tidy," he conceded, before pausing for a moment, "…meaning someone's been rummaging through the contents, looking for something?"

"Bingo. And I have a sneaky suspicion *that* person has also taken the second book, the purse, and the phone. We got here too late."

"But we have the book containing the diagrams and notes. I'll bet the intruder was really looking for those," Mark reasoned. "What do you think was in the drawer? What sorts of things do you keep in yours?"

Sandra gave Mark a look. "Never you mind, nosy. And the answer to your first question is, I don't know… a notebook, or diary, perhaps? Maybe a receipt or even a photo? Who knows?" She shrugged. "The one thing I do know is that this makes the investigation more complex."

Mark nodded, sighing.

"And here's another oddity: if there has been an intruder, where's the sign of a break-in?" she asked. "There isn't one. That would indicate that the deceased knew the person. Relatives and trusted neighbours might have keys. A friend may have known where a spare set was hidden."

Sandra's eyes suddenly focused on a small plastic box that had been revealed when she'd nudged one or two items in the drawer. "And here's yet another oddity," she declared, examining the contents of the box through the transparent plastic lid.

"Is that a St Christopher?" enquired Mark. "That seems a little out of place when you consider the books she likes to read."

"That's what I was thinking. Odd. Still, it could be something she was given in her previous life, so to speak."

"I've got a few of those," admitted DC Box. "We have quite a few leads to follow; I'll get on to them as soon as we've finished here."

"Agreed. And there's also the book, and the drawings Victoria was making. I can't help thinking they will hold the key to our little mystery."

* * *

Detective Inspector Beechcroft looked at the evidence gathered so far, his demeanour noticeably circumspect. There were a few hopeful leads and one or two issues to be followed up – the possible break-in at the cottage being the most pressing – but the forensic team hadn't been able to declare the death as anything other than an accident. He therefore needed convincing that the police had any further interest in the case.

He was just tidying the papers when Detective Sergeant Baines and Detective Constable Box entered the room. He waved aside all formalities and urged them to sit down. He sat on the edge of his desk, adopting a casual, friendly approach. Stuffiness was not in his nature – and, in any case, he admired and enjoyed working with both detectives who sat facing him.

"I see that we now have a name for this unfortunate girl… Victoria Kent. Do we know anything about her?"

"We've managed to build a reasonable picture of her life, sir." Sandra pulled an A4 sheet from a file and paraphrased, in a deadpan voice, "Lived just outside Mary Tavy on the edge of the moor… aged 31, fit and healthy… we think she was single… she worked as a scientist for a company in Plymouth… she loved the outdoors… she liked to read and she kept herself to herself."

She broke the monotone voice and adopted a chirpier tone. "The cottage is immaculate. It's so tidy and well-organised; I've never seen anything quite like it. The neighbours said she seemed very pleasant, but they hardly knew her. Her parents live in Kent, but they're currently on holiday abroad."

"Anything at all in her life that made her a target?" DI Beechcroft asked.

"Not really. We didn't uncover anything of interest, but it's worth mentioning that she was found with a book on the occult," DC Box informed him, wanting direction about that aspect of the case.

"Ah yes, you've made reference to that in the report," replied Beechcroft. "She was designing symbols of some kind. I think you referred to them as sigils, is that the word?" The others nodded. "Was this occult business a casual interest of hers, or was it more serious? We obviously need to be careful here. We don't want the press to get a hold of a wild fantasy."

Sandra nodded. "Absolutely. She has a library of books in her house, and a large section of them are esoteric in nature – at least to my untrained eye. Let's say that she knew what she was doing. What do you think about trying to decode the sigils? Is there any mileage in that?"

DI Beechcroft thought about it for a moment and then nodded. "Yes, we ought to follow that lead, but I can't give you much time on it. The break-in certainly adds weight to proceedings. Maybe, as you say in the report, the two are linked. What's missing from the house?"

"We think another book on the occult, her phone, and her purse. I also reckon something was taken from her top drawer—"

"A trophy hunter perhaps?" Inspector Beechcroft interjected.

"I think we can all rest easy that we're not dealing with an individual who has progressed from stealing from washing lines. I rather think the person was after a notebook or diary – something that would reveal their identity." Sandra was amused by the inspector's possible Freudian response. But thinking more deeply, she recognised that it was a possibility they should take seriously.

"Er… yes, of course. Now, equally pressing is Jack Reilly. What do we think about him? Can we be sure he isn't our burglar?"

Sandra thought for a moment. In truth, his evidence troubled her. "We're investigating that as we speak. He has a campervan, and he's staying at a pub in Lydford. It shouldn't be hard to find out what he's been up to in the last 24 hours. Also, we ought to try and track down this girl he claims to have met on the tor. With a name like Ruthven, it shouldn't be too difficult to find her. If she turns out to be fictitious, I think we ought to bring him in for questioning."

"That sounds good," replied Beechcroft. "We don't have any forensic evidence linking him to the death, and until we can nail him for the break-in, it would be foolish to bring him in at this stage. However, let's find out if there was a link between Jack and Victoria. Explore the usual avenues: work, rest, and play."

***

Jack's sister, Beth, was already at their old home sifting through things. He opened the door with his key and stood in the hallway. The familiar smell sent him into a brief maelstrom. What was it about your old home when you returned after a prolonged absence? Inevitably, his thoughts raced to when he was younger. It all seemed so much larger in those days – not that the house was small.

He called up to his sister, "I see that you've ordered the skip!"

"Hi, Jack! Come on up!" came the response.

Jack climbed the staircase and met Beth on the landing. They embraced and held each other for a while longer, acknowledging the emotional task that lay before them.

"It's a big skip," he said. What he really meant was that the job of clearing their mum's possessions was going to be a difficult, onerous task.

"How much are you going to keep? We have to lose it, Jack. There's no other way," Beth pointed out.

He knew there was no arguing. It had to be done. His sister was always stoic in the face of adversity, and he liked and admired her immensely because of that. He was struggling to come to terms with selling the house and moving on. He was also rather on edge about his time on Dartmoor. He knew it was only a matter of time before the police would want to question him again. He hadn't told his sister about it, and he dreaded her finding out. She had enough to cope with, let alone having to rescue a naïve younger brother who should have handled the situation he'd found himself in so much better.

SIGIL

"I'll handle her clothes," said Beth, before reeling off the plan she'd formulated in the car on the way to the house. "I'll save the best dresses, coats, and shoes and give them to the charity shop. I'm going to throw all the rest. I'll strip the bedding from the bedrooms and get rid of that as well. Can you sort out the garage? I don't want anything from there. So, any tools that are any good, keep. Otherwise, if they're no good, bin them. By the way, I've got a buyer for her runaround."

Sparked into action, Jack pulled out some gloves from his pocket. "Great. That sounds sensible. Let's give it an hour, then we'll meet in the kitchen for coffee."

With that, Jack went to the kitchen and located the garage door key. He was grateful that he didn't have to make many decisions. He would save one or two tools that might come in handy, but the rest would be consigned to the dump.

He wondered whether this task would bring him some valuable thinking time. After all, he could do with a breakthrough. All his internet searches on social media for a girl named Ruthven had been fruitless. He'd asked in the pub where he was staying if anyone had heard of a girl with that name, but to no avail. He chastised himself for not taking a photo of her – that was a schoolboy error of massive proportion. He was beginning to think that Ruthven wasn't even her real name, and that she'd just used it to enhance the fantasy. He needed new ideas, and quickly, because he couldn't stop thinking about her; it was getting to be a problem. And, as he was hopeless at hiding his worries, it was a problem his sister was bound to detect.

An hour later, Jack hauled the faded orange hover mower over the lip of the skip and tossed it in. It was the last bulky item to be dealt with, and he needed a drink. He slapped his gloved hands together, almost in triumph, and made his way inside the house. The hallway was lined with black sacks.

His sister was attempting to bury a mound of clothes into the last one when she caught sight of Jack. "Put the kettle on; I've got something to show you."

Jack dutifully retreated into the kitchen, wondering what his sister had found. He was preparing himself to be embarrassed by a dreadful school report, or a toy he'd played with as a small boy. He had a feeling that Beth hadn't found a roll of fifty-pound notes tucked into an item of clothing.

He was busying himself making a pot of coffee when his sister sat down at the kitchen table and produced a photo album.

"I found this, amongst others, tucked away in a drawer in the back bedroom," Beth said proudly, knowing that Jack would be intrigued.

"Old photos? Why this album especially?"

"Because you've just been down to Devon, and this book has photos from our old holidays there… on Dartmoor."

Jack suppressed his anguish as he tried to act in keeping with his sister's expectations. He opened the book and gazed at images that sent him right back to his past. "Oh my goodness, take a look at me there!" Jack blurted, pointing at himself in a picture.

"You were quite cute, if I remember correctly. Do you remember the caravan?"

"I loved that caravan," Jack replied, smiling. "I remember the bunk beds at the end and the little table we had for drawing and playing games. Truly happy days."

"And the campsite by the river. Do you remember much about that? We stayed there, every August, for three or four years in a row." Beth turned the pages of the album, highlighting various pictures with her finger.

"The campsite was awesome," said Jack, thinking back. "We had so much room to roam. Do you remember the games of cricket? And the ice creams from the little shop by the tennis courts?"

"That's right, we used to play cricket on that large open field that led down to the mini hydroelectric plant. They must have been getting power for the campsite from the flow of the stream. I think there was a small lake there–"

"The inflatable boat! It was yellow and we had a paddle each," Jack cut in, as the memories came flooding back.

He stood up and poured the coffee, wondering where that little carefree boy had gone. Nostalgia, even for a few minutes, had been a marvellous antidote to his woes. It was also healing to interact so positively with his sister. They had always got on, but now that both parents were no longer living, they would need an even closer bond to support each other in future times.

"Jack, do you remember any of the friends we made there? The Taylors, for instance?"

"I remember that our two families got together for a few of the holidays. It was Georgie and Oliver, wasn't it? I know I was very young."

"That's right. Oliver was roughly my age, and I think Georgie was a year older than you. Here, look." She pointed to a photograph of the two families together. "The four of us used to ride all over the campsite on our bikes. Then, as two families, we'd go out on the moor and have a picnic."

Jack nodded; it was all flooding back.

She turned the page. "Oh look, Jack… here." Beth drew his attention to a series of images. "Do you recall the time we met up with the Taylors' friends for the day?"

"Not really, no." Jack's brow furrowed as he tried to recollect the event.

"We'd all gone out for a walk… three families. There were six of us kids: you, me, Georgie, Oliver, Rachel, and Jacqui. Look, Mum's written notes in pencil underneath. Anyway, we ended up climbing the rocks of a tor. Jacqui – she would have been about your age – slipped and fell. She hit her face. Her dad had to take her to hospital at Tavistock. She was given stitches, and when we saw them later that evening, she had a dressing over the wound."

Beth's words – 'slipped and fell' – reverberated inside Jack's head like a coin being rattled in a tin.

"I don't think I remember," he mumbled as a holding comment.

Flashes of Ruthven's account came to him like a ghostly voiceover in a movie. He felt a fog descend, and he was struggling to think straight.

His sister, oblivious of Jack's mental anguish, continued trying to jog his memory. "Here she is, Jack. That's a good picture of Jacqui before the accident, and over here," she turned the page, "is her with the dressing. I must say, she was a pretty tough cookie. She didn't make much fuss at all. I think *we* were more alarmed about it. I can't believe you don't remember it!"

Beth turned back the page and Jack found himself staring at the photograph. It wasn't Jacqui's eyes he was hypnotised by – it was Ruthven's. He couldn't quite believe it, but it was definitely her. He would never forget that face, and even though she was a child in this picture, it was unmistakably the girl he'd met on the tor the other day. He stared at the picture and tried to imagine the slight mark that would emerge high on her cheekbone – that tiny scar, that beautiful blemish. In that moment, Hardy's words – 'It was the touch of the imperfect upon the would-be perfect that gave the sweetness…' – came to him. He was spellbound.

"Are you alright, Jack?" his sister enquired, a little alarmed. "You've lost your colour."

Jack paused for a moment, desperately trying to rescue the situation. He cursed the fact that his face always seemed to betray his thoughts. "Just thinking about Mum," he lied, "those were great holidays that Mum and Dad gave us."

Beth placed her hand on his and spoke tenderly as she said, "I know, I feel it too."

He felt dreadful; he had been disingenuous. He had used the very people whom he loved to dig himself out of a hole. He reasoned, however, that there was no point in involving his sister until he was sure his theory was correct. So, in an effort to cull more information, he casually asked about Jacqui's parents. "Where did the family come from, again? I remember that Georgie and Oliver came from The Wirral near Liverpool…"

Beth thought for a moment. "I think the dad owned a bookshop in Farningham, Kent. I only recall that because our dad ordered a book from him to help me with my dissertation at university. He gave it to me wrapped in the shop's paper bag, and I still have it at home. I think he specialised in niche interests – you know, odd stuff."

Jack was struggling to believe his luck. His sister had given him a golden nugget. Surely there couldn't be many bookshops in Farningham? He didn't know the town or village, but seeing as though he'd never heard of it, he reasoned it had to be a reasonably small, out-of-the-way place. Of course, Ruthven's parents might have sold up and moved, but he could probably secure a forwarding address.

"Odd stuff? What do you mean?" he asked, trying to sound nonchalant.

"Books on alchemists, psychoanalysts, conspiracy theories, ley lines –that kind of thing," Beth explained.

"I guess internet bookshops have stolen the market on popular fiction. Small independents have to specialise," Jack murmured.

"Yes, but you'll be surprised just how many people are seriously interested in esoteric literature and 'the auld ways'," Beth pointed out. "It's all rather hidden, and below the surface, but it's there. Actually, you won't be surprised by this – you write and take photographs for online websites that deal with this kind of stuff, don't you?"

"Indeed," Jack said. With that, he finished his coffee, stood up, and gathered his sister's mug. He then walked over to the sink and began to wash up.

Without looking at Beth, he asked, as casually as possible, "Could I have that book for a while? I'd like to have a proper look later. I don't want to keep it – it's as much yours as it is mine."

Beth was touched that he was as interested in their childhood holidays as she was. Of course, she had no idea that Jack had an ulterior motive for the request. "Yes, of course. There are another couple of albums. Why don't you have them for a bit, and maybe we can swap in a few months? I know you'll look after them."

"Thanks." Jack picked up his gloves and began making his way back out to the garage.

Beth spoke to him as he opened the door. "Jack… I'm really glad that you and I can talk to each other and share things," she said softly. "Many siblings would be at each other's throats, fighting over their parents' money and possessions. I love that we trust each other and that we don't hide secrets. Mum and Dad would be proud of us."

Jack blew his sister a kiss. He was lost for words.

* * *

Detective Sergeant Baines took the difficult decision to leave work on time. Her hours were officially flexible but, as she maintained, they were – all too often – floppy. There were always loose ends to tie up, colleagues to give advice to, and deadlines to chase. Secretly, she loved her work, but there were times when her resolve was pushed to the limit. An ever-increasing workload created tiredness, and tiredness created mistakes. Mistakes could be catastrophic and very public. Sometimes she wondered how the wheels kept turning, but they did.

Sandra had arranged to meet her older sister for a drink and a 'something' at a little independent coffee shop, over the county border in Launceston, Cornwall. That was the plan, anyway. What would normally happen is that the 'little something' would end up being more involved than a snack, but not enough to become an evening meal. As they ate and drank, they would while away the hours catching up on recent news.

The rather homely bell above the door chimed as Sandra entered the tearoom. The smell of freshly brewed coffee permeated the room. Individual tables were beautifully bedecked with stylish placemats and fresh flowers placed in small, decorative, porcelain vases. There were old-fashioned Tilley lamps, oak wood panelling, Art Nouveau figures, and subtle uplighting on Liberty wallpaper-covered walls.

Sandra searched the busy room and soon spotted her sister, Megan, sitting at a table in the far corner. She waved back, sporting a huge grin. Although two years older, she looked fairly similar to her, and people often commented on the family resemblance. Like her sister, Megan was reasonably tall and slim. She was also very attractive – not because she was classically beautiful, but because her face was expressive and interesting.

"What time do you call this?" Megan teased.

"Are you kidding? I'm early," Sandra replied, playing the game.

"Exactly. It's got to be the first time ever!"

"Very witty. Criminals don't usually pack up and go home at five, you know."

Megan looked her sister up and down and said, "You're looking great. Have you taken up walking or something?"

"It's funny you should say that. Actually, I'm still trying to get rid of the Christmas excess. I didn't really stop when everybody else did!" She pinched some skin around her midriff.

"Oh, you poor thing. You're wasting away!" Megan joked, before quickly adopting a more serious tone. She looked at her sister's face for clues. She sensed that Sandra was looking for reassurance about something. It was difficult to define, but it was there.

"What are you looking at me like that for?" Sandra asked, laughing defensively.

"Something's bothering you. I can tell. It's that older sister's sixth sense."

"What, just because I wanted to see you?"

"Tell me I'm wrong."

Sandra hadn't been expecting Megan to pounce so quickly, and she wasn't really sure she was ready to discuss what was on her mind. She should never have arranged to meet. As she could never lie to her sister, she would have to parry the ultimatum. She shrugged. "There's always stuff going on. I'm never without things to worry about. Anyway, let's eat; I've been at work all day and I'm starving."

With that, Sandra picked up the menu, signifying that she wanted the questions to cease.

For now, Megan dropped her concerns, knowing they would return to them later.

It was the usual pattern of events. The two sisters would clear the decks of minor chit-chat about work and friends, and then tackle any heavier matters after they'd eaten. They ordered cakes and coffee and quickly slipped into light conversation.

After the plates had been cleared and the second pot of coffee had been served, the casual, free-flowing dialogue seemed to peter out.

Sandra stared at her drink, deep in thought, as she stirred it.

Megan broke the brief pause in conversation, sensing that Sandra was now more ready to talk openly. "So, I take it you've split up with Sam?"

"Yes, a couple of weeks ago. I meant to tell you, but it wasn't that serious. It just fizzled out," Sandra said, unemotionally.

"Crikey, Sand – he was gorgeous! He had everything going for him. He was marriage material."

Sandra sighed. "And maybe that was the problem… I don't fit into that mould."

"What… he got all heavy, and scared you off?"

"No, no… nothing like that. I just wanted to keep it a bit more open," Sandra offered, obliquely.

"What… casual, you mean?" asked Megan.

Sandra sighed. "Look, I know you'd like to see me settle down because you care for me, but I can't see my life heading towards a wedding and babies," she replied, shrugging. "I'm not knocking it – you chose that path, and I'm so happy for you – I'm just made a little differently."

Sandra's statement was not a revelation; they'd had similar discussions in the past. Megan had hoped that her sister, now in her thirties, would have softened her position. After all, she knew that a woman's body clock tended to shape her thinking.

"I get that, but you could have dated him for while… see if you felt more deeply about him," Megan pointed out.

"I only ever wanted him to be my 'erotic friend'," Sandra stated, punctuating the words with greater strength as if it had been an effort to say them.

"Your what?" Megan asked, laughing.

"Erotic friend is the current terminology for 'friends with benefits'," Sandra explained. "You get intimate with them when the time suits, but they don't frame the whole of your life. Some folks don't like to be penned in."

"And he didn't fancy sharing you with others…"

"The *possibility* of others," Sandra clarified. "I don't want you to think my house is a cesspit of writhing bodies."

"I didn't mean it in that way," Megan said gently. "Sand, I'm not against however you wish to live your life. Hell, do you remember me at nineteen? I was a right randy cow. I'm just concerned because you seem a little unsettled."

Megan's sincerity always touched Sandra. Although they lived their lives differently, they shared similar attitudes and values. Sandra smiled at her sister to indicate that they still had a strong bond, and that – even though she might rail against her at times – she would always welcome her sister's guidance.

"I know, thanks. I appreciate it." Sandra paused for a moment. "Look, Megan, there's one other thing I've never told you…"

The comment made Megan straighten her back in anticipation as she held her sister's gaze. Sandra had let her sentence hang in the air because she needed affirmation. She knew that her announcement might be too much, and she needed to know whether Megan was prepared to take the risk of knowing something that, once said, could not be unsaid.

"Go on…" Megan replied, in a voice that was clearly uncertain.

Sandra paused. Even with permission to open the bomb doors and release the incendiaries, she struggled to press the button. "I'm attracted to women as well as men," she blurted out. "I haven't acted on it, but I feel it. It's a rather perplexing place to be in, and I don't really understand it. I'm… very confused."

"Oh, thank God for that," Megan sighed.

"What?" asked Sandra, wondering whether her sister had heard her properly. It was certainly an odd response.

"Thank God for that," she repeated. "I thought you were going to say you'd slept with Freddie."

They looked at each other and burst out laughing so loudly that they managed to disturb a few neighbouring tables. Not that they were at all bothered.

"You're safe – he's not my type," joked Sandra, "and, besides, there's no way I'd be messing with my brother-in-law."

"Glad to hear it." Megan grinned. "Incidentally, what is your type?"

Sandra thought for a moment. "Well, that's a bit complicated. I don't always know. Gay and straight people are quite wary of people like me; it's like you can't support more than one football team. I don't fancy joining the hedonistic crowd either. It's all a bit artificial and flaky. Besides, I have to be very careful, being in the force. You're the only person who knows."

As Megan reassuringly touched Sandra's hand, she spoke steadily. "I understand. But I won't lie to you – I'm worried about you." She paused, wondering how to clarify her thoughts without being too overbearing. Then, a thought came to her.

"Isn't it crazy," Megan continued, "that when we were young and we'd be out with Dad on those long moorland walks, it was you who was the worrier? You used to panic about getting lost. You wanted to return in daylight so you didn't get spooked. I was the carefree one, keen to push the boundaries. How we've changed in adult life!"

Sandra nodded before saying, "I had an unexpected and uncontrolled outpouring of grief for Dad the other day. It hit me like a sledgehammer; it was completely out of the blue. It lasted for a couple of minutes, and then it passed."

SIGIL

"I get that sometimes, too," Megan admitted. "It hurts. That's why we have to look after each other, Sand. Dad would want that. I'm here for you, but I can't give you much advice. You have a bumpy road ahead of you."

With that, the sisters lightened the conversation, knowing it was time to leave. Sandra felt as if she'd offloaded something that had preoccupied her thoughts for quite a while, and she was relieved that her sister had understood. Megan, on the other hand, had left the meeting with more worries than when she'd arrived. In truth, her younger sister had not greatly shocked her. She had always rejected the accepted path of others, and she knew that their lives would never align.

Outside the coffee shop, Sandra hugged her sister and promised to stay in touch. As she watched Megan walk away, she blew out a sigh of relief. She'd been right to confide in her sister. To hide that part of her life would have been an intolerable strain.

A moment later, Sandra turned and headed back to the car park. Suddenly, out of the corner of her eye, she noticed a small independent bookshop nestled between two larger concerns. She was surprised because she'd never noticed it before.

She looked up at the name, 'Farningham Books'. Outdated, second-hand hardback books dominated the window display. Behind, the interior looked fusty, but comfortable and welcoming. Dark wood shelves were filled with jacketless books that had presumably changed hands many times over the years. It was the kind of establishment that attracted the initiated; she doubted whether its 'chick lit' section would be overly comprehensive.

Noticing that one or two of the books featured the word 'magick' in the title, it occurred to her that the owner might be able to explain the significance of Austin Osman Spare, the author of the book Victoria Kent had been reading before her death.

At that moment, a man moved out of the shadows and opened the door. He was dressed in a long overcoat, corduroy trousers, a scarf, and a hat. He was clearly about to lock up the shop and leave.

Sandra looked at her watch and was surprised that the shop could still have been open. Seizing the opportunity, she approached the bearer of the keys. "Excuse me… may I have a word…?"

The man turned around in surprise and clocked Sandra, who was moving towards him. "Er… well, I'm afraid we've just closed. I should have shut at five-thirty as it is."

Sandra produced her badge and smiled gently. "I'll only keep you for a moment."

Chapter 6

Jacqui turned into the car park opposite Brentor Church. It was a lonely spot, several miles from a town or village of any size. In daylight, you could see the 12th-century building perched on top of the mound from miles away, dominating the skyline. In darkness, it was bleak, especially if the weather was poor. Tucked into the far corner of the car park was the grey Mazda she'd been expecting to find. It was the only car parked there.

She slid her diesel Ford Ka next to it, switched off the engine, and glanced nervously at the adjacent motor, hoping she hadn't made a mistake. It was dark, so it wasn't at all easy to make out whether or not the car was occupied.

Suddenly, the rear door opened – an obvious signal for her. So, Jacqui grabbed her shoulder bag, got out of her car, and slid into the leather seat that was awaiting her.

By the time she'd composed herself, she realised there were two occupants sitting in the front seats. "Chris… you as well as Ross? I'm honoured."

The driver of the car leaned around and met Jacqui's gaze. He spoke a little gruffly. "One, he needs to hear what you have to say, and two, he's my cover. Wifey thinks I'm out for a drink."

"So considerate of you, Ross."

"Damn it, Jacqui, what the bloody hell is going on? I've had a visit from the CID this afternoon. They're sniffing around about something."

"CID? What did they want?" Jacqui asked, concerned.

"As it happens, some reading about Osman Spare, and some general chit-chat about the kind of things customers are interested in," Ross explained nervously. "Do you know, I have a feeling they'll be back. And what the hell happened to Victoria? Didn't you hear that she'd drowned in a brook on Dartmoor?! She's dead, Jacqui! My God… and we're talking about the most experienced hiker I've ever met. The two incidents have got to be related. The CID isn't likely to pop into the shop just for some light reading. I don't like it at all."

Jacqui had to think quickly; she needed to shut the whole business down in one fell swoop, otherwise information would trickle out and eventually place her in a very awkward situation. "I was there," she admitted, "but I didn't see it happen."

"You were there? My God… you didn't…" Chris trailed off, struggling to compose himself.

"I said I didn't see it happen," she stated forcefully, before pausing to figure out what to say next, "but I heard her behind me… some way off."

Ross frowned. "You're not making sense. What are you talking about? Now I'm really getting worried…"

Jacqui took a second to compose herself. She knew she had to sound convincing. "Vicky had planned to bivouac on the moor around Great Kneeset," she explained. "It's a fantastic spot, right in the heart of the moor. It was part of her work – you know, testing something or other. She is…

was... tough, as you know, and would think nothing of venturing out alone. She had all the gear and all the survival skills necessary. She was a pro."

"So you tagged along to keep her company...?" Chris asked.

"No, not exactly."

"But after the four of us had made our pact, you became really good buddies. Didn't you want to go with her?" Chris persisted.

"I was good friends with her... but she was becoming more and more intense," Jacqui replied. "You see, I made the mistake of telling her something... very personal... about my situation. After that, she wouldn't let go. It was kinda suffocating."

"I don't understand. What do you mean, 'suffocating'?" asked Chris.

"She'd suggest that we meet up every five minutes... you know, kept texting... she wanted to buy me things... she became overly motherly. It was getting on my nerves."

"But you did go... you said you heard her?" Ross pressed, trying to steer the conversation back to its original course.

Jacqui took a deep breath. "Yes. I've done a lot of walking on the moor, so I told her I might venture out and see her. To be honest, I was never sure I wanted to meet up that day. She was getting more and more crazy about sigils; the Osman Spare stuff was beginning to shape her everyday thinking. She was texting me at all hours of the day – on her burner phone, I might add, as we agreed. She seemed to be on a mission to be my saviour, and it was all getting way too heavy."

"So you walked out and then changed your mind to meet up?" Chris summed up, trying to fathom what she was saying. "Is that what happened?"

"I was never going to camp overnight. I thought I'd meet up with Victoria as she was packing up. The trouble was, Great Kneeset is damned near to Fur Tor, and that's the place I've always wanted to get to. So I just thought, eff it – I'll meet up on the way back… only I met someone at the tor. We arrived at the same time, it was pretty weird."

"You met somebody? What the hell? What are the chances of that?" Chris asked, wondering where Jacqui's version of events was going.

"Exactly. And, to my surprise, he was quite adorbs. So I thought, eff it, I'm staying. We ate lunch together and he took loads of photos. We spent a good hour nattering, maybe more; it was as if we were locked in some sort of parallel universe," she added, staring into space for a moment. "And then the weather changed. We'd been lucky until then. Suddenly, the sleet and hail began to swirl, and the sky became moody and dark; typical Dartmoor weather. It was time to go, and when it's time to go, you have to move quickly. You must know that."

"So when did you see – or 'hear' – Vicky?" Ross asked.

"Well," she explained, "I parted ways with this guy as he was taking the route back to Postbridge. In the increasingly bad weather, I trudged back down the slope, heading towards Hare Tor. I knew it was unlikely that I'd find Victoria because it was getting harder and harder to see. I wasn't going to risk getting lost and, quite frankly, by that time, my head was full of that dishy guy I'd met.

When I eventually reached the Amicombe Brook, I was dead lucky." Jacqui's eyes began to glaze over as she recounted the drama. Her eyes looked upwards at the courtesy light in the car as if trying to scrape every last detail from her memory.

"How so?" Chris asked.

"I stumbled across a great crossing point – about four or five conveniently placed stones. I had to jump the last bit and I got wet, but it saved me bags of time. It was then a straight march across to Deadlake Foot. From there, the journey home is a bit easier."

"But you heard her, right?" Chris asked again.

"Yes, she must have still been on the east side of the brook, a little way back. I turned slightly when I thought I heard her shouting. I couldn't really see much, though, because the sky was full of hailstones crashing down. As I turned to look, they stung my face. I think she was waving her arms at me. She sounded quite exuberant, not screaming 'help' or anything."

"So you ignored her and walked on," Ross said in a flat tone. It wasn't accusatory, but rather a statement of fact.

"Yes, Ross, I ignored her. At that moment, it was easier to plough on. I still had a long way to walk. If I'd stayed, I could have lost valuable minutes of light; it was getting quite dark by then. I just figured she was so experienced that she would easily be able to follow the brook all the way down to Sandy Ford and then through to Tavy Cleave. I wished I hadn't done that, but sometimes in life, you have to look after number one. I was getting… just a little… scared," she admitted.

Ross shook his head. "Only, she tried to cross the brook in order to catch up with you. That's right, isn't it?

And," he added, "as she was so pleased to see you, she lost her concentration… for just a second."

"And in that second, she lost her balance," continued Chris, picking up Ross's train of thought, "and, as her bag was so heavy, she toppled and fell into the very cold water. She probably hit her head on a stone or something."

Jacqui nodded, looking back at Ross and Chris. "That's about it, I guess. I didn't hear any shouts or screams. The weather was getting very bad, as I said, so I just carried on walking. I had no idea what happened to her until I heard the news a few days after," she finished, summing up. "I must admit, I did think it strange that I hadn't heard from her for a while."

There was an uncomfortable silence while everyone digested what had just been said.

"I didn't kill her or anything," Jacqui said after a moment, "so stop looking at me like that. I'm telling you… that's what happened."

"But if you'd been with her, you could have saved her," Ross retorted.

"Yes, but she was driving me a bit crazy, and how was I to know she was going to fall? She was the experienced hiker – not me!"

"Poor, poor Victoria. I can't stop thinking about her lying lifeless in the icy water until she was found. I was only speaking to her a few days before," Chris said, lost in his own thoughts. "It's terrible. Truly shocking."

Jacqui sighed. "Look, there hasn't been a moment since when I haven't thought about it, but it's just one of those things. That whole day, for me, was one bizarre series of events that should never have happened."

"But drama seems to follow you, Jacqui. People who appear in your life seem to be beguiled by you," Ross pointed out.

Jacqui turned her head to face him. Then, she spoke in a voice that disarmed both men in the car. "But Ross, that's why you asked me to join your group: you, Chris, Victoria, and then me." She bore her eyes into his. "Remember, over a glass of wine, after the presentation about Austin Osman Spare… you whispered to me," she mouthed the words, "'I… need… your… sexual… power'."

She let the words linger, knowing the effect they would have. Her tone then became more strident. "Ross, the magus, exploring astral and earthly landscapes in search of gnosis, and the three acolytes hoping to find enlightenment in a world of the mundane; four people, bound by a pact, in search of a route through their collective subconscious to a higher plane. Don't blame me. You needed me. You wanted me. Remember?"

Chris and Ross were stunned into silence; neither could find an adequate reply.

Eventually, Ross attempted to clear the air. "I knew it as soon as I set eyes on you – when your father employed me to manage the bookshop. You knew quite a bit about Crowley, Osman Spare, and the others. When you began to attend some of the talks, I knew you wouldn't be shocked if I asked. There was, and is, something about you," he admitted. "When you enter a room, the energy increases immeasurably; I felt it the very first time I met you. I've seen others affected by it too, but you're bloody difficult to manage. You can be so elusive at times."

"I need my space. I need to make my own decisions. I don't just follow," she replied.

"That's all very well, but where do we go from here?" Chris asked. "I was totally committed. We had a union: a brotherhood. It's what I've been working towards my whole adult life. It felt like a calling. Victoria was an essential part, and I know she was ready to sacrifice everything." He paused, shaking his head. "And now she's dead."

"What we do now is finish this conversation, and then shut the fuck up," Jacqui snapped, realising that the two men needed herding.

"And the police?" Ross asked. "When they come knocking again… as they will?"

"You say nothing except that you knew her. You saw her once or twice at talks. She bought some books from the shop, that's all. You say nothing about me."

"But you said it was an accident. Shouldn't you be helping the police with their enquiries?" Chris pointed out. "What's the problem? That was our friend, face down in a brook. Why don't you care?"

Jacqui laughed sarcastically. "You know, for a bright guy, you're amazingly naïve and dim at times. Have you thought about what would happen afterwards?"

Their failure to reply immediately spoke volumes. Both men's faces revealed an increasing realisation that they hadn't thought it through. Not at all.

Sensing this, Jacqui pushed on. "You mention me and they'll start digging deep. They'll discover my relationship with the bookshop. That will lead to you two. They'll find out from people who attended meetings that we know each other rather well. If the press get hold of it… well, do you want me to elaborate?"

Her explanation was met with continued silence, so she ploughed on. "The press would have a field day – they love a bit of sex and magick. Ross, does your wife know how deep you were getting? Did you tell her about the ultimate ritual?"

Even when openly taunted, Ross refused to be drawn. His head was now dizzy with the scenario confronting him. He stared at the floor, deep in thought.

Jacqui turned to Chris. He blinked nervously, sensing that she was about to descend upon him with a stinging attack.

"Does your partner know that you were about to perform rites that involved sex magick with two other women? Let me answer that for you: No. She just thinks you give Tarot readings and talk weird stuff with a bunch of strangers."

Out of fear that the situation was getting out of hand, Chris tried to rally around the oath they'd made to each other. "But we agreed that secrecy was paramount. We each committed to higher authority. We didn't choose; we were chosen. It was to be our ultimate sacrifice."

"So keep quiet and say nothing, otherwise you'll become the West Country's latest celebrities – for all the wrong reasons. If I become the focus of a police investigation because either one of you blabbed, I'll bring the whole show down!" Jacqui threatened.

"And our mission? What happens to that?" Ross enquired.

Jacqui shrugged. "Let the dust settle and we'll see. I'm not promising anything."

As Chris turned and faced the front of the car, he spoke with sadness. "How on earth do we replace Victoria? Can we start again?"

Jacqui opened the car door and got out, pausing momentarily before departing. "I know she was becoming a nuisance, but our friend has just died. How can you talk of a replacement so soon? This isn't fantasy league football. You two do as I've said. I'll call you in a week or so. Don't contact me."

With that, she closed the door, wondering if her threats would be sufficient. She was amazed at how easy it had been to dominate the conversation. Both men were compelling and persuasive in talks and lectures on a subject they were passionate about, but they were surprisingly meek and lacking focus when confronted by a crisis. Once again, she felt oddly energised by her boldness.

Jacqui climbed into the driver's seat of her car and watched the grey Mazda reverse out of its space and leave the car park. With any luck, she had bought their silence for a crucial period.

* * *

Jack carefully weaved the van past the parked cars down the narrow street next to The Pied Bull public house in Farningham. Looking ahead, he saw better opportunities to stop. A church came partially into view on the left. A high wall and trees obscured the body of the building, yet the tower stood proudly above. Along the street, larger houses were set back from the road, fronted by large grass verges. He knew it was only a very small village, so he began searching, in earnest, for a place to park. Ahead, he could see a bridge spanning a river and an ideal spot to leave Smudge, his VW campervan.

The village was an unexpectedly glorious place – and quite hidden away from the nearby busy roads that could, unfortunately, still be heard. He walked over the bridge and was tempted by the riverfront Lion hotel. If he hadn't been pushed for time, he would have taken a few photographs and then sat by the Darent with a coffee, watching the world go by.

He continued past the river and noticed, to his left, the white weather-boarded houses of a new development where the old mill had presumably once stood. They had been tastefully designed to blend in with the characterful nature of the existing housing. There was certainly a rich history to be discovered lurking beneath the façade of the village; it seemed like the kind of place you had to live in before you could discover its secrets. All in all, he thought, this was just the place for a bookshop that specialised in esoteric literature.

As he climbed the incline that took the road away from the river and out of the centre, he began rehearsing his opening lines. This was not going to be easy. He would need the full cooperation of the family if they were to disclose details of Ruthven's whereabouts.

The bookshop was one of the last buildings on the left side of London Road, before the delightfully named Sparepenny Lane took the traveller off towards Eynsford, a slightly larger North Kent village. It was a small shop with an attractive bay window and glass-panelled door.

As Jack crossed the threshold, a mellifluous, high-pitched bell announced his arrival. He wiped his feet purposely on the decorative mat and then strode into the quiet space. There was something almost museum-like about the library of books that surrounded him; each tome would no doubt reveal a treasure waiting to be discovered, though their plain, hard-covered exteriors revealed few clues.

There was a couple that looked as though they were just about to leave, so Jack decided to immerse himself in a section of books he knew nothing about. He'd hoped to speak to the owner without fear of being interrupted, so he knew he had to pick his moment carefully. He tried to look erudite, but he couldn't concentrate on any piece of text for long enough.

Suddenly, the bell rang and Jack held his breath. He raised his eyes from the page and was expecting to see another customer. However, much to his relief, he realised that the couple had gone and the shop was now empty.

Waiting a while in an attempt to conceal his real motive, Jack closed the book and replaced it on the shelf. He then turned and ambled over to the till, where the shop owner was poised, ready to be of assistance. He was a relatively tall man, dressed smartly in a bottle green corduroy suit with a mustard-coloured waistcoat. Although he was nearing retirement age, he looked sharp, agile, and very knowledgeable.

"Not found what you were looking for?" questioned the owner. "Or perhaps you need some help?"

Even though he had rehearsed his lines, Jack found himself a little flustered. When it came to it, he changed his mind about his prepared opening and awkwardly blurted out the first thing that came to mind. "You won't remember me… but we have, in fact, met before."

There was an awkward silence.

"And I have a feeling that you're about to tell me when and where…" replied the owner.

"It was a long time ago," said Jack, not wanting to play a game with oblique comments but struggling to be lucid.

"Yes, I figured that, because I have a very good memory for faces. You haven't bought a book from me, have you?"

"Err, no. It's a super shop, but I haven't been here before."

"Then…"

"My parents knew the Taylors," Jack explained. "We used to spend time together on holiday. My sister Beth and I got on very well with Georgie and Oliver Taylor. I seem to remember that, one year, you visited us, and we all spent some time walking on Dartmoor. It's Mr Rourke, isn't it?"

"It is. By golly, then you must be David Reilly's son, Jack! You were only a young whippersnapper, of course. That was some time ago, but I do remember it."

Jack could sense that Mr Rourke wanted to say more, but that he needed to collect his thoughts for a second.

"Jack," he said after a moment, "we heard about your father… and the recent loss of your mother – such a dreadful event. We still see the Taylors, you see. In fact, we saw them last week. I think your sister must have informed them. It must be painful for you. We are so very sorry."

Jack nodded, smiling slightly. "Yes, I think Beth let them know. She's the reliable one." He was temporarily thrown by Mr Rourke's sympathetic comments, and he found it difficult to regain the flow. "And thank you, I appreciate that… but it wasn't, in fact, the purpose of my visit," he added, regaining confidence.

Mr Rourke looked straight at Jack, trying to fathom what else he could be interested in discussing. He searched his expression for clues, but couldn't find any. "Well now, I'm sure that you need my help in some way, but I can't quite see where this is all heading."

Jack placed his shoulder bag on top of the wooden counter. He then reached inside and revealed a package. "I would like you to look at these old photos, Mr Rourke." He spread them out for easy viewing.

"Oh my goodness, I remember that day quite well – for all the wrong reasons, I might add," said Mr Rourke, lightening the mood with a chuckle.

"I was young and I can't remember much. I'm sorry, but I can barely remember your daughters' names. My sister showed these to me; we found the album when we were sorting through Mum's things."

Mr Rourke nodded. "It started, as I remember, as a marvellous day," he began. "We joined your family and the Taylors for a long walk and a picnic. We parked up at Merrivale, near the Dartmoor Inn. On the opposite side of the road, there's a path that leads down the Walkham Valley to Ingra Tor. From there, it's a glorious walk along the old dismantled railway line to King's Tor. Well, you kids being kids climbed all over every rock we could find that day. It was all going swimmingly well until my younger daughter slipped and fell. She was always bordering on the reckless – great fun though!"

Mr Rourke transferred his gaze from the photos to the shop window, as if deep in thought.

"I remember messing about amongst the rocks, but I don't remember the fall for some reason," Jack said, attempting to fill an awkward silence. He didn't really remember much about it at all, but he used his sister's account to appear warm and interested.

"Of course, I had to get her to the nearest hospital," Mr Rourke continued. "She had a cut that looked rather too deep for a plaster. I left my wife and eldest daughter with you lot. Then, once they'd patched her up, we rejoined the party later on that evening." He flicked through the album. "You don't seem to have photos of that."

In response, Jack reached into his jacket pocket and produced the before and after photographs of Mr Rourke's youngest daughter. The concealment of the treasures did not go unnoticed; he demonstrated considerable puzzlement at the drama.

Jack got to the point. "This, Mr Rourke, is your daughter, Jacqui, but I know her as Ruthven. I desperately need your help in finding her."

Without a word, Mr Rourke came from behind the counter and strode purposefully over to the door. He turned the latch to lock it and then flipped the 'open' sign to 'closed'.

"You'd better come through. We have something to discuss," he said, gravely.

Chapter 7

DC Mark Box took a sheet of paper out of a box file and placed it in front of DS Sandra Baines, who had just sat down behind her desk with a cup of coffee. "I've made a copy of the tattoo, as it's easier to explain using paper than referring to a computer screen," he explained.

"That makes sense," Sandra replied, eagerly anticipating his findings. She then fumbled in her bag for a pair of reading glasses that would hopefully make his explanation even clearer.

"To be honest, this isn't rocket science at all, and I'm surprised Geoff didn't point this out when you last saw him. Although, in his defence, the sigil doesn't make immediate sense when viewed from below – as the camera reveals. The tattoo was obviously designed to be looked at by the person who had it, and that was Victoria, of course. Let me show you."

Sandra was glad that an actual demonstration was forthcoming as she was struggling to follow along. She took a large gulp of coffee to wake herself up.

"I'd never even heard of these symbols before; it's been quite an education for me," Mark said, as he spun the diagram around and waited for Sandra to sport her new reading aids. "See, this is the way the sigil would look if you were… er…"

"Staring at her pelvic region," Sandra cut in with a wry smile, understanding Mark's embarrassment.

"Yes, quite. And as you can see, the letters don't leap out at you. Especially if you're not looking for them."

"Okay, I get that."

"Now, if I turn it around – and this, of course, is the view that Victoria would have if she was… er…"

"Looking down at her pelvic region…"

Mark smiled, acknowledging the awkwardness. "Indeed."

"Oh my goodness!" Sandra exclaimed, seeing it clearly. "There's a J, an R, a K, and possibly a C or D, depending on whether the J includes a horizontal line or not."

Mark nodded. "That's what I thought, and given that you omit any vowels when you create these sigils, it doesn't exactly take a leap of faith to insert an A back in there to create JACKR."

"Jack Reilly. It's got to be," Sandra said, almost under her breath, not really believing the evidence.

"Well, I figure it's a heck of a coincidence if it isn't. Only thing is, there's something else – another development."

"Well, it's all happening this morning. Do tell me more." Sandra leant back in the chair, wondering what else there could be. On the one hand, Victoria's death could be explained very simply; on the other, it seemed to be getting ever more complex. "Have we found the mystery girl, Ruthven?"

"No such luck. But we have uncovered Victoria's keys and phone."

"So where did they surface?" Sandra asked, knowing it was unlikely that they'd missed them when conducting the initial search of Victoria's house.

"A stroke of luck, really," Mark replied. "A dog walker was making his way through Tavy Cleave when his Labrador started sniffing too eagerly at a pile of stones, a little way off the main track. When the owner of the dog removed the small rocks to see what all the fuss was about, he discovered a hidden waterproof container buried in the ground. Inside he found a phone, keys, a small amount of money, and a snack bar. Apparently, judging by the look of the box, she'd been using this system for a while. Crazy, really. All in the name of authenticity – I mean, why not carry them, but just not use them?"

"I'd say it was lucky that a conscientious citizen handed the box into the police station. What are the chances of that? This is an important breakthrough, Mark. If that mobile contains text messages between Victoria and Jack, it will confirm what we're suspecting."

"Our IT guys are examining the phone as we speak," Mark told her, knowing that speed was of the essence. "It was also lucky that the dog walker had heard of the unfortunate death of the girl and thought his find might be relevant to the investigation. If he'd got it wrong, some hapless hiker would still be scrambling around the moor for his house keys!"

Standing up and walking over to the map on the wall, Sandra pointed to the area in which the box was found. "It tells us that Victoria definitely walked through Tavy Cleave on her outward journey, *and* that she intended to return in that direction. I guess, because of where she lived.

We'd worked that out already, but it's good to establish one or two facts." With that, she picked up her coat and bag to indicate she was leaving the building.

"There's still nothing on the Ruthven girl. If she exists and that's her real first name, she's rather elusive," Mark said, "but I'll keep trying."

DS Baines nodded. "Yes, and see if you can crack the sigil on the paper found in the Osman Spare book; that might give us further insight. Right, I'm off to the weird but wonderful bookshop in Launceston. I want to know if Victoria had ever bought any books from there, or if they knew her. Who knows," she added with a grin, "maybe there's even a secret society to uncover!"

* * *

The elderly – but surprisingly sprightly – Mr Rourke seemed to age within seconds, the colour having drained from his face. He ushered Jack through a kitchen area and a courtyard to a converted annexe that had originally been the village's forge.

Jack sat at a fine oak table, in one of a matching pair of chairs. Mr Rourke filled the kettle and picked up a French press. Jack raised his eyes and nodded, understanding that the bookshop owner wasn't yet ready to converse.

Mr Rourke then sat opposite Jack, waiting for the kettle to boil.

Jack passively played his part in the ceremony, remaining silent. He knew that the older gentleman would reveal all once the social niceties had been performed. Even though it seemed charming – if a little outdated – it was an awkward and rather uncomfortable wait.

"Of course, she was always a free spirit," Mr Rourke said, as he plunged the cafetière. "Great fun though. Always laughing, never serious." He poured the coffee and sighed.

"She was just the same when I met her recently…"

Mr Rourke appeared not to process Jack's comment, and he ploughed on regardless. "We always felt we were on borrowed time with her. She was happy enough, but somehow she never seemed to fit the family mould. Of course, we had to tell her."

"Had to tell her what, Mr Rourke?" Jack decided to add the 'Mr Rourke' this time, because he wanted to be heard – and included. He didn't fancy listening to a long monologue.

It had the desired effect.

"Oh… err… that she was adopted," he replied. "After we had Rachel, our eldest daughter, my wife couldn't have another child – it was such a terribly difficult labour. We nearly lost her, you know."

Jack shuffled nervously in the chair, feeling it wasn't his place to hear such information. Thinking it necessary to say something, he mumbled, "Sorry to hear that," plugging the silence with a phrase he wasn't very happy with.

Mr Rourke shrugged sadly. "Well, you get over these things, and life goes on. Jacqui came along and we became a family of four. It was only when she reached her mid-teens that it started to feel like a family of three and a half. When we sat down and told her – when she was eighteen – it was as if she finally understood something she'd secretly known all along."

"It's not an easy age for anybody," said Jack gently. "It must have been a shock. Did she try and trace her biological parents?"

"Well, that's the thing," Mr Rourke cut in rather quickly, "it wasn't a shock to her at all. And no, she didn't want to pursue finding her 'real' parents. She just became more and more rudderless. To say that she wasn't risk-averse would be an understatement. At times, she became a nightmare."

Jack smiled inwardly and tried not to derail Mr Rourke's train of thought. He had only met Ruthven for an hour or so, but in that time he'd been bewitched by her confidence and almost recklessness. Jack desperately needed to ascertain Ruthven's whereabouts, and he didn't want to upset his host in any way, so instead he said, "I think you're about to tell me that she left the family home soon after."

Mr Rourke shook his head. "No, not straight away – that came much later. She stayed at home, but was hardly ever there, if that makes sense. My relationship with Jacqui spiralled when she lost all interest in her desire to study for her exams. She's so bright; she could have achieved so much. It became a… tension… between us."

"So, when did she finally leave?"

"Oh, she came and went all through her twenties. She'd stay for a bit while she arranged her next flat share, or if she needed to save some money. Sometimes we'd lose contact for up to a year. And then we lost total contact after her ill-judged engagement – well, that was my opinion anyway. It didn't last long, thank goodness, but it was yet another point of conflict. She knew that my wife and I didn't think it would last. I'm afraid that 'I told you so' doesn't really promote harmony." Mr Rourke stood up and walked over to the window, gazing out as if searching for something. "It was the diagnosis that really drove the wedge between us."

Jack reeled. He wasn't expecting Mr Rourke to divulge anything medical. "Was she ill?"

"Not *was*, Jack, *is*. That's all I can say. I'm only telling you because I know you through your parents, and I know the effect my daughter can have on the people she meets. She can be… unpredictable. Ever since Jacqui received the diagnosis, she's been hell-bent on living life on the margins. If I were you, I would be very careful not to get sucked into her world. It's sad for a father to have to say that, but it's true."

For a few moments, Jack reflected on what had just been said. Thoughts of Ruthven on the tor came flooding back. She had seemed so alive – how could she be ill? And then there was another thing: amazingly, he had been correct about an engagement.

"If her real name is Jacqui, why did she tell me it was Ruthven?" he asked after a while.

Mr Rourke's mood altered in a flash. He chuckled. "So, she's reinventing herself by using the traditional family middle name, is she? It's from our Scottish ancestry. I didn't know she was doing that. Jacqui Elizabeth Ruthven Rourke. Her biological mother had chosen the 'Jacqui', of course."

"Ruthven is a lovely name. I'd never heard it before," Jack said, rather wistfully.

"And she's a lovely girl. I wish I could help her." Mr Rourke sat back down at the table and opened the photograph album. He flicked through the pages and found the set of photographs they'd been looking at in the shop. "Such lovely memories. How young we all look." He paused briefly, then said, "Now, Jack, do tell me where you met my daughter."

Jack had to think very quickly. He didn't want to lie to Mr Rourke – who had, so far, been very candid and helpful. However, he certainly didn't want to spook the old gentleman with mention of the dead girl or the police.

"We met, amazingly by chance, on top of Fur Tor on Dartmoor. Do you know it?"

"Fur Tor? Yes, I do. So she managed to get there? Well, I never! Was she with someone?"

"No, she was alone. I think we were both surprised to see another soul; it's pretty bleak in February."

"Cranmere Pool and its letterbox used to be the great challenge on Dartmoor. In all honesty, if you take the military roads from Okehampton Way, it's a long walk – but not that tough to find. Fur Tor, however, is difficult from every direction. Well done you! So, did you recognise her from these photographs?"

"Not at the time, though I noticed the faint scar on her cheekbone. We talked about our childhood memories of the moor. She even spoke of falling from the rocks. When I saw this photo album at my Mum's and talked to my sister, I made the connection. It's pretty unbelievable, I know." Jack shrugged.

The bookshop owner gave a perfunctory nod, as if he was trying to understand the remarkable series of events but wasn't able to do so.

Expecting a more explicit agreement, Jack hurried on to avoid an awkward pause. "Mr Rourke… the weather turned bad, and we had to leave in a hurry. We came from different directions. I didn't share any contact details with her, but I'd like to meet her again."

For a moment, Mr Rourke remained deep in thought. After a few seconds, he appeared to rally his composure, as if he'd decided on a course of action. "Didn't I hear you say that you *desperately* need to speak to Jacqui?" he asked. "Tell me… is she in some kind of trouble? Are *you* in some kind of trouble?"

"Mr Rourke, Ruthven is in no trouble as a consequence of our meeting. We only spoke for an hour or so. I hardly know anything about her. That's the truth. It's just that she could help me with a small situation I've – inadvertently – got myself into."

Mr Rourke closed the photo album and pushed it gently across the table towards Jack. "To be honest, she's sent me and my wife in a spin for so long that I don't want to know the details. Jack, you seem to be a balanced chap, and I wish you well with your difficulty. The trouble is, I can't help you with Jacqui's whereabouts. I can give you her last contact address and mobile phone number, but she's purposely distanced herself from her old life. I wouldn't hold out too much hope that the phone is still operative. Leave me your email address and I'll send over what I have."

Jack nodded, taking the photo album and placing it back in his bag. He then stood up, indicating he was about to leave. "Well, at least that's a start. Thank you for discussing your daughter with me; it must be painful revisiting old times when the more recent ones haven't been so happy for you. I'll leave you my email address and mobile number. If you can think of anything that would help me find her, I'd be extremely grateful."

Together, they made their way to the shop through the courtyard.

"Look, Jack," said Mr Rourke as they headed inside, "this is a long shot… but I own another bookshop in

Launceston, Cornwall. I don't know whether you're familiar with the town. It's not at all far from Dartmoor in Devon, which is just the other side of Tavistock. Jacqui lives in that part of the world – or, at least, she did. If she's been walking in that region… well, someone connected to the shop might have heard of her. She might have used the shop for contacts; she's interested in esoteric literature, and she might have made some friends there. If she has been using Ruthven as her name, it's sufficiently rare enough for someone to take notice. I'll give the shop a call for you."

Jack's mood lightened at the prospect. This represented a very small breakthrough. "Mr Rourke, that would be great, thank you! I'll be travelling to the West Country very soon, so if there's no immediate joy, I can follow up by visiting the shop myself."

Jack left the premises with a little more understanding. At least he hadn't been wrong about Ruthven being Jacqui; he'd known it as soon as he saw the old photographs.

When he stopped to think about it, the coincidence of meeting her on the tor was really quite something. No wonder people talked about fate. His fate was certainly bound by her existence, and he had to find her quickly. He knew it would only be a matter of time before the police summoned him for more questions.

The most troubling aspect of the visit had been Mr Rourke's mention of a 'diagnosis'. Understandably, he didn't want to elaborate, but he made it clear that it was significant. That meant there was even more need to find her quickly, he thought, as he made his way back through the village.

* * *

Jacqui Rourke searched keenly for a telltale sign of Mr Harrison's body language, but she found nothing. Was it good news or bad?

As a gastroenterologist – a doctor specialising in the treatment of diseases of the digestive system – he was used to delivering news in a deadpan fashion. 'You don't find many adjectives in science', he would say to his friends at the tennis club. They would reply that he saved them up to describe his game instead: a weak second serve, a wild forehand, a soft backhand, a poor volley.

"Is it still benign?" she blurted out, unable to contain her anxiety any longer.

Resisting the temptation to become derailed, Mr Harrison opened the large envelope that contained the papers. He drew a deep breath. "You know I can't say that the GIST is benign… erm, I'm sorry, Gastrointest–"

"Yes, I know, Gastrointestinal Stromal Tumour," said Jacqui, abruptly.

"Yes, that's right." He started again. "One can never say that the tumour is benign because they can reoccur at any stage. For instance, a recorded case found that the patient's tumour had returned after seventeen years. All we can say is that you appear to be clear right now. I really can't be any more precise than that."

Jacqui allowed herself a brief smile. Her life had been turned into a tightrope walk these past five years; one foot in front of the other. Look ahead, not down. "It's very frustrating, but I'm very grateful that you have me in the system," she lied, wishing the whole experience would just go away.

In reality, she wondered whether total ignorance would be the better bet. It was mentally exhausting and, in order to combat the stress, her life had become more and more chaotic. She had never been risk-averse, but her recent escapades had been highly charged and in danger of getting completely out of control.

Mr Harrison cleared his throat. "Well, reading your notes, and if I can remember correctly… we discovered by chance that you had a GIST." He scanned down the page, searching for the relevant details. "Ah yes, it says here that it came to light during a computed tomography scan–"

"A CT scan, yes, for something completely unrelated," Jacqui confirmed. "That was a stroke of luck… or not, whichever way you look at it."

"You were certainly fortunate to find it in its infancy, but unlucky to get it in the first place; this diagnosis is incredibly rare for one so young. Twenty-five, wasn't it?"

Jacqui nodded.

Mr Harrison continued to skip through the notes. "We removed the GIST. It was small and localised, which meant it hadn't spread into surrounding structures." He looked up. "As you know, we don't use chemotherapy and radiotherapy for this type of cancer, because they simply don't perform well. We can offer you regular check-ups – and this is one of them – but little else, I'm afraid. We just have to hope that it isn't a recurrent cancer – especially if it returns in another part of the body."

Jacqui should have found the meeting to be a positive experience, having been given news that no recurrent GIST had been detected. But the truth was, she knew that – in all probability – she was on borrowed time. Treatment was always surgery, and if the resultant biopsy of any tumour indicated an aggressive form of the disease, she knew she'd be in trouble; long-term survival rates were not encouraging.

Mr Harrison returned the papers to the envelope as if to conclude the first part of the check-up. Somehow, Jacqui sensed that the next issue would be regarding her welfare.

She braced herself for yet another bout of 'fatherly' advice. Just lately, more than a few interested parties had tried to influence her, and she intensely hated the feeling of being crowded. This was the trouble with having a medical condition: you had to rely on people.

"Now, how about your emotional well-being, Ms Rourke? I know this can't be easy for you, but I've just given you the best news I can, and you still seem a little down. Of course, anxiety, anger, and fear are all normal reactions, but you must allow yourself to feel positive about the years to come. This is a very rare cancer, and we are learning more about it all the time. A medical breakthrough is eminently possible in the future. Just imagine how HIV patients felt in the 1990s."

Jacqui knew that, at this point in a social situation, it was correct to smile. It wasn't that she didn't like Mr Harrison – he was actually quite personable – it was just that if she could see something coming, she had less respect for it. Mr Harrison's attempt at a good bedside manner was a little flimsy.

Encouraged by her slightly changed demeanour, he decided to offer her some counselling. "Why don't you let your hair down a bit? Have some fun. Perhaps take up a new hobby. Feeling a little better about yourself will help – trust me."

Jacqui laughed inwardly at the irony of the genial doctor's comments – if only he knew. How about a solo hike to one of the remotest parts of England, offering sex to a stranger on Dartmoor, or partaking in occult practices and the theft of various items from a dead girl's house? How was that for starters?! He didn't have a clue. Even so, she had no choice but to continue listening to his pleasant – but redundant – advice.

"Above all, you need to talk to people – a significant other, perhaps. Do you have anyone who fits the bill? A parent, work colleague, friend, or partner?"

Jacqui took a deep breath while trying not to let her exasperation show. Most people who'd figured in her life had either tried to control her or had been giddily affected by her. The only significant other she could think of was Ruthven: her newly identified alter ego. Now, *she* was a force to be reckoned with. She gave another faint smile. "There is someone who is helping me, thank you."

"Not surprised," he said, "not surprised." With that, Mr Harrison stood up and offered his hand. "Now, unless there's anything else, we'll see you again in six months or so. The team will be in touch."

After her amusing thoughts of the rejected sexual advances she'd made on Dartmoor, Jacqui recalled the awkward handshake with Jack. It surprised her that she'd thought of their meeting on quite a few occasions lately. There was just something about it that she couldn't quite put her finger on. He was strangely familiar, but maybe it was just the fact that they'd both shared similar holiday experiences when they were younger.

She offered Mr Harrison her hand in response, pleased that the meeting was drawing to a close. She chose a fairly bland statement to sign off with. "No, thank you, doctor. You've been very clear. Thank you for your time."

Jacqui made her way out of the clinic and into the chilly air. She fastened the top buttons on her coat, buried her hands into its deep pockets, and found her car that was parked on the far side of the car park.

There was no doubt that this was certainly a reprieve; she'd almost talked herself into believing a GIST had returned, mentally preparing herself for the worst possible news. She ought to have felt elated now, yet the death of Victoria weighed on her. It was very troublesome, and more than a little unnerving.

As Jacqui turned the key, a cloud of diesel particles puffed into the air, and as she manoeuvred the impish Ford Ka out of the parking bay, she reflected on her afternoon.

Actually, it had gone remarkably well. In fact, analysing it further, she realised she could look forward to another six months or so of worry-free living. By now, she was sporting a broad grin on her face. She pumped the air with her right hand and then turned up the radio.

Tonight she was going to celebrate with Ruthven, and it was going to be different.

Chapter 8

DS Sandra Baines had agreed to meet Ross Raymond – the manager of the bookshop in Launceston that specialised in esoteric literature – during his lunch break. Once she was inside, Ross flipped the 'open' sign to 'closed', turned the latch, and beckoned her to a small room to the rear of the store. He had certainly been expecting a return visit from the CID, but the presence of the police in his place of work seemed uncomfortable. Selling books about alternative religion, the occult, the afterlife, conspiracy theories, and so on was not against the law, but he had a feeling that the visit was not concerning issues of legality.

DS Baines took a seat and agreed to share a pot of tea that Ross had prepared for the interview. He was just about to offer some shortbread when it occurred to him that this might be construed as bribery and corruption and that he had something to hide! He thought he'd better not rile the very attractive lady who was about to interrogate him.

At that point, he began to worry that he'd already betrayed his thoughts about her appearance, and that she would mercilessly tear him to shreds if she detected even the faintest whiff of a lack of respect. His recent experience of the formidable Jacqui had made him nervous.

Sandra accepted the offer of tea, even though she was desperate for coffee, and wondered how anyone could omit offering accompanying biscuits. She knew it was probably a mistake to attempt to shed a few kilos starting that week, but the hike across Dartmoor a few days previously had provided her with the impetus.

"Thanks for the tea. I haven't drunk out of such a fancy cup since my father's wake," Sandra said.

"The tea set was passed down to me by my gran," Ross replied, glad that he'd impressed her.

"I'm honoured. I usually get given a chipped, stained mug."

"Some criminals have class," he joked, spurred on by her disposition.

"Well, you may be, but you're not under caution – this is just to help us with our enquiries. Thank you for seeing me during your lunch break."

"Not at all. How can I help you again?"

Sandra reached inside her bag and withdrew a recent photograph of Victoria Kent. It had been provided by the company she'd worked for, and was used for brochures and other advertising material. She placed the picture on the table in front of Ross, who was just about to sit down. "I'm wondering if you know, or have seen, this individual," Sandra said, in her well-practised voice.

In reality, Ross had known what was coming, but it was still a shock. He had practised this scenario many times in his head, but the real event superseded the imaginary. If he were to be anything but convincing in the next few moments, hell and damnation would descend upon him. The image of Jacqui – sitting in the rear seat of his car, clearly stating the desired roadmap ahead – was never far from his thoughts.

"Well, if I'm not mistaken, that's Victoria Kent. She's bought a few books from here and attended one or two evenings when we had guest speakers," he offered in a mix of surprise and calmness. "What's this all about?" He felt his face beginning to increase in temperature, and he prayed it wasn't visible.

"Do you know most of your customers by name?" Sandra asked, ignoring Ross's plea for more information.

"Not at all but, like I said, she's attended a few talks by various authors and eminent practitioners. It's always nice to welcome new people into the fold. It's my business to get to know them and help them in their particular voyage of discovery. Is she in some kind of trouble?"

DS Baines took the photo and placed it back in her bag. "I'm afraid she's dead, Mr Raymond. Her body was found on Dartmoor in a remote location." As Sandra finished her sentence, she carefully gauged his response.

Ross left a respectable pause as he adjusted his focus to a blemish on the table, avoiding eye contact. "I'd heard some gossip about a girl dying on Dartmoor… talk can get pretty salacious and exaggerated to be honest, but, my God, I didn't know it was Victoria." He looked up at Sandra. "How can I help you with this? I haven't been up on the moor since last autumn."

"I don't think you can help us with her death, Mr Raymond, but perhaps you can help us with some aspects of her life."

"I'm not sure what you mean… sorry, this is all a bit of a shock," Ross said truthfully. After all, Victoria's death had been a devastating event, and he hadn't quite recovered. "She only discovered us about a year ago… I don't know much about her life at all. Wouldn't colleagues at her place of work, or her family, be in a better position to inform you?"

"Yes, but I'm here to discuss with you aspects of her life that her family and work colleagues knew little, or nothing, about." She delved into her bag and produced more photographs. "This book, wrapped in a Farningham Books paper bag presumably bought from here, these drawings, and this metal dish containing fragments of charred paper were found in her backpack. She had been camping overnight near Fur Tor," DS Baines explained.

Ross stared at each photo in turn. Jacqui, of course, had alerted him to Victoria's intentions, but it was still surprising to see the evidence. "It's a book by Austin Osman Spare," he told her. "These drawings look like sigils. Spare is one of the most important writers in this field. I remember her telling me that she was becoming more and more interested in his work, but I never knew she was practising–"

"Practising what, exactly?" Sandra asked, sensing that Ross was becoming increasingly uncomfortable for some reason.

"Well, rituals involving sigils. It's one thing to read literature and be interested in the subject, but it's quite a step up to enact and be involved. Most people don't reach that point. I'm very surprised that Victoria felt ready to do that." Ross was becoming more nervous because he knew he had to be very vague. He desperately wanted to avoid further scrutiny – and the possibility of revealing how heavily he was involved in her 'education'.

"So, one might conclude that Victoria was receiving help in her quest for enlightenment. You said that she'd attended talks, here at the shop, some evenings. Were you involved?"

"Look, after a talk, everybody mingles and discusses. From time to time, I had conversations with her about sigils and Osman Spare. I helped her in her quest by introducing her to other guests and speakers. These events are designed to be a melting pot of ideas and experience. It's not against the law."

"I know it isn't, Mr Raymond, but what I'm trying to understand is whether others were involved in this activity, and if it had any bearing on her untimely death. Now, please give me your thoughts on *this*, if you will." She took out a piece of paper that had a copy of Victoria's tattoo printed on it.

Ross stared once again at the evidence placed before him. It didn't take him too long to recognise a very elementary sigil, and he immediately deciphered some of the letters. "Okay, so that looks like an homage to a sigil, as it's rather simple in form and doesn't contain many letters."

"It's actually a copy of a tattoo found on Victoria's body. So, who is Jack Reilly? Sandra probed forcibly, hoping to throw Ross completely off balance. She traced the letters with her finger, adding weight to her question. "That's J… there's the C… that's a kicking K to add artistry… and there's the R. Being a vowel, the A is, of course, missing. That gives us JACK R."

Ross wasn't expecting DS Baines to be quite so well informed, and he reeled from the sudden line of questioning. For a start, he had no awareness of Victoria's tattoo, and he really had no idea who Jack Reilly was. He opted to stay silent and examine the drawing in more detail.

After a while, he conceded to himself that DS Baines could be right. However, knowing that Jacqui had told him about Victoria's increasing obsession with her, and that she used to call her Jac, the sigil could, in fact, stand for JAC ROURKE. If you omitted the vowels and the repeated R, you were left with the same letters: JCRK.

He became instantly aware that this actually represented an enormous piece of luck.

"I understand your reasoning, but I have to tell you that I have no idea who this Jack Reilly is," he told DS Baines. "How do you know the R stands for Reilly, anyway? You must know who he is."

"So you never heard Victoria mention a man named Jack?"

"No, never."

"And, when I examine all your records of attendance for these talks, I won't discover a Jack?"

"Well, I don't recall a Jack, but I'll certainly look for you." Ross began to get out of the chair.

"Look for me later, Mr Raymond. I can see that this avenue of questioning is not going to be very fruitful."

Sandra cursed her eagerness in trying to wrong-foot Ross. Somehow, something wasn't quite right. Maybe they'd been too willing to believe that JCKR placed Jack Reilly clearly in the frame. What else could it stand for?

"Yes, of course, but you're quite welcome to send somebody over to search anything we've got here," Ross offered, a little nervously. He couldn't imagine, even for a minute, that his records were in a suitable state for close scrutiny.

"Oh, don't worry, we'll do that if it comes to it," Sandra replied, trying to sound bullish. She gathered the various documents from the table and replaced them in her bag. It was an obvious sign that the meeting was about to close, but she hadn't quite finished yet. She knew that her line of enquiry had proved to be a dead end, but something still didn't seem quite right. She wasn't in the habit of being so spectacularly off-beam.

"Did you ever take Victoria out for a drink?" Sandra asked as casually as she could.

Ross, still on his guard, knew where the conversation was heading, and decided to meet it head-on. "I'm married."

"That doesn't stop you from having a drink with somebody, does it?"

"But what you really meant was: did I have sex with her," Ross said in a manner that betrayed his frustration. He cursed himself inwardly for taking the bait.

"You seem to be putting words into my mouth," said Sandra, "but I seem to have hit a nerve."

Ross stood up and positioned his chair under the table. It was a move to draw the conversation to a close. He smiled. "Look, after the lecture, a group of us would go across the road for a drink to extend the evening for a social. I think she was there on one or two occasions. I never took her out alone, and I certainly didn't have sex with her."

Sandra looked squarely at Ross, trying to read if he was being economical with the truth. She placed her chair back into its place and politely mirrored his facial expression. "It was good of you to see me during your break. I'll let myself out."

"Yes, I have to open up for this afternoon, but I doubt there's a queue stretching down the street! I hope I've been of some use. Sorry I couldn't help you with this Jack fellow."

"Well, if you bump into him, you'll know whom to contact. Perhaps you could ask around for me."

Ross nodded.

DS Sandra Baines opened the shop door and walked out onto the street. Something wasn't quite right; she knew that. Her line of questioning about the sigil had drawn a complete blank. She cursed herself for being overconfident of a breakthrough. However, the throwaway comment about Ross's possible involvement with Victoria had produced an unexpected reaction. Even if Ross was telling the truth about no romantic liaison, he was guarding something. He had been decidedly uncomfortable and very defensive.

Ross turned the 'closed' sign back to 'open' and watched DS Baines as she merged into the people and parked cars on the street. He'd had a lucky escape, but he knew the detective hadn't been completely thrown off the scent. If she'd managed to dig a little deeper and find the connection between Victoria and 'Ruthven', his whole world would have come crashing down.

Jacqui would blame him for talking too much. She wouldn't be easily pacified. The problem was, the more troublesome she became, the more he couldn't stop thinking about her.

* * *

Seemingly unable to operate her left eyelid, Jacqui opened her right eye. A shaft of sunlight beamed through a tiny gap in the curtains. She blinked rapidly and scanned the room, beginning to identify features. Gradually, the left side of her face – the one buried in the pillow – began to function.

What time was it? Where the hell was she? These thoughts entered her head as she turned over, but then a wave of nausea rushed through her body, the sudden movement causing her head to reel and spin. Almost as if suffering from a bout of vertigo, her stomach reacted violently to the unwelcome sensation. She avoided the calamitous act of vomiting by taking in rapid deep breaths and repositioning her now thumping head.

As Jacqui stared at the ceiling, the events of the previous evening began to surface. It was a case of trying to piece them together so they made some sense. Her first panic came when it occurred to her that she might have shared the bed with a complete stranger – or, even worse, a friend. She desperately searched for clues.

She moved her head to the side to detect any signs of human habitation. Once again, her head thumped alarmingly, but she ascertained that the bedclothes had remained tucked in that side, giving her the impression that she'd been the single occupant the previous night. Her sense of relief was marred by the failure to remember who her host was. Someone had obviously looked after her, and judging by the fact that she was clothed in a t-shirt and yellow pyjamas, that person was clearly female.

Jacqui didn't need a PhD to figure out that her crashing headache was the result of alcohol abuse.

Once again, she steadied herself with deep breaths. On the bedside cabinet, to the right, she noticed a life-saving pint of water resting on a cork placemat. That was another reassuring sign. She took eager gulps, knowing that dehydration was adding to her discomfort.

Suddenly, there was a knock on the door and a face peered into the room.

"Lucy!" Jacqui cried, in a voice that betrayed her bewilderment.

"Well, don't sound so surprised," Lucy replied. "Who did you think it was?"

"I don't recognise this room… these clothes… I feel awful."

"Well, this is my new flat, and you were completely trollied. You deserve to be very ill. What a night, though."

"Was I very embarrassing?" Jacqui asked, not really wanting to know the details.

"You can't remember, can you?" Lucy asked, enjoying the situation.

"No, not at all – well… perhaps a little. Do I want to remember?"

"Hell yes! You were outrageous, and you drank like a fish. I've never seen you like that before. It was as if you were a different person."

Jacqui closed her eyes for a moment as hazy – yet strangely familiar – faces flashed before her. "Did we come back here with a couple of guys? I remember snogging somebody in a taxi."

"He was like an octopus; his hands were everywhere. Mind you, you did say, 'I'll bet you can't find the front door key!' It's not even your house, you minx."

"No way!"

"Yes way!" Lucy hit back, indicating that there was more.

"So… did they stay?" Jacqui nervously probed. "Did I sleep with…?"

"You owe me, Jacqui Rourke. I met the cutest guy I've met in a long time, and you just happened to pass out. That kinda killed the mood!"

"Whoops."

"We dragged you up the stairs, but the lads left me to get your clothes sorted. I think they realised the party was over because they left soon after."

"I'm so sorry, Lucy. I just can't remember much. I can barely recall the taxi ride." Jacqui rested her head back on the pillow. "God, I feel wretched. A hangover is worth it if you can play back events and have a laugh, but I can't recollect anything beyond that first pub."

Lucy stood up and laughed. "That's because, in the first twenty minutes, you downed a large red wine with a gin chaser. What were you celebrating? Or maybe you were commiserating? Come to think of it, you didn't say."

Jacqui took a moment to reply, indicating that it was complicated. "Just life, really." It was a bit feeble, but it was all she could muster under the circumstances.

The catch-all response didn't fool Lucy, who was used to Jacqui's guarded comments. She knew that with her mercurial friend of many years, you could only ever scratch the surface. Their relationship was never founded on emotional reciprocity; they simply enjoyed each other's company when it was convenient.

Lucy smiled, signalling that it was fine to be evasive. She wasn't going to push for more information. "I'll make some coffee. If you can face it, the shower's good. I've left a towel there for you." She then turned and opened the door, before hesitating and adding, "Somebody asked me to give you a message… I'll tell you all about it when you come down."

She retreated quickly, leaving Jacqui unable to quiz her further on this intriguing announcement – she was feeling too groggy to protest and shout after her, but now she felt apprehensive.

Her friend had shielded her from the news for a reason; it obviously wasn't frivolous gossip. She could have shared that last night. Initially, she worried that it concerned the death of Victoria, but – to her knowledge – Lucy had no connection with that part of her world. She couldn't think of a mutual friend who might want to pass on a message.

The identity of the mystery messenger certainly spurred Jacqui on to confront the day and get out of bed. Her head was still in a poor state, but she was now less worried about vomiting. Some toast and strong coffee would help revive her constitution, but first, she needed a shower.

The shock of the hot water, almost stinging as it cascaded all over her body, had the desired effect. She wasn't sure whether it was cleansing or rousing, but it made her feel better and more prepared for the emotional rollercoaster her life had become.

A few minutes later Jacqui descended the stairs, clothed in a bathrobe that had been left out for her. She lingered in the hallway, looking at the framed photographs hung on the wall. She recognised herself in some of the older group pictures, but she was conspicuously absent in the more recent ones.

She had known Lucy a long time, but as they'd both grown older, contact had become more sporadic. Jacqui mused that this was inevitable, given her newly found penchant for accelerated life. Lucy was hardly going to hang onto her coattails; she had her – more conventional – life to lead, searching for a partner and pursuing her career in law.

As Jacqui entered the kitchen, the welcome food smells reassured her that she was feeling better. She sat down at the small wooden table that was set with a pot of coffee, fresh orange juice, a rack of toast, and various condiments.

"Take your pick – that's if you feel up to it," Lucy said, pleased that her friend had surfaced.

"It's like a hotel… and, yes, I feel up to it. I'm going to take that coffee black and grab some toast, if you don't mind," Jacqui replied, feeling the warmth.

Lucy rolled her eyes. "You deserve to be poleaxed today, but it always surprises me how chipper you are after a night out. I'd be like a zombie."

They laughed, and then spent the next few minutes sharing stories of their history together. After one too many 'Do you remembers?' Jacqui turned to face Lucy and said, "You've been a great friend over the years. I want you to know that."

Lucy stopped pouring the coffee. "My God, Jac – you make it sound like it's the end or something. You're being a bit dramatic, aren't you?"

"You're one of the few people who know about my adoption and my birth mother leaving me money," Jacqui continued. "You've never pried into my personal situation. You've always taken me at face value, and I like that. I know I've been all over the place these last ten years, and it hasn't made the slightest bit of difference for us. I know that, of late, I haven't been around much, but when I needed a night like last night, you were the first person I considered asking. We always seem to pick up from where we left off. No pressure."

Lucy's eyes began to water; this unexpected outpouring of emotion from Jacqui had taken her completely by surprise. She tried to say something worthy in response.

"I'm just proud to know you. We all are, though I don't think any of us feel we've got particularly close to you, Jac. But you're so vibrant and fun to be around that you take us all along for the ride. You have this ability to engender self-belief in people; you empower them. I won't lie, though… without meaning to, at times, you suck people into your world; you captivate them. Then, before they know it, they find themselves stranded. So… what happens to Jacqui Rourke when you wear us all out, and we find partners and melt into suburban bliss? Are you going to inveigle our husbands, wives, and dogs?"

"Great word, but I prefer 'seduce' – like a siren," Jacqui said. She mimicked the beckoning motion of the hands. "Come to me… Come to me!"

They both laughed.

Lucy finished pouring the coffee and, for a moment, the two sat in silence.

Jacqui broke the brief period of much-needed reflection. "Who knows? I might meet somebody and it will all change. I might get there before you. How do you spell commitment, by the way? Is it one 'm' or two?"

Lucy laughed. "Err… yeah, says Jacqui, conveniently sidestepping her engagement…"

"Oh, cripes, that was a disaster… moving on…"

"Exactly. Sooner or later, you need to stop searching. Maybe we all do." Lucy paused, wondering whether it was the ideal moment to furnish details on the announcement she'd made in the bedroom. "Look, I received a message on my phone, from your dad…" She let her words trail off, as she knew Jacqui would be alarmed.

Jacqui stopped chewing her toast. Her mouth was full, but she abandoned all protocol. "My dad? What the heck?"

"I know, it was out of the blue," Lucy said, trying to place it in context.

"I didn't know he had your number."

"Well, he obviously doesn't have yours. I thought you were still on speaking terms?"

"We are, but I've changed my phone a few times and, anyway, I don't like him fussing after me. I haven't seen my parents for quite a while now. He's probably trying to build bridges," Jacqui reasoned.

"It wasn't about that at all. He said that someone urgently needed your help and was desperate to talk to you. You are to go and speak to Ross at the bookshop – apparently, he'll fill you in on all the details."

"Why didn't he ask Ross to get in contact with me? Not that I mind you passing on the message, of course," Jacqui added, keen to let Lucy know there were no hard feelings.

Lucy shrugged. "Maybe because he knew I'd be far more reliable getting the message to you; he knew I'd go out of my way to speak to you about it in person. I like your dad, Jacqui. He really cares about you. I don't think this is trivial. He obviously thinks it's important, otherwise he would have chosen a different path."

Lucy was going to ask what Jacqui thought it was about, but she knew better. Her friend's affairs were often cloaked in secrecy.

Jacqui nodded. "Yeah, that figures. He always thought you were reliable. If only he'd known what a tart you were!"

Lucy saw the irony and laughed.

Jacqui smirked at her own savage humour, but deep inside, her mind wandered to the issue at hand.

The last thing she wanted to do was contact Ross.

Chapter 9

Ross placed the handset back on its base. He didn't get many calls on the landline these days and, when the phone had rung, he knew it was most probably Mr Rourke, the owner of the shop.

He might have been forewarned about the identity of the caller, but he wasn't at all prepared for the content of the call. It was a surprise, and very worrying on many levels. Not only did Ross not want to contact Jacqui, but he had also nearly dropped the phone at Mr Rourke's mention of Jack Reilly. Things seemed to be getting very complicated, and Ross couldn't see an easy way out.

Firstly, Jacqui had warned him to lie low and stay 'out of her hair' for a while. He had known her long enough to respect her wishes; she was extremely fiery when rattled. She would have expected him to be clever enough to parry her father's request and persuade Mr Rourke of another course of action.

Secondly, and even more troublesome, the CID was obviously interested in Jack Reilly for some reason. Yesterday's meeting with DS Baines had convinced him that he could get into a lot of trouble if he didn't divulge the kind of information Mr Rourke obviously had. In order to remind Jacqui who Jack was, Mr Rourke had given Ross details of her chance liaison with him at Fur Tor. Ross remembered her talking about this encounter when she was explaining Victoria's tragic death. It must be the same person, he thought, trying to fit all the pieces together.

Ross stared at the piece of paper that lay next to the phone. Jack's contact number appeared to him like a safe code to Pandora's box.

It was a good job the shop was empty, because he desperately required some thinking time. On the face of it, he thought, Jacqui may well be pleased with the opportunity of a reunion with this stranger. Mr Rourke had said that he desperately wanted to speak with her, so he obviously had something on his mind. However, what if their meeting was in some way tied up with that fateful afternoon on Dartmoor? Ross knew that Jacqui wanted to avoid attention at all costs. She certainly didn't want the police sniffing around – she had made that perfectly clear.

Ross cursed his luck. Either way, he was bound to upset somebody. Somehow, he had to find a solution that would cause the least damage. It was tempting to phone the police and contact Jacqui and let them all sort it out. He wondered, though, if he could survive the fallout: it would be catastrophic.

It didn't take him long to figure out that he would, in all probability, lose his post as shop manager – and his marriage. His wife would be horrified to learn about his increasing interest in performing rites and rituals involving nakedness with three other people in some weird secret pact. And then there were the local newspapers and media. They would have a field day; Jacqui was certainly correct about that.

Ross decided, rather apprehensively, to break the radio silence with Jacqui and contact her. For sure she would be annoyed, but at least he could try and explain. The ball would then be in her court.

He reached for his burner phone, hidden in a secret compartment of his leather man-bag. The four of them had each agreed to have one so they could privately message each other without fear of being compromised by partners, nosy friends, or work colleagues. The contractless, pay-as-you-go system worked perfectly. 'Perfectly', that was, until the demise of Victoria. It suddenly dawned on him that the police might have discovered her burner phone – unless it had been well hidden.

Ross closed his eyes and placed his right hand on his forehead, desperately trying to keep his woes from escaping, but it wasn't working. The creation of the pact had been incredibly exciting and the result of some very careful planning. He'd really thought he was going to achieve a lifetime goal. After all, he'd felt the calling for many years, but until recently he hadn't been in a position to share his passion with such like-minded individuals.

However, he hadn't bargained with the stress of such a clandestine operation. He kept reminding himself that he hadn't broken the law in any way, but even so, it didn't seem to help.

Just at that moment, the mobile phone in his bag began to ring. Out of sheer surprise, he took a step backwards and almost dropped the bag on the counter. Once he realised what was happening, he frantically rummaged through the compartments and negotiated his way into the false bottom. Grabbing the phone, he answered it before it made any more noise.

"Jacqui? My life, that nearly frightened me to death," he said, slightly out of breath with nervous energy, "I thought we were only using text. There could have been a shop full of people… I could have been with Claire!"

"Well, that's a laugh, seeing as though whenever I've been in your shop it's been empty. Anyway, relax. I knew you were working, and that you didn't have anybody there."

"How come?" Ross asked, rather bemused.

"I've just walked past."

"Don't be daft. Why are you calling me then? Why didn't you just drop in and speak to me?"

"Just in case the police are watching. Unlikely, but I'm not taking any chances. You said that they'd called…" She paused. "You're wearing a rusty red jumper and jeans, just in case you don't believe me."

She waited for a response, but Ross was desperately trying to gather his thoughts.

"So, have they been back?" she asked, more forcibly.

Ross failed to answer in time. All he could muster was an incriminating, hesitant breathing sound.

"They bloody well have, haven't they? I hope you kept your lips buttoned, Ross."

He cursed his luck. She'd always had the knack of knocking him off balance. "You don't have to worry; I didn't mention your name. They are way off track," he replied as calmly as he could, though he didn't sound very convincing. "Anyway, what did you want? Because I have something for you," he continued.

"I know you do," Jacqui replied.

"I don't understand… how?"

"Never mind. I'll be parked in the track that leads to the equestrian centre at Polson Bridge. Six o'clock. I gather it's only a message and a few details, so you'll be home in time for dinner with wifey." With that, Jacqui hung up, giving Ross no time to react.

Ross cursed Jacqui's tactics; he hated being at her beck and call. He was going to message her, saying that he had to make a delivery after closing and that it might be better to arrange another time, but then he thought better of it. He did, after all, want to get shot of this whole sorry business. There was no doubt that recent events had been playing on his mind – and his wife, Claire, had begun to notice.

Ross placed the mobile phone back in its cunningly devised secret space in his leather bag. He then glanced at his watch, seeing he had two hours before he had to leave. He knew one thing for certain: he was going to find out as much as he could about this Jack Reilly character before making his mind up whether or not to inform the police. The question was: Should he share with Jacqui the details of DS Baines's interest in Jack Reilly and the sigil?

Lots of questions, he thought, but no answers.

* * *

As she drove, DS Sandra Baines saw DC Mark Box at the agreed meeting place. She indicated, slowed, and parked the car just ahead of where he was standing.

"I thought you'd forgotten about me," he said as he climbed into the passenger seat.

"Usual problems… hair, make-up, and making my bladder gladder." She laughed. "You need a girlfriend, Mark, then you'd know that ten past really means half past!"

Sandra drove away from the kerb and proceeded down the narrow high street that wound itself past the church and several local public houses.

"Hey, watch that parked car, boss – do you need to go back for your specs?"

"Cheeky, cheeky! You know they're for reading. I can see perfectly well when driving, thank you. You're just a nervy passenger."

Sandra had gone out of her way to give Mark a lift to work; her longer-than-normal journey would give her time to get up to speed with any developments. First of all, though, she needed to admit to the errors she'd made interviewing Ross Raymond. She could easily have spun them differently, but that, she felt, would disrespect her partner. Playing it straight at all times meant they could depend on each other in a tight squeeze. Besides, as her father would say, 'A problem shared is a problem halved'.

"Damn, damn, damn!" Sandra shouted, thumping the steering wheel with both hands.

"Steady. What the heck's up? That lady is allowed to come in front of you; the traffic is merging from the left."

"It's not that; it was yesterday," she told him.

"Your interview with Ross Raymond? Or another less-than-promising night out looking for romance?"

"Very funny. The former, as it happens – although, knowing my luck at the moment, it could easily have been both," Sandra replied, concentrating on the road.

"Mr Raymond not very forthcoming with information, or are we barking up the wrong tree?" he asked.

"I played it badly, Mark. I was too eager. My sixth sense told me he was being very economical with the truth, so I thought I'd unseat him with Victoria's sigil tattoo and the link to Jack Reilly."

"How did he react?"

"All rather impassively. He agreed that the tattoo could be a very basic sigil and he confirmed the letters, but he really didn't have a clue who Jack Reilly was. Either that or he's an amazing liar – and I've not met many of those. It was almost like a relief to him when I mentioned Jack's name."

"Maybe we really are barking up the wrong tree," Mark concluded.

Sandra drove the car up to a busy main road junction and signalled left. DC Box thought it prudent to cease conversation until Sandra had safely negotiated the hazard. Once they were gathering speed on the A road, he spoke again.

"Perhaps the letters stand for something else."

Sandra had considered the same thing, but was keen to argue the reason for their continued interest in the case. "There are too many coincidences at play here. Jack says he met a girl, by chance, at the tor; a girl dies less than a quarter of a mile away on the same day. It's in the middle of nowhere. She has a tattoo of a sigil bearing letters J C K R. We know she's into that stuff because we found a book by Osman Spare, and the burnt paper in a silver dish as an offering of some sort in a weird ritual. It's a big ask to put all that down to 'sometimes it happens'.

Sandra thought for a moment and, as Mark didn't respond, she continued. "Do you know what? I'll bet anything that Ross doesn't just sell books about 'weirdness'… and I reckon there's definitely some connection between him and Victoria."

"When you say 'connection', do you mean he was having an affair with Victoria, or he was embroiled with her in the dark arts?"

"Maybe not the first, but most probably the second. I just have a feeling that I touched a nerve." She shrugged. "Anyway, fill me in on any developments about Victoria's notes on the papers found in the Osman Spare book."

"Okay, so I've been busy…"

"Good. I like the sound of 'busy'," Sandra said, excited by the prospect of a breakthrough.

"…trying to unravel what was going on in her mind as she was camping overnight out there in the wilderness. If you don't mind, may I continue?"

"I'm all ears, Mark; you have my full attention."

"I reckon she was working on creating a pair of earrings to be used as a sigil. I'm no expert on jewellery, but the teardrop design and the detail of the hole at the top, so they can be suspended from a hook, point clearly to drop earrings. I must say, they look rather beautiful."

"Earrings?" Sandra queried. "I take it they contain letters? And you said they were designed to be a sigil? It sounds complicated… are you sure?"

"It is complicated. The capital letters are worked into a creative design, and a teardrop of – presumably – gold borders the work to create the earring. It really is intricate. If they had been made, they must have cost a packet."

"That's good thinking. There's no point in crafting a design for earrings if you're not going to get them made. You might just as well create a drawing of the sigil on paper and leave it at that."

"Exactly," Mark said, pleased that Sandra hadn't

dismissed the idea out of hand. "And… what's more," he continued, "there's a note by the drawings: 'Chagford handmade jewellery'."

"No number or website?" Sandra asked, surprised by the omission.

"Nope. Just that. I will, of course, get on to it today. Presumably, she had located an independent jeweller who has a small workshop at home. Something like that. If we're very lucky, Victoria had them made very recently. If they exist, the jeweller should be able to furnish us with some details."

"If they're as intricate as you say, there won't be many jewellers who could take on such a task. Somebody in the trade will be able to narrow the search. This is a good lead."

"Of course, it's only a hunch that they exist. All her notes and scribbles could easily be works in progress," Mark pointed out.

Sandra nodded. She knew that investigations often involved 'one step forward, two steps back'. There was a danger of getting ahead of oneself and, for some reason, this case had exposed her tendency to be too urgent. It was one thing to be proactive, but quite another to be reckless. She had already made too many uncharacteristic errors of judgement. In fact, she was beginning to think she was losing her touch – her instinct for reading people.

"What about the letters? Have you been able to decipher anything at all?" Sandra probed, hoping for another lead.

"The good news is that I reckon I've worked out the letters to the sigil…"

"And the bad…?"

"Well, even if I've correctly identified all of the letters, I still have to place them in order and work out which vowels and repeats are missing. From the top of the diagram, I have S, G, H, T, R, V, M, N, F, probably a D that's reversed, and possibly a Y." He shrugged. "I work in a police station, not GCHQ."

"Okay, I'll have to have a look at those over a coffee. Meanwhile, get some help from some geek who loves to crack codes," Sandra suggested. "Seriously, they love that kind of stuff. There might even be some kind of computer algorithm out there that could help narrow down the options." She thought for a moment. "Let's check the gaming community as well. The message hidden in the sigil might be dynamite and, to be honest, it's all we have right now."

Mark made notes as the journey continued. Sandra often had the habit of rapidly firing off ideas and lines of enquiry as they occurred to her. Sometimes her thoughts were barely connected, or at least rather obscure, as if they'd been subconsciously pulled from a thought stream. He didn't mind this approach at all, however; it kept investigations lively.

As the familiar shopfront of the bakers came into view, Sandra indicated and slowed to a halt.

"Same rolls as usual, boss?"

"Yes, but tell them to go easy on the butter. I'm on a health regime."

Mark got out of the vehicle, shaking his head in disbelief at Sandra's comment. "You go on ahead and park up at the station. I've got to nip into the newsagents. I'll only be about five minutes… oh, and thanks for the lift."

"No worries. I'll get the coffee on."

***

Jack decided to stay at a cheap hotel even though Smudge, his campervan, had a cosy – but chilly – sleeping option.

He quickly recalled his last fateful journey to the West Country. How could he forget? The Dartmoor break had been bittersweet. Even as he thought about the visit, images of Ruthven came flooding into his consciousness, though the subsequent horror at the police station annoyingly began to nibble away at the dream sequence. It had also been cold, and even though the diesel heater would provide some all-night comfort, he didn't, on this occasion, feel like having a camping experience.

This trip to Launceston was all about trying to link up with Ruthven – or Jacqui, her real name, as he'd recently discovered. Her father's offer of contacting the bookshop at Launceston had produced promising results. She was obviously known there because Mr Rourke had told him that he'd left his contact details. However, Jack had hoped she might have contacted him by now.

Jack left the hotel and glanced up at the castle perched high on its conical mound. It dominated the town like a towering adult looking down over children. He couldn't see much of it, however, due to the rapidly fading light.

He hadn't been in the town since he was a child, here on holiday. He must have taken a ride on the steam railway, but all he could remember was his mother buying a saffron cake from a baker and eating a pasty. He passed the war memorial and started searching for signs of his destination.

Jack had only briefly thought about which actions he should be taking. He knew he should have contacted the police the moment he'd finished speaking to Mr Rourke, but he felt happier taking matters into his own hands.

Firstly, he felt inclined to discuss with Jacqui what had happened after they'd met on Fur Tor. Even though their meeting had only lasted an hour or so, he somehow felt responsible for her. At the end of their chance liaison, she had betrayed a glimpse of vulnerability. Jack certainly didn't want to frighten her with the inevitable visit from the police.

Secondly, and purely selfishly, he wanted to see her again. Deep down, he knew this was the driving factor.

Jack glanced at his watch and knew he was cutting it fine. He'd hoped that the check-in at the hotel would be straightforward, but there'd been a mix-up about the car parking space for his campervan. Eventually the problem was solved, but now time was running short if he was to reach the bookshop before it closed.

Luckily, Mr Rourke's instructions were concise and accurate; he was soon striding down a side street searching for a similar shopfront to the one he'd visited in Farningham. Several doors up from a very promising-looking café, he spotted a rather indistinctive façade: one that was clearly designed to appeal to the initiated rather than the speculative. A sign above the window sported, rather incongruously, the name 'Farningham Books'.

The shop bell rang quaintly as he entered the establishment. It was empty. Jack wondered how such businesses survived. But then again, he mused, online literature surely didn't possess the same attraction. There was something about old books. The touch. The smell. The history.

Jack strode purposefully through the shop and made for the counter where purchases were made. The gentleman behind the desk looked up, not expecting such an immediate call for assistance. Most customers spent ages perusing every corner, nook, and cranny.

"Mr Raymond? Ross, I believe? I'm Jack Reilly. Mr Rourke said that you'd be expecting me," Jack announced, offering his hand in welcome.

"Err… no, he's not here at the moment," replied the gentleman, shaking Jack's hand rather limply.

"Oh… err… that's really unfortunate. I've travelled quite a distance. I was hoping to catch him…"

"He's just left the building to make a delivery. I'm so sorry. He asked me to look after the shop for the remaining ten minutes and to lock up at six. I know he has a meeting after, so there's no use trying to contact his mobile. He won't be back this evening."

Jack processed the information but said nothing. He was considering a response when the gentleman spoke again.

"I can tell him you were here. He could see you tomorrow, I'm sure."

Jack cursed his luck; if only he could have reached the shop in time! Sure, he could call again tomorrow, but he'd been hoping to make contact with Jacqui tonight. He couldn't hang around indefinitely. And then there were the police. He still had this nagging feeling that they'd want to speak to him again; they hadn't seemed to believe his story.

Jack nodded. "It's not ideal, but I'm staying for a few nights at the Castle Hotel, here in Launceston. I'll call again tomorrow morning. Can you tell him that I called, and that I need to speak to him? It's rather urgent."

"I'll make a note right away to remind him. Sorry, what's your name again…?"

"Jack. Jack Reilly."

"My name's Chris, by the way. I'm just a friend doing a favour. Sorry that your time has been wasted."

Jack nodded again and turned to leave. As he moved towards the entrance, it occurred to him that he hadn't had a hot drink for a while. He spun back around and called out, "I don't suppose there's a café open around here, at this time of day?"

Just as he'd finished his sentence and before Chris had a chance to respond, Jack noticed – through the translucent glass of the shopfront – a girl moving quickly across the other side of the street. His heart began to race as his eyes focused on the female form. As she swept past, she appeared to glance at the shop. Her hair. Her face. How she moved. She looked very much like… it had to be…

"Well… most places are shutting about this time, but just around the corner, there's a lovely little old-fashioned teashop. I think they stay open until six thirty on a Friday. You could be lucky."

Jack wasn't really listening. He was now cursing his luck that he'd ever even asked the question. He knew that each passing second increased the likelihood that he'd struggle to catch up with her.

"So, you need to go left from the shop entrance and follow the street–"

"Thank you so much. I've got to go…" Jack cut in, now abandoning all forms of social etiquette. He turned and practically flew out of the building.

As Jack vanished without the complete set of instructions, Chris stared after him in amazement. It was most unusual.

Jack knew he had to hurry; the girl was moving quite quickly past the window, as if she needed to be somewhere. She was heading back to the main shopping area – which was good, on the one hand, because he'd come from that direction himself. On the other hand, however, it also gave her plenty of opportunity to slip away unnoticed.

Jack scanned the road ahead, but he couldn't see her.

If only I'd left the shop a second or two earlier!

He retraced his journey and was pleased to see the iconic hexagonal war memorial and the town square. Surely, he thought, in an open space he must be able to spot her. She'd appeared to be moving with purpose, but he couldn't believe he hadn't caught up with her. Perhaps she'd entered one of the many shops he'd just passed.

It then occurred to him that she could have been heading back to her car. He hadn't logged any signs for car parks but, then again, he hadn't been looking. It was entirely possible that she'd dived down a small side street – or a locally known alleyway – to her car that was parked conveniently in a road away from the throng of the town.

Jack turned 360 degrees, desperately seeking a sighting of Ruthven, but to no avail. Practical options were now very limited. Even if she hadn't left the road beforehand and had reached this spot, she could have chosen any direction to go in next.

Knowing that time was of the essence, Jack decided to go with his hunch about Ruthven returning to her car. The only way he could narrow the odds was by retracing his route to the bookshop and taking the most likely side street. It was a shot in the dark, but it was his only chance. At least, he figured, he might see her in her car, emerging from one of the small lanes.

So, he set off with long, purposeful strides, almost breaking into a run. He sensed that she was close.

Chapter 10

Ross turned onto the A388 out of Launceston and headed towards Polson Bridge, his given meeting place. It was only a few miles away, and that represented very little thinking time. He hadn't yet decided whether to divulge all the details of DS Baines's visit or not. Laying all the cards on the table had a certain appeal, but to imagine that it would end his participation in the matter was fanciful. Inevitably, Jacqui would be alarmed to hear about the connection the police had made between the sigil tattoo found on Victoria's body and this mysterious photographer, Jack Reilly. That would surely send her into a tailspin. It might signal that the police knew nothing significant about Victoria's private life, but it would send a clear message that the net was closing in and that Jacqui's mercurial lifestyle was about to be shattered.

To say nothing about the tattoo conversation with the police, and to merely repeat the request given to him by Mr Rourke, would be easier. However, knowing Jacqui's frequent ability to pull the rug out from under him, he would be highly unlikely to deliver the message without betraying his unease. In the long run, that course of action could end up being even more problematic.

As the road entered a straight section, Ross's thought stream was rudely interrupted by the worryingly familiar outline of two round headlights coming towards him. The beams, rather poor by modern standards, caused his heart to race. If he wasn't mistaken, it was his wife's rather clapped-out 1970s MGB GT that was approaching. He knew that she would return from visiting her friend in Lifton along this very road, and he cursed his stupidity for not taking an alternative country lane. Because the day had been hijacked by circumstances beyond his control, he had forgotten that morning's conversation with his wife.

In the fraction of an instant before the cars passed, Ross decided to divert his gaze and fiddle with the entertainment system. With any luck his wife would fail to notice his silver hatchback as they passed – or see him driving it.

It was definitely his wife's car. Even in the fading light, Ross recognised the shape. As he nervously glanced at the rear-view mirror, he expected to witness the green sports car's brake lights fill the frame. The last thing he wanted was for her to turn around and follow him. With any luck, she'd been too busy mulling over the details of her chat with Diane to notice oncoming traffic; his wife's confidant had enough troubles to occupy her thoughts for days.

Realising it was now unlikely that he was going to be tailed, Ross accelerated away. Time would be of the essence, and he would have to conclude his business with Jacqui and return home before it would be too awkward to explain where he'd been. The day had sprung one too many surprises already, and he was becoming tired of firefighting.

* * *

Jacqui placed the ticket into the machine and waited for the barrier to rise. Edging slowly out of the car park, she resisted the urge to duck, illogically anticipating the arm to crush the roof upon its descent. She was just about to weigh the options of turning left or right upon exit when, at the junction at the top of the road, she caught sight of a man striding in her direction. He was forty metres or so away, but he seemed worryingly familiar. His purposeful gait, his flowing hair, his height... it had to be...

Desperately trying to make sense of his presence and anxious not to get caught up in yet another drama, Jacqui indicated right and drove away from the town, into the maze of back roads. In a mixture of emotions, she cursed her luck and praised her fortune at the same time. She was reasonably confident he hadn't seen her face, but she was bemused by his direction of travel. Perhaps he, too, had parked his vehicle in the tiny backstreet car park, but what were the chances of that? You would have to know the town well to know of its existence, and she wasn't aware that Launceston was that familiar to him. He had spoken about Dartmoor and Devon, but not Cornwall.

Jacqui darted in and out of the side roads until she joined the main thoroughfare leading out of town, heading towards the Devon border. The further she distanced herself from the sighting, the hazier she became about the identity of the individual. One chance encounter on the moor was one thing, but a second freak event was too much to contemplate. It reminded her of far too many books she'd read where the pace of the plot-led novel encouraged the reader to suspend reality. Maybe she was developing a 'thing' for a certain type of man, and she hadn't been aware of it until Jack bloody

Reilly turned up. He had a lot to answer for, she thought, especially as she remembered his name so easily. When did that ever happen?

Common sense persuaded her that she was becoming too easily distracted. However, it was undeniable that she'd experienced the same frisson, the same momentary loss of clarity. She knew it had affected her, but even if it was Jack, now was not the time to meet again. Her life was still too messy. Things needed to calm down a bit first.

* * *

"Where on earth do you park in a place like this?" DS Baines asked, driving further and further away from their intended destination.

"Chagford is a very small market town, boss," replied Mark. "They're not big on multi-storey car parks in this part of the world. It's best to head up to the church over there; there's a car park just beyond." DC Box was amused that Sandra had expected to find a place on the street. He found her occasional impatience quite endearing.

"Know it well, Mark? Some floozy of yours lived here?" Sandra taunted.

"Floozy? No. A girl I used to know? Yes."

"It's a bit off the beaten track. Helping her with her homework, were you?" she asked, enjoying the fact that Mark seemed vaguely uncomfortable in the direction the conversation was heading.

"Up here… on the right. I'm sure your legs will manage the short walk back. If you're lucky, I'll take you past the bakers." Mark allowed a gentle smile to surface.

He knew he was pushing his luck. He knew that Sandra hadn't long begun a new fitness regime as she wasn't happy with her post-Christmas appearance.

"You're that far away from a clip around the ear," she laughed, holding her thumb and forefinger just millimetres apart. "Now, show me the way – seeing as though you're obviously a celebrity in these parts."

"It was a long time ago, and it didn't last; another one of my spectacular failures. When I told her I was joining the force–"

"Ah, yes," said Sandra, "I know how that sentence ends."

They both stepped out of the car and made their way through the narrow side streets to the main throng of the market square. The iconic market house – with its octagonal slate roof and matching conical dovecote tower – was English country quaintness personified, and it dominated the view. Although, at first glance, it looked every bit like a destination for the well-heeled and retired, it was actually a place of activity and life. The ancient stannary town was now home to many pubs, hotels, and excellent shops. Its charm drew people from far and wide to experience its delights.

Alsop's, the jewellers, was tucked away in the far corner of the square, next to the art gallery. The shop, in need of modernisation, was nonetheless in keeping with its surroundings: functional, yet homely. These days, most customers were interested in mementos and accessories. Gone were the days of selling yellow gold signet rings, bracelets, and necklaces. Silver and white gold Celtic knotwork earrings, brooches, and pagan-inspired rings and badges adorned the displays. The arts and crafts were alive and well, the profit margins less so.

Michael Alsop, wearing two sets of spectacles – one perched jauntily like sunglasses on the top of his head – lifted his eyes from the back of the watch that had been removed for internal inspection. "Can I help?" he offered. Clearly, the couple before him was not interested in browsing the slightly dusty-looking additional trays of jewellery inside the shop.

"Mr Alsop? I am Detective Sergeant Baines and this is Detective Constable Box. I gather you phoned the station about helping us with our enquiries?"

"Oh… oh yes, indeed. I remember." Michael took both pairs of glasses off his head and popped them into the top pocket of his shirt. "I thought you might be interested. It was a great shock, you see… when I saw it on the news… you had better come this way. Sophie will look after the shop for a few moments, although I don't suppose we'll be that busy."

Sandra and Mark nodded in agreement and followed Mr Alsop into his backroom workshop.

"So, Mr Alsop, I gather this is about a certain pair of earrings?" Sandra prompted.

"And so it is." He ushered DS Baines and DC Box towards two chairs and then sat on a wooden stool next to the worktop. "It might be nothing, but when the news broke… err… of the death of the poor lady, I thought it best to contact you. I wasn't going to say anything at first, because it's nothing really. It's just that she collected them the day before she was found. Such a shock."

"You did the right thing, Mr Alsop," Mark told him. "Any information, even seemingly trivial, is of interest to us. It could be a vital piece of the jigsaw that we're missing."

"Was it an accident?" asked Michael. "The poor girl. That's a lonely place up there near Fur Tor. However did it happen?" As he spoke, he opened a brown folder that was on top of a pile of papers.

"Well, that's what we're trying to establish," Sandra explained. "Let's say we have an open mind at present."

"I see," Mr Alsop said, disappointed. He took out three sheets of paper from the folder.

"Why don't you tell us everything – about the earrings and the contact you had with Ms Kent? Or maybe you knew her as Victoria? DC Box is going to take a few notes, if you don't mind."

"Yes, of course. Ms Kent visited the shop about three weeks prior to the… er… accident, or whatever." Alsop took a deep breath and continued. "I am used to creating bespoke jewellery for clients, but this was an unusual brief. The earrings had an incredibly intricate design containing letters in various positions. A framework, in the shape of a teardrop, bound the letters. Quite beautiful they were, too. Ms Kent was adamant that there was to be no flexibility in the position of the letters, or their inclusion. In other words, I couldn't move a letter or miss one out to make my life easier. I wasn't about to, of course, but the reason I'm telling you this is because it was all so very important to her."

Even though the old gentleman paused at that point, Sandra and Mark remained silent, neither wishing to break his train of thought.

Taking the cue to continue, he pressed on. "Now, let me show you the design, and it will make more sense." Michael spread the three sheets of paper out on the worktop. The drawings were familiar to the detectives;

they resembled those left inside the book found inside Victoria's backpack.

"The thing I found strange," he continued, "was that the letters didn't seem to make any sense. It wasn't as if they spelled 'Victoria', or perhaps her mother's name, if they were intended as a gift. Most odd. Still, they really were attractive, and they are, perhaps, some of the best earrings I've ever created. They were a devil to make, though. Very time-consuming."

Sandra looked carefully at the designs, hoping for some extra information. At the bottom of the second sheet, she caught sight of a list of letters. Mark, also noticing them, pointed them out to Mr Alsop.

"Oh yes, these were the letters. She was most insistent," Michael told them. He went on to show where each letter appeared in the design. Some were cunningly placed and not at all obvious. One was reversed and a few were much larger than the others.

"Who were the earrings intended for? Did she say?" asked Sandra, knowing it was a long shot.

Michael gathered up the papers. "Not really. She said they were a special gift… that's all. I'll get these copied for you." He stood up and shuffled over to the photocopier as he carried on talking. "Victoria turned up after three weeks, as we agreed, and paid in cash," he said. "I found her a lovely red box to keep them in. She was very happy indeed."

"Did she try them on?" DC Box asked.

"No, it was all very transactional. I got the impression that she had a few things to do. Picking up the earrings was probably one of a list. I noticed that she checked her watch a few times. That sort of thing." Mr Alsop handed the copied design sheets to Sandra.

"You've been most helpful, Mr Alsop," Sandra said. "It all helps us build a picture of her last movements. Thank you for your time."

"Yes, I don't think there's any more to say… well… perhaps I should mention her reaction when I placed the earrings in her hand…"

"Go on," Sandra encouraged, fearing he might shy away from revealing something important.

"I've seen the world, Detective Sergeant, and I've created many strange pieces of jewellery in my time, but I think I know when I'm dealing with the occult," he told them. "She received the earrings in her hands almost like a child cradles a tiny rabbit. And… I swear she began to radiate. If I didn't know better, I'd say they began to glow in her hands. She tilted her head up and gave me a knowing grin. Then she whispered, 'Thank you'. It was as if I had enabled her in some way. I can't really explain it, but there you are – I felt it."

Sandra and Mark looked at each other, each knowing that, yet again, something had come to light that made the death of Victoria anything but a straightforward case of an unfortunate accident.

"If you think of anything else, Mr Alsop, you will give me a call, won't you?" Sandra said, passing the jeweller a card with her contact details. "Anything at all…"

* * *

Jack crossed the road rather recklessly, forcing cars to slow down on either side. He then strode purposefully down a small side street, knowing that time was of the essence. He considered it the most likely looking place to find a car park; however, nowhere looked at all promising. For a start, a large 'P' sign at the road junction would have been helpful, but then again, he wasn't thinking straight. He could have missed it. He couldn't stop thinking about the girl, and he felt – somehow – that she was very close. Not only did he want to see her again, but she could also confirm their meeting on the moor with the police. It would be so easy if it wasn't so difficult.

Ahead, he could see a break in the rooflines of the houses. This looked promising. He quickened his pace, and at that moment two things happened simultaneously. First, further down the road, a blue Ford Ka exited what looked like a car park barrier. Secondly, an elderly lady crossed the side road and approached him, raising her hand. He desperately trained his eyes on the car, hoping to detect details of the driver, but the lady closed in on him, forcing him to divert his attention.

"Young man, you have a lot to live for. You must take more care. Didn't anybody teach you the Highway Code? You could have caused an accident," she remonstrated.

Jack cursed his luck; nothing seemed to be going his way. He wanted to scream at her to mind her own business and leave him alone, but he found himself apologising profusely. "I'm so sorry. I'm in a dreadful rush. You're absolutely right, it was terribly dangerous."

The apology took the wind out of the old lady's sails and she nodded, rather surprised. "So well spoken as well…" she muttered as she continued up the road, "…wasn't expecting that."

Jack looked back towards the barrier and saw the rear of the blue Ka disappearing from view. At that range, he couldn't see the driver or read the registration plate.

He would have kicked something if there'd been an innocuous object lying on the pavement.

Instead, he hastened his footsteps and reached the car park, scanning the space and hoping that the blue Ford had been a mistake. It could have been anybody. He didn't have a clue if she'd been heading towards her car. In fact, he didn't have a clue about much at all. What was it – a hunch, a sixth sense, or desperation that drove him beyond his usual, rational self?

The half-empty car park gave him no clues, and he stood in silence for a moment, pondering his best course of action.

* * *

Ross drove across the river at Polson Bridge, leaving his home county behind in the rear-view mirror. The River Tamar – the natural boundary between Cornwall and Devon – flowed onwards to the south, towards Plymouth Sound and the sea.

As he crossed the stone structure, he couldn't help but recall that the ancient name for the river meant 'dark flowing'. Like the water beneath him, he felt he was being carried away by a strong force. No longer was he in control of events. His lifelong ambition to form a secret pact with like-minded individuals – searching for and shaping sacred truths, and involving sigils and chaos magick – was in tatters. Victoria Kent was dead. The detectives investigating her demise were getting perilously close to uncovering some awkward revelations. His wife, already moody about his lack of regular hours and odd appearances at the shop, was becoming more and more suspicious; his marriage wouldn't survive the salacious gossip. And then there was Jacqui…

He parked in the lay-by, just before the trackway that led north to Welltown Farm. The area had been reasonably quiet since the Launceston Bypass had been built in the mid-'70s. It was, however, busy enough for a clandestine meeting to go completely unnoticed.

Ross smiled at Jacqui's adroit planning. She really was something else. He'd known that the first time he'd met her. She wasn't physically stunning in the traditional sense; it was something far deeper than that. Her directness, her ability to flirt almost unnoticed, her intelligence… he'd been instantly spellbound. But he also knew she was trouble. Like a siren, men and women were drawn to her rocks, and his ship was sailing dangerously near.

There was no other car in the parking spot, so Ross switched the engine off and waited for Jacqui to arrive. Finding music a distraction, he preferred to mull over various scenarios in silence.

It wasn't long before headlights flooded the inside of his vehicle and, looking in the mirror, he saw a car gently rolling up behind him. He was greatly relieved when the lights were doused and he could detect the familiar shape of the small Ford he was expecting. Just for a brief moment, he thought his wife had retraced her route and was about to ask for an explanation.

Thankfully, the headlights behind him flashed, indicating that the coast was clear for the meeting. He approved. This way, his car wouldn't be invaded by the waft of perfume or the presence of female hair. After the last meet at Brentor, he'd spent a frantic twenty minutes opening all the windows and brushing down the rear seat. Even though he'd done nothing wrong, it would be difficult to explain. His wife's surname ought to have been Holmes or Watson: nothing went unmissed.

Ross exited his car and walked as casually as he could around to the passenger door of Jacqui's Ka. Before he could lift the handle, the door sprung open and he heard Jacqui's familiar bark.

"Hop in!"

Jacqui intended to control the meeting right from the start. She knew she had to be very direct with Ross – otherwise, he would find ways of opting out of difficult decisions… or he'd tell her half-truths.

Ross slumped into the front seat and exhaled.

"You haven't done anything yet. Save that for later – after I've finished with you," Jacqui told him.

"Charming. I love you too," he replied, jolted that there wasn't even a customary greeting.

"Hello Ross. How are you? What's your day been like? Has your wife caught up with your secret life yet? How's that? Will that do?"

"Very funny," he retorted. He was always put out when she made him feel like a hen-pecked husband. In reality, his wife was more gregarious than he was.

"Now then, back to business. I gather you have some information for me," Jacqui said, purposely establishing eye contact so that she could read his reply.

"Your father phoned–"

"He owns the shop. He speaks to you all the time," she pointed out.

"Yes, I know that, but this wasn't about the business. It was about contacting you. Somebody wants – no, *needs* – to meet you. And quickly."

"What? *He* wants to meet me, you mean. That's a new one, pretending to be somebody else." She recalled that Lucy had relayed her father's message about a mysterious person eager to meet her, but she was keen to test the legitimacy of it.

"No, Jacqui… I don't think so."

Jacqui stared at the steering wheel of the car, hoping she hadn't overplayed her response. After a moment, she decided to test the truthfulness of his reply by continuing with her line of attack. "I love him dearly, but now is not the right time to play happy families. I told him I had things to do; I needed the freedom to break loose for a bit. I said that I'd be the one to regain contact… when I was ready. I'm not falling for that one," she reiterated.

"Jacqui, it's about the photographer you met on the moor. He's the one who wants to meet you – Jack Reilly."

She turned back to face Ross. So Lucy's message had been accurate, and it wasn't all about her father re-establishing contact. This was certainly explosive; she wasn't expecting Jack's name to feature in their conversation. "Don't be daft. That's a wind-up. How has Jack been talking to my dad? There's no connection."

Her mind was working overtime, desperately trying to establish if there was, in fact, a link. Had she missed something when they met at Fur Tor?

"Look, all I know is that he called in at the Farningham shop. Your dad said that you wouldn't believe me so he told me to mention King's Tor. Does that make any sense? Is that a code word for something?"

Ross waited for a reply but Jacqui was speechless. King's Tor was the place where she'd slipped and fell when she was ten, maybe younger. She had to be taken to hospital and she received stitches. Subconsciously, two fingers of her left hand reached for the scar high on her cheek; they brushed her skin as if to remind her that the blemish was still there.

"Anyway," continued Jacqui, "how did my dad know that you knew me? We said we'd keep that a secret for a while. Have you been talking to him about me?"

"Relax. He phoned on the off chance. I haven't ever mentioned you to him before, I swear. I was going to, though… at some stage… we discussed that."

"On the 'off chance'? What does that mean? It doesn't make sense at all," Jacqui said. "You don't phone somebody at the other end of the country and say, 'Do you know Jacqui Rourke?'"

"Look, apparently, this Jack Reilly is in trouble in some way, and you can help him," Ross continued. "I guess your father thought, as he owns the shop, you might have popped in… met some people… exchanged a few numbers and so on. He said that if you've been using the name 'Ruthven', it might be sufficiently rare enough for somebody to notice. He's not wrong, is he? Did you use that name when you met Jack?"

Jacqui ignored the question, and instead tried to piece the fragments together. Why had her father used 'King's Tor' as a code name for evidence that the request was bona fide? It was all such a long time ago… though obviously meaningful.

"Okay, so here's what happens," Jacqui said in a measured voice. "When Jack calls at the shop, you'll explain that I'm not readily available owing to unknown circumstances. You'll tell him to write a note explaining his predicament and how I can help. He is to slip it into an envelope and seal it. He is then to place the envelope in a waterproof green plastic sandwich box and leave it hidden by the bridge that crosses the old Great Western Railway track bed at Liddaton. That's just down from Brentor Church, heading towards Coryton. It's out of the way, but he'll find it."

"Jeez, Jacqui," exclaimed Ross, "it's like something out of a spy film. You're kidding me. Can't you just meet him?"

"Oh, and tell him not to try any fancy stuff, otherwise I'll leave the box there for some nosy teenage girl to pick up and read all about his predicament."

Ross held his hands up in mock surrender. "If that's the way you want to play it, that's fine with me. I guess he should be thankful you didn't just refuse."

"Yeah, well he's a nice guy, but I don't like the way everybody's trying to crowd me out. That's you, Dad, Victoria, the police… and now, Jack."

"The police don't know about you, Jacqui. They know about Victoria and her interest in Osman Spare, but not about you." Ross started to sweat. What he hadn't dared share was that the police were flailing in the dark trying to establish a link between Victoria and Jack. With any luck, the case would go cold and Jacqui could remain anonymous. Whatever was good for her well-being was good for his.

Jacqui turned her head to the left and studied Ross's face. She smiled reassuringly, nodded her head, and then turned away again, facing the front screen of the car. A moment later, her left hand shot out rapidly and cupped his crotch, pressing him against the seat of the car. "You're keeping something from me. You said, 'they don't know about you' twice… and you're sweating ever so slightly. I can read you like a book."

Ross squealed. It had been so sudden and had come as such a shock that he listened to her reasoning for a moment before pushing her hand away. "Aaargh, that hurt! You wouldn't know how much that hurt! I could have you for molesting me."

Finding the power game interesting, Jacqui acted coy. She gently moved her hand away, instead placing it high on his inner thigh. In a softly spoken voice, she whispered, "Sorry, Ross, I don't know what came over me… shall I rub it better?"

Ross looked at her to check how sincere she was being. He was helplessly beguiled by her soft tones. "That might be some recompense," he said. His hand moved towards the zip of his trousers.

Jacqui's facial expression changed, aware that he'd played right into her hands. She couldn't believe how easily such an intelligent man could be strung along. A year ago, when she'd first met him, she was almost starstruck. He had the looks and an air of mystery about him. He had led her into a voyage of discovery: a world of new possibilities. Victoria had also taken that journey. Now, Jacqui found him laughably puerile and rather pathetic. In a crisis, he flapped around like a seal.

"That just about sums you – and most of the male race – up: one minute you're whingeing about being molested and roughed up by women, and in a nanosecond you've got your pecker out."

"I was just attempting to rearrange myself…" Ross pleaded unconvincingly.

"This is what's going to happen, Ross: you are going to tell me all about the police visit. If that is not forthcoming *and* satisfactory, your life will need rearranging…"

Chapter 11

Sandra could hear her mobile ringing, but she couldn't quite detect its whereabouts. She scrambled around her kitchen, desperately trying to identify the direction from which the sound was coming. Somehow, her personalised ringtone seemed to be defying physics. It was, annoyingly, the same volume everywhere.

"Everywhere but nowhere," she cursed.

Suddenly, Sandra caught sight of the phone's plastic protector sleeve peeking out from under a pile of utility bills. She grabbed the rectangular life support machine and just about managed to hit the green 'call receive' button – even though she wasn't wearing her glasses – but before she could answer, a voice cut in:

"Is that Detective Sergeant Sandra Baines?"

"Speaking," Sandra replied, trying to regain her composure. She was running late again this morning, and she was mildly irritated at being hijacked before coffee.

"Do you have a minute or two to spare? It's Michael Alsop, the jeweller. I spoke to you yesterday at the shop."

"I have, but you'll have to give me a second while I pour my coffee. It's a lifeline in my profession." Sandra held the phone to her ear as she filled her favourite mug to the brim.

SIGIL

Although Mr Alsop said nothing as the fluid splashed and gurgled, filling the vessel, his pattern of breathing indicated that he was very anxious indeed.

"Okay, go on," she told him, once she was ready.

"Look, this is all rather difficult, but there's something else… more about Victoria. I really need to get this straight," he said, mustering all the courage he could.

"Is it something we can deal with here and now, or can you come to the station?" Sandra asked, keen that it would be the latter. She had a busy day ahead of her.

"Can you come here again?" he asked instead. "There's something you need to see."

Sandra took a deep breath. She didn't have time to make visits to all and sundry. Small details could be processed and logged by others. On the other hand, she couldn't dismiss his request out of hand. In her experience, virtually all cases were plagued by sloppiness. How often had the police overlooked a statement or a piece of evidence? How often, after the event, had a member of the public screamed that he or she hadn't been listened to? A vital clue, filed and forgotten?

Something in Mr Alsop's edginess alerted Sandra to take his request more seriously.

She was just about to ask him to offer more details when he blurted out, "It's a video… of Victoria."

"Okay, I wasn't expecting that."

"And it's… shall we say… highly sensitive. I'm not sending this over the internet."

* * *

Although the market town of Chagford was frustratingly charming, Detective Sergeant Baines hadn't anticipated visiting it two days running. She promised herself that when she finally managed to find a partner, she would return to soak up the ambience and discover its hidden gems. It wasn't difficult to understand why, all year round, tourists came to experience the hustle and bustle of this quaint place. There was something so gloriously old-fashioned about most of the stores – despite the obvious architectural reminder – though calling it a 'living museum' would be a little crass. The people who lived here worked hard to preserve the community, and they had no intention of changing. Many had moved to this Devonshire idyll *precisely* because of its sepia-tinged outlook and lack of convenience.

Sandra pondered the effect that a double visit would have on Michael Alsop. She hadn't detected twitching curtains or shopkeeper stares, but she knew nothing here would go unnoticed.

Even though Sandra and Mark were in plain clothes, they would, by now, be marked as unlikely tourists. She knew that much. Sandra adored working with her junior detective, but they didn't exactly look like a couple. Their business-like stride to the jewellers would certainly promote the odd whisper or two.

Mr Alsop, eager to receive the pair, opened the door before they'd reached the entrance to the shop. Rather than showing them the way into the workshop, as before, he ushered them upstairs. This different strategy heightened the drama somewhat, and Mark gave Sandra a raised eyebrow.

"This is a delicate matter. We'll be more private here," Michael Alsop explained.

Sandra nodded.

They sat in three prearranged chairs, looking towards a flat television screen. Unfortunately, the scene resembled a seedy X-rated cinema club from the 1970s. The décor of the room added to the unfortunate experience.

"I need to explain," confessed Mr Alsop.

"That might be helpful," Sandra agreed.

"During this morning's telephone conversation, I tried to intimate that this was going to be difficult and very embarrassing for me. Well, I came to the conclusion, after you left the premises yesterday, that I must set aside my own misgivings and tell the whole story…"

Michael paused for a moment, trying to ascertain how to continue.

"Go on," Sandra encouraged.

Mr Alsop regained some composure. "After you've seen this, you might think poorly of me – that I should have been such a fool. Maybe, you might feel that I coerced this lady to satisfy my own lust, but I can assure you that is not true. This was her idea, and it was spontaneous, as I shall later explain. Yes, I know I should have resisted. My age, experience, and stature in the local community should have equipped me to deal with the issue, but I'm afraid I succumbed to my intrigue and interest in all things strange and unexplained." He paused for a moment before adding, "Victoria Kent was also very persuasive."

"Our role is not to judge people, Mr Alsop. Whatever happens between consenting adults is of no interest to the police," Detective Constable Box explained.

"I am also about to break a promise I made to Victoria," he said quietly.

"Promise? What, to destroy the video?" Sandra asked.

"Indeed. I made a promise that I would erase my copy, but before I could, I discovered that she'd perished up on the moor. After that, I was in a bit of a quandary – I didn't know what the best course of action was. I hardly knew the lady, of course, but it seemed a betrayal… you know… to show you this."

"But Mr Alsop," said Sandra, "it's not as if you're selling salacious porn to the newspapers. Presumably, you're sharing it this morning because it has additional information to what you gave us yesterday. I think your conscience can rest easy. Now, can you tell us what happened after you gave Victoria the earrings?"

Michael nodded. "Yesterday, I said that I've been crafting jewellery for minority 'fringe' interests for some time. Pagans have been using my services for years. I gather that, locally, I have gained a certain reputation. They know that the items they're interested in aren't going to be available to purchase from high street stores, and so they ask me to make them. However, some examples are so bespoke, they are beyond… er… pagan-style trinkets…"

"I don't follow," Sandra said.

"Well, I get many requests for inscriptions on rings and bangles, images of the green man, Ogham tree alphabet paraphernalia, zodiac nipple rings, and so on. But, now and then, I get commissions for something rather… shall we say… more niche…"

"Meaning the occult," Mark clarified, "and Victoria's earrings were one such undertaking?"

"Indeed they were, although that was never discussed at the outset. But I knew. All through their construction, I was aware that I wasn't merely crafting an accessory to be worn down the pub. I was creating an enabling force. And, in the hands of the initiated, they could become very powerful. Not malignant, you must understand… well, that's my belief anyway." With that, Michael Alsop stared at his hands, looking deflated. It was as though the very same hands had been responsible for something beyond his control.

"When you gave the finished article to Victoria, you mentioned that you'd noticed something out of the ordinary," Sandra pressed.

"I just saw the glow," he explained, "and not just from the gold. The radiance was incredible. It shook her too. It was a combination of her aura and my crafting of, dare I say, something so beautiful. Her design had come alive in her hands. It was somehow tangible. She looked me in the eye and said, 'You know, don't you?' I nodded. Then she said, 'You knew from the beginning, and now you must help me further'. I was, at that point, eager to follow. I wasn't going to say, 'Now you've got your earrings, clear off'." He cleared his throat. "So, rather timidly, I said to her, 'What do you mean? How can I be of further assistance?'"

"How did she know you'd be able to film her? She must have taken quite a chance. She hardly knew you at all," Sandra pointed out.

"Ah well, she saw the camera that I have downstairs in the workshop. I use it to take pictures and videos of jewellery for my website and social media. She asked me about it, in casual conversation, when we discussed her design proposal. I thought nothing of it at the time, but now I know that she was sizing me up, so to speak."

"You were a stranger to her, and – if you don't mind me saying – quite a few years older. Didn't that strike you as unusual?" Mark asked.

Michael Alsop paused to consider his response, wondering how he'd managed to land himself in such an awkward situation. He cleared his throat and spoke in a measured tone. "Do you know, I think it was *because* I was older and a relative stranger that it made it easier for her. I think – or rather, I hope – she didn't consider me as predatory. She trusted me to film her without expecting… anything else… shall we say."

"And did anything else happen afterwards?" Sandra asked.

Michael was so abrupt that he almost answered her before she'd finished her question. "Absolutely not. I did what she asked." He lowered his voice again. "She was emotionally and physically exhausted, after she'd finished. I made her comfortable. Then I packed up the gear and left."

"I understand," said Sandra, shuffling about on the chair and trying to settle herself for the viewing. "Now, describe what we're about to witness and tell us what to look out for. Presumably, there's something of *particular* interest here."

Michael nodded, happy that Sandra had not continued with her line of questioning. He was also encouraged by her respect for his version of events. She would, no doubt, suspend judgement until they had seen the footage.

"She invited me to visit her house, later that afternoon," he explained. "She said that she would prepare the room for the ritual. All I had to do was set up the lights, and sort out the camera lenses and so on."

He took a deep breath and continued. "She entered the room, turned on the music, and signalled for me to start filming. I had read about this kind of thing, but I had never witnessed it before. It was shocking, exhilarating, beautiful, scary, and life-changing – all rolled into one. Of course, I have been a non-practising, casual student of the occult all my life. To others, this may seem like 'mumbo jumbo', but the ritual is all about using the earrings as a sigil. You may want to do some research on that…"

Mark gave Sandra a knowing look. Neither, however, wished to acknowledge their familiarity with the concept for fear of prolonging Mr Alsop's introduction.

"She uses another sigil, which appears to be a tattoo, just below the bikini line," Michael explained. "She enlarges this sign by writing it on her torso with body paint. At the climax of the ritual, please note the 'telos' she uses – that's the raison d'être, the goal, the purpose. She shouts and moans these words. They mean something to her. If you can decipher the sigils and understand the telos, it might unlock the mystery of her death. It was not my business to ask, and it would have been wrong of me to try to delve into her secrets."

"Thanks for that, Mr Alsop," Sandra told him. "It's always useful to have background information. It also puts the whole scenario into context. Perhaps now we can run the video?"

Her thoughts flitted inappropriately towards darkened cinemas, popcorn, giggling fits with friends and being remonstrated by stony-faced couples sitting behind. She hastened the images away and readied herself for some uncomfortable viewing.

Mark, who knew Sandra too well, stared ahead at the screen so as not to fan any flames. At times like these, it was hard to remain totally professional. It reminded him of watching awkward nude scenes on the television with his parents in the room.

Mr Alsop selected the file on the computer and clicked play.

The video had been shot in Victoria's back bedroom, but you couldn't really tell. She had erected screens to hide the incongruent wallpaper, and there was neither a bed nor cabinets and cupboards to clutter the scene. A large, decorative mirror was hanging on the left wall. A table, draped in a black cloth, was positioned at the front, leaving space behind for movement. On this table there was a silver goblet, some kind of large pen, an array of lit candles, and some incense sticks burning – their smoke drifting upwards, undisturbed. Music thrummed discordantly, virtually inaudible at first but rising noticeably. Carefully positioned uplighters threw colour around the room, creating an atmospheric mood.

The visual feast was cleverly created; this was no hastily cobbled together, amateurish home studio fit for webcam consumers.

Victoria entered the set from the right-hand side. Wearing only a black mask, she held a silver dish out in front of her as if carrying a coronation crown. On the small platter lay the earrings that Mr Alsop had so amazingly crafted: the sigil. Her slender, reasonably tall body moved gracefully towards the table. She knelt before it and held the dish aloft.

Rhythmic drumbeats now pulsated as a wash of ethnic synthesised keyboard sounds ebbed and flowed with the stereo panning effect. Strange bowed instruments, like cellos, added to the drama. Victoria gazed directly at the camera and held a stare, her eyes fixed as if her mortal body was earthly but her mind was elsewhere.

Victoria's black mask was magnificent. Pearl and black beads dangled in vertical lines to adorn her cheeks. The feathers and delicate lace sections were hiding so much and yet, tantalisingly, so little. The nose section was pointedly arched like an upturned prow of a sleek ocean yacht. Her eyes, now dominant, pierced the incense haze like a raptor.

She lowered the plate and rested it on the black-clothed table. Then, taking the silver goblet in her right hand, she placed the silver lip to her open mouth and tipped the vessel back violently. The torrent of red wine filled her mouth and cascaded across her chin and down her throat, before running in multiple rivers over and between her breasts. The careless abandon demonstrated by the event was a portent, and perfectly timed.

Leaving the lines of 'blood' to reach her belly, she lifted the large pen from the table and stood up. She placed the tip at the base of her ribcage, and – with careful, obviously practised precision – she drew bold lines and curves to form a larger version of the sigil tattoo that embellished the skin above her pelvic region. It was seamlessly performed and strikingly effective.

The music, now louder still, spurred Victoria to sway and dance. It was almost as if she had just dressed in a new item of clothing and wanted to show it off. She began thrusting and gyrating her hips. She was spinning and arching like a performance artist as she started shouting,

'Jac… Jac… you must harness the power within you! You must not leave. Thou wilt live, thou wilt live!'

And then, almost as if there'd been a given signal, she stopped and held her head perfectly still.

The name 'Jack' jolted Sandra and Mark. They turned to acknowledge that the other had heard the significant call.

Next, Victoria bent down and picked up the earrings. She held each one in turn by the hook and dangled it close to her eyes. It could have been a shaft of light from the window, or a reflection from the uplighters, but her face glowed each time. She secured each earring into her lobes and adopted a star-shaped pose. This announced that the first part of the ritual was about to give way to the next phase.

The room was becoming ever more atmospheric as beams of light lanced their way through the translucent film. The music, now more manic and discordant, took the experience to another level.

As she fell to her knees, Victoria's hands started exploring her body. Her upper torso writhed and pitched in line with the jarring rhythms. Her face was, at times, contorted with the pain of ecstasy.

"Jac… Jac… I will hear you, see you, breathe you, touch you… live!" Victoria exclaimed, repeating it numerous times. At first it was just a low moan, but then it started building in intensity.

Without warning, Sandra stood up and turned her back to the screen. "Okay, okay, that's enough for me," she proclaimed. "I get the idea, and I know where it's going to end. Cut the video."

Rather surprised by the sudden interruption, Michael left his seat and quickly scurried over to the computer. The abrupt cessation of the thunderous, discordant rhythms and the rapid flickering light emanating from the screen left an equally disturbing silence and stillness in the room.

Sandra felt the need to fill the void. "Does she say anything else after that?"

"No, she repeats the phrases over and over until…"

"Yes, quite," said Sandra. "Mark can take a copy of the file and watch the whole thing through again just in case we've missed something."

Mark nodded, still surprised by Sandra's reticence to witness the whole video. She wasn't easily embarrassed, and certainly not squeamish. He'd seen her operate in the most desperate moments. This piece of evidence had obviously hit a particular nerve.

"Mr Alsop, you were right to show us this. It could be important, and I know it was difficult for you. Now, she mentions a 'Jack'. Do you have any idea about this person? Has he been a client of yours at some stage? People of similar interests will use known, bona fide establishments that are sympathetic to their needs."

"Well now, I've been thinking the very same thing," he replied, "and I've been racking my brain, but I can't come up with any such candidate. As I said earlier, I never asked at the time because it would have been impertinent of me to do so. This ritual was deeply personal to Ms Kent. People interested in the occult do not practise because it titillates; it's meant to facilitate something… in a positive way, of course."

"You say '…in a positive way', but Victoria Kent ended up lying face down in a river in the bleakest part of the moor very soon after. Could this ritual have led to her demise?" Mark asked.

"No, I don't believe so, but the two events in quick succession shook me," Michael admitted. "I didn't feel it was my place to dismiss them as a coincidence; I knew I had to refer the matter to you. In my view, this was nothing about demons and devils," he added.

The two detectives nodded in acknowledgement.

"Thank you, Mr Alsop. We'll let ourselves out… oh, nearly forgot the copy of the file," DS Baines added jovially, trying to lighten the mood.

"I knew you'd be wanting that, so I've copied it onto a pen drive for you," said Michael as he passed the small object to DC Box.

Sandra noted the irony of the situation; the device may have been amazingly compact and light, but the load lifted from the jeweller was sizeable and heavy.

The detectives threaded their way back through the town to the car park. There was much to assimilate from the experience they'd just shared, but neither felt the need to talk about it until they'd reached the sanctity of the car. Somehow, discussing such a private event in the street seemed inappropriate.

Once they were safely cocooned in the vehicle, Sandra addressed the 'elephant in the room'. "Sorry, Mark – it just felt so… voyeuristic. I was a bit hot under the collar back there. I don't know what I was feeling. Once we had the nugget, the reference to Jack, that was enough for me."

"It was certainly strange and very real – not like some Hammer Horror movie," he agreed. "If I'm honest, I'm glad you stopped the show. It was very weird there with him in the room. Even though it wasn't remotely like sex on the telly, it was highly charged. I've never seen anything like it. Very uncomfortable," Mark added, feeling equally confused.

"And the reference to Jack?"

"Ah yes," he acknowledged, "now that was of significant interest. I hadn't anticipated that. Quite a shock."

"So, what did he call it – the telos? The mention of Jack, coupled with the sigil tattoo, points to Ms Kent knowing Mr Reilly. He was there on Fur Tor at the same time. It's only a spitting distance away from where she was found."

"It's certainly looking more likely," Mark said, "but–"

"I know what you're going to point out," Sandra interrupted. "We still don't have any forensic evidence."

Detective Constable Box stared out of the windscreen. The mundane views of shoppers returning to their cars and the darkening grey skies were perfect for quality thinking time. Even though Sandra, sitting next to him, was a slight distraction, he could let his mind drift into a world of possibilities. Mark always found staring at a computer screen, or a sheet of white paper, rather limiting. Memories of exams and assignment deadlines flooded back to him. He knew that cases could be won without forensics, but circumstantial evidence had to be cast iron.

He tried to sum up their position. "If we could crack the sigil code for the earrings, that would help enormously. If it confirms that Jack was the focus of the ritual we just witnessed, that would strengthen our case against him immeasurably. However, we have to establish a link between Jack and Victoria. We could do with an email trail, text messages, witness statements, photos and so on… but, frustratingly, we don't have any. What if it's a different Jack she's referring to? Do we have enough to bring him in and question him?"

"We could do with something a little more tangible," Sandra admitted. "Evidence of him being in her house, for instance. Somebody broke in and was interested in something…"

"The earrings!" exclaimed Mark. "He was after the earrings. The sigil must be important, otherwise he wouldn't have risked visiting the house."

Sandra's face lit up, recognising the breakthrough. "You beauty… that's it," she said. "So that's the reason why her top drawer was all in a mess – he was in a panic trying to find them."

"The only thing I'm not sure about is why Victoria put the earrings in her knickers drawer. Isn't that odd? Why not use the jewellery box? Do you keep earrings there?"

Sandra feigned shock at the suggestion. "As I said before, 'Keep your nose out of my top drawer', Box," she remonstrated, before laughing. "However, you make a good point. I don't keep mine there. Perhaps the mystery burglar, being a bloke, thought otherwise."

"Maybe he was looking and was disturbed. He became a little frantic, found what he was looking for, and then scarpered before he could tidy up. That's the reason nowhere else is ransacked," Mark suggested.

"Sounds logical. Do you know, I think we ought to pay another visit to the house and conduct a more extensive search. You were right when you thought the back bedroom had been used as a home studio. I didn't understand the significance of that then, but it's much clearer now."

Mark nodded. "I think you're right. If we can find evidence of Jack being in the house, it would make the case against him very strong."

"What about the recovery of her phone? Have they managed to establish whom she'd been contacting prior to her death?" Sandra asked.

Mark shook his head. "Not yet, but I'll chase that later. I'll try and sweet-talk the department to place us further up the queue."

Sandra started the car and coasted up to the barrier. She smiled to herself as she noted that the mechanical arm provided a poignant metaphor.

It was time, she thought, for a few restrictions in her life to start lifting.

Chapter 12

Jack lay back on the hotel bed; waiting for the phone to ring had been mentally exhausting. He was consumed by the need to make contact with the elusive, and fiercely private, woman who had pretty much taken over his life. She – fortunately, yet unfortunately – held the key to his future well-being.

He had followed her bizarre instructions to the letter. He had written a brief note to explain his predicament, and had told her where he was staying. He had then put this note in a waterproof plastic box, which he'd placed amongst the long grass by the road bridge that crossed the disused Great Western Railway track bed at Liddaton. Now all he could do was wait and hope.

Deep down, Jack had admitted to himself that he would gladly spend a week more in Cornwall if it meant he could track her down and see her again. Realistically, though, he could stay for only a couple more days – unless, of course, the police had other ideas.

Jack had just settled himself down for a pre-dinner snooze when the telephone sprang to life. The screen lit, and an annoying buzzing sound made the instrument almost dance on the bedside cabinet.

Apprehensively, Jack reached out and pressed what he hoped was the appropriate key. "Hello, Jack Reilly speaking."

"Okay, Jack, so this is how it works. You meet me at Combestone Tor on Dartmoor at eleven tomorrow morning. You remember that place?"

Jack sat bolt upright, hardly believing what he was hearing. He was too stunned to answer quickly.

Jacqui filled the void with more information. "It's just up from Venford Reservoir. There's a place where you can park your car just in front of it… remember?" She waited for Jack to respond.

"Yes. It's been a long time since I've been there, but I do remember it."

"Good," Jacqui replied. "Remember: eleven o'clock."

"It's good to hear your voice–"

"Save that stuff for tomorrow, Jack – but remember, we're not there for a picnic. I'll explain when I see you."

Before Jack had a chance to say goodbye, Jacqui had gone.

* * *

"Do excuse the mess; I'm in the process of boxing everything up for a move," Jenny Jones said apologetically as she ushered DS Baines towards a chair at the breakfast bar in the kitchen.

"Thank you," replied Sandra, climbing onto the seat.

"So what's this all about, Detective Sergeant? From Devon and Cornwall? You appear to be off your regular patch." Jenny pointed to the teapot and then the coffee jar, raising her eyebrows.

"Coffee, if it's not too much bother. It's been a long drive." She waited until the owner of the flat had gathered the mugs together and switched the kettle on before she attempted to answer.

Jenny, however, jumped in first, rather nervously. "I gather it's not me you're enquiring about. I was hoping I'd got away with that spot of skinny dipping at Maidencombe, a few years back."

Sandra laughed. "Corfu maybe, but not Maidencombe. You were lucky we didn't section you for reckless behaviour, or endangering your own life – even in summer, the water is freezing."

Jenny sat down and placed the drinks on the bar. "You said it was a matter pertaining to Jack Reilly, but I'm not with him anymore. We broke up before Christmas last year."

"Yes," Sandra said, "I'm aware that your relationship ended. I'm here to gain your insight into him as a person – what he was like in the relationship, so to speak."

"Is he in some kind of trouble? He is okay, isn't he?" Jenny asked, alarmed. "I don't understand."

"He's perfectly fine, as far as I'm aware. We're just trying to establish some facts about a situation that happened on Dartmoor… we're trying to rule him out of our enquiries," Sandra answered, tactfully.

"A situation?"

"A woman tragically lost her life on the moor. We believe that Jack was working – taking photographs, that is – in the vicinity. We like to conduct background checks on key witnesses and suspects. It helps us create a picture of the people we're dealing with," Sandra told her, trying to be as vague as possible. She took a well-timed gulp of coffee; the M25 had taken its toll.

Jenny frowned in concern; the police asking questions about Jack was the last thing she'd expected. "I'm not sure how I can help. Jack is the most passive, charming man I know. He wouldn't hurt a fly. I certainly can't imagine him being in any sort of bother."

"But you're not together now. Did he end the relationship?" Sandra asked.

"No, we're not together now, and I'm sad about that. We made a joint decision… we thought our relationship had run its course…" Jenny's facial expression betrayed her feelings. It was clear that she felt her words were an admission of failure.

"How so?"

"We knew each other way back… at school. We had a six-month romance, but when school finished, separate universities at opposite ends of the country split us up. We tried to keep it going, but we drifted apart."

"But you found each other again?"

"Yes, many years later. I stayed up in Durham for five years or so. I found work up there and another partner. I returned to Surrey when that relationship ended. It's also very cold up there!" She took a breath as if summoning strength. "I bumped into Jack, here in Sutton, in one of the local pubs, and we hit it off straight away… as if we'd never stopped."

"Sounds like a lovely story, but it doesn't have a happy ending. What happened?"

"We decided not to marry, and babies weren't a priority. We enjoyed the lives we were living. I guess we both immersed ourselves in our work. More and more, Jack wanted to roam about the country, taking photographs for his blog. He was beginning to get approached by publishers and was networking with other authors who could use his material…"

"And you?" Sandra pressed.

"My work is with rare diseases – research and so on. I had an opportunity to take up a post at Brandeis University in Boston, Massachusetts, specialising in health policy analysis. A big step, going to America and all that."

"I take it you accepted the invitation, and this is you packing up?"

Jenny scanned the room. There were boxes everywhere. "Yes. I knew that I had a very good chance of securing the post about a year ago. We talked about it at length. It's what I'd been striving for… but Jack, obviously, didn't want to sacrifice his interests. His line of business is all about the myths, legends, and rural life of the UK. Neither of us could see him thriving in the States – he loves stone circles and warm, flat beer too much." She shrugged, sighing. "So, we'd reached an impasse. We knew that our own projects were too important to us. From that moment, it was inevitable that we'd go our separate ways again. But it hurt us both, terribly." Jenny pursed her lips in a forced smile. She was finding it difficult talking about this to a relative stranger.

DS Baines nodded. She could see that the conundrum had weighed heavily on the woman sitting opposite her. Quite often, Sandra found that ex-lovers would sound off about a previous partner to make themselves feel better about a breakup.

"So Jack didn't press you to put your career on hold, have a family, and settle here in leafy Surrey?" Sandra asked, trying to veer the conversation towards Jack's temperament.

Jenny smiled at the irony of the question. "Jack didn't press me to do anything… ever. He's a free spirit and he always encouraged me to be whatever I wanted to be. Unfortunately, because we'd previously broken up when we were younger, it made it easier to do so again. We'd already set a precedent."

"Was he ever jealous of you in any way? Did you argue?"

Jenny paused to reflect on the line of questioning. She was bright enough to understand where the detective was nudging the proceedings.

"Never jealous… absolutely not. And we only argued about really silly stuff like tidiness or being late. That's what makes the whole thing so tragic."

"So, presumably, he didn't have a temper… he never lost it?"

"Goodness gracious! No, never. I could never be with anyone like that. And, before you ask, he was never violent towards me. If we ever had cross words, he would remove himself from the situation and go into himself, if you know what I mean."

"Yes, I get that," DS Baines said, scribbling down a few notes. She looked up and tried another avenue. "What about money? Was Jack ever seriously in debt?"

"Well, we never had loads to spare because of student loans and our carefree lifestyle," Jenny explained. "We both worked hard and partied hard as well. At times, the car would go wrong or the washing machine would need replacing, but that was all. Jack has just recently lost his mother," she added, "so when he and his sister sell the house, he'll have fifty per cent of that. His work is patchy, but he's building up a reputation and he can be well remunerated for serious articles and publications."

DS Baines took a mouthful of her drink and then carefully framed the next question. "Do you think he was seeing someone else while he was with you?"

Jenny locked her eyes onto Sandra's, hoping to be able to read her. Was this for real, or was she just fishing? "Look, if I said, 'There's no chance of that', you'd be thinking, 'How many times have I heard that? The poor delusional princess'. But Jack was such a rubbish liar; he wouldn't have been able to juggle two lives. I never had any doubts about his commitment to our relationship. To be honest, this is the first time I've even considered the possibility. I'm not sure where he would have met somebody else either. It's not as if he had the opportunity to chat somebody up next to the photocopier. And to guess your next question, yes, our sex life was good. No complaints there!"

Sandra held both hands up in surrender with an accompanying smirk. She had no intention of giving Jenny a hard time and was amused by her perception.

The gesture had the desired effect; Jack's ex-partner smiled at her embarrassing outburst.

"When did you see him last?" Sandra asked, keen to establish if Jack's behaviour had changed in recent weeks. It was also meant to sound like a last question. She was keen to re-establish a calmer atmosphere.

"Oh, that would be… four or five months back. We agreed to make a strong break so it wouldn't be so painful. I phoned to check that he was dealing with his mother's death… oh, and I got a Christmas card from him." Jenny paused for a moment, trying to remember any other relevant details.

DS Baines drank the last few mouthfuls of coffee. She then popped her pen into her bag and closed her notebook. "You've been very helpful, thank you," Sandra told her, weighing up the complete lack of breakthrough with her inner voice telling her that Jack Reilly was an unlikely murderer.

Jenny showed DS Baines to the door. As she twisted the catch, she felt the need to strengthen her evidence by delivering a parting shot. "We were two adults who realised our time together had come to an end. We both had dreams of the future that involved us being on different continents, thousands of miles apart. There was no acrimony. We had no children. We agreed to cherish the time we'd spent together, while also moving on. And we parted on good terms – I even gave Jack a gift when we said our goodbyes."

"Oh yes?" asked Sandra politely.

"It was insignificant, really, and certainly not valuable. I knew that mainstream religion wasn't important to him, and I knew he would never wear it. It was just a token – almost a talisman. I gave him a St Christopher necklace for safe passage…"

* * *

Jack crossed the River Tavy and took the right-hand turn out of Tavistock up onto the moor road. It headed eastwards, climbing majestically for a few miles until it levelled off to what seemed like the top of the world. If he had been pleasure-seeking, he would have parked Smudge in one of the parking bays created for sightseers and walkers, and gazed at the panoramic landscape. At this height, on a clear day, you could see for miles. To the left, Cox Tor and the two Staple Tors dominated the view.

To the right, Sharpitor was clearly visible, although it was many miles distant. Straight ahead, the television station mast at North Hessary Tor acted like a beacon.

Jack marvelled at the view, but his mind was elsewhere. It had only been just over a week since he'd seen her, but those eight or nine days had been spent in complete turmoil; his world had been turned upside down. He'd been relieved to hear her voice again and he felt cheered at the prospect of another meeting, yet issues remained. The tone of her message had been rather curt and transactional; he had hoped for warm and embracing. Clearly, there was much he didn't understand about her.

Ideally, the conversation would flow as it had when they'd first met at Fur Tor. She would offer to speak to the police and he would be cleared of any involvement with the tragic death of the hiker. After that? After that… he dared not contemplate.

The quarry at Merrivale soon came into view and he carefully negotiated the campervan around the windy bends of the Walkham Valley floor. As the VW California accelerated up the steep hill, he noticed the ancient stones to his right that had first ignited his passion for photography.

As a teenager, he'd always been thrilled to discover the enigmatic Dartmoor granite structures, often in desolate places. As soon as he'd been given his first serious camera, he had delighted in capturing their drama by utilising the barren landscape and brooding moorland skies. He hadn't yet decided upon the purpose of stone rows, huge menhirs, barrows, and granite circles, but he felt their energy. It was almost as if a baton had been passed to him by an ancient culture, and now it was his duty to preserve their reason for being by representing them faithfully in modern media.

It wasn't long before he indicated right and took the narrow lane towards Hexworthy. The bridge at Huccaby was so narrow it required careful attention to cross, and Jack was relieved that the way was clear. Underneath, the West Dart River meandered its way towards Dartmeet and beyond. Huge boulders littered the riverbed and made for spectacular childhood rock hopping. As he passed the Forest Inn on an extremely tricky bend that also elevated alarmingly, he knew that his goal would soon be in view. The very narrow road, with few passing places, would continue to rise for a mile until it levelled off at his destination.

Combestone Tor was best viewed from the other side of the Dart Valley. It was nestled on the steep hillside but, from the road behind, it appeared as just another set of large rocks. It was popular because it was easily accessible, and its structure was easy to clamber over. This made it an ideal picnic spot for families.

Jack was relieved to see that the designated meeting place was going to be private; there were just two cars parked in the bay. As both were empty, and he couldn't see evidence of life, he figured Jacqui hadn't yet arrived and the visitors were walkers.

He parked the campervan in an open space and spied a string of Dartmoor ponies ambling nosily towards him. He remembered, as a child, just how crestfallen he'd been when his sister told him the ponies weren't pleased to see him personally –they just wanted his apple core.

He was anxious that Jacqui wasn't in a car waiting for him, but happy that he'd arrived on time. If he'd been late, and she'd already gone, it would have been very difficult to establish contact again.

He was just about to open the door and start searching for her amongst the rocks when he heard a knuckle tap on the sliding door window, causing him to almost jump out of his seat.

He held his chest. "My God, I swear my heart missed a beat. Where did you come from? I didn't see you arrive!" he said through the window.

"I walked. I saw you arrive. I was just making sure you didn't have company," Jacqui answered.

"Walked from where?" he asked, lowering the driver's window.

" I'm here, aren't I?" She raised a faint smile, not answering his question.

"Do you often make sudden appearances, hang around for a while, and then disappear without a trace?" asked Jack.

"Of course. I do it all the time. You're lucky you got a second shot. I usually open the wrapper, chew the contents, and then spit them out."

Jack got out of the campervan and stood before her. Once again, he was totally captured by her directness. "I've been thinking about you a lot this last week," he said, trying to hold himself together. "It's been tough."

"The police? I read your note."

He nodded. "So, what's with sending me down narrow lanes, and hiding messages in a sandwich box?"

"There are things about my life that I only want a few people to know," she said carefully. "I had to be sure it was just you I was meeting, and I wanted to know what the problem was. Look, it's a lovely sunny day – rather rare on Dartmoor for this time of year. Let's perch on the rocks and talk. I know of some large flat stones to the right over there."

Jack nodded and Jacqui led the way. They climbed over a few low rocks and manoeuvred through gaps to find a reasonably level slab that jutted out over the falling ground below, at which point they sat, dangling their legs over the edge. The view down to the River Dart and across to the distant tors to the right was amazing.

"Now I remember this place," Jack said. "I got stuck trying to find my way through those huge stones over there. I was really young. My dad had to come and rescue me."

"You said… when we met. That's why I chose here. I thought you knew it well."

"I haven't been back since then," Jack said wistfully, wondering how the years had slipped away so fast.

They both scanned the horizon, trying to take in the grandeur.

"I need you to help me," Jack said in a low voice that betrayed his embarrassment for asking. "The police… they think I had something to do with the death of a hiker not far from Fur Tor."

"How did the police know you were on the moor at the same time?" Jacqui asked.

"I went to them," he admitted, shrugging. "I heard about the death of the girl on the radio… the local news. That was another time I nearly had a heart failure – I thought it was you! I thought you'd slipped and fallen on your way back, you know, when the weather had deteriorated. It was really rough. I couldn't just forget about it and drive back to Surrey. I couldn't leave you. I felt honour bound… seeing as though we… we…"

"That's very sweet of you, Jack, but now we're in a bit of a hole," Jacqui told him. 'I take it they didn't believe you because it was such a coincidence?"

"…And they couldn't find anything about you because your name isn't Ruthven and there were no witnesses," Jack blurted out. "I didn't have any proof of your existence – no photos or even contact details."

"But you haven't told them that my name *isn't* Ruthven, have you?"

"No," Jack replied, "I found that out from your father. I went to see him at the bookshop in Farningham."

Jacqui had already heard this from her meeting with Ross, but it still shook her. She couldn't even begin to fathom how Jack knew that her father owned a bookshop in Kent.

Instead of sounding peeved at the breach of her 'world', however, she decided to mount a charm offensive. "So, Jack Conan Doyle, how did you work that one out? Perhaps I should have arranged the meeting at Hound Tor? You might have felt more at home there."

"I got lucky. I was given a photo album to look at," Jack said, knowing that Jacqui would be desperate for more details. Quietly, he was relishing the fact that she might be impressed.

"And…?"

"And, amazingly, there were instantly recognisable photos of you as a child."

Jacqui tried to digest this information, but it didn't make any sense. She didn't particularly like having her photograph taken, so it was unlikely that her image had been readily available to anyone outside her family. It was at that moment that her father's code word – 'King's Tor' – nudged her thought process. "My accident at King's Tor…"

"That's correct, and what's more, I was there with my family," Jack told her. "What are the chances of us meeting again as we did at Fur Tor? Probably more than you think, but it's still very weird. What are the chances that when my sister and I were clearing my mum's possessions from her house, after her death, we came across old photo albums of our holidays in the West Country? When I saw you in one of the books – those photos of our day out with the Taylors – I knew it was you. It had to be. The picture of you with stitches high on your cheek, when you came back from hospital, was the giveaway. I recalled your story about falling on the rocks… it had to be you."

Jack was almost breathless after rattling the sentences off in quick succession. He turned to face her and couldn't help gazing at her now faint scar – the telltale blemish.

"That's pretty unbelievable," Jacqui said, trying to assess the ramifications. "So how did you manage to track down the address of the bookshop? I don't remember our families having any contact over the years."

"My sister said she remembered ordering a book from the shop when she was studying; I think our father gave her the heads up that your dad's bookshop specialised in the kind of material she needed. I think the paper wrapper still survives. 'Farningham Books' is a bit of a giveaway. I used the internet for the rest. Farningham is not a big place."

"So Dad recognised you?" asked Jacqui. "He believed your story?"

"I showed him the albums. He remembered the day very well – for obvious reasons. He was sad that I'd just lost my mum. He had heard about my dad's passing from the Taylors. When I said I needed to contact you because I needed help, he promised to do all he could. However, he knew that you didn't want to be contacted, and he didn't have an up-to-date number for you anyway."

"That's quite a story," Jacqui said, using a well-worn phrase because nothing else seemed to fit. It was, after all, extraordinary.

Jack nodded. "It's been a chain reaction of coincidences, and although I hardly know you, I feel that we're connected in some way."

"And now you want me to present myself to the police and tell them how we met on Fur Tor," Jacqui said.

"That's about it," answered Jack. "Then my account bears scrutiny. It all fits."

Jacqui remained silent for a few moments. She'd already known that this would be the likely outcome of the conversation; once she'd read about Jack's predicament from the note in the sandwich box, it didn't take a rocket scientist to work out he needed her to make herself known to the CID.

She cursed her feelings for Jack. He was sensitive, interesting, intelligent, handsome… and now there was a historical link thrown into the mix too. But this was not part of the plan at all. She did not want to feel duty-bound to family, friends, or lovers. She didn't want to be accountable to anybody.

"I want to help you, Jack," she said, "I do. But I have a problem…"

Chapter 13

"A problem?" asked Jack, incredulously. "What kind of problem? You only have to show the police your face, tell them we met, and that I left heading towards Postbridge." Her blank expression was not encouraging, so he continued, "In fact, thinking about it, you left the tor and headed in the direction the girl was found. You must have crossed the brook – it's amazing you didn't bump into her."

"That's the problem, Jack."

The disappointment in her voice was evident, and it took a second for her statement to sink in.

"What the hell does that mean? You saw… her body?" he asked, alarmed.

"No, I didn't, but I did hear her calling me… in the distance… or, at least, I think I did. I knew her, Jack."

Jack paused for a moment. "I don't understand. Did you walk the moor together and then split up because you had an argument, or something?"

"No, but I knew she'd camped over the night before at Great Kneeset – that's a hill about a mile north of Fur Tor. She was a very experienced hiker. I'd told her I might meet her the following day – the day I met you, that is – but that was a big mistake."

"A mistake? Why?"

"Because I didn't want to commit. I made a last-minute decision to cross the Amicombe Brook and climb Fur Tor. I'd always wanted to see it."

"I'm really glad about that, because we met, but now you're going to tell me the awkward stuff," Jack said, in a subdued voice.

"Yes," Jacqui replied, "this is where it gets awkward. You remember when I left? The weather was closing in. You said we'd better be leaving."

"Yes, I remember that well. It was a difficult journey back."

"So, I scrambled down the slope of Fur Tor," she explained. "There's not really a path – at least, I couldn't see one. There's clitter everywhere, rocks, boulders… it's a bit of a nightmare. Anyway, I reached the brook and surprisingly found an easy crossing, but at that point, it began to sleet heavily. My face was stinging as I was walking into the driving icy rain. I could just about see the direction I needed to travel, but I could hardly hear myself think. It was very disorientating. As you know, Jack, the weather up here can change in an instant."

He nodded, reliving his own troublesome journey through the hail, sleet, and snow. "That's where she saw you. She called out," Jack surmised.

Jacqui sighed. "Well, this is where it gets a little muddled. I thought I heard her, but when I turned to look, I couldn't see a thing. It was like something out of a horror movie, only it was real. The light was beginning to fade, and I desperately wanted to push on back home. I didn't want to spend ten or fifteen minutes trying to hook up with her. It's easy to lose your bearings."

"Did it sound like she was calling for help?" Jack asked.

"No, just my name, a couple of times – to attract my attention, I think. I figured she'd understand that I needed to cut across to Deadlake Foot and find the path up and over Hare Tor. I was parked over Lydford way. She was going in a different direction – to Mary Tavy via Tavy Cleave. Honestly, Jack, she was so experienced. She tested equipment for organisations and expeditions… you know, serious cold weather stuff. That was her job. She wrote reviews for magazines and websites. I never even gave it a thought that she wouldn't make it back."

"The police think she slipped and fell… and that I might have pushed her," said Jack quietly. He wanted to shout out, 'If only you'd stopped to talk to her!' but he knew there was no point.

"Obviously, now I wish I'd tried to find her, but at the time I just wanted to make it back to the car. I was on the edge of my capability out there," Jacqui explained. What she didn't want to say was that the woman had been getting on her nerves, lately. Victoria hadn't understood that you had to let a friendship breathe.

"I reckon she must have been excited to see you, and in trying to attract your attention, she lost her concentration and fell," Jack suggested.

"But why didn't she pick herself up? That's what I keep asking myself."

"Perhaps she hit her head on a rock, or something."

They sat in silence for longer than was comfortable.

Jack assessed the implications of Jacqui's testimony. She hadn't really explained to him why she had a problem helping him out of his predicament.

Jacqui, on the other hand, didn't want to let Jack down, but she certainly wasn't going to divulge information about the nature of the relationship she'd had with Victoria, the secret pact they shared with Ross and Chris that she was now very much regretting, or any other reason why police intrusion would be severely unwanted.

"You see, Jack," said Jacqui after a while, "it wouldn't have changed anything if I'd told the police. I couldn't have saved her because I was unaware that she'd fallen. If you hadn't shown up, the police would have announced that it was an accident – as it was. It's the same result. I didn't want the police raking over my life. I didn't want what you've suffered. I need to do things, and I only have a short amount of time to do them."

Jacqui let the last sentence hang in the air, hoping that Jack wouldn't demand more clarity. She hadn't intended to venture into her personal welfare, but she was running out of road.

"I heard that you were ill, from your dad," he said quietly. "Is it serious?"

"My God! What has he been telling you? He had no right to discuss those details!" Jacqui barked.

Jack cursed himself for his insensitivity, but he felt that she had almost invited him to respond. "We didn't discuss anything – that's the truth. I didn't ask, and he wouldn't tell me. He just said that when you became aware of something serious, health-related, you decided to spend even less time at home. He was trying to explain why he couldn't furnish me with any contact details for you. I think he was a little embarrassed, to be honest."

Jacqui searched the expression on Jack's face. She knew she could read him; he might have been a relative stranger but he was an open book. She laughed inwardly at her inappropriate suggestion when they'd previously met. It was an obvious sign to her that she found him instantly trustworthy and discreet.

He smiled gently, offering reassurance that he wasn't lying, and she demonstrated acceptance.

"I would never let you sink, Jack," she told him. "I would come forward and tell the police about our meeting – if it was necessary. You have my word on that. However, that time isn't now. The police won't find any evidence against you because there isn't any. They're just being diligent. It's their job to look at everything."

"So you want me to just sit it out, and hope it blows over?"

Jack knew the answer, but he wanted her to realise the sacrifice he'd have to make.

"Yes, that's what I want you to do. Can you do that for me, Jack? We're not hiding anything. The girl, Victoria, died as a result of an accident: pure and simple."

"And if I need you to speak to the police because they're trying to pin something on me? How will I reach you?"

"Call my dad. I think I need a word with him anyway, so I'll leave a contact number with him. But Jack… no socials. I'm going to need to disappear for a while."

Jack looked down, crestfallen. He'd been about to ask if he could see her again, but he could tell his chances weren't good at all. "Does that mean we won't meet again? Only I'd really like to… you know, when this is all over." He spoke softly, desperately trying not to betray how crushed he was feeling.

Jacqui pushed her hands flat into the stone slab and sprang down from the elevated platform. Performing a perfect dismount, she smiled at Jack so as not to alarm him of her sudden move. "Come on, Jack, let's walk," she said. "There's a small path next to the road."

Jack followed her lead and jumped down onto the springy moorland grass. Then, together, they made their way through the bracken towards the road that led to Venford Reservoir.

"You're sweet, Jack, and I do want to keep in touch, but I can't allow myself to be emotionally tied to anybody – not yet, anyway. When I found out about my illness, I made plans to live a carefree life. I'm financially independent, and I come and go as I please. My long-term health may not be that promising; things could change at any time, I'll tell you that much." She sighed loudly. "I feel closer to you than I'd like to admit, but that doesn't change anything. Selfishly, there are things I want to do, and I don't want you to feel responsible for my behaviour. I really wouldn't be good for you."

"I've just finished a long-term relationship," Jack said. "It was a mutual decision. She's a great girl but, going forward, we wanted different things. I get what you're saying. I wasn't looking to find something on the rebound… it's just that it took me by surprise, you know, when we met. I was just up on the moor taking pictures. You certainly left an impression on me because I couldn't get you out of my mind… I still can't."

They strolled beside the roadside, carefully adopting the narrow desire path worn by sightseers travelling to and from the reservoir.

Jacqui broke the silence. "There's a delightful walk along the leat over there, but I didn't fancy scrambling through a load of bracken to get to it."

Jack looked over to where she was pointing and acknowledged her comment, even though his mind was elsewhere. He couldn't help feeling that he needed to make his position clearer. "I'm not going to stalk you or anything," he told her. "I may well need your help, but I'm going to respect your privacy. I think it's the only way I can stay in the game. Who knows, our paths might collide again someday! I certainly hope so."

Jacqui stared at him for a moment. "Yes, I hope so too, Jack, but don't waste your life hanging around waiting. I generally leave a trail of destruction behind me. You see? It's happened again. I've inadvertently got you into a mess. There are quite a few bruised individuals who feel let down by me. And then, of course, there's Victoria – the girl on the moor. What could be worse? Everybody seems to want to save me from myself, but I'm happy with what I have left of my life."

She turned to face Jack and held both his hands in her own. Once again, a hug seemed inappropriate and almost patronising; somehow, locking eyes and squaring up face to face was far more intimate.

In that moment, Jack desperately wanted to kiss her, but he was aware that such a move might not be received well. It could undo the trust he'd garnered by agreeing to her demands. Instead, he asked, rather nervously, "What you have left?"

"You, however, have been different from all the others," Jacqui continued, ignoring his question. "I thought you might pile the pressure on. We both know how we felt after our meeting. Our past history, unbeknownst to both of us, seemed to draw us together in some crazy way. Also, you were the voice of reason at the tor… in so many ways!"

They both laughed at the memory and then walked on in silence, taking in the surprisingly warm, but watery, sunlight. It was the kind of day you always hoped for on the moor but rarely saw.

Jack knew their time was now very short; he could sense that Jacqui would be announcing her departure imminently. At that moment, he felt it might be the last time he would ever see her. Once again, he couldn't find the right words to say. He cursed himself for his lack of faith in his own lexicon.

"Do you need a lift somewhere? I'm going to cut loose now," he said, surprising himself with his decisiveness.

Jacqui felt wrong-footed, even though she, herself, was about to declare a parting of ways.

"…No thanks. I'll walk here for a while longer." She smiled uneasily, trying not to show her disappointment; she hadn't expected Jack to call time. "You go. I'll be fine. I'll try not to have any dramas this time."

"That might be helpful," he said, appreciating the light-hearted comment.

"You look after yourself, Jack."

"I promise," he said, turning to go. His voice was unsteady.

With his back to her, he raised his hand. It was given as a gesture of farewell but, in reality, it was his only remaining coping mechanism. He couldn't bear to see her stride away into the distance again. His eyes watered as he marched purposefully away from her.

"I'm sorry, Jack," she muttered under her breath, hoping he might turn around.

For several moments, Jacqui stood still and watched his shape gradually diminish and then disappear.

* * *

When the class ended, Sandra began to roll up her purple mat. She was sure that the early 20th-century German developer of the exercise, Joseph Pilates, would not have been terribly impressed. He might have forgiven her lack of core stability, flexibility, and muscle control – owing to her novice status – but he may have despaired at her failure to push herself beyond her limits.

This was her third visit, and Sandra reasoned that although the process was good for mind and spirit, it was really friendship she was seeking. She had worked alongside too many career policemen and women who had become almost institutionalised. It was why people who worked for the force were predominantly sociable with their own.

Sandra scanned the room and quickly found a friendly face. Hannah, an athletic-looking vision of happiness and well-being, strode towards her.

"I'm glad you made it, Sandra. I was worried you might have bailed."

"Ah, thank you," Sandra replied. "I must admit, my dismal performance last week didn't exactly inspire confidence. I nearly went 'A over T' several times! A little bit better this week, though."

"You'll get used to it. I was rubbish the first few times. Still am really," she laughed.

Sandra subconsciously cast her eyes over Hannah, unable to imagine that the toned specimen standing before her could ever be uncoordinated.

"I do find it strangely calming and peaceful," Sandra told her.

Together, they made their way through the double doors of the studio and quickly crossed the floor of the gym. Sandra had anticipated the clanging of weights and noisy exhaling of the muscular elite, but the room was surprisingly empty. They found it easier to speak in the foyer, though.

"I've had to deal with a lot of aggravation recently, so I use it as a means to steady my head," said Hannah.

Sandra smiled at the unintended pun. "Aggravation can only mean partner, parents, or pennies," she postulated, pleased with the off-the-cuff alliteration.

"Probably all three, but mainly the first. Five years and then it… just… fizzled out."

"Five years? Wow, I've never got beyond one. Must say something about me."

"…That you have standards? Unless you keep being dumped… but looking at you, Sandra, I can't imagine that," Hannah said, with a cheerful laugh.

"My boredom threshold is usually the culprit… not that I want to be disrespectful to my exes. I don't know what I want most of the time. It drives my sister mad," Sandra admitted.

"Does your current partner know they're on a twelve-month deal with little chance of an upgrade?" Hannah teasingly probed.

Sandra recognised that Hannah had respectfully avoided the 'he' or 'she' in the question, and enjoyed the witty, cutting remark. "Closed for trading at the moment. Repair and refit. Footloose and fancy-free, me. How about you? Any sizzle replaced the fizzle lately?"

Sandra was chuckling inwardly, unable to fathom where her sudden passion for literary devices had come from. She was also finding the conversation relaxed and easy – which was new.

"Assonance in addition to alliteration. Check you out! No, is the answer, and although you're going to say, 'Yeah right', I'm really loving the freedom."

"Is that a teacher marking my homework? I appear to have made a 'Charlie' of myself."

"For my sins," acknowledged Hannah. "And *I* appear to have been boring. I don't want you to think I go around correcting apostrophes all over the place."

"Even though you do…" Sandra said, knowing it was very likely.

"Guilty as charged. Arrest me," Hannah pronounced in a comedic voice, offering her wrists to be handcuffed.

Sandra cocked her head slightly and, with a knowing smile, let the silence hang. "Well now…"

"You're kidding… you're not, are you? You're in the force? Oh my God, I walked right into that one."

"For my sins… I have been known to apprehend the odd pedant."

They both laughed.

Together, they strolled out of the building and into the car park, stopping at a bollard when it became obvious that their respective vehicles were in different directions.

Hannah was the first to point out their parting of ways. "I'm over there, and you're over there because I saw you arrive."

"Good detective work, Hannah. I'm impressed."

"Next week?"

"I should be okay unless my shift gets changed," Sandra said. "Yes, I really enjoyed that session."

Hannah reached into her bag for her car keys as Sandra walked towards her parking slot. She called out before Sandra had taken too many steps.

"Hey, and you'll have to come out one evening. I have a load of girlie mates who like to let their hair down once in a while. I know you'd get on with them!"

Sandra turned and smiled.

"What do you think?" Hannah pressed, now more confident of an affirmative response.

"Yeah, I'd like that a lot. Thanks for the offer."

* * *

From Forda, a tiny little hamlet that straddled the River Lew, Jacqui walked up the lane to the A386 at Sourton. She had left her car precariously parked, but figured that the thoroughfare was so out of the way it wouldn't be a problem. Anyhow, she reasoned, she didn't intend to stay long. Whatever Chris had in mind wasn't going to distract her from her chosen course. She was determined of that.

When she reached the junction, she could see Chris ahead; he had perched himself on a hexagonal bench that surrounded an ancient tree. As it was on elevated ground, it afforded marvellous views of the edge of Dartmoor. It also overlooked the highly surreal Highwayman Inn that occupied a prominent position on the main road. The architecture looked utterly bonkers and Jacqui knew that the establishment was equally quirky inside. As much as she fancied a drink in the strange and wonderful place, however, she had business to attend to.

She climbed the tiny access lane that led to a few houses, and – further on, as a track – to the local beauty spot, Sourton Tors.

Chris waved as she approached. He was keen to indicate that the meeting was not meant to be confrontational, and he also knew she'd already seen him from the road.

Jacqui slumped down on the seat next to him, slightly out of breath from the steep incline. "May I congratulate you on choosing what is obviously one of the worst meeting places I could ever imagine?" she puffed.

"Really?" he whined, slightly disappointed that she wasn't in a better mood.

"Well, it's not exactly clandestine; just about everybody in the vicinity can lay their eyes on us. What were you thinking?"

"Ahh… everybody but nobody. It's so public it's–"

"Don't give me that bollocks," she snapped. "And don't think I've brought my sarnies with me so we can look like a couple of 'dinks' midway through a hike."

"A bit harsh. I *am* actually halfway through a walk. I've got *that lot* to do later." He pointed behind him.

The trackway from Sourton Tors to the Nodden Gate near Lydford was a breathtaking undertaking. The path upwards to the tors was painfully steep.

"Yeah, well, forgive me if I pass on the Julia Bradbury bit, but I've got stuff to do. Presumably, you have something to give me. So come on, hand it over." She held her hand out, waiting for the contraband.

"I don't know how you do it."

"If it was you whinging about something, you would have sent a text. It's hardly rocket science," Jacqui pointed out.

Chris sighed. "Okay, so I do have something, but I want to explain the situation first…"

"…So it won't appear to be something so trivial and so I won't think I've wasted my time getting here…?"

"Jacqui, don't be so aggressive," he told her, "and it's not trivial; we were all in it together, remember? I'm doing this because of the lecture you gave Ross and me in the car park at Brentor."

Jacqui lightened. She recognised that she'd given both of the men a bit of a roasting in order to make them compliant. "A fair point, Chris, so please explain. I'll try and behave myself, but you boys make it so difficult."

Chris drew a deep breath and pulled a small package out of his rucksack. "Okay, so you know how Victoria wasn't exactly about to start working for a phone company on the help desk…"

"Her mobile wasn't her most treasured possession, if that's what you mean," Jacqui replied, quickly matching the size of the package to the topic of conversation.

"Quite…"

"Oh, I get it, this is her burner phone… one of the four. How did you get hold of it?" Jacqui asked, thinking back to when she'd searched Victoria's house.

"She was having problems with the battery life," Chris explained. "She asked me to find out if she was doing something dumb that was causing the juice to plummet. I didn't get the chance to give it back to her before she… before…"

Almost as if it were too hot to handle, Chris nervously passed the package to Jacqui. Then he looked down, avoiding eye contact.

"Yes, well, we're all trying to come to terms with that, Chris." She thought for a moment before continuing, "So why offload it to me? Why not keep it, or destroy it?"

"When we met at Brentor you made it pretty clear how you wanted to proceed. I believe your account, Jacqui, so when I realised I still had the mobile and it was of obvious interest to the police, I began to panic. It's too hot for me, but I don't want to cause you grief. I guess, what I'm trying to say is, it's now yours to do with as you see fit. I don't want to keep looking at it thinking I should do something with it. I thought you'd be pleased… you know, that I trusted your story. I haven't even told Ross about this."

"So, basically, you're passing the buck so it's not your problem anymore?" Jacqui said, a little unkindly.

"Something like that," he answered, "but like I said, I thought you'd approve."

"It's akin to reverse pass the parcel. I'm ecstatic, Chris. However, I'm glad you didn't give it to the police. What's on it?"

"All of our WhatsApp messages and emails. It's difficult to tell, of course, but it doesn't look like she's deleted anything at all. There are no huge gaps. Trust me, I've only read the last few messages. It seemed disrespectful, you know, trawling through her personal life when she's no longer with us."

Jacqui read his face. He seemed genuine.

"I haven't touched it in case you wanted to check it out," Chris continued. "We all know each other's passwords – that was the deal when we bought them. It's going to be very difficult to trace." He shrugged. "You could destroy it. We could destroy ours as well. I'm sure Ross would agree. Just give the signal."

Jacqui sat silently for a moment, processing the information. She found it mildly irritating that, through no real fault of her own, she was having to cover so many tracks and deal with so many loose ends in order to get her life back on an even keel.

"You saw the barrage of messages she sent me in the weeks preceding her death?" Jacqui asked, ignoring the discussion about destroying phones. She knew it was important to maintain 'private' communication with Chris and Ross for the time being.

"Yes, it did look like she was sending a lot of traffic your way… was she hitting on you, or something?"

"That's interesting that you think that was possible. No, I don't think so, is the answer. It was more like mothering."

"Mothering?" he repeated, surprised. "Why did she feel you needed to be mothered?"

"Because… in the early days, when we first became friends, I made the mistake of opening up quite a bit about… 'stuff'," Jacqui explained. "The friendship soon became obsessive: the mothering, the *smothering*."

"I really liked her."

"I know you did, Chris," Jacqui said, "so did I. But you weren't at the receiving end of her obsession." She shook her head, sadly. "At first, I didn't realise she was like that. I guess she was one of those all-or-nothing types. I mean, her interest in Osman Spare and the occult became a passion in such a very short period of time. One minute she was introducing herself to Ross at the bookshop… the next… she was planning sex magick with him."

Chris winced at Jacqui's scant regard for subtlety, though he desperately tried to hide it.

"You and Ross loved it," Jacqui continued, "a beautiful woman thrusting herself into your world, lapping up everything you said…"

Chris stared at her. "But don't forget, Jacqui, that because Ross regarded you as the most gifted psychic he'd ever met, you gave it legitimacy. Victoria was utterly captivated by your aura. It was much more than admiration."

Without warning, Chris stood up and slung his rucksack over his shoulder. Jacqui, although surprised by the sudden movement, was pleased that proceedings were drawing to a close.

"I'm going to take advantage of the good weather and push on," Chris said, checking he hadn't left anything on the bench.

"That's timely, Chris, because it's not exactly warm here."

"Sorry this was all a bit awkward, but I do want to help you. Perhaps when this has all died down, we can meet up with Ross and discuss future plans?"

Jacqui stood up and faced him. She touched his sleeve as a mark of gratitude. "Let's hope so," she said, knowing that by the time normality was resumed, the moment would have passed, "…and thanks."

"Take care of yourself, Jacqui. Stay in touch, and if you need anything, you know how to reach me."

With that, Chris took the steep track behind them. He didn't turn around; he just strode on purposefully and was soon out of view.

Secretly, Jacqui was thrilled with the outcome. She now had the one piece of evidence that, if the police had discovered it, could have caused her a major headache.

After their earlier meeting, she knew Jack wouldn't volunteer evidence to the police about her identity. She could rely on him for that much. Besides, the whole thing had been an accident, so why would she have to worry about the police interviewing Jack again? Surely they were just interested in ruling him out of their enquiries. With any luck, the whole thing would die down and she could resume her carefree lifestyle.

There was just one problem – she was having nagging doubts about something she couldn't quite put her finger on…

Chapter 14

DS Baines and DC Box sat opposite a rather peeved-looking Jack Reilly in the interview room. He had taken advantage of the presence of a duty solicitor but he wasn't about to reel off 'No comment' at every turn, because he knew he had nothing to hide. It was, however, the very situation he was dreading. He knew that Jacqui was desperate to remain anonymous and, if things took an ugly turn, it would be difficult for him to remain silent.

DS Baines opened proceedings with a hammer blow.

"So, Jack, we have evidence of you being inside the home of Victoria Kent. She, if you need reminding, is the deceased female who was discovered – barely a quarter of a mile away – lying face down in the Amicombe Brook on Dartmoor on the day you admit to being at Fur Tor. Both places, for the benefit of the recording, are extremely remote. Now, you say that you have never met her before and have no knowledge of her being there on that day. How do you respond?"

Jack took a few seconds to digest this information. He was utterly baffled – and very worried. It began to dawn on him that the police considered him guilty and were about to fabricate evidence in order to make everything fit.

"That's nonsense," he protested. "You haven't got anything because there isn't anything to have. I've never been there. I haven't a clue where she used to live because I never knew her."

Despite his bullish response, he had a feeling that the police were about to go for the big reveal. He wasn't wrong.

DS Baines carefully took two photographs out of a folder that was lying on the table next to her. She placed them in front of Jack. "Image one reveals a box containing a St Christopher medallion. Image two is of the medallion itself."

Sandra let the evidence sink in for a moment and then continued. "We know this is yours, Jack, because your ex-girlfriend, Jenny Jones, told us she gave it to you. In a rather touching addendum to our interview, she described how she gave you an object like this as a gesture of safe passage. It's going to have your prints all over it."

Somehow, after the initial shock of seeing the gift, Jack was able to rapidly process all available options. He knew there were no messages inside the box. He also figured that it could only have been Jacqui who'd placed it in the house because he gave it to her on the tor. She was so careful about preserving her anonymity that it was highly likely that she'd wiped the box clean and used gloves to place the object somewhere in the house for some – baffling – reason. In reality, it was his only hope.

"There won't be anything to link me with that particular box," he blagged, hugely against type. "There must be hundreds of those in people's houses, dotted around the countryside."

A wave of guilt hit Jack as he played back the moment Jenny gave him the talisman. Even though it signified the finality of their relationship, it was one of the most precious times they'd shared together. How could he have so casually let it slip through his fingers?

"But you do have one," reasoned Sandra. "So you could produce it as evidence that this is not your box, couldn't you?"

"No… no, I couldn't."

"No?" asked Sandra. "Why would that be, Jack? You don't look like the kind of guy who accepts a present and then throws it in the bin five minutes later," she added, tightening the grip.

"I don't have it anymore," he said, shrugging. "I gave it to Ruthven, the girl I met on the moor. The weather came in bad, as I told you. I gave it to her because I was worried she'd get lost. I don't believe in that stuff, but I wanted her to feel as if a guiding spirit was seeing her home. Her need was greater than mine at that point."

DC Box wasn't impressed with the explanation, and he was quick to pile on the pressure. "Ahh, the mysterious girl you met at the tor. The only problem is, Jack, we can't trace this person; she seems to be a figment of your imagination. You're expecting us to believe she simply disappeared without a trace, clutching an identical St Christopher to the one found in Victoria Kent's bedroom?"

Jack wanted to shout out that Ruthven must have put it there, but he didn't want to incriminate Jacqui, or draw the police's attention towards her in any way. So, at his own – potential – personal cost, he decided to continue with his line of defence.

"Well, what can I say? That's what happened. Yes, my ex gave me a box like it. Yes, I gave it to the girl I met on the moor because I was a little worried about her. No, I didn't visit the dead girl's house and leave it there. No, the girl who died on the moor is not the same girl I spent time with at Fur Tor. Now, I suggest you check the box for fingerprints because you won't find any of mine on there. Perhaps then we can end this charade."

Jack felt better for his outburst, but he wasn't convinced that the police would leave it there.

Sandra gathered the two photographs and placed them back into the folder. After pausing briefly, she pulled out a sheet of paper, placed it on the desk, and rotated it 180 degrees.

"For the benefit of the recording, image three is a copy of some earring designs that we believe were created by the deceased woman, Victoria Kent. Do you recognise these?"

Jack, who'd been trying to steel himself for the next revelation, wasn't expecting to comment on women's jewellery. "Er… no. Not at all. They look beautifully ornate, but what have these got to do with me? I don't understand."

"We believe Victoria had these made. We also believe they were in her house when you broke in. Someone had clearly been rummaging around in her bedroom. Does that jog any memories?"

"This is incredible. So… I break in, deposit a St Christopher necklace for some reason, incriminating myself in the process, and then rifle through her cupboards to nick a pair of earrings? Do me a favour, Detective Sergeant. Listen, I'm a photographer from Surrey. I'm not some Devonshire petty thief."

Sandra had been expecting denial, and now she wanted to shake him by revealing the earrings' true purpose. She didn't think he'd be expecting them to have that knowledge.

"These aren't just any old ordinary earrings, Jack, as you well know," she continued. "This pair of 'beautifully ornate' – as you put it – earrings constitute a sigil: an occult symbol used in ritual. We believe you stole the physical earrings in order to remove incriminating evidence."

Jack was in a daze. This was all too farcical for him to comprehend. He was lost for a sensible reply and merely shook his head.

"For the benefit of the recording, the accused is shaking his head."

"For the benefit of the recording, Jack is shaking his head in disbelief!" he shouted. "How on earth would they be incriminating? I don't even know what a sigil is. I've never heard of it. This is madness!"

"For the purpose of the recording, I'm now going to play an excerpt of a video of Victoria Kent in the throes of a performance," Sandra stated. "She is naked and we have doctored her appearance in order to preserve her modesty. We believe that what you are about to witness is part of an occult ritual. At the crescendo of the proceedings, she shouts out a name. This is further proof that you, Jack, knew the deceased."

Jack, now overwhelmed at the possibility of another trumped-up revelation, just stared at the laptop.

The show began. Immediately, flashing lights stabbed at odd intervals, making him feel further on edge. Discordant music jarred. The woman's face and body contorted. The intensity grew with each wave of sound and light. It was unbearable. Jack wanted to look away, but he was aware that this might signify guilt. He was no Richard Dadd, but this felt like Bethlem.

Jack was almost at the point where he wanted to scream, 'Enough!' when the naked woman – wine cascading over and between her breasts like Blood Falls, pen in hand, and tattooing a strange symbol on her stomach – cried, "Jac… Jac…!"

She continued to utter lines, but Jack had finally heard and seen enough. He stood up. DC Box turned off the machine. The room fell silent.

Judging his movement, DS Baines spoke softly. "So, you see, Jack, we know that you knew her. The St Christopher, the vanishing earrings, she called out your name… she dies just a stone's throw away from where you acknowledge that you met a girl… it all adds up. It's time to tell us exactly what happened."

* * *

Jacqui picked up the red jewellery box that had begun to gather dust on her bedside chest of drawers. Surprisingly, she hadn't examined the contents since the larceny. She smiled at herself in the mirror, wondering whether 'burglary' was a more realistic description. Yes, Victoria had confided in her that she kept spare keys in a magnetic box under her car, but did that amount to permission to enter her house? Certainly not to most people, yet her newfound friend had become almost obsessive, inviting her around at every opportunity.

Jacqui gazed at the beautifully crafted container. In reality, a lot had happened over the past week or so, and she knew she could only confront the contents when she had enough headspace. Her medical reprieve, Jack's understanding, Ross's submissive behaviour, and a little luck had bought her that – for a while, at any rate.

The pace at which Victoria had progressed from neophyte to practitioner had unsettled Jacqui. When she'd first made her acquaintance, their discussion had centred on a lack of fashion sense and failed relationships. They'd shared jokes and observations. They'd questioned the real motives of Ross and Chris. However, within months – after Jacqui had unwisely shared her medical condition with her – Victoria had devoured the entire canon of Austin Osman Spare, created sigils, and designed jewellery fit for a ritual. Who knows, thought Jacqui, perhaps the reason she'd hiked to such a remote spot on Dartmoor was to perform the 'sacred' burning of the drawings. It seemed likely.

Anticipating the powerful spring, Jacqui tentatively prised open the box. Two immaculately crafted teardrop earrings nestled in their pearl satin bed like Hollywood lovers – their radiance difficult to comprehend. She was shocked by their energy.

This was no ordinary trinket. No lover's largess or family heirloom. In that one fleeting moment, Jacqui recognised that she'd severely underestimated Victoria, and she cursed her own intolerance and need for such control.

For several moments, Jacqui held the visual wonders by their hooks, the golden teardrops dangling beneath each thumb and forefinger. She raised them to eye level and the movement caused both to turn. Just a fraction. Like sleeping princesses awakened from their golden slumber.

Remarkably, as if scripted in a gothic play, the sun's rays caught the sigil and its reflections bounced, in turn, off the mirror. The shafts of glowing light seemed to explode into the room, now dancing, as Jacqui eased her grip on the pair of twins.

She turned her hands palm upwards, the earrings resting in the hollows. She stared at them. She was now acutely aware of the heat and effulgence given off by the force within. With respect – and awareness that she would have to learn how to manage the adornments – she laid them on the bedspread.

Jacqui took a deep breath; she hadn't been expecting that. Sure, she thought, landscapes can energise one; clothing can empower; love and loss can evoke feelings difficult to quantify; sex can take you to places that transcend the body… but this was different: a subtle release of *something*. In order to be felt, and realised, it somehow needed to be harnessed.

Now casting a critical eye over the recumbent earrings, Jacqui could clearly identify some of the letters that formed the sigil.

"You beauty," she whispered to herself. "You absolute beauty."

An S was immediately discernible at the top of the teardrop. A, G, H, and T appeared clearly underneath. The main 'bulb' of the design was more crowded. Jacqui knew that letters could be reversed, or even bent, to maintain the line of the artwork, so it wasn't difficult to unearth an R, F, and Y. An upside-down V could also house an M. An N and a reverse D, according to her first pass, completed the set. Of course, she could easily be wrong.

Jacqui wrote the letters S G H T R F Y V M N and D in a notebook that she kept handily in her shoulder bag. She then grabbed her mobile phone and typed into the notes app: 'Decode letters'.

Finally, she set an alarm for seven-thirty that evening.

* * *

Jack paced around the confines of the police station cell. It was crushing. How had it all come to this? Things were getting serious.

He trusted Jacqui and believed her account, but – to say the least – many aspects of it were highly unusual. He just couldn't understand how the St Christopher had come to be in the dead woman's home. The only possible explanation was that Jacqui had visited the house after the tragedy and left it there as a sort of penance. It occurred to him that Jacqui, after a death, might have imitated what he and his ex-partner had done: gifted the needy a token of safe passage. However, it amounted to a lot of risk and must have been quite an undertaking. *Why would she do that?* he questioned, frantically trying to get to the heart of the issue. A simpler way of honouring a fallen comrade would have been to post something online.

So maybe… maybe she had been economical with the truth.

Perhaps she hadn't just put the St Christopher necklace there; perhaps she had *planted* it there. To frame him.

And it was working.

Jack shook his head; he couldn't allow himself to go down that route of thinking. He couldn't bring himself to believe it. After all, he didn't believe Jacqui had murdered that woman on the moor, and why else would she need to frame someone?

He knew, instinctively, that Jacqui hadn't done anything untoward to her fellow hiker. If he had that wrong, it would plague him forever. They shared a strange historical connection, and she had explained the sequence of events to him, face to face. He acknowledged to himself that he possessed many faults, but grossly misjudging character wasn't one of them. He also knew that she was fiercely independent. The bar she'd set for anonymity was higher than anyone he'd ever met. The trouble was, Jack concluded, now feeling sorry for himself, *he* was the collateral damage in all this. He wasn't sure whether he should shoulder that.

Perhaps he was being soft, Jack mused. Maybe even beguiled. It was true that he'd become mildly infatuated with Jacqui. Their chance meeting, decades before, had almost lured him into the thought that fate was at play, but he'd always scoffed at the notion that his life had, in any way, been mapped out before him. Coincidences happen, he reassured himself. Just reach for a tome on probability and discover how seemingly unlikely events are far more likely than one would think.

Coincidence.

He rattled the word around in his head, almost blaming the very existence of it. The meeting at Fur Tor, their meeting as children, the tragic accident happening at the same isolated location on the same day, the discovery of the photo album, and how the St Christopher had afforded the bearer very *unsafe* passage…

And then it hit him. The final coincidental gift to the prosecution: she had cried out Jack – his name, only it wasn't referring to him. It was Jac, short for Jacqui!

Jack stopped pacing. The revelation had begun to unfurl everything. His mind was going into overdrive.

He wondered what on earth Jacqui had got herself into. He then tried to play back the conversation they'd had when they'd met for the second time. Jacqui had confessed to knowing the dead woman, but he couldn't remember anything being said about earrings, sigils, or occult rituals.

Earrings.

At that moment, he understood who had taken them. He realised why she'd entered the house. The St Christopher must have been an afterthought.

It began to dawn on Jack that he didn't really know his newfound, mercurial friend at all. But did that make any difference?

The point was – he readily admitted to himself – he could see why DS Baines had her claws in him.

He could picture her exact thought process…

He was there. He pushed her and panicked when she fell and became lifeless. He found her keys, phone, and credit cards in her rucksack. He deposited the St Christopher at her house to justify to himself that it had been some kind of accident. He had taken the earrings, hidden her belongings, and left the area.

That was the 'tidy' series of events. It was plausible. That explanation involved no coincidences. Who wouldn't go along with that? he reasoned.

And then it occurred to him, as he played back the possibilities, that he almost believed it himself. This is exactly how one could fall into line, agree under stress, begin to wonder if it had all happened in a trance-like state and that Ruthven was, indeed, a figment of his imagination, fuelled by turmoil and the need for escape.

He had only been confined for an hour or so, but he reckoned that, come the morning, he'd be requesting a pen to sign his confession.

The rigid structure that was designed to be a bed offered no solace, so Jack continued to move within the confines of the empty room. As the movement of his feet seemed to propel his thought process, he decided that sitting down would encourage resignation. Giving up.

By continually revisiting the issues, he hoped that, eventually, he would experience that 'light-bulb moment'… but it never came. He just couldn't solve the conundrum: how to provide proof of Ruthven/Jacqui's existence without compromising her. She had asked him to protect her anonymity, and had assured him she would be there for him if it became really serious. Well, things were certainly serious alright. But how could he deny her? How could she ever trust him again if he played the role of Judas?

Jack's mind roamed to the consequences of playing the long game. It was just about possible that Jacqui had wiped the box clean and left no trace. He wondered if the police could bring him to trial with such a lack of physical evidence. After all, there wouldn't be any DNA at the scene of death because he wasn't there. There would be no evidence at the house if the box had been dealt with. There would be no witnesses attesting to his relationship with the dead woman because he never knew her. No phone records. Nothing.

Surely, he thought, there was no case. However, a carelessly placed jewellery box with his fingerprints all over it would change everything.

He could already hear the damning whispers that would soon become raised voices.

"Even if she tripped and fell, Jack, why didn't you wade in and rescue her? Why didn't you call for help? How could you just leave her there? No decent human being would ever do that."

He knew he wouldn't be able to bear the injustice. He also knew that if he 'sold' Jacqui to gain his freedom, she would be subjected to similar noise.

With his back to the door, Jack started another lap of the cell floor. Although he knew he wasn't going anywhere soon, he needed to settle on a plan. Not only was his freedom at stake, but also his mental well-being.

He hadn't convinced himself that any line of defence was particularly favourable, but by the time he reached the bed again, he'd finally made up his mind.

* * *

DC Box glanced through the cell door's peephole. Jack's body language told him all he needed to know; it didn't shout guilty or not guilty, but it did indicate he was in a state of flux. There was clearly something on his mind other than, 'They have the wrong man'.

This was an odd case, he thought as he walked away.

Sandra was waiting for Mark in her tiny backroom office. He shut the door and sat down opposite her. There was an air of unease in the small space.

When presented with such damning evidence of his presence in the house – along with Victoria's outburst – Jack had seemed remarkably resilient. They had expected a series of, 'No comments', or a capitulation. Jack didn't seem like a hardened individual; he was clearly an emotional type.

The lack of a confession – or an explanation of the tragic accident he'd run away from in a panic – meant that the St Christopher box was now crucial. The final nail…

"You think we should have waited until we had confirmation about his dabs, don't you?" Sandra said.

"I must admit, it did seem a little hasty."

"Only I could see Beechcroft pulling the plug… any moment," Sandra explained. "Come on, what are the chances that she owned the same St Christopher? We know his ex gave him one when they parted. Victoria shouts out his name. It's all there."

"I get it, boss. He should have realised that the game was up. He's a bright boy."

"Only he didn't," Sandra said slowly.

By the tone of her voice, Mark could tell she was having second thoughts. "You mean, what if the box comes back clean? Like he said it would?"

"Exactly."

"Well then, we'd have nothing," Mark said, sighing. "The CPS isn't going to proceed if we have no DNA at the scene and no concrete evidence that he knew Victoria Kent. Her mobile phone records aren't helpful at all; the analysis just came in."

"Perhaps she used a burner phone?" Sandra flimsily postulated.

"Boss, as you well know, she wasn't a drug dealer or a spy. She wasn't even with a partner. She had no reason to be below the radar."

"That all makes sense, Mark, but why do I continually think there's more to this than meets the eye?"

"Because Jack Reilly doesn't fit the norm?"

"Middle class, well spoken, and polite, you mean? We've had those before. Anyone can snap in an instant. It's in all of us. An advance rebuffed; a belittling rejection; a sudden rush to the head; a feeling of despair… No, it's not that, Mark."

"Because the occult is hanging over this investigation like a dark cloud?" he suggested.

"A bit melodramatic, maybe, but there are certainly aspects that colour the thinking. If we probe a little harder, we might uncover all sorts of unimaginables. However, I'm not sure whether they have any bearing on the death of the girl."

Mark let Sandra's comments hang in the air. He then reached for a file that was tucked away in a bag by his feet. "That more or less leaves the mystery girl, Ruthven," he said, landing the paperwork in front of him. "Perhaps Jack's account is real."

"Wow, as if by magic…" Sandra teased.

"Not really, boss. It's the work I've been doing on the sigil. I haven't got very far because it's almost impossible. I've consulted a few experts in the field. However, I do notice that the letters R, T, H, V, and N appear…"

"And if you add the vowels…" Sandra said, thinking out loud.

"Exactly. Ruthven. Of course, that still leaves S, M, F, Y, D, and G. Goodness knows what they amount to. You could probably make a case for hundreds of possibilities."

Sandra picked up the sheet of paper and studied the letters. Mark, impressed that she'd countenanced a possible change of tack, waited for her response.

"Of course, it could stand for Roti Heaven."

"Boss?"

"I could demolish a curry right now; I'm starving."

"This case has pushed you over the edge. The things you think about," Mark said, shaking his head in disbelief.

Sandra laughed.

Chapter 15

Jacqui turned her Ford Ka away from the fuel pump queue and headed towards the customer parking bays on the far side, away from the throng of the services. The annoying buzz and rattle of her burner phone had heralded a caller, and it wasn't exactly welcome.

She snatched the device from the glove compartment and tapped the green button. She then placed the handset to her ear but said nothing.

"Jacqui?"

"I'm not exactly going to announce myself, Ross. That's the whole point of the phone."

"Ah, yes. I get that. Sorry. Can you speak?"

"I can now that I've parked up. Okay, what's happening? No more messages from my dad, I hope. Have the boys in blue paid you another visit?"

"Rest easy, Jacqui," Ross said, surprised that she was being so convivial.

"No text message means you need to talk to me about a problem – so let's hear it."

Ross took a deep breath. He knew that what he had to say would upset her. "Your Dartmoor acquaintance, Jack Reilly, is being interviewed by the police again."

Jacqui paused for a moment. "How on earth do you know that? That's a worry."

"That I know it? Or that it's happening?"

"Both."

"Very witty. Claire told me. She was out with her rambling set yesterday. One of her fellow walkers is a journo from the local newsfeed; seems they were discussing it over lunch. The news is that he might have known Victoria, broken into her house, and stolen something. And that… perhaps he killed her."

"Did–"

"Don't worry," Ross cut in, acutely aware of what Jacqui was about to ask, "I acted suitably nonplussed. She's used to me switching off when I'm eating."

"Your wife is no fool, Ross, and you are not a good liar. If she even gets a faint whiff of a connection…"

"I know, I know. Trust me."

"Trust you? Now you have me very worried."

"Listen, Jacqui," said Ross, ignoring her comment, "I've never met this Reilly character, but you're not going to just hang him out to dry, are you? I mean, you said it was an accident, and he wasn't even there. What if they charge him?"

"Call off the dogs, Ross. The police won't charge him because there's no evidence. You can't invent DNA. He never knew Victoria, and he certainly didn't break into her house. Honestly, how did the police arrive at that angle?"

Jacqui certainly wasn't going to declare her own role in the scenario, and she was desperately trying to ascertain how the police had managed to connect Jack with the event. It was deeply troubling.

"Maybe it's just a case of Chinese whispers. You know how journalists try to make it all seem larger than life," Ross suggested.

"Indeed."

"Jacqui, there's one other issue…"

"Go on…" she said, bracing herself for another bombshell.

"It concerns Victoria's burner phone. If the police find that… There must be a load of stuff on there. Do you know where she used to hide it?"

"You mean you, in the early days, inviting Vic for a drink in out-of-the-way locations? Claire would love to read those messages. What were you doing, Ross, trying to get into her pants?"

"What the heck?! Did Victoria tell you that?"

"I have the phone…"

"You have the what?!" Ross asked, almost shouting.

"It makes for some interesting reading."

"It's not what you think, Jacqui," he said quickly. "I never… I used to give her books to read. You know, as a kind of course. She was devouring them. We just talked."

"Of course you did, Ross. Farningham Books' mobile library? My, your community outreach efforts are really impressive."

"How did you get it?" he asked, trying to swerve the obvious slight.

"Never you mind," Jacqui replied. "I have it, so just you be a good boy."

* * *

A knock at the open door interrupted DS Baines's lunchtime reverie. Detective Inspector Beechcroft poked his head around the corner, signalling he had an item to discuss.

Sandra admired his consummate professionalism. Unlike other higher-ranking officers, he always treated her tiny office space with respect.

"I have an update on Jack Reilly. Do you have a few moments?"

Sandra, mouth full of tuna melt, ushered him in using semaphore.

DI Beechcroft sat on the edge of the table, indicating that the meeting was going to be brief. "The box has come back clean. It's obviously been wiped. The case against Jack was flimsy enough with it, but now we don't have any evidence at all to connect him to the burglary or the death. We have to release him. It would harm our reputation with the CPS if we tried to push this through."

Sandra sighed. "I get that. I had a nagging suspicion it would turn out like this."

"You've worked hard on this, Sandra. Nobody can say that you didn't exhaust all possibilities. We'll arrange a press release."

She nodded. "How are you going to word that?"

"Well, the usual for these situations. 'There's not enough evidence to prosecute. We're not looking for anybody else, unless witnesses come forward with any further information'… that sort of thing."

"I understand," Sandra said. "What about Jack's story about the girl? Isn't it worth letting the press know that a girl called Ruthven could help us with our enquiries?"

"Giving the press a name would take the focus away from Jack. If it wasn't an accident, he's our man. If she exists, and hears or reads about the press statement, she'll surely come forward. Why wouldn't she?"

Sandra wanted to point out, 'What if she was implicated?' but she knew that the likelihood of a female murderer stalking the moor was extremely low. In any case, the forensic team hadn't detected a scuffle or a push.

In the end, she just nodded. It was hard walking away from a case when a few ifs and buts remained, but you had to know when to stop. "Shall we carry on trying to decode the sigil?" she asked, even though she knew the likely response.

"No," replied DI Beechcroft, "we have more pressing engagements. Even if you could solve the riddle, I don't think it will amount to much. The girl screaming out Jack's name tells us all we need to know. It's frustrating, but there we are. Until somebody comes forward with something really interesting, we're done."

* * *

At the beginning, there had only been a few reporters standing outside the Castle Hotel. However, the sight of professional-looking cameras with long lenses draped around the necks of seasoned photographers encouraged a few inquisitive shoppers to see what all the fuss was about. Consequently, the numbers grew. Most of the crowd had no idea why they were standing there, but they didn't want to pass on the possibility of catching a glimpse of a celebrity.

You didn't see many famous faces in Launceston; it wasn't that kind of place. Like in other towns in the county, they tolerated new people visiting for a short while, but they didn't like you hanging around. In the summer the numbers swelled, but come October, the 'emmets' would return to their Home County nests, and the locals – weary of traffic delays, parking difficulties, and busy streets – would sigh with relief.

The babble of voices and the increasing throng of the gathering attracted yet more townsfolk. It was mid-February, and excitement on the streets was unheard of.

Caught unawares, the local beat officer rapidly contacted the station for further details.

Jack Reilly, sitting in the back of the approaching taxi, looked out of the window; he could see a number of people milling around, obviously waiting for something to happen. After his unexpectedly quick release, he was overjoyed, assuming the whole charade was over; as much as he adored the West Country, he couldn't wait to leave and return home to a more mundane existence. Even thoughts of Jacqui were now locked away. After all, the thought of tracking her down and pursuing her was just too exhausting. Well, he thought, for the moment anyway.

Naïvely, he hadn't considered the hellish reality of the situation. The taxi driver, beginning to understand that the object of the crowd's curiosity was currently in his back seat, stopped the car just before the hotel. Besides, too many people were spilling over the kerb and onto the road, making it unsafe to get any closer.

Jack released his seat belt, reached into his pocket, and offered cash to the driver. "Keep the change and thanks," he said.

"Right ho. Thanks. Er… listen, I've got to shoot off…"

"No problem," Jack said, opening the door quickly so as not to delay the driver any longer.

No sooner had he stepped onto the tarmac than the cameras started flashing and the shouts rang out. At first, it was the local hacks who initiated the barrage.

"Are you a murderer, Mr Reilly?"

"Can you tell us why you left a girl dead on the moor?"

"Did you push her?"

"Why didn't you call the police if it was an accident?"

"Mr Reilly?"

"Mr Reilly?"

Jack instinctively made a move to get back into the taxi but, as he'd shut the door behind him, he couldn't grab the door handle before the car sped off. He looked up at the faces of the now baying assembly, feeling like he was standing naked before them.

Spurred on by the initial outbursts, people in the crowd started adding to the attack.

"How could you leave her to die?"

"You filthy animal!"

"Killer!"

"Lock 'im up!"

If Jack had had a scarf, he would have shielded his eyes from the madness. Instead, he stuck his elbow out and covered his face with his forearm. He couldn't believe what was happening.

More yells and camera flashes heightened the fray as Jack made a move for the door of the hotel. He quickly realised the scene was about to get ugly.

Out of a sense of entitlement, one of the journalists attempted to block his path in order to ask a few more questions. Jack pushed him aside. The lone policeman, cursing his luck that he was still without backup, opened his arms wide to hold back a group of people who were now closing in. However, he was powerless to stop others from getting close.

Jack, now riled by the injustice, abandoned his 'quiet man' persona. He had never faced a situation like this, and he found reserves in himself that he'd never explored before.

As he turned and snarled at the mob, he roared in defiance, "I'm not a killer! I don't even know this girl. I'm innocent!" And then, appealing to them, he softened his approach. "Please… you have this all wrong."

The confrontation and the shock of the emotion in his voice made several people take a step back, which was enough of a signal for others to recede. The pack seemed to lose its herd mentality, and the aggression notably faded. Disgruntled mutterings now replaced the previous vitriol and rage.

Now tearful, Jack took advantage of the lull and pushed through the door.

The porter, who had heard the commotion, met him in the foyer. He tried to offer some advice. "The management think it would be beneficial if you were to leave the establishment as soon as possible."

"Don't worry; I'm getting out of here right away." Jack didn't even look at the man as he marched towards the staircase. His plan of action was very simple: pack, get to Smudge, and get the hell out of there.

* * *

When Ross heard the door open, he casually glanced towards the front of the shop. He was not expecting to see his wife battling her way through the entrance with two large bags. He couldn't remember the last time she'd set foot on the premises, and he began to prepare himself for an awkward situation.

"Busy?" questioned Claire sarcastically. She could see that the shop was empty.

"Quiet…" he answered, looking down at her shopping, "…until you appeared. Been on a tour of the town's charity shops?"

"It's called husbandry. You should try it sometime."

Ross would normally have found a good retort, but he was getting impatient. Clearly, his wife had come bearing news, and he was eager to deal with it. "To what do I owe the pleasure?"

Claire set the bags down and walked over to the counter. "Charming. Actually, it's more news about this Jack Reilly character. Seems as though the police have let him go."

"And…"

"*And*, you had better make sure that this house is in order."

Ross frowned. "I don't follow. What has this fellow's guilt or innocence got to do with me?" He was finding it easy to act bemused because he couldn't follow Claire's logic at all.

"How many bookshops are there like this one? You know… west of, say, Exeter?" she asked.

"There's a handful around, but nothing as specialist as this one. Even though you don't take much of an interest, you know that, Claire. What are you driving at?"

"The police may have let him go on a technicality. However, I'm hearing that the local press are far from giving up."

"Yes, but that local hack – to whom you were referring at breakfast the other morning – probably has nothing better to write about. Honestly, Claire, I wouldn't take much notice of that tittle-tattle." Ross, still trying to grasp the connection, was keen to stay faithful to his usual response when confronted with gossip.

"The thing is, Ross…"

"Go on…"

"… the girl who died on the moor was carrying literature associated with the occult."

Even though Ross knew from DS Baines that the police had found a book in Victoria's rucksack, the statement shook him. He knew she'd probably performed an occult ritual the night before her death – Jacqui had told him that – but how did anybody else know? Chris wouldn't have spoken to the media. That was a definite. "Well, I wonder how they found that out?" he asked, trying to think fast. "Did that come from the police?"

"No, not directly," Claire replied. "However, journalists have a habit of extracting information from loose-tongued individuals. Seems as though he knows someone in the forensic team. Apparently, a very delectable brunette…"

"And sometimes the police let the press get hold of information they don't want to handle," Ross added, thinking aloud, speculating whether it had been leaked on purpose.

"Indeed. However it happened, though, the local papers and newsfeeds are going to be thirsty for knowledge. Where did she get the book? Was anybody else involved? What local contacts did she have? Ross, they might be knocking on your door, quite soon. Thought you'd be interested. That's all."

"Thanks, I am. But I remind people that we're not living in the Middle Ages. It's not illegal to read this material, and there's an appetite for it! Millions of people want an alternative to what has controlled their lives for centuries. I don't tell customers what to do. That's their own business."

"Yeah, well, good luck with that one," said Claire. "I'll remind you of that when you appear on the evening news. I should get your hair cut if I were you."

Jacqui had warned him to remain tight-lipped; she knew there would be salacious gossip. Ross was now very worried that his wife's interest had been piqued.

"Don't forget we're at Mum's at eight." With that she picked up her bags, made for the exit, and opened the door.

Just before vanishing into the late afternoon February gloom, she turned and said, "Come to think of it, you may have actually known the dead girl. Now there's a thought. One of your acolytes, was she?"

Claire let the question percolate for a fleeting moment, knowing he'd be short of a reply.

Ross froze.

"Sort this mess out," she said firmly. "Don't make me dig any deeper…"

* * *

Jack almost ran down the corridors leading to the rear entrance of the hotel. Fearing that the angry crowd was reassembling in the car park, he decided to reconnoitre the situation first. So, he left his holdall and camera bag by the door and crept out. It was only a small parking area and his campervan was clearly visible. There were a few other vehicles, and they didn't impede his view. The coast appeared to be clear.

Over the past few minutes, as he'd packed, Jack had chastised himself for being so trusting. The earlier experience of the baying crowd had shaken him to the core, and now, he thought it couldn't hurt to take a more thorough approach. He desperately wanted to just open the sliding door of the VW, sling his bags onto the rear seats, and drive away. But how often did a promising situation appear too good to be true? They could still be out there.

So, keeping to the periphery of the compound, and ducking low behind several parked cars, Jack gained a better view of the way out.

His heart sank. Straddling either side of the exit barrier, two motorbikes loitered, ready for action. A helmeted rider and a pillion sat on each machine, waiting patiently. Jack instantly dismissed the idea that they were simply joyriders when he noted their zoom lens-equipped cameras and gimbals. Evasive action was needed if he were to avoid more unwelcome scrutiny.

Pleading with the paparazzi would only give them extra footage, and trying to drive through the gates at speed would be reckless. No, he reasoned, the only way to evade the hounds was to get the hotel management to move them. And that would involve subterfuge.

Jack kept his head low and slowly worked his way back to the rear entrance. His plan might work, he thought, but would the hotel support him? Wouldn't they just want him out of the way? Out of sight, out of mind, so to speak.

He stood back in the corridor with his bags. Then, taking his mobile phone out of his rucksack, he punched in the numbers for the front desk. After a few nervous moments, the call was answered.

Jack spoke with authority. "This is Jack Reilly. It seems that journalists are blocking my way out of the car park. I need to speak to the hotel management at once, otherwise there will be an almighty ruckus. May I remind you that, as I was a paying guest, you are responsible for my safety. I was also advised to leave immediately."

"I'll get the manager to call you right away, Mr Reilly," came the response.

Jack sensed the urgency in their voice – that was a relief. He didn't want to waste time on an uncommunicative hotel receptionist.

It wasn't long before his mobile phone rang.

Jack didn't observe the usual niceties and, instead, launched straight into his demands. "This is what I want. Firstly, an attendant is to move my campervan around the corner to a side street. I have the keys here, by the back door. Anyone waiting by the barrier will think that the van is a shuttle bus for the hotel.

"Secondly, you are to speak to the paparazzi outside and invite them into a small conference room. You will say that I want an interview to set the record straight, and that I don't want to be hijacked on the street again.

"Thirdly, you will call me when the journalists are gathered inside. I will then exit casually through the front door, walk around the block, and recover my vehicle. Do you think you can do that for me? Because, if you can't, there will be another very angry scene outside your hotel."

Jack, who was used to bumbling through life, was amazed that he'd been so direct.

There was a short pause and then an equally short answer.

"Yes, we can do that for you."

* * *

Visiting Alsop's the Jewellers had been quite an experience, and Jacqui's assessment of Victoria Kent had grown immeasurably. She stood outside the shop, staring at the darkening sky, and then blew a kiss – surreptitiously, as if to indicate, 'I should have done better by you'.

After the 'unboxing' of the earrings, Jacqui knew she had to visit the place of their birth. She had to meet the creator and witness his hands at close quarters. She had to stare into his eyes and *understand*.

Of course, she'd had no intention of revealing the true nature of her visit; a casual enquiry about a made-to-order ring had sufficed. She would have loved to have discussed the sigil's inception – perhaps even garner a snapshot of what was in Victoria's mind – but Jacqui wasn't going to compromise her anonymity, and some things were simply best left unsaid.

Yes, thought Jacqui, *Victoria had chosen well. Very well.*

As she had time to spare, she decided to relive one or two childhood memories. Jacqui had visited the endearing moorland town before, but that was long ago; she'd forgotten the narrow streets and how individual all the independent shops were.

She walked along the left-hand side of the square that led up to the Three Crowns Hotel and St Michael the

Archangel Church. As she neared the peak of the rise, her mobile phone pinged, indicating an incoming message:

Fancy a girls' night out with a new crowd? Love to meet up again.

It was Lucy. Jacqui smiled, acknowledging the craft of the message. She had proposed '…a night out with a new crowd', indicating a less intense evening of banter and silliness. Lucy had correctly assumed that she would shy away from another heart-to-heart so soon after their last meeting. The last time had also been about shameless flirting with guys; Ruthven had been in town.

Jacqui was very tempted to accept. An evening with a group of girls could be fun; she'd spent far too much time worrying about the opposite sex lately. Her father, Chris, Ross, Mr Harrison, and especially Jack had all occupied far too much of her 'hard disk drive'. They all wanted, assumed, or needed something from her. Perhaps she was just afraid of commitment, she reasoned.

An affirmative was easy enough, but Jacqui wasn't at all pushed for time. So, she dialled Lucy's number, hoping her friend was available. The call was answered immediately.

"Jacqui?"

"That was quick. Were you sitting on it?"

"Just powdering my nose. I'm in the lav on a break. Trust you to call me now," Lucy replied.

"Ewww, that's weird."

"Get over it. Hold on while I dry my hands."

The industrial sound of the hand dryer made Jacqui hold her phone away from her ear. After an uncomfortable wait, she could hear her friend's voice again.

"Soz. You have to get your hands dry otherwise the phone slips through your fingers. Done that a few times."

Jacqui laughed, recounting her own experiences with wet-fingered mishaps. "Lucy, your proposition sounds interesting. Tell me more."

"Are you coming?"

"I said 'interesting'. Give me something to chew on. Who are these people?"

"Just casual mates I've met from all over the place," explained Lucy, trying to keep it light. "Some of them are friends of friends, if you know what I mean."

"So, not a chamber of legal buddies, if that's the correct collective noun?" asked Jacqui.

"Hah, very funny. No. The idea is to widen the circle. Take Hannah, for instance. She's a teacher. I met her in a gym a few years back. We don't meet up that often, but when we do it's great. She doesn't want to hang around with fellow teachers all the time. I think she's invited a few of her newfound chums. They're not likely to be dull."

"Well, I'm certainly warming to the idea," Jacqui admitted.

"Cherise runs her own doggy daycare business," Lucy continued. "Now, she's a blast. I met her at a cold water swimming event."

"Jeez, Lucy, I think I'll stick to hiking across Dartmoor. Are we eating, by the way?"

"Well, we could do. Let's see how many of us are up for it. Otherwise, we'll find a happening bar so we can have a bash."

Jacqui could see the appeal: a new group of people that she could dip in and out of. Nothing heavy. And if it didn't work out, Lucy wouldn't mind.

She started walking over to a quiet corner, in between shopfronts; she felt exposed standing in the middle of the pavement. "I reckon you can count me in, Lucy. Send me some dates and times."

"Oh, that's great, Jacqui. We'll find somewhere new to go; it won't be the usual haunts. Trust me, it's going to be fun!"

"Well, thanks for thinking of me. I know I can be flighty with friends… I don't know how you put up with it," Jacqui told her, more seriously than she'd intended.

"Forgiven. Hey, we go back a long way, remember? In any case, what am I like?"

"How long is your break?" Jacqui teased, feeling pleased she'd managed to round the conversation off nicely with a joke.

"Get out of here, JR. I'll send those dates. See you soon."

As she watched life go by on that cold February afternoon, Jacqui slid the phone into her back pocket and scanned the streets. It had been a very worthwhile trip.

Chapter 16

Jack strode out of the front entrance of the Castle Hotel. The first part of the operation had gone well. He had given the keys to the valet and, from a safe vantage point, had watched his campervan pass unchallenged through the exit barrier. Ten minutes later, he'd been given the all-clear. Presumably, the journalists were now waiting for him to show up at the spurious interview. He would have laughed at his audacity, but he wasn't at all confident it would end well. He certainly didn't have any time to lose; he had to get to his vehicle and be away before the hounds found his scent again.

Once he'd stepped over the threshold, he didn't know what to expect. In truth, bedecked in a waxed jacket with a woolly hat and scarf, and carrying his large holdall and rucksack, he resembled a typical visitor. Inside, however, he felt like an overdressed fugitive.

The streets were surprisingly quiet, yet only an hour previously there had been tumult. It was raining and the light was beginning to fade. For the first time in memory, Jack championed the inclement weather; it would be easier for him to slip away in the drizzle.

His footsteps hastened as he recognised the name of the approaching side street. He didn't dare look back as it would seem like he was running, guiltily, away from capture. So, like Orpheus seeking to escape the underworld, he tried to hold his nerve.

As soon as he turned down the narrow avenue, he spotted the unmistakable outline of his dark grey van. So near and yet so far! His mind raced. At any moment the roar of motorbike engines could deny Jack the peace and solitude he craved.

Once he was there, Jack slid back the side door of the campervan, hastily threw his two bags onto the rear seat, reached for the keys in the glove box, puffed out his cheeks, and blew out air in relief. Success!

After throwing his damp hat and scarf onto the passenger seat, he started the engine. The click of his seat belt, like the drop of the conductor's baton, signified that all was good to go. Still expecting trouble, Jack quickly glanced into the rear-view mirror, but all was clear. Pressing his right foot on the accelerator as calmly as possible, he manoeuvred out of the parking slot and drove ahead.

It wasn't long before Jack realised he hadn't connected his phone to the cradle on the dashboard; he'd left it in his rucksack. Like Tantalus, the answer to his problem lay teasingly out of reach. He cursed himself. After all, no mobile phone meant a lack of directional assistance. He didn't know Launceston at all well, especially the back roads to the north and east of the town.

Even so, he drove blindly on, preferring to put some distance between himself and the hotel.

The rain, which was now falling significantly, soon became a challenge. As soon as the roads had turned greasy, the driving of those around him had become more erratic. Jack swore at the late braking of the car in front only to realise it had stopped to enable an elderly gentleman to cross at a junction. Trying to maintain a safe distance behind the vehicles in front meant he hadn't been paying enough attention to the signs.

He was pleased to merge onto a more mainstream thoroughfare, but he had, by now, completely lost all sense of direction. The A30 – the artery that would guide him back towards Devon and London – cut across to the south, but he was now travelling north towards Riverside.

Oblivious of this fact, he drove on until he realised he was in the vicinity of Launceston's steam railway. There was little time, however, to reminisce. Jack gave the memory a half smile and then realised that if he continued on his trajectory, he would end up crossing the River Kensey. In order to take evasive action, he decided to take the next left.

Checking his mirror, he was shocked to see the outline of two motorbikes weaving through the traffic several cars behind. The valet must have tipped them off. Besides, it was obvious that he would drive away from the vicinity of the hotel; the chasing hounds didn't need to be psychic.

Jack knew that his VW van was too visible to miss; even in the rain and gloom, he was a sitting duck. His only hope was to make the turn and try to seek sanctuary. For a moment, he toyed with the idea of hiding in a pub car park. Perhaps they'd be too far behind to notice he'd left the road.

He tried to rationalise the situation.

What are they after?

In an instant, he saw how it would play out. The bikes would follow him until the roads became quieter. Then, one would overtake and slow down while the other would draw up alongside the van. They would flag him down, knowing he wouldn't topple them over to escape. Once stationary, the pillion riders – armed to the teeth with cameras – would capture the look of anguish on the driver's face. He could even write the headline for them: *Released Suspect Flees in Spite of Pressing Evidence.* If they pestered him enough, he might even give them a roadside interview.

Well, there was no chance of that, he told himself. He knew how they could quote out of context and edit to advantage.

Jack took a chance and darted through a gap in the traffic. An indignant driver sounded his horn, wound down his window, and clenched his fist in anger. It was close. Jack was expecting to hear the sound of graunching metal and broken glass, but he'd somehow evaded an accident. If lucky, he might have bought himself just enough space and time to shake off the closing motorcyclists.

The move had taken Jack out of the town and down towards the valley floor. With the river to his right, he was penned in by steep-sided hills to his left. He was hoping for a five-way junction, or at least a crossroads. His only possible relief was a turning up the hill to his immediate left, or keeping straight on along the appropriately named 'Under Lane'. In other words, a fifty-fifty situation: heads or tails, hero or zero.

Jack chose the immediate left turn, hoping that the chasing pair would assume he hadn't seen them. It was a very steep hill that initially swung to the right and then curved dramatically to the left. It was amazing that no traffic was coming down the hill, as passing places were few and far between.

Just as Jack thought the steepest sections of the road had been negotiated, the road lurched to the right and the gradient further increased. Already in second gear, the vehicle whined noisily as the increasing revs pushed the vehicle on. The conditions were horrible now and, as Jack felt the lane level off, a sudden unwelcome 'ping' of three warning signs appeared on the dashboard.

Known, ironically, as the three amigos, the ABS, skid symbol, and tyre pressure indicators glowed like stray embers falling onto your favourite fireside carpet. Jack knew that the faulty ABS sensors wouldn't affect the drive of the van, but they would make the braking much less precise. In heavy rain – and on an undulating country lane, where the road surface was poor – he would have to be careful.

Now Jack faced the dilemma of either pushing on away from those pursuing him or having to find a place to pull off the road and hide. The faster he went, the less time he had to react to less obvious unmetalled driveways that might lead him to safety. Honestly, he didn't care where he was heading so long as it wasn't back to town.

Jack searched his mirrors for signs of two single beams dancing behind him. To his relief, he found only darkness. Thinking that the bikes would easily have made up the time they'd lost in the traffic back in town, he reasoned they must have carried straight on along Under Lane. In all probability, that meant the bikers were now ahead of him, travelling westward.

Jack pinned his hopes on the rain-sodden, leather-clad marauders realising he'd outwitted them and therefore abandoning their quest. Besides, he was beginning to feel more positive about the increasingly foul weather. Wouldn't it make their pictures unusable?

The hedges and trees of the lane gave way to buildings on the opposite side of the road. Jack now felt happier, assuming he was approaching a village – and a village, he thought, might mean a pub.

He braked as he came to a crossroads. Slowing down on the wet surface, the campervan felt less assured but not dangerous. Instinctively, he turned right, thinking that the centre of the village lay in that direction. He didn't realise that turning left would have taken him, very swiftly, to the safety of the A30.

It became immediately apparent that what lay before Jack was either wishful thinking or a mirage. A handful of buildings surrounded the crossway, but little else signified human activity, and in no time at all, Jack had passed through the tiny community. He pursed his lips and shook his head, wryly assessing the way the balance of luck seemed to even itself out. His left-turn decision up the hill had produced some promising results, but now he was heading back towards uncertainty.

While ruminating, Jack soon found himself dealing with a more pressing issue: he was plummeting down a very steep hill. The sudden descent took him completely by surprise, as he'd just accelerated away from the hamlet out of sheer annoyance. In a fraction of a second, a sharp bend to the left caused the van to wobble. He had braked but, fearing the lack of ABS, it wasn't as sharply as he'd have liked.

The curve proved to be far more extreme than he'd predicted; after somehow exiting the ninety-degree turn, the campervan gained momentum and surged ever downward. Jack was more than a little alarmed. He was amazed that he'd managed to negotiate the bend, but now he was travelling way too fast. Another bend loomed.

This time he applied more pressure to the brakes, his heart in his mouth because he had no idea whether there were any oncoming cars. The lane was very narrow at this point and, this time, the VW swung more violently. The front wheels skidded on the wet loose stones that had gathered on the inside of the curve. The rear of the vehicle rocked both ways, trying to deal with the extreme camber and quality of the tarmac, and then – as it briefly left the other side of the lane – it clipped some overhanging shrubs with the back of the metal awning casing.

Jack had survived, but the situation soon became even more perilous. He pumped the brakes, but he couldn't seem to slow down enough. Furthermore, Smudge had not regained equilibrium and disaster was inevitable. With little – or no – control, the van reached the bottom of the hill.

Horrified, Jack glanced to the right, realising he was about to merge into another road. Everything was happening too quickly. Failing to brake at all, he shot across the oncoming lane.

By sheer fortune, there were no cars travelling in either direction. His second stroke of luck was the absence of hedging.

He had no time to turn the wheels. Jack left the road, his front tyres smashing against the raised grass verge. The front fairing crumpled, the energy of the vehicle sending it upwards and onwards. All Jack could do was hold his arm across his face and brace himself. Catastrophe was imminent.

The VW California crashed back down but tipped uncontrollably onto its side. It slewed across the saturated grass and sliced through the farmland fencing designed to keep cattle away from the road. Seconds later, a momentous crunch of metal, plastic, and glass punctuated the gloom.

The heft of the ancient granite wall, demarcating the flood plain fields, had proven one barrier too many. The engine had stopped, but the grey, twisted bulk was creaking and hissing. Contracting metal ticked like a mantelpiece clock. The nearside wheel turned its last few revolutions. The pulse was fading.

And then, silence.

* * *

The two pillion riders dismounted their motorcycles and lifted the visors of their helmets in order to speak. The engines were still running, making conversation difficult.

"We would have caught up with him by now; he must have gone a different way out of town."

The second photographer nodded. It made sense.

"Let's turn around and take the next right. He might be lurking up there somewhere."

"This sodding rain needs to stop. Is it worth it?"

"Know what you mean, but I hate the thought of him laughing. He made a right monkey out of us back there. Besides, I want the money shot. I haven't had a front page for a while."

"Yeah, well, just twenty minutes more. My gear's getting wet."

"Agreed. If we don't see him around here soon, he's probably made it to the A30... or he's tucked up somewhere."

The two men returned to the riders and explained the plan. Once the two photographers were back on board, the motorcyclists made a U-turn and roared back the way they'd come. It was only a few miles back to the junction.

The lead bike indicated right and slowed down to take the turn. The second motorbike, adopting the same line, followed suit. As they readied to cross the road and take the lane up the hill, the pillion rider on the lead bike tapped his partner forcibly on the back and pointed to the left.

He could see the obliterated verge, wrecked fencing, and muddy track caused by the snowplough effect of the overturned vehicle. As the bike moved on, he craned his neck and peered backwards, following the trail of churned-up grass.

There – resembling a World War Two crash landing – was, unmistakably, the mangled wreckage of the dark grey campervan they'd been pursuing. It had ended up against the dry stone wall. And it had only just happened.

The pillion rider shot his left arm out and pointed to the horror.

Understanding that there was some kind of problem, the motorbike rider indicated and pulled over. The two riders behind immediately saw the carnage.

Both bikes mounted the grass verge and set down a safe distance from the lane. It was easy for the four men to gain access to the field because an entire section of wired fencing and posts had all but disappeared. They ran as best as they could across the field, but the rain had made the surface very slippery. As they approached the crash site, they began to see what had happened.

The impact of the van colliding with the granite wall had crushed the engine compartment. However, the cabin was largely intact – save for the windscreen, which had disintegrated. The safety airbags had activated and, although they'd subsequently deflated, it was very difficult to see inside.

It was an absolute mess. The vehicle had toppled ninety degrees and taken down a small tree on its journey. The boughs and branches were strewn across the smashed windscreen area. 'Easy' access was therefore only possible from the passenger door, and that was locked.

"Is he alive?" one of the riders yelled.

"I can't get to him," replied another in a panic-stricken response, trying frantically to find a way in.

"Call 999!" cried one of the press to his fellow photographer. "I'm checking that the fuel tank isn't ruptured. I know it's a diesel, but I'm not taking any chances."

"I'm on it," the other replied, walking away so he could hear the response of the emergency services.

"No one could have survived that. I can't hear him. If he was hurt, he'd be shouting."

"He might be unconscious. But even if we could get in, we can't move him. We could smash the passenger window, but we can't drag him upwards. Neither can we get him out through that jungle in front of the cabin."

The two riders surveyed the scene, helpless to do anything.

One pointed back to the lane they'd been about to turn into. "If he'd lost control and hit the verge, he would have just been wrapped in the wire fence. Look at the angle of the tyre marks."

"Yeah, it looks as if he's come down the hill at a rate of knots and hit the grass head-on, taken the fence with him, and smashed into the wall."

Moments later, the pair could see one of the pillion riders walking towards them, still talking on his mobile phone.

"With any luck, the muddy field and fence would have soaked up a lot of energy. He might have a chance… if he hasn't hit that wall too hard."

The photographer slid his mobile into his back pocket and, as he came closer, he spoke to the two riders. "Ambulance, police, and firefighters are on their way. I said we were just passing… that's not a lie, is it?"

They shared a knowing look, the implication just beginning to become apparent.

"Hey Paul, what the fuck do you think you're doing?"

Hearing his name, Paul walked towards the others. "No leaking fuel. That's a relief. I don't trust this 'diesels don't catch fire' malarkey. I was just taking a few shots," he explained incredulously.

"You ghoulish freak. There could be a dead man in there. What were you thinking?"

"My job is to record, and that's what I'm doing," he replied with total disregard. "You never done that before, Phil?"

The other cameraman was aghast. "It's not a warzone, Paul. Joe Public doesn't need to see this," Phil answered, pointing towards the distressing scene.

"Yeah, well, I can soon erase them. Now that I've done that, let's get the hell out of here."

"We can't leave him. It doesn't seem right," said one of the riders.

"Wakey wakey. Do you want to be interviewed by the police? I can tell you what they'll be thinking," Paul said.

"He's right, you know. Even though we weren't on his tail, we'll be blamed for this."

They looked at each other, waiting for someone to make the first move.

"We don't have long. You've done the right thing, Phil. The ambulance will be here any minute. We've got to go, lads… Tom? Jon?" Paul prompted, knowing that Phil would be the hardest to convince.

"Something must have been wrong with his van. We didn't chase him down that hill. I don't want to take the blame for that. Let's go," Jon said, setting off for his motorbike.

Phil wasn't at all happy with the situation, but he realised he was outnumbered. He loved his job. He enjoyed the cut and thrust of real stories – moving situations. And it was exciting following the lives of others. However, right now, he felt sick, and nothing more than a voyeur. What if Jack really had been innocent? Did he deserve this?

Phil was the last to climb onto the waiting motorbike. The riders flicked the stands back into a horizontal position. Then, scoring deep tyre tracks into the muddy grass, they accelerated away.

* * *

It wasn't long before the disgruntled crows took to the skies again. Preferring lower elevations and moist locations, this particular dry stone wall, on the flood plain, had been a favoured place to perch. The highly intelligent corvids hadn't bargained for yet another disturbance and, owing to the excessive human presence, they would soon be heading for roosting sites in nearby trees.

The emergency services arrived in a blaze of flashing lights and sirens. Before long, the field was a hive of activity.

Chapter 17

As Jacqui made her way back to her car, a nagging doubt – the one that had been bothering her for days – surfaced once again. She had felt uneasy after her meeting with Chris, and doubly uneasy after the morning's conversation with Ross. Generally, she prided herself on making well-thought-out, smart decisions that kept her ahead of trouble. Usually, her nimble, fleet-footed approach kept her moving forward. She wasn't used to mopping up errors of judgement, and the last thing she wanted was scrutiny. That meant somebody cared and, if a person cared, it meant that a failure to reciprocate would disappoint.

Jacqui couldn't understand why she'd been experiencing flashbacks of the jewellery shop's interior. While she'd been waiting to be served by Mr Alsop, she'd spent the time perusing the array of items on sale. She hadn't really been interested in buying anything, however; she'd been preoccupied with taking in who he was, listening to his voice, identifying his mannerisms, and so on.

She thought back, remembering the layout of the shop from earlier that afternoon. It was perplexing, and the more she tried to divert her mind to something else, the more it would flash images that were seemingly unimportant. Jacqui reasoned that it must be guilt. What else would prompt unwanted memories? What else appears out of nowhere like a ghostly visitation, or an unwanted guest? Don't we all try to lock that particular genie in a box even though we don't have the key?

Box.

Jacqui mouthed the word to herself, realising it was the beginning of a chain.

Box…

Blue-based jewellery box with a clear lid… St Christopher … Jack… Victoria's house…

Guilt.

Once the connection had been made, the word association tumbled out like sugar cubes from a jar.

She reached her car in a daze, the impact of the discovery palpable. She unlocked the door and sat inside, casting aside anything she could fidget with. The confines of her compact vehicle acted like an exclusion zone. It was time to think. Time to process. The world outside could go and hang itself.

Jacqui held her head in her hands and cursed the one act of sentimentality she'd been responsible for in all the years she could remember. Jack had so touchingly given her the St Christopher at Fur Tor, and she, in turn, had passed it on as if it were Charon's obol: Victoria's assured passage to the next life. She allowed herself a fleeting half smile; it was hardly a religious rite if you placed the *viaticum* in the deceased's knicker drawer.

She knew that guilt had driven her to act in such a manner. Jacqui also acknowledged to herself that passing on the box was a way of enforcing the severance of relations with Jack. She knew, after all, that she'd become dangerously attracted to him. Like a smoker discarding half a box of cigarettes when trying to kick the habit, drastic measures were sometimes required.

Sighing, she looked out of the windscreen, searching the middle distance, though she wasn't actually taking anything in. That was the point. If you could bypass actual detail, it gave your mind a chance to burrow more deeply into its hidden depths. She recognised that the box was the only link Jack had with Victoria. There was nothing else. There couldn't be. However, Jacqui couldn't fathom how the police had made the connection. She knew that the CID would have searched the property, but would the St Christopher box have been so incongruous? Even if it was, how did the police make the gigantic leap that it had once belonged to Jack? It was hard to realise how such a little thing could prove to be so significant.

Jacqui distinctly remembered taking great care to hide her identity when entering Victoria's house. As she sat in the car, she convinced herself that she'd removed all traces of fingerprints and DNA from the amulet. Jacqui also recalled wiping the box and the St Christopher and subsequently treating both with bleach. At the time she wondered if she was going mad; she was aware that such behaviour could be construed as paranoia. She used gloves and even protected her feet with plastic disposable overshoes when breaking in. If her anonymity had been preserved, then so would Jack's.

Jacqui breathed out, pleased that she'd given herself the all-clear. Nothing to worry about, she affirmed. Only, she did worry. And it was concerning how much she felt for Jack. Indirectly, she'd been responsible for all the trouble he was facing, and it didn't seem right at all. She had asked a lot of him to trust her so.

She took a moment to calm herself. The storm had passed, but she felt deflated. She felt like the tourist who had avoided the plane crash by narrowly missing the flight; there was nothing to celebrate.

Jacqui picked up her phone, which she'd tossed onto the passenger seat, and cancelled the alarm set for that evening. There was no point in trying to decode the sigil's letters today; she had to be in the correct frame of mind.

That would have to wait.

* * *

It was one-thirty in the morning, and Jacqui had fallen asleep on the sofa. Suddenly, her pay-as-you-go mobile announced a message. For just a few seconds, the occasional table next to the sofa was flooded with light, but it was enough to stir Jacqui from her slumber.

The flickering light of the television screen made her look away and, grabbing the remote, she extinguished the annoyance. Then, in a slightly confused state, she picked up her phone and saw a message. It was Ross. The news was good:

They've let Jack go. No charges.

Jacqui had to read the message twice before she sported a tired smile.

"Fly back home, Jack. Don't look back," she whispered.

* * *

Sandra crossed the River Tamar, and therefore the border between Cornwall and Devon. On her way back to Tavistock and beyond, she chose to cut across country using the delightful B road that wound its way through Milton Abbot and skirted small villages such as Lamerton. It was probably quicker to take the major roads out of Launceston, but it was much further that way, and they didn't provide many opportunities to stop. Sandra needed to speak to her partner, DC Box. She had information she wanted to share, and it couldn't wait.

She approached Eastacott Barton and indicated right as if to visit the luxury apartments set back from the road along an entrance driveway. By all accounts, it was a fine spot for a holiday break. Right now, thought Sandra, it was a fine spot to pull over and park her car. She disliked speaking whilst driving, and generally preferred 'old school' forms of communication. Besides, she laughed, thinking about her habit, there were times when it was impossible not to wave your hands about in fury or glee.

The mobile rang twice before a familiar voice answered.

"Boss? What's up?"

"You sound busy, Mark. That's unusual," Sandra commented.

"Very funny. Where are you?" he asked.

"On the Milton Abbot road. Just been to sort out a domestic at Lifton."

"That's a bit off track – no need to be there coming back from Lifton. A cake shop or fancy man?"

"You keep pushing your luck, Box… I've been to Launceston…"

There was a pause while DC Box processed the statement.

Sandra continued before he could respond. "I thought that, as it wasn't very far, I'd pay Ross Raymond another visit."

Mark paused for another second before replying, "Boss, we're supposed to be off that case now."

"I know, but I had to get one or two things clear in my mind. Unresolved business, so to speak. In so doing, I've unearthed some truly shocking news."

Mark Box could hear the urgency in Sandra's voice. She clearly needed to share a heavy load. "Go on…"

"Ross Raymond informed me that Jack Reilly is in hospital. He's critically injured. They've induced a coma. It's that serious, Mark."

"He's what?!" asked her partner, unable to believe what he was hearing.

"Apparently, his campervan left the road, crashed through a fence, and smashed into a wall."

"Where and when?"

"Now, here's where it gets very strange," Sandra replied. "I got that information from our friends across the border. Seems as though it's all very cloak and dagger, which is odd. The Cornish boys in blue want to keep it very hush-hush."

"Intriguing," said Mark, knowing that she would elaborate.

"It's all a bit sketchy, but Jack left custody in a taxi and returned to his hotel in Launceston. Somebody must have tipped off the press about where he was staying because they were there waiting for him. Apparently, a crowd gathered. It got a bit nasty."

"So Jack left the hotel in a rush," stated Mark. "Who wouldn't?"

"Exactly… only it gets worse…"

"Go on…"

"He was followed by the local paparazzi on motorbikes," Sandra told him.

"Oh no, I know where this is heading…"

"In an effort to evade them, he managed to lose control of his vehicle," she confirmed. "It all happened in a country lane heading west out of Launceston."

"And because this is very embarrassing for us, the top brass want to keep a lid on it," Mark said, assessing the situation correctly. "But what about the press?"

"Probably a small paragraph on page four. This doesn't look good for them either. After the furore in Paris over Diana's death, this sort of harassment is very frowned upon."

Mark sighed. "I don't know what to think, boss. It's all a bit of a mess. How did it turn out like this?"

"That's exactly what I was thinking," replied Sandra, shaking her head.

"How did Ross Raymond get to know about what happened?" Mark queried.

"He said, 'Word on the street'," Sandra explained, "but that's rubbish. I was pressing him about Victoria Kent and Jack and so on, and he soon realised that I didn't know about the accident. It took the wind out of my sails."

"I can imagine. You weren't expecting that."

"He seemed very prepared, Mark. You know, everything in order. Mailing lists, people attending courses and events, social media followers, et cetera…

Victoria Kent features here and there, but there's no mention of Jack Reilly anywhere."

"He knew you'd be back, boss. He'd met you before."

"Yeah, well… he even confidently evaded suggestions that he knew Victoria a little better than his wife would be happy with. He said that she was wildly enthusiastic about the study, and that he met her on an intellectual level, passing on and discussing new reading material. I think there might have been some funny stuff going on, but if we can't prove it had anything to do with Jack, we have to leave it."

"Did you mention the video or the sigil?" asked Mark.

"No… I thought about it, but I couldn't really ask him to comment on highly personal details about the deceased. He isn't a suspect." She sighed. "Perhaps I was hoping for too much, but I was counting on Ross telling all. He's had a while to think about it, and he's definitely holding something back. But now that Jack is on the critical list…"

"We've hit the buffers," Mark finished.

"Indeed, we have. It's a shame because, if he doesn't pull through, there will always be a question of guilt hanging over him that he won't be able to answer to. I wanted to clear it all up beyond reasonable doubt, give Victoria's parents some peace of mind. And, to be honest, I want to know that I can still read people. This case has been like no other in that respect. Why do I feel a bit sorry for Jack when there is pretty damning circumstantial evidence that he was involved?"

"I can't answer that, boss, but I feel the same. Everything does point in that direction." Reading Sandra's mood

– and knowing she'd said all she'd wanted to say – he knew it was time to change the timbre of the conversation. "Wise words, boss, but your pressing issue now is to get back here and write up that report on the domestic in Lifton. I'll get the kettle on."

"Agreed. I'll catch you in twenty minutes or so. See you back at base."

Sandra placed her mobile phone on the passenger seat, opened the door, and stepped out of the car. It was a crisp February day and visibility was very good. The sky was clear, unlike the day before when it had been wet and gloomy.

She looked out and over as the ground fell away before her; the view across the Tamar Valley was spectacular at this point. She had travelled on this road many times, but she hadn't really taken the time to notice before.

Sandra took in the meandering river as it snaked beneath her. Like an adder, its coils were almost touching. She began to understand how some people became recharged when in contact with such wonder. She had felt it when walking across the open moor after witnessing the lifeless body of Victoria Kent. She had missed that interaction with nature. Somehow, Sandra thought, the last ten years of her life had flown by. What was worse… she didn't seem to have much to show for it.

The brief interlude was enough for Sandra to reset for the rest of the day; in that ephemeral episode, she had managed to gain some perspective and resolve. She pledged to herself that she *was* going to take more risks in her personal life, and that she *was* going to break out of her comfortable-but-going-nowhere bubble and meet a more diverse crowd.

Sandra unlocked her car and sat inside, smiling – then, a pang of guilt descended as she realised that Jack Reilly, right at that moment, was fighting for his life.

* * *

Jacqui sat on the edge of her bed. She had been careful to make it properly that morning because everything had to be in order. Her life, she admitted, could be a bit chaotic at times, but this morning it was to be different. 'Tidy bedroom, tidy mind', she heard her father say. She chuckled to herself, realising that – over time – she had begun to adopt more of his foibles than she'd be prepared to admit.

She reached for the Austin Osman Spare book she'd taken from Victoria's house and placed it on her bent knees. She then opened the top drawer of her bedside chest and found the small ring binder notebook she'd put there a few days previously. Jacqui found the relevant pages and settled it on the flat surface of the book. Next, picking up her shoulder bag that had been lying on the floor, she selected a sharp pencil from the zipped compartment. Her movements were purposeful; this was to be no casual affair.

She cast her eyes over the notes she'd already made. There was a list of letters she had identified in the design of the earrings. She'd written them as a row of capitals:

S G H T R F Y V M N D

Jacqui knew that trying to decode the sigil would involve prior knowledge, some hunches, and a lot of guesswork. She also knew that if Victoria had chosen something very obscure, her chances of success were non-existent.

Jacqui's first stab at inserting missing vowels into letters to form a word involved her alter ego: Ruthven. The letters R, T, H, V, and N jumped out at her immediately. Victoria was one of only a handful of people she had trusted with the name. So, it was obvious that if the sigil were to be highly personal to her, she would choose that. It also occurred to her that there was no 'Q' or 'C', so Victoria couldn't have used 'Jacqui'.

Sure enough, by using a U and an E, Jacqui wrote the name RUTHVEN in her notebook. By process of elimination, that left:

S G F Y M D

Jacqui placed the capitals underneath the name of her alter ego. She was excited about the possibility of finding her first word, but she knew that, in truth, it was easy to find names from that list. She toyed with other possible outcomes and immediately found FROGGY for a nickname, although not hers. MINDY, MAVIS, VERA… the list was endless. As it was possible to use repeat letters, the sheer number of potential iterations was mind-boggling. It served as a salutary reminder that the next stage was not going to be so straightforward.

If a hunch had been used to identify the first word, Jacqui decided to adopt prior knowledge as her second tool. She recalled some of the heart-to-heart discussions she'd had with Victoria. They had shared hopes, fears, and secrets in those heady days. Some were alcohol-induced slips of the tongue. Others were clear-headed, rational barings of the soul.

Jacqui remembered how Victoria had become highly emotional when she'd revealed the nature of her cancer.

It was probable, she concluded, that the sigil had something to do with her well-being. So, she wrote down the phrase that was common to all sigils:

IT IS MY WILL TO

Jacqui then attempted to complete the sentence by using likely words. She ran through possibilities such as, 'It is my will to cure Ruthven's illness', 'It is my will to give Ruthven lasting life', or, 'It is my will to kill Ruthven's cancer'. It was hopeless: a never-ending task. Jacqui realised very quickly that all of her examples used letters that didn't figure in Victoria's sigil. However, she reasoned, if she could complete the infinitive 'to _', the other words might fall into place.

Jacqui stared at her notebook, trying to solve the puzzle. She noticed that her complete examples of infinitives used four-letter words: '…to cure', '…to give' and '…to kill'. They seemed to roll off the tongue incredibly easily. Perhaps Victoria had used the same technique. So, Jacqui wrote down the incomplete sentence:

IT IS MY WILL TO _ _ _ _ RUTHVEN

As a visual learner, Jacqui found this more helpful. Of course, she realised, the missing word could contain five or more letters, but it was a start.

She scanned the list of letters again for clues, and it quickly became apparent that she would need to fine-tune her search even further. She posed the question: Does the missing word begin with a consonant or a vowel?

She spoke softly to herself, "If it begins with a vowel, it could be something like 'ease', as in, 'It is my will to ease Ruthven from pain'…"

In the blink of an eye, Jacqui caught sight of the word 'from' and, all of a sudden, thoughts of vowels and consonants were abandoned. She immediately cast her gaze back to her list of remaining letters and saw an 'f' and an 'm'. This was a breakthrough – or at least it could be, she reasoned, trying not to get ahead of herself.

Jacqui thought about the three tools she would need to solve the conundrum. She decided to add a fourth – 'from' had been a slice of luck.

The sentence was still far from complete, but there were now fewer letters to deal with, and these had to be used at some stage. Jacqui wrote out the revised version and the remaining letters:

IT IS MY WILL TO _ _ _ _ RUTHVEN FROM _ _ _ _ _

S G Y D

She discounted 'ease' because it wasn't a dynamic word and, in any case, after you omitted the 'S', it left a rather unhelpful list of 'G', 'Y', and 'D'.

Jacqui stared at the four letters and then glanced back to the unfinished sentence. She tried to form words but nothing came.

Her mind raced back to all those deep conversations with Victoria. She recalled when her friend had announced that she'd designed a sigil in the form of a pair of earrings; it had come as quite a shock. Victoria had spoken to her about 'saving' her through 'sigilisation'. She was to have the earrings made and then, in a ritual, as the creator, she was going to 'charge' the sigil. She spoke at length about the unconscious manipulation of the symbols. She had been deadly serious.

The combination of the flashback and staring intently at the four letters for a few minutes led to the second revelation. It was like trying to remember someone's name for half an hour and then, for reasons unknown, it simply appeared.

"'Save' has got to be a candidate," she enthused. Victoria had definitely used that word. Jacqui remembered being very apprehensive at the time because it represented yet another person trying to interfere with her life. If somebody saved you, you owed him or her something. That was uncomfortable.

Jacqui calmed herself and double-checked her logic. 'Save' used the 'S'. The 'V' was a repeat letter. All was good. 'Save from' what? She pondered this for a fraction of a second. 'Dying' was the answer; it almost presented itself. The word was charged enough because it was a concept she'd been trying to come to terms with.

Jacqui wrote the words down, her hand shaking:

MY WILL IS TO SAVE RUTHVEN FROM DYING

The words appeared like a message from a séance. It had to be correct.

Instinctively, Jacqui reached for the red jewellery box that she'd positioned next to her bedside lamp a few days previously; she felt a deep desire to verify her solution by moving her fingers gently over the golden glyphs. She prised the lid away from the base of the box as the strong spring tried to conceal its treasure.

Like two pearls in a shell, the earrings, once again, more than delighted her as she gazed at them. Each time Jacqui examined them, the experience became increasingly more powerful. The reflection from the gold lit her face and she grinned, engorged by their radiance.

As before, Jacqui held the teardrops aloft, but this time she watched them pirouette gracefully. It was as if she had now acquired the right to handle them; she had unlocked their secret. The first time Jacqui had held them, they had been almost unruly. But now that they were 'complete', they purred with a simmering force that she knew she could harness. She sensed that, when worn, the influence of the earrings would be even greater.

Jacqui gathered both of the teardrops and placed them in the cup of her right hand. She could feel the sigil teasing, almost goading her to insert each golden hook into her lobes, but she resisted. Instead, she returned the earrings to the box and closed the lid. In that moment, she knew she must preserve the integrity of the sigil and only unveil it in very special situations – times when all her senses were heightened to the extreme. They were to be no fashion accessory.

The experience of decoding the sigil and handling the enigmatic jewellery had left Jacqui feeling rather profound. She felt a rush. Dynamism. Spirit. Life.

She considered whether it could be psychosomatic or not, recognising that Austin Osman Spare was onto something – knowing that the subconscious world was worth mining.

Jacqui placed the notebook and pencil in her bag, leaving the book and jewellery box on the bedside cabinet. Then she stood up, walked over to the window, and looked out. It was a bright day. The watery, mid-February sun was forming weak shadows that barely hid the details, but it was a world away from the previous day's dimness.

Spring was a way off yet, but Jacqui could sense that it would soon be time to develop a new awareness: a DIY project of the mind, so to speak. Maybe, she thought, it was time to invest in delayed gratification and think about planning for the future.

In that short moment, the power of the sigil had allowed her to feel less urgent. It had given her a calmness that she'd never thought possible. Ruthven – her adrenalin junkie alter ego – had given her life, but it was all about the moment: short episodes she could walk away from. Jacqui recognised that she would need to stop hiding behind her – increasingly dominant – friend.

With a wry smile, Jacqui decided that all that could wait for a few more weeks. She wasn't quite ready to retire her hedonistic other self… not just yet.

There were, after all, a few more cigarettes left in the box.

Chapter 18

Beth Gibson stepped nervously into the intensive care unit where Jack Reilly was being cared for. The cleansing of her hands with an alcohol-based hand sanitiser was a precaution she was familiar with, but she hadn't bargained for the wearing of a gown and gloves. She had already deposited her coat and personal belongings outside. She had assured the ICU nurse leader that she hadn't any signs of illness or a cold and had left her husband to look after their son, Charlie, in the downstairs waiting area. The seriousness of the situation was evident.

On hearing the news, Jack's sister had done well to keep herself together; she had focused on getting her family to the hospital as soon as possible. On arrival, Beth hadn't known what to expect, as the details given to her had all been rather vague. There had been an accident. Jack was in an intensive care unit. But he was being given the very best support available.

'Intensive care' indicated to Beth that there was an obvious threat to life. However, she had no idea whether he was conscious or not. She was also in the dark about the extent of his injuries. As his next of kin and older sister, she knew it was important to fight the urge to break down.

A nurse ushered Beth into Jack's individual room. As she entered, Beth caught sight of the lifeless form of her brother lying supine, head elevated, on the hospital bed. Her right hand immediately flew to her mouth as she took a sharp intake of breath. It was more than a shock; it was crushing. The nurse leader had told her, just before coming into the room, that he was in a coma, but Beth hadn't internalised that at all. From the time of her being informed to her standing before her sibling, it had been a total blur.

Jack's eyes were closed, his face expressionless and his skin colour drained of any signs of vitality. She thought that he'd just died, unnoticed.

The nurse squeezed Beth's left hand in reassurance as she led her closer to her brother. The nurse's gentle handling made Beth compose herself.

"Sorry, that's not helping at all, is it? It's just… I thought he was…"

"He's in a coma, Mrs Gibson. It's quite normal to have that reaction."

"Will he… is he going to… will someone tell me all about it?" Beth asked.

"The neurologist is here. He will see you shortly, Mrs Gibson."

Beth moved closer to Jack, trying to detect a flicker of recognition. She wondered whether he could hear her voice.

"At the moment, Mr Reilly is in a constant state of unconsciousness," the nurse told her, gently. "He's not going to be able to respond to instructions of any kind. However, there is some evidence that patients in comas can hear loved ones, and that it gives them comfort."

"Thank you, nurse, that's a comfort for me as well," Beth said, appreciating the remark.

"Ah, here's Mr Stanway, the neurologist. He'll be able to answer any questions you have. I'll pop back in and see you after Mr Stanway has finished." With that, the nurse moved politely away to take some readings from one of the many monitors in the room.

Mr Stanway strode purposefully towards Beth and offered his hand. "Mrs Gibson. Richard Stanway, neurologist."

Beth shook his hand and was immediately taken by his warmth. She searched his face for hope. "Is there anything you can tell me?" she asked desperately. "As you're a neurologist, I take it the major concern is damage… to the… brain?" Beth's voice trailed off. It was almost too painful to confront the obvious.

"Okay, let's clear up a few points," he said, his voice calm. "I'll establish where we are, right now, and then say what we hope will happen as the days progress."

Beth nodded.

"Firstly, we need to make a complete assessment of Jack's overall health. We'll also need to find out more about the condition and intensity of the coma. In order to gather the information, we'll be running various scans. Jack has had a serious accident, and his body has shut down all but necessary functions. He can't tell us anything at all."

Beth looked over at Jack, desperate to hold him – but even if it were allowed, the cables, tubes, monitors, and stands prevented any chance of that. She fought back the tears. "Will he wake up? Will he pull through?"

"It's early days; I'm afraid, at the moment, there's no way of telling," Stanway told her. "Once we've completed our tests, I'll be in a better position to answer that. Let me tell you that he could wake up in a minute, next week, or never. But before I worry you too much, you should know that Jack could easily have died in the accident, but he didn't. The safety airbags did their job. He was also driving a van – a bigger vehicle, generally, affords more safety. The rain-soaked ground may have slowed his vehicle down. He has bruising from the seat belt and on his legs, hands, and face. He may well have broken ribs, and so on. Put it this way, Mrs Gibson: I've seen much worse. What I can't comment on *yet* is how much the impact has caused significant trauma to the head."

"Jack's my baby brother," Beth said quietly. "He's young, very fit, and in good health. He'll be trying to find a way back, Mr Stanway."

"Positive thinking, Mrs Gibson," the neurologist said, smiling. "Those are all qualities that give him the very best chance of recovery. Now, let me explain what all this paraphernalia is all about." He moved over to the hospital bed and pointed to the many monitors and leads.

"So many wires, tubes, screens… my poor bro," Beth whispered.

Mr Stanway nodded. "Okay, so this is no ordinary hospital bed," he explained. "It can be adjusted in a multitude of ways. It's important to keep the head in an elevated position; it helps to reduce the amount of intracranial pressure. It will also let the blood and cerebrospinal fluid drain from the brain."

Beth winced, though she realised that Mr Stanway was – in his own way – trying to explain that the unit was doing everything possible. "And this tube?" she asked, keen to understand. She knew that the more she understood, the less likely it was that she would panic.

"Ah, that one measures the pressure in the skull." Stanway quickly pointed to the breathing apparatus, realising that a prolonged conversation about skull pressure might become too distressing. "The ventilator helps the patient breathe. It sends oxygen to the lungs. We don't want Jack to accidentally stop breathing. We've also got the nasogastric tube, here, if we need to feed Jack with liquid food."

Beth nodded, happy that she had recognised 'naso' for nose and 'gastric' for stomach.

"We're monitoring his heart rate and rhythm with these leads…" Mr Stanway pulled back the sheets to reveal several small black patches attached to the skin around the chest.

Beth's eyes widened. This was beginning to resemble Jekyll and Hyde. The room whirred and beeped with electronic noises. Monitors displayed constantly changing readouts. All that was missing were steam-emitting conical flasks, test tubes, and a head clamp.

Mr Stanway continued his tour. "This machine here vibrates. We use it to help loosen the phlegm inside a patient's chest. Hopefully, we won't need that, but it's there just in case."

"Just in case of pneumonia?" Beth asked, trying to think things through logically.

"Top of the class."

Beth sported a faint smile – it was all she could manage under the circumstances. She realised, in that moment, that there were so many ways in which Jack could succumb. It would be a miracle if he survived.

Mr Stanway pointed to the tubes that led from below the sheets to various bags underneath the bed. "As

SIGIL

I said, Jack's body has shut down. That includes the control over his bladder and bowel. Of course, we're able to measure the amount of urine passing through."

Beth nodded again. It all made sense, but she doubted she'd remember half of it later on. She was deeply impressed that Mr Stanway had taken the time to explain and demystify how they were attempting to save Jack's life. It was comforting to know that he was receiving the best possible care.

She pointed to her brother's hand and the catheter that was taped securely to the skin. "I recognise the intravenous drip. I know what that's for."

"Yes, we insert nutrients and medicines directly into the vein."

Stanway knew that Beth would not immediately respond, so he left her to process her thoughts for a few seconds. "We have everything covered here, Mrs Gibson," he said after a moment. "This is the best place for Jack, though I can't guarantee anything, I'm afraid. We think he has a good chance of recovery, but until we see the results of the scans, we won't know the extent of the damage. Being in a coma is not a death sentence. Many people regain their health. Of course, it will take time."

"Thank you, Mr Stanway. I appreciate everything that you and your team are doing for Jack."

"That's very kind of you, Mrs Gibson, but it's just what we do here. Now, I'm going to leave you alone with your brother. If you have any questions at all, please ask a nurse. This is a specialist unit and they are highly trained. Oh, and one other thing: you must look after yourself, Mrs Gibson. Jack could be with us for quite a while. You won't be able to come and visit every day because you have family, friends, work, and so on. You mustn't feel as if you are abandoning him if you miss days."

"I'll try and remember that, Mr Stanway. Thank you."

With that, the neurologist nodded and left the room.

For the next few moments, Beth tried to take in the enormity of the situation she and Jack now faced. She looked over to her brother and wondered how it had come to this.

Beth moved closer to him. She would have loved to have held his hand or wrap her arms around him, but the danger of infection prohibited such a move. She stared at his face, studying the features she knew and loved so much. His eyes were closed and he looked at rest, but she wondered what was going on behind the mask. Would he know that she was standing next to him? Could he really hear her voice?

"Jack, I have no idea about what's been going on, and I don't know how you got into this mess, but we're going to get you out of it."

Beth searched for a twitch of recognition – a flicker of the eyelids, increased activity on the heart rate monitor – but found nothing. His body remained stiff and inert.

As she tried to find the right words to say, tears welled up in her eyes. The suppressed emotion within her was now reaching almost uncontrollable levels. "Look, now you've made me cry!" she spluttered. "I'm trying to hold it together, but I can't. You're all I have now, Jack. Mum and Dad are gone. It's just you and me. You have to find a way out. I promise I'll look after you."

Beth knew that Jack wasn't going to suddenly open his eyes and smile at her, but it was still disappointing when he remained motionless.

The life support machines continued to deliver their digital symphony. They were strangely comforting; all the time she could hear beeps and whirring noises, she knew he was still with her.

Inevitably, Beth's mind flashed back to times when they were young. She stared at Jack's ashen face, wondering where the years had gone. As his older sister, she had looked out for him and had often kept him out of harm's way, but now she was powerless to do anything.

She wanted to scream, but she could only sob, desperately overwhelmed by her sadness at this tragic turn of events. In order to find comfort, Beth started to hum and sing the nursery rhyme she used to delight Jack with, all those years back.

> "Row, row, row your boat
> Gently down the stream.
> Merrily, merrily, merrily, merrily,
> Life is but a dream."

Beth imagined Jack singing off-key and trying to follow his sister's rowing action. He would ask for it again and again.

> "Row, row, row your boat
> Gently up the creek.
> If you see a little mouse,
> Don't forget to…"

She omitted the last word, even though she knew that Jack would no longer shout, "…squeak!" as he used to. The memory was rich, but it only hid her desolation for a minute or so.

However, if she'd been looking at the screen at that very moment, Beth would have noticed the tiniest spike in the heart rate monitor…

* * *

"Thanks for coming over, Chris!" Ross called out to his friend as he crossed the threshold of the bookshop.

"No worries; always happy to oblige. I can quite as happily eat my lunch here as back at my place. That's the beauty of working from home."

"As I explained, Chris, I just have a quick delivery to make and then I'll be back. I've had a few customers in this morning, but I don't anticipate a rush in the next hour."

"Trade picking up then?"

"You know how it is – the odd newspaper article, television series, or film can easily whet the appetite. We don't do so badly here."

Chris and Ross swapped places behind the till. The shop was empty. Outside, the weather looked dreary again, making the interior rather dark.

"Actually, Chris, there was something I wanted to run past you. It shouldn't take a minute…"

"Sounds serious. I'm all ears."

"It's regarding that Jack Reilly character," said Ross. "You know, the guy Jacqui said she'd met on the moor."

"Yes, I saw him in here, if you remember. He suddenly dashed off, which was a bit strange. In fact, that whole episode was mighty weird. Poor Victoria." He shook his head sadly. "You know, I keep thinking about her. I just can't believe she won't ever walk through that door again. It's such a terrible loss." He looked over to the entrance and the empty space in front of it.

Ross, prompted by his friend's change of demeanour, dragged a bar stool from behind the counter and sat down. He chided himself for thinking he could deal with the subject in a matter of minutes; he knew that Chris had deeper feelings for Victoria than he'd first imagined. Mentioning Jack Reilly had reopened a fresh wound.

"I had the police sniffing around here again," Ross told him, once he was comfortable on the stool. "DS Baines – she's rather formidable."

"Again? What was she looking for?" Chris asked, still replaying moments he'd shared with Victoria.

"Anything that could prove that Jack Reilly was interested in the occult. Also, anything that could link him to our Ms Kent. Of course, there wasn't anything. I've never even met the fellow."

"So, are they suggesting he might have been involved in her death? If so… that's incredible. I thought Jacqui had explained everything. I believed her, anyway…" Chris placed his bag on the floor and pulled a chair over to sit on it. He, too, had realised Ross wasn't about to leave anytime soon.

Ross took a deep breath. "A bit of background that you may not be familiar with: one of the walkers in Claire's ramblers' group has connections with the Devon police. So, listen to this: Claire's out walking with the group and he starts discussing stuff about Jack Reilly. The police had pulled him in for an interview – under caution, I might add. He obviously likes the sound of his own voice because he's got everyone agog about Jack and Victoria being involved in sex magick and occult rituals.

He said that the press would soon be onto it. It was meant to be a, 'you heard it here first, folks'."

Chris stared at him for a moment. "And because you haven't told me anything about this, I'm guessing there's an addendum to the story…"

"Correct. They kept Jack for a time and then they released him. The police issued some low-level press statement saying that they weren't looking for anyone else, but that there wasn't enough evidence to proceed with charges against him."

"You don't think there was anything in it, do you?"

"No. The police would have searched Victoria's house to rule out foul play. A casual glance at her bookshelf would have told them she was interested in the kind of books we sell. Somehow, they linked Jack to that. Goodness knows how, though."

"So we're back to the status quo then?" Chris asked, rather bemused as to where this was leading.

"Not exactly," Ross replied, sighing. "Apparently, the press knew where Jack Reilly was staying. Cameras flashed away as he entered the hotel. There was a bit of jostling and shouting. Quite a scene for this town. He left within the hour."

"So he scarpered back home?"

"He attempted to…"

"What do you mean? What stopped him?"

"He lost control of his vehicle. Turned it over. Crashed into a wall down by the River Kensey."

Chris's mouth dropped temporarily open. "What the hell was he doing down there?"

"I don't know, Chris. But, I do know it was a bad accident."

"When you say *bad*… do you mean fatal?"

"Honestly, I don't know."

"Wow. Like I said before, this whole thing is totally weird. I don't know what to say. Poor fella."

"Of course, there's the elephant in the room…"

Chris took a moment to work out what Ross was suggesting. "Jacqui?"

Ross nodded, indicating that he'd finally reached the point of the conversation. As he continued, he spoke more softly, almost as if he was worried she might hear. "I let her know that he was being interviewed. Then, as soon as I heard he'd been released, I messaged her to say he was driving home. I haven't spoken to her since."

Chris immediately understood the ramifications. He took a few seconds to respond. "You're thinking that, as far as she's concerned, it's all done and dusted. The whole saga is over. We can all get back to normal. So there's no point in telling her. It would only…"

"Exactly. She can't do anything about it. If he's still alive, she won't want to show her face at the hospital. She said she wanted no intrusion into her private life. Remember that chat we had over at Brentor?"

"I remember it well, Ross. She made it very clear. However, I know you well. Something's eating away at you. You want to tell her. You want that load lifted."

Ross sighed. "I won't lie, Chris – you're absolutely right. But it's not only that. If I don't judge it correctly and she gets ratty with me for not telling her, the whole thing will be over. Our pact. My life's work." He paused for a moment. "I've never met anyone like her, Chris. She has an aura I can't put into words. She is the one. I feel it. We were so nearly there."

"Are you thinking we can find a replacement for Victoria and rekindle what we had before?" Chris asked, eyebrows raised. "Jacqui's almost impossible to handle. Will she be up for it?"

"It might take time, but… yes, I think it's possible. It has to be, Chris."

"I'd like to think so too, Ross, but Jacqui is so unpredictable. Maybe the moment has passed. What makes you think she'll keep in contact? I know her dad owns this bookshop, but she doesn't exactly talk about him much."

Ross stood up and patted the sides of his jacket to locate his car keys. It had been good to air his concerns; Chris had always been a good listener, and Ross respected any advice given by his long-term friend.

He turned to face Chris and posed the necessary question: "Do I hide and risk the wrath that will inevitably descend on me if she finds out, or do I inform and risk the fallout and potential disintegration of our pact? What would you do?"

Chris stood up in order to give his answer more gravitas. "You have to tell her, Ross. I don't think either of us will want to bury that news too deeply. I, for one, would rather play it straight. Que sera, sera, and all that."

Ross nodded in agreement and placed his right hand on Chris's shoulder. "I was hoping you'd go for the former. That means I'm going to have to call her now. But you're right, Chris, it has to be done."

Ross made a move for the door, but turned just before he reached it. "I'll give her a ring later this evening. Let's hope she's had a good day…"

Sigil

* * *

Sandra and her sister Megan dangled their legs over the North Teign River as they sat on the ancient Teign-e-ver Clapper Bridge. Two massive flat slabs of granite supported by a single pillar of odd-shaped stone blocks spanned the fast-flowing water. A lone, windswept hawthorn, skeletal in February, watched over the pair like a chaperone. The distant Watern Tor to the west could be seen on a clear day, but as March approached – like on most Dartmoor days – the visibility was severely restricted by mist.

"Remember coming here with Dad?" Megan asked.

Sandra smiled. "I do. It's such a lovely spot. There's just something about water winding its way down from the hills…" She found a small stone lying next to her and casually lobbed it into the stream. Her overstretched arm caused her necklace to become more visible.

"Check that out!" Megan said, spying the jewellery.

"What, my secondary school, rounders team, boundary throw? Impressive, huh?" Sandra laughed.

"No, I could beat that with my left hand. Your rather swanky necklace is what I'm finding interesting."

Sandra looked down, realising it had become visible. "Megan… it's just a necklace. Don't be weird."

"Just a necklace? But you don't wear necklaces…"

Sandra didn't answer her sister but smiled teasingly at her.

"So… somebody nice bought it for you?"

Sandra tucked the necklace behind her sweatshirt before her sister became too interested in its history. "Nosy. Wouldn't you like to know? Actually, I bought it myself."

"Let me see it; now you've *really* got me interested."

Sandra reluctantly reached behind her warm layer and revealed the item. "Happy now?" she asked.

Megan edged closer to get a better view. "That is the cat's meow. That's rad, sister!" She was more than a little surprised.

Sandra shook her head. Her sister's attempt at cutting-edge street parlance was woefully out of date. "What's the big deal? You've been encouraging me to doll myself up for ages."

"It's really lovely, Sand. Where did you get it?"

Sandra was chuffed at her sister's approval but was wary about revealing too many secrets. "I found it online. The actual shop is in Chagford."

"Two crescent moons, joined back to back… that doesn't seem like something your typical small town jewellers would sell…" remarked Megan, intrigued by her sister's choice, "…very unusual."

Sandra let her older sister's remark hang in the air, but Megan continued to enthuse.

"Those three gemstones are beautiful. What's that… a pink topaz at the top, an amethyst where the moons join, and a sapphire at the bottom? Hot dang, that looks like platinum as well. Sand, that must have cost an absolute fortune."

Sandra shrugged. "When I saw it, I loved it. It was one of those impulse buys. I liked it because it was different." Being economical with the truth, however, didn't sit too comfortably with Sandra, so she tried to offer a better explanation. "As well as the usual stuff, the shop sells more niche designs… you know that I've always been drawn to the fringe."

"So how did you find this place?" pressed Megan. "Since when has Chagford been your go-to place for purchases? This is becoming more interesting by the minute."

"Shall we walk?" asked Sandra. "We can go back via Batworthy Corner, over there." She pointed to the clump of fir trees in the distance. "We can cross the river again further up, and get back to the car via the Gidleigh Park Hotel. Remember that way?" With that, she stood up and gathered her rucksack, indicating that the answer to Megan's questions might involve a lengthy response.

"I remember getting our feet wet trying to cross the river using the stepping stones," said Megan. "You and dad just laughed."

Sandra held out her hand and helped pull her sister to a standing position. Together, they trod the well-marked trail to the distinctive dark green smudge that was the fir plantation half a mile ahead. It was wet underfoot, but exhilarating. The air was fresh and unsullied by pollution; the atmospheric views up to Shovel Down, quite magnificent.

The three-mile walk back to Megan's vehicle afforded Sandra time to explain the recent series of events that had consumed her working life. She skirted around the role of Mr Alsop and the true significance of the earrings, but it enabled her to put into context her knowledge of the local jeweller.

"My goodness, that's quite a story," said Megan, once her sister had finished. "I read about the girl being found near Fur Tor, but all this other stuff… well, it's baffling."

"To be quite honest, Megan, it's made me want to quit the force."

"What the heck!" her sister exclaimed. "That's a bit extreme! I mean, the force… your job… it's who you are…"

"Exactly, and right now, I don't much like who I am." Sandra sighed. "Failure to nail a criminal happens. Failure to conduct a crime scene properly happens, but I've never before experienced such a low after a case has been dropped. It's made me feel empty. It feels so… unfinished. And then, of course, there's the tragic accident."

Her sister stared at her for a moment. "I recall the last time we met. You indicated that it was time for 'new horizons', so to speak." Megan's delicate use of the euphemism didn't go unnoticed. "Perhaps this new feeling is all part of that?"

Sandra acknowledged the comment with a smile. "That's very perceptive of you. Whatever happened to the girl who couldn't see beyond an iced bun?"

"Ah, well, when her father died, she had to grow up and look out for her little sister."

They hugged each other in the middle of the narrow lane that led to where Megan's car was parked. It was so out of the way, they didn't anticipate an agricultural vehicle coming. The tractor, on its way to Scorhill Farm, slowed down, allowing the driver to blast the horn.

As it passed, the farmer grinned at the pair and raised his thumb in approval.

Chapter 19

"Where did you say?"

"Mannequins…"

Jacqui couldn't make sense of the answer. It didn't seem a likely name for a cocktail bar. She held her mobile phone closer to her ear. "What, Mannequins as in tailors' dummies?"

"Yup, that's right," replied Lucy. "It's pretty whacky. They have these mannequins all over the place: on tables, behind the bar, in alcoves… some in the middle of the floor space. What's more, they frequently change the position of them, so every time you go in there, it's different. Clever, huh?"

"Dressed mannequins?" enquired Jacqui.

"Some are… boxers on the blokes, lingerie on the girls, that sort of thing," Lucy explained. "A few are completely naked. You can guess what some people have done with a felt pen…"

"Hah, sounds hilarious. Trust you to sniff out a place like that."

"Well, that one's just for starters. There are other surprises…"

"Listen, Lucy, I won't be there until a bit later; my dad's down from Kent, and you know I haven't seen him for ages. I think he's checking out the bookshop in Launceston, running through the accounts with Ross. I said I'd meet him for a drink and a convo."

"Oh, I'm so happy for you, Jacqui. That's great news! Try to be gentle with him, though…"

Jacqui never ceased to marvel at her friend's empathy. Lucy could easily have been miffed that her fast and loose friend had changed the arrangements – and not for the first time.

"I will be there, but don't hang around waiting for me. I'll find you if you've moved on," Jacqui said, keen not to complicate Lucy's plans.

"No probs. I'll drop you a line. Hey, just wondering… how did your dad get your number?"

"He didn't. I listened to what you said when we last met; I got in contact with him. He nearly dropped the phone when he heard my voice!"

"Good girl. Hey, Jacqui, I've got to go now. See you later."

Jacqui smiled at the 'good girl' reference. She wouldn't have accepted that from anyone else. She couldn't remember ever being anybody's good girl.

* * *

The evening at Mannequins was in full swing. Lucy and Hannah, who barely knew each other, had assembled a group of similar-aged women who knew each other even less. It was a brave experiment that could have gone horribly wrong.

Each participant had willingly entered the fray in an effort to change up an increasingly tired social scene, and it was instantly agreed that a few ground rules ought to be observed. There was to be no mention of work, politics, or religion. However, humorous tales of failed relationships, sexual encounters, holidays, and overspending were to be encouraged. All of the invited happened to be single and so they were all, in a sense, footloose and fancy-free. If any group member felt uneasy, they could retire without recrimination. Well, that was the theory anyway.

Lucy and Hannah's initial fears that setting 'rules' would stifle conversation were quickly allayed. The choice of venue was also an instant hit. Even at the start, when the venue was only half full, it looked lively. The fibreglass dummies added to the mix, looking like a host of scantily clad street performers. The effect was occasionally unnerving but hugely entertaining.

As early starters, the group managed to commandeer a corner of the L-shaped space, sitting on two large Chesterfield sofas divided by a long oak table. The furniture was well worn but supremely comfortable. The cracked lines of the leather seating may have looked like the skin of fading film stars, but they held the full panoply of tales to match their years of service. The industrial modern décor and lighting provided extra ambience; it was moody enough for secrets to slip, but light enough to gauge reaction.

It was primarily a cocktail bar, so after two hours, a variety of different-shaped glasses furnished with bent soggy straws, cocktail sticks, spent citrus fruit slices, and depleted ice cubes adorned the table. It was already looking deliriously chaotic.

Carmen had confessed to backing out of a threesome at the last minute. That had left two guys, who were complete strangers, staring at each other dressed only in their underpants. Cherise tried to up the ante by admitting she'd been duped by identical twins. Hannah, realising it was her turn to confront the confessional, recounted falling asleep, stark naked, on her made bed, on a hot summer's day, only to be awoken by the window cleaner. Anecdotes were traded and stories were embellished while the listeners – holding their sidecars, mojitos and Singapore slings – shrieked and squirmed in equal measure.

The pair of mannequins, directly next to their sofas, soon became objects of attention. The male – dressed in black boxers, a bow tie, and a pair of sunglasses – provoked much drunken hilarity. The 'pouch' that protruded encouraged several of the women to share details of various unwanted pictures they'd received via WhatsApp.

Sandra, however, although sharing the fun, was more interested in the female dummy, dressed in a blonde wig and lingerie. Whilst the others sensibly slowed down, knowing they had other bars to visit, Sandra was just hitting her stride. The effect of the sizable quantity of alcohol had made her carelessly and dangerously drawn towards objects of desire. She began to secretly revel in the fact that while her friends were drooling over the muscular chest, biceps, and sturdy thighs of the male, she was transfixed by the curves, clasps, and lace of the adjacent figure.

Unconsciously, her left hand went straight to her newly purchased necklace. She caressed it almost as if it were the comfort to a nervous habit. As a child, she would clutch a tiny felt rabbit that held all of life's familiar smells. Unlike the previous outing with her sister, she let the platinum necklace sit loud and proud over the top of her short black dress.

After Lucy had 'plumped up' the dummy with a few tissues under its boxer shorts, she checked her watch. It was time to move on to the next bar, but Jacqui still hadn't showed. She looked across at Hannah's newly found Pilates friend, Sandra. She was becoming very animated, which was hardly surprising; she had complemented each of the last few rounds with chasers. Lucy thought that Jacqui would have latched onto her in an instant, and she could imagine them becoming partners in crime. She had a great sense of humour, but wasn't in the least bit shallow.

Her real worry was that Jacqui might arrive too late… or not at all. It was one reason why she hadn't announced to the group that they were incomplete.

Hannah sidled up next to Lucy, moving her hips and arms in a drunken imitation of the Twist. "Time for a dance and a mingle. How about 'Toots', across town?"

"Yes, I'm with you on that. It's not too far and the fresh air will do us good," Lucy replied. "Cherise and Carmen are in the lav. Where's Sandra?"

"Over there, by the door. She's just seen an old school friend who was just about to leave. She's starting to sway a bit." Hannah laughed.

"Well, I've had a few, but she's been drinking in between rounds."

Lucy and Hannah observed Sandra's ebullience. She was clearly enjoying herself. However, the warning signs were not difficult to detect. They looked at each other knowingly.

"Okay, let's round up the troops," Lucy declared.

Sandra could see the girls collecting their bags and making their way over to her, so she broke away from her conversation and called them over. "Hey girls, I've had the time of my life, but you go on without me."

"Don't be daft – we'll wait for you," Carmen spluttered, still giggling from the conversation she'd had with Cherise in the ladies' toilets.

"Girls, I'm not used to this, and I'm nearly done," Sandra admitted. "I'm just signing off with an old school chum and then I'd better grab a taxi home. Honestly, it's been a blast, but I'm getting a bit wrecked; I should have paced myself a little better."

Feeling responsible that she hadn't gauged Sandra's lack of experience in boozy evenings, Lucy managed to get serious. "Sandra, that's a real shame, because you've been such a laugh. But now, listen to me: you must promise to get that taxi. No walking anywhere alone. If you change your mind, a couple of us will come back for you."

"Thanks. I'll do that… I promise."

Hannah moved closer to Sandra and touched her arm affectionately. "It was great to have you along, Sandra. I'll catch you later."

Sandra hugged the group and watched them leave. She then returned to her friend, who was laughing.

"A good bunch of mates there. Do you meet in here often?"

"No, that's the first time. I haven't had such a good 'crack' for ages."

"Well, I come in here from time to time, so perhaps we'll bump into each other again. Look, I have to go. I've got a lift waiting for me." With that, her friend opened the door, turned, and waved goodbye.

Sandra – who was standing in the doorway – gave a thumbs-up signal and was just about to return to buy another drink when a taxi stopped in the middle of the road, slightly ahead of where she was standing. For some reason, Sandra felt the need to see who was getting out of the vehicle. She recognised, immediately, her habit of becoming more interested in people-watching after she'd consumed one too many drinks. It was bordering on being nosy.

The occupant leant forward to pay for the ride and then opened the rear door of the car. The swivel of her legs, and the consummate ease at which she exited the taxi, took Sandra by surprise. It should have occurred to her that the woman was heading her way, but when she strode purposefully in her direction, Sandra instinctively turned to see her friend disappearing down the street. Being nosy was one thing; being caught out being nosy, quite another.

Without making eye contact, the woman breezed past Sandra, who was still holding the door open. The waft of her scent was intoxicating. Sandra found herself tilting her nose up a fraction, trying to gather in more of the heady fragrance.

It all happened in a fleeting moment, and by the time she'd gathered herself, Sandra realised she'd missed the opportunity to take a good look at the woman's face. Instead, she found herself staring at the rear view – fuchsia-pink trailing hair, long flowing coat, military-style camouflaged leggings, and DM boots – of the dreamy apparition that had just sailed past her.

* * *

As the taxi drew up outside the fashionable, newly opened bar, Jacqui checked her phone – it was late. It had been a very constructive meeting with her father, but it had been quite a rush to get ready for the night ahead. She also noted that there were no new messages; presumably, the gang was getting deliciously merry inside. However, the mobile phone signal was known to be very unreliable in these parts, and they may have already flown the nest. She leant over to the driver and gave him more than enough for the ride.

Eager to join the action, Jacqui then exited the cab and made for the entrance. She cheekily brushed past a stunningly dressed reveller holding open the door. It would have been polite to say, "Thanks", but the woman was looking elsewhere and didn't seem to be paying much attention. Secretly, she was hoping her Alice Roberts-inspired hair colour would have attracted at least a glance.

Jacqui scanned all that was before her as she made her way to the bar. Lucy was correct: the mannequins that were dotted around the space looked amazing. It was a great concept. She laughed at the absurdity of it all. An approaching coat stand to the left prompted her to make herself more comfortable. She checked she had her phone in her bag and then found an available stool.

Although the bar wasn't crowded, several mixologists were busy creating cocktails. Desperate for a drink and waiting patiently for the never-before-tried lotus martini, Jacqui pulled her mobile from her bag to check again for updates. There was nothing, though it was obvious that Lucy and co. had moved on. As there was still a lack of comms, she decided to stay for one drink and then re-evaluate.

Ordinarily, she would have welcomed attention from a man chancing his luck with the odd crass chat-up line; usually, it was highly amusing and a lot of fun. This evening, however, she wanted a night free from the dating game. Making instant assessments and adjusting your own behaviour could be very tiring if you weren't in the mood.

Jacqui braced herself for the inevitable, 'Can I buy you a drink?' when – to her delight – the girl she'd seen at the door climbed onto the seat next to her. At that moment, the bartender delivered the cocktail Jacqui had ordered, placing it before her. The V-shaped conical glass containing the indigo-coloured lotus martini looked suitably striking.

"You beauty…" Jacqui raised the glass to eye level in order to assess the translucent shade. She couldn't decide whether it was blue or purple.

* * *

Sandra moved away from the door and examined the room for a suitable place to stand and make a phone call for a cab. Perhaps another drink was going to be one too many. The sensible course of action – which she'd relayed to her newly found friends – was soon abandoned, however, when she caught sight of the shock of fuchsia-pink hair in the bar area. It was enough to set her mind racing again. She had only seen a fleeting glimpse of the girl's face as she left the taxi, and was intrigued to find out more. She couldn't seem to stop herself – even though she knew it could end in disaster or, at the very least, severe embarrassment.

As Sandra closed in, she expected to see the girl in conversation with a group of friends – or a guy who was easy on the eye – but, to her surprise, she was alone. Furthermore, the bar stool next to her was available.

Wanting to capture the prize, Sandra almost lurched towards the seat. In her woozy state, she awkwardly sat on the stool. Luckily for Sandra, the girl next to her was more interested in the cocktail she'd ordered and failed to notice her lack of finesse.

Sandra settled herself and watched intently as the girl raised her drink, admiringly, to eye level. Sandra was just about to utter her favourite phrase for such situations, when, to her amazement, the girl used the very same line.

"Hah, that's something I say," Sandra said, pleased to be able to use such a convenient conversation starter, "…and it certainly is a beauty."

"Never had one before, so this ought to be interesting. Care to join me, or are you waiting for someone?" the girl asked in a friendly tone.

After her near accident climbing the bar stool, Sandra was caught off guard. She had expected the girl to smile politely and ignore her comment. In a fluster, she started to apologise. "I've already had one too many, and I was just going to order a cab. You probably saw me looking a little unsteady by the door… the fresh air and all that…"

As soon as she'd uttered the words, Sandra regretted her overly subtle, trying-not-to-be-too-eager approach. It also betrayed that she'd marked the woman's arrival. That was embarrassing.

"Don't be too hasty. How about you have one more with me, and then I'll get that taxi? You look as though you might need some help."

Sandra couldn't believe her luck – she thought she'd messed up.

She caught the profile of the girl's face as she took a sip of her martini. She was relieved to see that she wasn't a pin-up beauty; neither was she a clone of the fashionable girls who paraded around the local town centre. Everything about her was wonderfully interesting, yet strangely arcane. She felt a rush of excitement.

"Do you know, I think I will," Sandra gushed. "Nothing doing tomorrow, so who cares?" Sandra caught the eye of a bartender who had just served a customer. "Can I have the same cocktail as this lovely lady sitting next to me, please? Sorry, haven't a clue what it's called."

"Ooh, fiercely independent, are we?" the girl said, surprised. "The pleasure was mine."

"They cost a fortune, and I might not live up to expectation…"

"Sounds interesting," said the woman. "What am I expecting?"

Instead of floundering, Sandra tapped into the flow. "Oh, I don't know… stimulating conversation that lasts as long as it takes for you to finish your drink. Something like that?"

"I'm intrigued. Where shall we start?"

Given an open invitation, Sandra glanced at the girl. Her fuchsia shade of pink hair was too obvious to comment upon, and it would have been too weird to compliment her leggings. She wasn't about to comment on the state of the nation, or why Christianity was on the decline in the western world. Then, out of the blue, she found a suitable response. "I love the way you get out of the back seat of a car…"

* * *

Jacqui wasn't expecting such left-field flattery. It made her laugh out loud and she almost failed to reposition her glass safely on the bar. "I get out of the car just like everybody else," she defended, still giggling.

"Well yeah, but you keep your knees beautifully together, turn, plant your feet on the floor, and then spring upwards and out. It's like a film star. I'm like an octopus…" Her neighbour swivelled towards her and imitated the action. Jacqui caught sight of the woman's shapely legs, clothed in fishnet tights and boots.

"Wow… someone's been a tad nosy. Do you make a habit of spying on women getting out of cars?"

"Not guilty," she laughed. "Just spying on women, generally."

A spotlight from overhead caught the woman's necklace and the reflection dazzled Jacqui's eyes for a fraction as it moved. It was enough for her to reach out and place two fingers underneath the pendant.

"Back to back crescent moons, eh? Nice necklace. That's a beauty as well. A real beauty. There's nothing quite like a piece of jewellery that tells a story…"

Their eyes locked for a brief moment.

Jacqui could feel Ruthven rising. She felt the unannounced upheaval: the glorious sticky sweat and increased heart rate. The flood of dopamine. She knew Ruthven made her behaviour risky, but she loved it. She hadn't anticipated a new adventure, but one had seemed to fall into her lap. Really, it would be rude not to…

The girl in the black dress held the pendant and looked straight at Jacqui. She was dying to intimate its code but she knew that, like a French courtship ritual, the occasion required oblique references and knowing glances.

"I like to think of it as representing the new me," she announced, coquettishly.

"So what would the old you have been like?" Jacqui teased, trying to glean more information. "Tell me more."

"Safe... afraid to cross the Rubicon. Living a good life, but only half a life."

Ruthven tapped Jacqui on the shoulder, indicating it was time to take the wheel. "And once you cross... do you plan to return?"

"Ah, now there's the rub," the woman replied, "I haven't thought that far ahead. What's your take on that?"

"I don't plan anything. I go wherever the prevailing winds take me. But be warned: I often leave a trail of destruction behind me." Ruthven winked, teasingly burrowing her eyes into the girl sitting next to her.

"So you've been there? What's it like?" the woman asked, finding the thought of wanton behaviour very alluring. After all, she had lived her whole life following convention.

"Well now, perhaps the wind has never blown me in that direction... I'm not giving away *all* my secrets."

* * *

Sandra was utterly transfixed, but still wary. The woman sitting beside her was either leading her a merry dance for the thrill of it, or she was laying it on thick because she might be up for fun and games later on. She certainly had more 'rizz' than the labels on her father's old Genesis LPs – the last few minutes had been a euphemism fest. The lexicon gymnastics had been so deliriously intoxicating – and she loved playing those games, especially when she'd had a few drinks.

When Sandra's cocktail arrived, it seemed to herald a lighter tone of conversation. Picking up the glass, she looked closely at the contents. She tried to take a demure sip, but it turned into more of a slurp. "Wow, that's not bad at all. Good choice. More indigo than blue, I'd say."

The girl laughed and touched Sandra's knee affectionately. "How many have you had? If I let you phone for the taxi, you'd end up ordering a takeaway."

"That's food for thought..." Sandra replied, quick off the mark.

"Kerching! An attempt at humour, eh? Perhaps you're not quite as juiced up as you appear. Maybe you're quite capable of fending off all these predatory males around here."

They both looked around the room for a few moments.

"As an old boy I once met said, 'Men: mean, envious, and nasty'. Guess I'll take a rain check this time." Sandra fixed her eyes back on her cocktail, nervously twiddling the stem of the glass. Perhaps she'd been too obvious.

"Well said, that girl. They can be a little predictable... and persistent. But then again, if I inspired no reaction at all, I'd be as miffed as hell! Guess that's just girls." She raised her glass.

Sandra raised hers to join the mock toast. "Guess that's just girls..."

Both women tipped back their glasses. It felt like a celebration of sorts, though neither could quite fathom what they were celebrating.

Sandra felt like she was standing on the edge of a chasm. She simply didn't know how to take it to the next stage. She wanted to invite the captivating 30-something back to her place, but the girl hadn't long arrived. Presumably, she was meeting someone and was just filling in time. Although things had worked out better than she could ever have imagined, she was preparing herself for the fall.

It always seemed to turn out that way.

* * *

Jacqui would have been delighted with the edgy fun she'd just experienced, but she could feel that Ruthven wanted to push the boundaries. Out of the corner of her eye, she saw a tiny flash of light emitting from her bag. More than likely, she figured, it was Lucy messaging her about where to find them. Ruthven, however, had other ideas…

"Hey hun, I have to powder my nose. Can you save this seat for me? Don't go wandering off now," she said to the woman sitting next to her, who smiled in response.

Jacqui needed the break to consider her next move.

She made her way to the toilets and weighed up the two options. The sensible course of action was obviously to meet up with Lucy and the others. She was guaranteed a few laughs and would, no doubt, meet some new, like-minded souls. That could be very beneficial going forward. However, she was already late to the party, and it was always difficult joining the throng when you'd already missed so much of the action.

By the time Jacqui had rationalised Plan A, she knew it was a non-starter; Ruthven was itching to push things forward at a pace.

She had considered what it would be like to have a same-sex encounter before, but the opportunity had never presented itself. Although Ruthven enjoyed taking risks, they were never pre-planned. Never forced. The thrill of it came from the moment.

Ruthven could feel the sour taste in her mouth that always preceded a thrust into the unknown. The situation was ideal: the girl was alone, very attractive, intelligent, and interesting. They hadn't even shared names, so the affair would be containable. The girl had also intimated that she hadn't popped her same-sex cherry either. If it didn't work out and turned into a fiasco, therefore, there would be nothing lost apart from a few hurt feelings and some embarrassment.

And then, of course, there was the sigil.

Jacqui reined in the force she felt within; there would be an opportunity to adorn the earrings later. Ruthven knew how to take experiences beyond the mundane, but it would be Jacqui who had the nous to make it happen. It was time for a cool head.

* * *

"Thought I'd scared you off – you've been ages," Sandra said as light-heartedly as she could.

"Queue in the loo. Same old SNAFU... so, while I was waiting, I booked that cab for you. And... as it happens, you won't have to wait long. It'll be here in five."

Sandra was crestfallen, but she tried to adopt a brave face. "Oh… thank you. I'd better drink up. That's… very kind of you. I've enjoyed our little chat. I wish I'd met you earlier."

Sandra looked across and saw that the girl had already slung her bag over her shoulder, her body language indicating that it was time to gather their coats and make for the door. She was confused. Was her newly found friend going to see her safely to the taxi, or was she going to move on to her next destination? She was so disappointed that her evening was drawing to a close that she remained silent. She couldn't muster the right words to say.

As they threaded their way through the now very busy cocktail bar, Sandra was desperately trying to work out how to maintain contact with the stranger who had captivated her for the last half an hour or so. It occurred to her that she knew nothing about her. What did you even say in these circumstances? Could you ask for someone's details when you were just about to be bundled into a cab? Something must have happened to change things – otherwise, how could she have misread the situation so badly?

Sandra opened the door and took some unsteady steps out onto the pavement. The cold air hit her, and her eyes took time to focus; the contrast between the dimly lit interior and the brightly lit street was traumatic. A further shock came when an arm reached out and held her around the waist. The feeling of warmth and being cared for travelled up through her spine to the nape of her neck. She wanted to reciprocate by resting her head on the girl's shoulder, but she saw a car approaching.

"You didn't have to do this for me. Thank you so much." By now, she had resigned herself to the fact that the girl was out of reach. She had slipped away… just like all the others.

"No worries, it was a pleasure." Her voice, although dreamily sensual, was no comfort.

Once the vehicle had stopped, the woman opened the door of the cab and ushered Sandra into the back seat.

She almost fell into the car – laughing at her own inability to negotiate the tricky manoeuvre – and didn't notice the driver opening his window to take instructions.

It all happened in a blur.

"Shift your arse, there's gotta be room for one more in here…"

Sandra was aware of a perfumed body edging up next to her. When the electric vehicle moved away from the kerb at a surprising speed, she found herself rolling around, trying to find the seat belt.

"Where are we going?" giggled Sandra, finding the whole experience rather amusing, yet also confusing. "You don't know where I live!" she yelled at the driver.

She turned, and was surprised see her cryptic Goddess looking at her.

"That would be my place, I guess."

Chapter 20

Sandra knew the area well, but she'd been more interested in her fellow passenger in the back seat of the taxi than trying to ascertain the postcode. The pair thanked the driver and made their way up the path to the front door. It was a modern ground-floor apartment in a reasonably affluent neighbourhood. Everything about the exterior was neat and tidy, but it betrayed no secrets about the owner.

The girl found her key and opened the door. She flicked a few switches and various rooms came to life, flooded with tasteful lighting.

"Nice place," remarked Sandra.

"Yeah, I like it. There's just me, so it doesn't need to be too grand. Give me your coat; I'll put it in the spare room. Why don't you take a seat in the lounge? I'll only be a jiffy."

Sandra handed her coat to her mystery companion, unzipped her boots, and placed them near the door. In her stockinged feet, she padded silently on the engineered oak wooden flooring and perched herself, nervously, on the edge of a comfortable-looking sofa.

As she was sitting there, Sandra played a few scenarios in her mind. Half of her was happy that her wooziness had allowed her to be marvellously carefree. The other half was trying to steady the ship and watch out for sandbanks. The interplay was intensely exciting.

It wasn't long before the owner of the house returned. Rather than sit on an adjacent chair, the girl crossed the boundary of social norms and sat tightly next to her.

The rhythm of Sandra's breathing leapt uncontrollably. Her vision swam in anticipation. An arm curled around her waist and she felt the strong command of the girl's hands. She moved willingly, tipping her head at an angle as she was sucked towards the embrace.

The two girls locked eyes in consensual, non-verbal play, both realising that the kiss was inevitable.

* * *

Even though Ruthven was bold and reckless, she searched behind the woman's eyes to see if the feeling was mutual. The rules of engagement could be very different with a woman. She knew they were complex creatures because her own mood swings were impossible to predict. When did a man ever turn down the opportunity for sex?

And then she thought of Jack. For a fleeting moment her confidence waned. However, the woman's desire to reciprocate and push things further had gone beyond the point of no return. She moved her head to the right and closed the gap to a mere finger's width, leaving Ruthven room for the final push toward the summit.

Ruthven met the girl's advances and their lips collided. At first it was surprisingly soft and touching, but then their coupling became urgent and hungry. Ruthven moved her right hand and pressed the girl ever closer.

SIGIL

* * *

Sandra felt the brush of soft lips and the smooth skin around the woman's mouth. She smelled the citrus notes of perfume from her neck. She felt their breasts crushing against each other in the warm embrace. It was a world away from her last experience with a man.

Unconsciously, they knew when to part. Sandra moved her head back a distance to where she could feast her eyes on the woman's features and begin to fathom her aura. She laughed in happiness. The girl, who beamed, mirrored the joy. Both were relieved at the outcome.

Sandra moved her hands and placed them onto the girl's shoulders, while she complemented her movements by wrapping both hands around Sandra's waist. It was a significant moment for both of them.

At that same moment, an ancient ringtone from an old mobile phone could be heard coming from another room. The girl was obviously embarrassed; her radiant smile turned into an awkward grimace.

"Why don't you go and answer? It might be important," Sandra said, understanding how she must be feeling. It was almost comical.

"It won't be as important as this…"

"Go on, I'm not going anywhere," Sandra reassured her. "We can resume when you come back," she added tenderly, touching the woman's face with her hand.

The caller was persistent and the phone was still ringing as the host disappeared into the room next door. Sandra couldn't help but overhear the girl's voice.

"Hello."

Intrigued to find out who could be calling at such an hour, Sandra strained her ears to detect a reply, but she couldn't hear anything. She was sitting too far away.

"Ross, look, this is really bad timing. Call me tomorrow – bye."

The level of the woman's voice and the abruptness reassured Sandra that this *Ross* was unlikely to be a lover.

"Ross, wondering where his girl is tonight?" Sandra called out, not being able to resist a tease.

The girl appeared at the doorway. "Ross? He wishes! He's probably had a few and decided, at this time of night, to invite me to some book launch."

"Hah, I know a few like that… hey, by the way, what's with the two phones? I hope I haven't just kissed a spy!"

"Just an old one that still works. I leave it here at home," she lied. "I've never been that savvy at transferring my contacts. Boy Scout, me: 'Be prepared'. Anyway, don't go anywhere, hun; I'm just going to be a few minutes." Seductively, the girl blew a kiss and disappeared into a bedroom.

Sandra knew that the excitement of the kiss and the amount of alcohol she'd consumed had totally affected her thinking. If she was nervous before she entered the flat, she was jittery and apprehensive now. She knew that it felt wonderful and natural, but something about the phone call had alerted her senses. Unfortunately, her role as a Detective Sergeant had always interfered in her modus operandi. Most of the time, it was a curse.

She dismissed the negative feeling as quickly as it had come.

* * *

Jacqui was used to late-night phone calls from Ross; he seemed to presume that everybody in his social circle would be on tap in the late hours. She also knew he liked to offload problems before he slept, which was a worry… after the good news he'd given her that Jack was heading home, she had begun to relax about any potential 'difficulties'.

She cut the phone dead in case the moment between her and the attractive woman currently sitting on her sofa had passed. It was just getting interesting. She then placed the phone in her top drawer and, in so doing, noticed the jewellery box containing the sigil. She felt an immediate draw towards it. If ever there was a moment to unleash its potential, it was now.

Her mind flashed back to its unveiling: the way the two teardrops had danced underneath her fingers. The woman wouldn't exactly be a willing participant in the ritual, but hopefully she would enjoy the outcome. Besides, Jacqui reasoned, her alter ego had already decided.

Ruthven threw a kiss in the direction of the girl and bought herself a moment or two to adorn the golden twins, diving back into her bedroom to replace her studs with the sigil teardrops.

It was emotional. Ruthven felt energised as she checked the effect in the mirror. They were stunning.

Forget the dopamine rush; these feel-good neurotransmitters that hung beneath her lobes were creating a storm.

And a perfect one at that.

* * *

Sandra tried to be as casual as possible, though the last minute had seemed like a lifetime. She couldn't recall a guy asking for a few moments by himself in the throes of passion. Not being at all skilled in the arts of wooing a woman, she resigned herself to the fact that these things were entirely plausible.

All of her fears were allayed when the girl appeared by the door again, raising her index finger in a beckoning motion. "Hey, honey, why don't you come into the bedroom? I think we'll be more comfortable here."

Sandra giggled at the cheesy, B-movie script line. Enjoying playing along, she stood up, straightened her dress, and strutted across the lounge with a seductive swagger to meet her temptress.

They kissed again by the doorway. After a few seconds, the girl withdrew from the clinch and held her hand out. Sandra willingly accepted the invitation and was led into a spacious, well-decorated room.

Sandra knew immediately that something was different about the second kiss, but she couldn't quite put her finger on what it was. Perhaps her fuchsia-pink-haired siren had applied more lipstick after the phone call.

After being motioned toward the bed, she perched herself on the edge, next to the pillows. The girl knelt on the floor before her. She looked down at her playmate, who had now inched Sandra's dress up so that she could rest both hands just above her knees.

Instinctively, Sandra looked away, nearly jumping it was so thrilling and intense.

At that moment, in her peripheral vision, she caught sight of a book lying on the carpet next to the bedside cabinet. Normally that would not have piqued her interest, but the name 'Osman Spare' – emboldened across the front cover – caught her attention.

Sandra knew at once that something was amiss, but she managed to hide her angst. The girl giggled, pleased to have provoked such a reaction. She moved her hands a fraction of an inch higher up Sandra's thigh. She was clearly enjoying the power play.

Sandra felt the girl pushing her knees apart and moving her body in between. She turned her head back towards the movement, wondering and waiting to see what was about to happen next. Normally, her vulnerability at being in such a submissive situation would have heightened her excitement, but she was still trying to comprehend her feeling of uneasiness. She found herself gazing at the woman who was looking up at her.

Something about her was different… and then she realised why.

Still staring into the eyes of the girl who was now moving in for another kiss, Sandra – in a power play of her own – moved her hands up and held the woman's head. She affectionately brushed away the hair of the girl to reveal her ear and neck. Again, a waft of perfume sent Sandra into a dizzy spiral. She leant forward, almost in slow motion, to kiss the soft skin.

In so doing, she couldn't help but take in the teardrop earring that hung exposed. She gasped. "Did you put these on for me? They're exquisite."

"My favourite earrings for a *very* special occasion," the girl replied, whispering in Sandra's ear.

Sandra placed her hand underneath the woman's left earring to examine it in greater detail. "The filigree is so fine. My god, there are actual letters in gold. What do they say?"

"You get to find that out after you've claimed your prize," the girl purred.

And then it hit Sandra. She recognised the unique design – the one-off masterpiece Jack had denied any responsibility for.

All the other oblique references collided and were processed into one clear picture. It couldn't possibly be coincidence. She glanced at the girl's upper cheek and detected the faint – but visible – scar. Her eyes fell to the woman's hands, still clasping her thighs. The brilliant, sky-blue nails appeared like the undersides of ten jet aircraft flying in V formations, homing in on their target: the Osman Spare book, the mention of 'Ross'… and then there were those spectacular earrings, hanging like ripe fruit, which had been crafted by the gifted but eccentric Mr Alsop in Chagford.

She didn't want to believe it – she didn't want to confront it – but it was inevitable.

"Gorgeous girl, I can only claim my prize if you tell me your name," Sandra said, her heart beating fast.

"My name?" The question caught the woman off guard.

"Only, Daddy told me to never go with strangers. I would never do that…"

"Your daddy was a smart man…"

"And?" Sandra asked, kissing her neck once more.

"…And, my name is Ruthven."

Chapter 21

Sandra inserted her key into the front door – taking a few tries to get it right – and let herself in. It had been a long and eventful night, and as she staggered into her seemingly desolate house, she was still under the influence of alcohol.

Tonight had been another close encounter, and equally, another failure.

Now, however, was not the time to pour herself another drink in the hopes of erasing the abject feeling of unfulfillment and loneliness; she was too aware of the slippery slope that awaited such an action. No, it was a hot beverage she was craving, and a black coffee was the obvious choice.

Sandra kicked off her heels, but – as the residual heat from the radiators had long since dissipated – kept her coat on for warmth. She made her way to the kitchen, turned on the lights, and unceremoniously dumped her bag on the worktop.

It occurred to her that it was the absence of connection, not the lack of people in her life, that made it so disappointing. Her sister and her colleagues, like Mark, certainly added colour to her world, and she knew that they cared for her. They were, however, not always available – or aware enough – to bolster her crumbling confidence; they had their own lives to lead. Also, Sandra knew how good she was at masking her mental deterioration.

She half-filled the kettle, flicked the switch, and prepared herself for the jarring cacophony she knew it was about to make – especially as there were no other sounds at this time of the morning to mask the hideousness.

Her thoughts inevitably flickered back to Ruthven – or Jacqui, as she had discovered her name actually was. The taxi drive home had given her some time to reflect on how the evening had come spectacularly crashing down without warning, but honestly, it was just too incredible for words.

Her role as a detective in the police force had, once again, scuppered any ideas of personal happiness, and she was deeply resentful of that.

As Sandra waited for the kettle to boil, she replayed moments from the evening in her head, like when Ruthven had floated past her at the cocktail bar, leaving 'contrails' of intoxicating perfume behind her; the knowing look on Ruthven's face when she spied her newly purchased necklace; their first embrace and the softness of her kiss; Ruthven's hands edging up her thighs, provoking an electrical charge that had taken her breath away; and then, the sight of the beautiful, enigmatic teardrop earrings – the unfortunate curtain call, without applause.

Sandra loaded her French press with a hefty scoop of ground coffee. *Desperate measures*, she thought, amazed that she could still think of puns, even at her lowest ebb. Maybe it was a habit. She poured the boiling water into the vessel and watched the grounds swirl and settle like a child with a sensory glitter bottle.

It was easy to float back to the extraordinary events that had followed the reveal…

Ruthven had proudly proclaimed her name, clearly expecting intrigue and wonder. Instead, Sandra remembered pulling away and hiding her face in her hands. At once, she had realised the ramifications of such an announcement. After all, the name was so unusual.

So, Jack had been telling the truth all along; Ruthven was no figment of his imagination, no lie.

From that certainty, like numbers falling into place at the end of a Sudoku puzzle, a series of unanswered questions regarding the case suddenly became clear: Ruthven had taken the route off Fur Tor as Jack had indicated; she must have seen, or met, Victoria on her way to her car; she knew Victoria because she had the sigil; Ruthven must have taken the earrings from her house; she knew Ross, because of the phone call…

Like shelling peas from a pod, Sandra had fired the statements off, bringing the crushing reality to bear.

Ruthven must have sensed, immediately, that something was wrong; she'd stood up and taken Sandra's hand away from her face, to see what was going on.

Sandra replayed the moment when she'd stared into Ruthven's eyes and said, "Tell me your real name – and sit down, because we need to talk… for Jack Reilly's sake."

Ruthven had blurted out, in panic, "Who are you? How do you know Jack? What is this – some kind of entrapment?"

Sandra sighed. That question had hurt, because she really did like her. Ruthven had truly captivated her… and then it had turned, all too swiftly, into yet another failure. It was the last thing that Sandra had wanted to happen. The word 'entrapment' particularly stung because she'd then had to reveal her own identity as a homicide detective. She knew it was going to take time to convince Ruthven that it was nothing more than a crazy coincidence, or at least, the fault of mutual friends of friends – as she had found out later. And then, of course, there was the possibility that Victoria's death had been no accident…

When Ruthven – or Jacqui, as she later revealed – had heard about Jack Reilly's plight and the connection between Sandra and the case, she had immediately crashed down to her own ground zero. There was no fight or pretence left. She had sat down beside Sandra and willingly retold everything she knew, convincing Sandra that, on that fateful afternoon, she'd only heard Victoria's distant shouts. There was no shove or angry exchange. She had simply pushed on towards Hare Tor and beyond due to the atrocious weather.

She had also admitted to using Victoria's key – which had been hidden under her car – to enter her house. There, she had deposited the St Christopher, and then taken the sigil earrings and the Austin Osman Spare book.

Of course, once Sandra had realised that Jack was telling the truth, all those details made perfect sense. What Sandra hadn't countenanced was Jacqui's motive for such extreme behaviour. What had she got to hide?

What followed was an emotional outpouring. She had told Sandra all about the original GST cancer diagnosis, the desire to live life as if there were no tomorrow, the realisation that she was adopted, her interest in the occult, and the clandestine pact with Ross, Chris, and Victoria, based at the bookshop. Jacqui had explained her changing relationship with Victoria, but recognised the deceased's altruistic brilliance in designing and creating the sigil for her enlightenment and benefit. She had recounted solving the code that unlocked the sigil, and the revelation of the words that emerged. She had admitted that she'd been too hasty in condemning Victoria as overbearing. Perhaps, in hindsight, her own demands had clouded her judgement. Sandra thought that her desire to remain anonymous was understandable, if a little wayward.

But Jacqui didn't stop there. She went on to flesh out the connection between her parents and Jack's parents, the origin of the blemish on her upper cheek, Jack's discovery of the photo in the album, and his detective work at finding her father's location.

It was incredible – and unbelievable, especially Jacqui's account of the meeting at Combestone Tor and the bargain Jack had reluctantly agreed to.

Once Sandra had grasped that Mr Rourke owned the bookshop in Launceston, the whole connection between Jacqui and Ross became clear. It was almost too much to comprehend. But, then again, she had guessed that Ross was being economical with the truth.

As Sandra poured the coffee as carefully as she could manage, she cursed the alcohol; the effects of so many cocktails had caught up with her. Once she had left the warm cocoon of the taxi, the cold air had hit her like a battering ram. Finding her key and identifying the slot in the door had been rather comical at first, but then very frustrating.

The hot drink tasted good, but she realised it was dripping on her dress; she could feel the warm dampness on her legs. Clearly, her first pour had partially missed its target.

In the grand scheme of things, it was nothing, but sensing the downward spiral, Sandra began to weep.

* * *

Jacqui couldn't think about sleep: it was out of the question. Her mind was racing, even after several hours of talking to Detective Sergeant Sandra Baines. As Ruthven, she had always been up for risky encounters, but what had just happened was out of even her league. And, of course, none of that really mattered after she heard the news about Jack.

It suddenly occurred to her that when Ross had phoned, he'd been intending to tell her all about it, but she'd shut him down because it was, quite frankly, bad timing. Typical.

Again, that didn't matter at all now. Jack was languishing in a hospital in a coma. She'd promised him before that if it got really serious, she would be there for him, and she wasn't going to let him down now. She had some serious making up to do – if, of course, he managed to survive. She coughed, almost retching at the thought of him lying there, connected to tubes and wires, his life hanging in the balance.

At three o'clock in the morning, however – or whatever time it was right then – she knew she wouldn't be able to see him. It would obviously have to wait until the next available opportunity, and that frustrated her like hell. Jacqui was used to living in the here and now.

Shaking her head, she admonished herself for her flippant attitude with the whole saga. It was almost like a game – but people had got hurt and, once again, she was at the centre of it all. She hadn't recognised the severity of the situation. Jack had tried to explain, but she just hadn't seen it… or, at least, she hadn't seen it his way.

Jacqui moved from her lounge to the kitchen. What she needed now was a large glass of Shiraz; that might help her sleep. It occurred to her that, apart from the cocktail at the bar, she hadn't drunk anything else that night. Once the lovebirds had left Mannequins in the taxi, the only heady mixture she'd been after was the delectable Sandra.

She allowed herself half a smile. It was strange that when she'd entered the cocktail bar, all she'd been looking for was a girls' night out, not a liaison. What was it that intrigued her about the possibility of something even slightly risky? Why did she leap at the opportunity? Was her life really that shallow?

She acknowledged that she had some personal demons to negotiate, which allowed her at least some defence, and – up until the moment that she'd revealed her alter ego – it had been a hell of a lot of fun.

Jacqui watched the rich, dark red wine splash into the glass. Then, having performed the task without spilling a drop, she raised the vessel and wondered if it was a good idea to drink it after all.

At that moment, she caught a fleeting image of her face; the reflections caused by the kitchen spotlights hitting the sigil earrings threw sparkles of light against the surface of the wine glass. Amongst the turmoil of the last few hours, Jacqui had forgotten she was still wearing them.

She reached up and felt the radiating metal dangling, like ripe fruit, from her left ear. Then, without ceremony – but with the deepest reverence – she removed the teardrops from her ears and placed the golden twins onto the worktop. She knew, at once, that their 'second outing' would be their most important undertaking: she would take them to see Jack.

As a recipient of the sigil, she was aware that any effect of the subconscious 'charge' that Victoria had gifted her was hardly likely to be transferable. If it worked at all, it certainly didn't work like that. However, just as Jack had passed the St Christopher pendant on to her, it was the thought – not the physical object – that mattered.

She also knew that she'd need to present the most positive version of herself at Jack's bedside if she were to be of any use to him at all. There was no doubt in her mind that the sigil experience had given her a different outlook on her future and, in that way alone, Victoria had managed to 'give her life.' There was, after all, more to living than the physical nature of being.

Jacqui concluded that she couldn't offer Jack much, but it was all she had to give him – and she was running out of time.

* * *

Jacqui strode purposefully towards the hospital entrance. She didn't want to be late, and it was imperative that Beth should see her as a dependable and unfailing friend to Jack – even though she had hardly been that before his accident.

Luckily, that very morning, Jack's sister had received a call from Sandra. In an effort to tie up all the loose ends, Sandra had explained everything. She had rightly concluded that Jacqui would want to see Jack and had therefore prepared the way for this to happen. Fortunately for Jacqui, Beth could see the bigger picture: even if there was just the smallest chance that Jack would react to his newfound friend's voice and awake from his perpetual nightmare, it would be worth it.

Jacqui didn't know how to recognise Beth, but a woman who looked slightly older than her sibling was waiting patiently by the front door of the hospital. Jacqui took a sharp intake of breath; she could see that days of worry and anguish had taken their toll on Jack's sister. It was amazing how the lines on one's face told so many tales.

Jacqui flinched, feeling the heavy weight of expectation. She needed to make a good first impression, though she understood that this visit was not all about her. She reminded herself that Beth had been gracious enough to allow her the opportunity to visit, and that most people would have slammed the door in her face.

Jacqui made a beeline towards the person waiting just outside the entrance. For reassurance, she patted the outside of her coat pocket that contained the sigil earrings, safely tucked away in their small red box. She would have worn them proudly, but she was frightened that Jack's sister would regard her as some kind of shallow 'fashion princess,' hideously overdressed for such a crisis. After all, since when did you dress up to see someone lying in a coma? It was going to be challenging enough sporting fuchsia-pink hair. Fortunately, the woman she was walking towards hardly looked demure.

As she approached, the lady looked up, and – much to Jacqui's relief – gave her a friendly smile. Not only that, but she extended her hand in a welcome gesture and said, "You must be Jacqui? Wow, I love your hair. I've never had the courage to do that."

Jacqui was not expecting such a positive start; she had braced herself for a frosty greeting. "And you must be Beth. Thanks. I've not long had it done, actually. Out with the old and in with the new, as they say…" Jacqui cursed herself for such a crass, throwaway comment. Feeling nervous in the company of strangers was quite a new experience for her.

Beth nodded, still smiling.

Jacqui clasped both of her hands around Beth's extended one. It reminded her of the awkward parting handshake with Jack on Fur Tor. "Listen, Beth, it's so good of you to let me come. I know it must be very difficult for you."

Beth pursed her lips and gave an appreciative half-smile. "Yes, it's been very hard, and when I heard from the detective that Jack had got himself into a terribly difficult situation… well, I didn't know what to think. I can't lie to you: I wish that you had done things differently. However, DS Baines reassured me that you'd made a great impression on Jack, and that you'd promised him you'd be there for him, if needed. I've never got involved in Jack's affairs and he's always been a good judge of character, so here we are. This is all about my brother, not me."

Beth indicated that it would be good to enter the hospital, rather than continue talking outside, and Jacqui could tell Beth was beginning to well up. Her eyes were glistening, and she looked very tired.

Jacqui followed Beth's lead as they made their way to the entrance of the building. Just as they were about to cross the threshold, however, they heard a voice calling from behind.

"Hey, hold up, you two!"

Jacqui turned around to see Detective Sandra Baines striding towards them.

"Is there room for one more?" Sandra asked, with a beaming smile. "Look, I know we can't all go and visit him at the same time, but I just wanted to be here – you know, to offer my solidarity."

Sandra moved towards Beth and offered her hand. "Detective Sergeant Sandra Baines. We spoke earlier."

Beth was surprised but elated by the gesture. "My goodness, you didn't have to do that. You must be busy with work and so on." She shook Sandra's hand. "It's lovely to meet you, though." Beth turned to Jacqui. "This is the detective who phoned me and explained everything."

Jacqui chuckled at the potentially embarrassing introduction. "Yes, we've met before…" She nervously exchanged a glance with Sandra who, in turn, was struggling to keep her composure.

"Oh… yes, of course," said Beth, realising that Jacqui must have been questioned at some point during the investigation.

"I have today off – which is just as well, as I enjoyed myself a little too much last night …" Sandra teased Jacqui with a knowing look. "No ill effects today, though, thank goodness. Now then, that makes three of us… and all here to help Jack. Surely any man couldn't wish for more," she added, trying to sound buoyant.

"Well, actually, it makes four," said Beth. "This morning, I received a video recording from Jenny, Jack's ex-partner. She's in America now. Would you like to hear it? It's such a tender message."

"Oh my goodness, that's such a lovely gesture," said Jacqui. "Shall we find somewhere we can listen to it properly?"

The trio moved to a quiet corner, away from the busyness of the main foyer. There, they huddled together and listened to the emotional, heartfelt tribute to Jack.

"You…"

"…beauty," completed Jacqui, in unison with Sandra. "I can see why they were together." She moved her hands to wipe her eyes. "I'm sorry, but that's made me all teary…"

"Yes, I interviewed her, and she is indeed a lovely lady. Don't some people do the most amazing things?" Sandra asked, adding weight to Jacqui's sentiment. She, too, was feeling the onrush of emotion, so she dabbed the corner of her eye with the side of her index finger.

"Come on," said Beth, rallying the troops, "he's got four of us to contend with now."

With that, the three unlikely amigos linked arms and strode down the hospital corridor, heading for the intensive care unit.

Acknowledgements

First of all, I would like to thank Nick Jefferson for encouraging me, and spurring me on, to complete Sigil. Without his help, my authorship would still be perilously becalmed, in the writers' Sargasso Sea, two thirds of the way through its journey. There were encouraging currents of thought lurking below the surface, but no winds to guide me home. Nick's highly positive critique of what I had started gave me the impetus to find the answers that I was searching for.

I had purposely not planned Sigil. I had firm ideas for my main protagonists, the opening scene on Fur Tor and the reveal at the end, but I thought I would let the rest evolve, the characters acting as I thought they would do given the circumstances.

This approach follows the mantra: if I don't know what is happening next then neither would the reader. It's all very exciting until you realise that at some stage you need your characters to head in the direction your ending demands. I'd like to think that I got there eventually, but for many months I just couldn't figure out how, plausibly, to get everything aligned.

Huge thanks also to Sean Jefferson for introducing me to the work of Austin Osman Spare and the concept of a sigil. I hope that I have been faithful to Spare's ideas. I fashioned the esoteric seal, involved in the book, as my character, Victoria, would have done so, designing it so that a jeweller could have actually created the earrings. Thanks, again, to Sean for interpreting my sketches and providing the artwork for the sigil used as a frontispiece in the novel.

I would like to thank my editor Jessica Coleman for her guidance and skill. Right from the onset she seemed to understand exactly what I was striving for. I can't remember disregarding a single suggestion that she made. I can still remember the thrill at reading through the 'clean copy' for the first time.

Caroline Roche, Sue Greenham and Sebastian Marris, thank you so much for reading my debut novel and providing me with your no holds barred opinions. You gave me enough affirmation to continue reshaping and honing the script. I found it surprisingly difficult to find people unknown to me willing to take on the task. Your role in the process cannot be understated.

Many thanks to the team at ebooklaunch for preparing the book for publication, and thank you to Jessica for recommending them.

Lastly, thanks to my parents for giving me a love of Dartmoor and the surrounding area. There was nowhere else that I was going to set my first book.

Printed in Great Britain
by Amazon